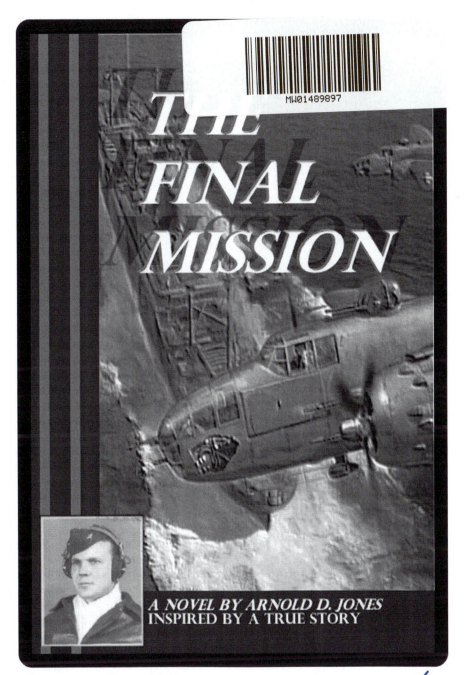

THE FINAL MISSION

A NOVEL BY ARNOLD D. JONES
INSPIRED BY A TRUE STORY

TO CHRIS Enjoy the Story

[signature]

Grey Wolfe Publishing, LLC
PO Box 1088
Birmingham, Michigan 48009
www.GreyWolfePublishing.com

© 2013 Arnold D. Jones
Published by Grey Wolfe Publishing, LLC
www.GreyWolfePublishing.com
All Rights Reserved

ISBN: 978-1-62828-016-6
Library of Congress Control Number: 2013954821

PRAISE FOR
THE FINAL MISSION

They came from all walks of life and from every part of this nation. They were rich, poor, upper class, middle class, young men and women of every race, culture, creed and class. They were the children of the doughboys and knew good times and what it meant to be in want. They were the men and women of the greatest generation. Men like J. D. Jones made up this generation. A man whose story was retold in "The Final Mission"; Jones epitomized character, courage, and sacrifice. Traits of that nature were common at that time. His actions and those of the men with him should remind us all as to why we should never forget the commitment of those who served in that war and should pass on their story and their legacy to succeeding generations, the children, grandchildren, and great grandchildren of those who served during the greatest struggle in our history.

~Staff Sergeant Jason Darryl Branch US Air Force (Ret.)

PRAISE FOR
THE FINAL MISSION

I thought that the combination of the military section with the espionage portion made the book an easy read. Jones was able to keep both plots going without losing focus on either part.

~Michael Shaw, Lieutenant; Michigan State Police
Veteran; Sergeant, US Army Military Police

The story includes crash landings, adventures on islands in the Pacific, romance, heartbreak, and a heroic return to the United States, only to fall into further adventure and intrigue in Chicago. Part of the story involves the Willow Run Plant, Belle Isle, and parts of Northern Michigan. The Final Mission, it turns out, is flying over Lake Michigan, and involves a fantastic battle. I don't know what parts of the story are real, and what are imagined, but it was a great pleasure to read, and left me wondering "what if this really happened?"

~Debby Retzer, RN, University of Michigan Health System
Veteran; Captain, US Air Force Nurse Corps

THE FINAL MISSION

ARNOLD D. JONES

DEDICATION

My Uncle, Joseph Dutton Jones Jr. (JD)
    United States Army Air Corps, WWII.

My Father, Gillas Denver Jones
    United States Army, WWII.

My Uncle, Bill (William Edward Jones)
    United States Navy, WWII.

My Uncle, Russell Jones
    United States Army, WWII.

My Uncle, Isaac Jones
    Tennessee Mountain Men, U.S. Revolutionary War

Mr. Kellogg, my teacher.

ACKNOWLEDGEMENTS

A special thank you goes out to my lovely wife, Josie, who has been ever patient and loving while I spent countless hours writing, and even more patient hours listening as I read each chapter aloud.

I am grateful for your encouragement and support.

I love you.

CHAPTERS

FOREWORD

This story began in the middle of the nineteenth century. My involvement however, is much more recent. It all started for me when my dad asked if I would be interested in joining him on a trip from our homes in Michigan to the place where he grew up. He wasn't the type to admit to being too sick to attempt the trip alone. Instead, he invited me to come along for company. In reality, Dad needed a driver and someone to be close by, just in case his strength gave out. I happily signed on, knowing full well why he had made the request.

The trip had been sparked by the passing of one of Dad's lifelong friends. Though my father's body was now frail, his drive and determination remained strong and evident. Throughout my life I had witnessed Dad's unwavering loyalty to his friends and family, so I understood that as long as Dad was still breathing he would be at that funeral.

We were on our way the next afternoon. About an hour into the journey Dad began to tell a story about one of his older brothers. The brother had, until then, been regarded as somewhat mysterious; very little had ever been said about him to anyone of my generation.   I suspect the passing of Dad's childhood friend triggered memories of my uncle, whom the family just called JD. I spent the next several hours being entertained and amazed as my father recalled the story in such detail that it was as if it had happened only yesterday. Little did I know, or even suspect, how much of what I was hearing would affect my life.

Dad's friend whose funeral prompted our trip had been the same age as JD and as young men they had joined the same National Guard unit. This long-ago connection apparently brought back to the surface the distant memory of JD and revealed for the first time since World War II the complete story of our mysterious uncle.

JD was the nickname given to my uncle as a child. Over the years, I had pieced together fragments of information that clearly indicated JD was looked upon as the family hero. On the rare occasion when a family conversation would turn to the subject of JD's military service, the topic would quickly change. Gaining a clear picture of exactly what he had done during the war eluded outsiders and youngsters alike. Those who knew weren't talking and JD never attended family gatherings. In fact, as far as I knew, like myself, neither my brother, sister nor any of our cousins had ever laid eyes on Uncle JD.

I have often heard that those who fought in World War II are America's greatest generation. Those of us who were spared from conflicts of that sort will never know or fully understand the reasons why they didn't talk about the war. Theirs was a story they kept to themselves. When it appeared that the mystery was about to be revealed to me I was excited to finally hear the story that had until that day been kept a closely guarded secret.

Dad and his siblings were raised during the great depression in the coal mining country of Eastern Kentucky. Opal was the first-born but she died an infant. Aunt Ann came next, then Uncle Arnold. JD was the second son. His full name, I soon learned, was Joseph Dutton Jones Jr. Next was Uncle Russell, shortly followed thereafter by Uncle Bill. Then my dad came along, named Gillas Denver Jones. The last child was a girl named Virginia Fern. Five boys and three girls blessed the home of my grandparents, Joseph Dutton Sr. and Maude Jones.

Being that Dad was much younger than JD, one might expect that his reminiscences of his older brother were from the perspective of an admiring child observing the accomplishments of a much older and wiser big brother. With this in mind, upon hearing my dad relate his memories of JD's adolescent years, it at first seemed to me that Dad's description of JD's accomplishments might be somewhat exaggerated. However, some time later, I had the occasion to interview people who had grown up with JD. These interviews confirmed Dad had been quite accurate in his recollections.

JD was always big for his age and he was well coordinated and very athletic. He played the three popular sports of the time, baseball, football and basketball. He lettered in all three in his freshman year. On the baseball field JD pitched and was the catcher when not on the mound. On the gridiron he quarterbacked a full house backfield which featured his size, agility and speed as the cornerstone of a running style offence. In those days players stayed on the field and played defense as well. On the defensive side of the ball JD was the team's middle linebacker. Most interesting was his role on the basketball court. As he was the tallest player on the team and usually the tallest on the court during games, one would expect that he played the center position. Long before Magic Johnson as a six foot nine inch point guard led Michigan State University to a national championship, JD filled a similar role for his high school team. With excellent ball-handling skills, speed, size and quickness, he could breakdown the defense from the backcourt and he was strong enough to take the ball to the basket with power.

His personality on the field of play was intense and competitive, but those attributes were in stark contrast to his normal character. To those that knew him growing up, he could best be described as a nice guy. Although he was not overly outgoing, he had little ego and possessed an engaging manner. His unassuming, charismatic personality made people comfortable and confident when in his presence. All of this, when added to his striking good looks, made him popular with the girls as well. JD was interested in the attention the girls showed but with his school work, farm chores, sports activity and church there was little free time to explore the mysteries the young ladies presented. My grandfather expected nothing less than outstanding grades on every report card, church attendance each time the church doors opened and he insisted that all assigned chores be done on time and correctly. All of the children knew better than to compromise in these areas.

In December of 1941 all of the boys were of military age with the exception of my dad. He was still in high school when the war broke out. Dad did eventually serve in the Army though too late to join the fighting. He was sent to Europe at war's end and served as part of the occupation forces. As for the others, Arnold was rejected by the military because his trigger finger was missing. The family rumor was that he cut it off himself to avoid military service. I never believed the story, but in Uncle Arnold's case it was difficult to be sure of anything. However, Dad confirmed that his brother lost a finger in an industrial accident well before the start of World War II.

Bill joined the Navy, Russell chose the Army and JD became a pilot in the Army Air Corps.

Uncle Bill served honorably on three different ships. The first two to which he was assigned were sunk by German U boats in the North Atlantic. Eventually reassigned to the Pacific, he served on a Navy Destroyer as a gunnery mate. He directed anti-aircraft fire until the day a Kamikaze pilot flew his plane straight into one of the gun batteries my uncle was coordinating. The ship was seriously damaged but remained afloat. However, Uncle Bill's combat days were over. It would take another book to describe all that he went through during the war, so for now, I will just say that Uncle Bill was seriously injured and knocked out of the war. He endured a long and difficult recovery in a Naval hospital. Only by the grace of God did he recover.

Russell piloted a landing craft, ferrying troops and supplies to the beaches of countless Pacific islands and carrying the wounded back to the ships anchored off shore. On one such trip, Russell's landing craft became hopelessly grounded on a beach at low tide. Without a weapon and under extremely heavy sniper fire, Russell was somehow able to find sufficient cover to allow him to make his way out of the stranded landing craft and off the beach. Avoiding the combat area, he slowly worked his way up into the hills. His parents were notified their son was listed among many others as missing in action. The news, as you might imagine, caused the entire family much concern and worry.

After several weeks of vicious combat, the main battle finally ended with a victory by the combined forces of the Army and Marines. Within a few weeks of the occupation the Army replaced the Marines who moved out to prepare for the next island invasion. The Army immediately began to fan out across the island, rounding up the few remaining Japanese soldiers still hiding throughout the island. Eventually, US troops patrolling up in the hills discovered Uncle Russell in a small village occupied by native women and children. It seems that he had made himself quite comfortable there for several weeks. From the reaction of the women upon his departure, it was obvious that he had developed quite a few new and very close friendships. His parents were relieved when informed that he was no longer missing in action, but safe in the brig for the next thirty days. Uncle Russell was given the opportunity to restart his military career as a Private. I mention this single incident only to shed some light on Uncle Russell's carefree spirit. It would be unfair if it were used to measure his contribution to the war effort. Instead it should be noted that he served his country honorably until the war was over.

JD was the pilot of a B-25 Mitchell Twin Engine Medium Bomber. JD's National Guard unit was called up for active duty within days of the attack on Pearl Harbor. Upon completion of basic training he was sent to Texas to attend flight school. He completed flight training, qualified as a pilot and was assigned to bombers. His training continued in twin engine bombers, and eventually JD was given command of a B-25 Mitchell. He entered the Pacific combat zone in the spring of 1943.

By that time the war in the Pacific was advancing much more quickly than had been originally expected. The Pacific Campaign was originally intended to be a holding action to allow Europe to receive most of the men and equipment. The strategy was to deal with the Germans and Italians first, after which the allies could turn their full might against the Japanese Empire. However, the shift by U.S. high command to follow an island hopping strategy shelved an earlier thought wherein troops would slug it out one island at a time. This change served to accelerate progress toward the intended objective of meeting the Japanese on their home turf. In any case, U.S. land based tactical air support resources were being stretched beyond their limits.

JD and the crew of his B-25 had been in the thick of the fighting for several months. They were seasoned veterans by this point in the war, all much older and wiser than their actual ages.

The determination, experience and skill of the Japanese on land, at sea and in the air had taken the lives of many B-25 crews. JD and his crew had experienced close calls on nearly every mission but somehow their luck was holding. This was serious business. You either grew up fast or died. It was as simple as that. There were no boys in JD's crew. These were men.

Combat limits were in place in the Pacific Theater. Pilots, as well as the other crew members, were required to fly sixty combat missions; after which an individual could choose to finish out the war in a non-combat assignment. These non-combat assignments were usually stateside and involved training new pilots and crews. After the successful completion of the first thirty missions it was customary that a thirty-day stateside leave be granted, after which the crew member would return to finish out his remaining thirty missions. Meeting the sixty mission threshold bought you a ticket home for good, if you were lucky.

With the first half of his sixty required missions completed, JD was all set to go home and meet up with his family in Kentucky for Christmas. To JD this was a dream come true. Earlier, JD had written to my grandfather hinting of the possibility that he might be home for Christmas, but asked his father to keep it quiet just in case the unspeakable were to happen. With the memory of Russell's missing in action report fresh in his mind, JD reasoned this would insulate my grandmother from undo worry and stress. Grandma knew that he was scheduled to come home; there was no keeping that a secret. It was just the timing around Christmas that would create the added stress. It was best to spare her the heartache if he missed the holiday season.

Then there was Susan, the Texas girl JD had met during pilot training. She had won his heart. They had continued to correspond regularly and the relationship seemed to be growing ever stronger. My grandfather, who was an engineer on the railroad, promised to get word to her when JD's schedule was firm and arrange a priority ticket for both Susan and her mother to visit Kentucky during JD's stay there. Anticipating the time at home as well as seeing Susan again occupied JD's thoughts. The waiting was almost painful.

The following story was told to me by my father on the way to Eastern Kentucky, detailing the events that led up the final mission, that mission and what transpired afterwards.

The Final Mission

PROLOGUE

He had seen sharks right here, lots of times. They cruised back and forth not twenty yards off the beach. He had never seen sharks in the bay but they had been here, on the sea side, just off the point. They were probably here now. He would soon find out.

A half-moon momentarily disappeared behind a cloud. The glistening reflection of the moon's glow upon the surface of the water immediately disappeared, turning the ocean to black paint. He couldn't see anything. If something was down there he wouldn't find out until it was too late. He tried not to think about it, opting to check his course instead.

The boat was making its way parallel with the shoreline about fifty yards from the beach. The point was now a hundred yards ahead. The water had raised high enough to cover his bare feet and ankles, now it was half-way to his knees. He turned the wheel to the right, bringing the boat even closer to the island. When the small craft had closed the distance from fifty yards to ten yards he turned the wheel a second time. The boat returned once more to a course parallel with the beach. Satisfied, he lashed the wheel down tight.

In the darkness he made his way aft, stumbling over the dead bodies. Taking hold of the cargo nets he hoisted himself up and over the drums. Near the stern, he climbed up on the starboard side rail. Crouching, he balanced his weight between the balls of his bare feet and his fingertips. The point was approaching, he waited. Within moments the bow was even with the spot where the sand narrowed before finally disappearing completely as it met the gently rolling surf. Coiled like a spring he took a deep breath, held it, and then launched himself into the blackness.

His head emerged from under the water five yards from safety. With an urgency generated by the fear that some unseen creature might already have him in its sights, he swam furiously in the direction of the beach.

He was out of the water in less than a minute. Standing on the sand in only his undershorts he heard the boat steadily making its way out to sea. He turned for a moment to watch while trying to catch his breath. Then he turned back and made his way along the beach. His breathing was better, more relaxed, but his heart was racing out of control. They would be coming; now they had a reason. He had to think, he had to prepare.

For the first time he wondered, had he made the right choice? There was a lot to do and very little time in which to do it. But he couldn't stop second-guessing his decision. It was much too late now to play the 'what if' game, but that was exactly what he was doing. He couldn't stop wondering if he should have taken the offer.

CHAPTER ONE
THE OFFER

"The Colonel wants to see you in the command hut."

JD half turned to see Sam Evans, the company clerk, standing in the wooden door frame of the tent. He was a tall, lanky guy with a big, toothy smile on his face which seemed to spread from one ear to the other.

"I'll be right there," JD responded while maintaining his focus on the duffle bag he was nearly finished packing.

Sam was still smiling when he added, "It looks like you could be home for Christmas, with any luck."

JD placed the last of his belongings inside the bag then grabbed his hat off the cot as he started for the door. "I sure hope so, I've already written to Dad and told him it was a strong possibility, but I'm sure if I miss it by a few days it's all the same to the family."

He stopped in midstride, taking just a moment to study Sam's face, "Sam, you look happier about this than I am." JD started once again to leave but paused to add, "By the way, you wouldn't happen to have any idea why the old man wants to see me?"

"No, he never tells me anything. But, I can tell you that he had me pull your file yesterday and put it on his desk. He's been going over it all morning. And yes, we're all happy, besides being a little jealous to boot. I mean what a break; Christmas at home sure sounds good."

JD slipped past Sam and headed for the command hut. His destination was a short walk through the jungle canopy which concealed several rows of tents, huts and out-buildings from overhead observation. The trees also supplied shade which provided some relief from the midday sun. It was hot; it was always hot.

Along the way he couldn't help but wonder why the Colonel had summoned him. It was unusual, to say the least. In fact, this was the first time he had been ordered to the Colonel's office. To this point JD had been careful to stay under the radar. Rather, he focused on doing his job to the best of his ability, ever mindful not to draw any undue attention to himself.

JD entered the command hut and stood at attention in front of the Colonel's desk. The Colonel was sitting while three other men stood gathered around the desk. One of those present JD knew to be the Colonel's aide. He was standing behind and to the side of the Colonel looking over his shoulder. The other two were First Lieutenants and pilots, like himself. Each stood on either side of the desk. Something was up. They were in deep conversation, leaning over, studying the papers spread out in front of the Colonel. JD didn't really care what was going on and had no difficulty blocking out the men's conversation. At that moment he was still thinking only about going home.

As he stood there, he noticed the Colonel's desk was cobbled together from an old door laid over some discarded shipping crates. The door still had its knob and the Colonel's shirt was hanging from it right in front of JD. He found himself staring at the makeshift desk while patiently waiting for the old man to acknowledge his presence. Somehow the shirt just hanging there didn't seem out of place. In the South Pacific formality had often been replaced by simple necessity. Improvisation was the standing order of the day.

JD's mind wandered to all the things around the base that were made from something else. Way out in the Pacific when something was needed a person either figured out how to get it or, more often than not, made it using whatever was at hand. JD's analytical mind began to calculate the percentage of tools, utensils, and all manner of things that were fashioned from something other than the object's original purpose. His thoughts returned to the present as the three men acknowledged him as they moved past on their way out of the tent. He smiled in return and then they were gone. The Colonel gathered the papers and stuffed them into a folder, sliding it to one side. A second folder with JD's name hand lettered on the cover was now in front of his commanding officer.

Colonel Fielder returned JD's salute. Then he stood up while at the same time extending his hand. JD felt a firm handshake that seemed to convey true warmth. In a forward combat zone everybody was forced to share the same challenging living conditions. The practice of adhering to strict protocols gave way to wartime decorum that was much more relaxed in the field, but still correct in maintaining military discipline. In this instant however, it did seem to JD that the Colonel was demonstrating more cordiality then he was accustomed to seeing.

The Colonel began, "Lieutenant Jones you've done well so far with thirty successful combat missions under your belt. You're half way home son just thirty more to go. How does it feel?"

The Colonel didn't give JD a chance to answer. JD could only assume that he probably wasn`t expecting one because he continued without pausing.

"You have done all that we've asked and performed your duties in a manner befitting an officer in this man's Army. You should be proud of your contribution to the war effort, as I'm sure you are."

JD acknowledged the Colonel's comments with a simple, "Thank you sir."

Now he waited for the other shoe to drop. He had no idea what it would be, but it had to be something. He had always been treated with respect since his arrival in the combat zone but the Colonel's approach seemed over the top. A simple, "well done", was the norm. There had to be more to this than merely a fond farewell from the officer in charge.

He didn't have long to wait. Fielder motioned for him to take a seat. They both sat down and the Colonel continued. "As you're aware, around here we are short on everything but Japs. We don't have enough equipment, crews or experienced combat pilots like yourself."

This time the Colonel waited for a response.

"That's certainly true sir." JD spoke as if stating the obvious.

"Because we find ourselves in this situation I have been authorized to make you an offer," said the Colonel.

He then rose to his feet and came around the desk where he stood next to JD. *This is it. The other shoe is about to drop.*

"If you will agree to forgo your stateside leave you'll be granted an immediate ten-day pass to be spent in New Zealand. I know this doesn't sound like much, but the good part is that when you return from ten days of rest and relaxation, you'll be credited with fifteen additional completed missions. That will leave you with only fifteen to fly to earn the full sixty. What do you say to that?"

JD didn`t answer immediately instead he tried to sort out how best to respond to this completely unanticipated offer. Going home for Christmas versus going home for good; now this was something to think about. Very few guys made the full sixty. If his experience from his first thirty completed combat missions was any indication of what was coming then his chances of survival were slim. This was an important decision. It could literally mean life or death. With thirty already in the bag and fifteen taken off the board, the sixty mission goal seemed reachable.

"Sir could you give me any idea of my next assignment? I mean, after I complete my required combat?"

Without hesitation Fielder responded, "With your record and experience I will recommend that you be assigned to bomber pilot training in Texas. That's where you received your training and where you can do the most good."

"Would I have an opportunity to get home to visit the folks before reporting to my next assignment?"

"We'll see that you receive that thirty-day pass. I'm sure your mother and dad are looking forward to seeing you," promised the Colonel; and then he added. "I suppose you have a girl back home as well."

JD took a moment before responding. "Actually, there is a girl, her name's Susan and I sure would like to see her."

"I'm confident that she'll wait a little longer if you write and tell her the good news. So what do you say Lieutenant, do we have a deal?"

There was really nothing for JD to think very long about. The offer was just too good to be true. "Yes sir we have a deal," JD answered as he reached out to shake on it.

The Colonel was pleased and said so with a smile and an even warmer handshake before dismissing the young Lieutenant. JD walked out of the hut and was greeted by another extremely warm tropical afternoon, just like all the rest. This time he was lost in his own thoughts, his mind was conflicted. The events of the last few minutes had flipped a mental switch requiring him to rethink an awful lot. For the past several days he had been focused on getting home to his mother, dad and Susan. That all changed after entering the Colonel's hut. He wasn't going home. There would be no sitting around the Christmas tree drinking hot cocoa, enjoying the people he missed so very much. That was all gone. He hadn't yet replaced those thoughts with anything else. He was feeling a combination of sadness and loneliness, which he concluded was caused by the sudden absence of anticipation. Surely, his overall situation had improved but, the boy inside him longed to have a real Christmas at home. It surprised him that he felt this way. The experiences of war had changed him but the boy wasn't really gone after all, just pushed so far back that he hadn't realized he was still there.

That evening he wrote a letter to his dad explaining his decision and asking for his understanding. JD was more like his dad in appearance and in personality then any of his brothers. He was comfortable sharing everything with his father. Dad could read the words and see the boy but he could also see beyond the obvious. He could understand JD's heart. He always had. JD also asked his father to explain to his mother the benefits of this change in plans, hopefully tempering her disappointment.

He wrote a second very long letter. This one was to Susan. In it he explained the situation and went into great detail covering all of the positive aspects of his decision. He was excited at the prospect of returning to Texas as an instructor and he told her so.

This fact alone eliminated the distance between them. Who knew where he might have been assigned upon his return if he hadn't accepted the Army's offer? His decision was bringing him back to her hometown. He hoped that his words and thoughts would be enough to help her understand.

With both letters finished, sealed and posted his thoughts turned to New Zealand and the next ten days away from the pressures of war. He was already packed and scheduled to fly out that afternoon. A transport plane was to have provided the first leg along an indirect route to the States. With new orders cut for New Zealand it was a simple thing to amend the flight plan of the transport. First stop now would be Auckland, New Zealand. He was on his way late that very afternoon.

CHAPTER TWO
THE SECOND HALF

On the flight to New Zealand the plane was forced to make an unscheduled stop due to engine troubles which delayed his arrival by several days. Once JD finally arrived in New Zealand, he used his ten days of R&R and then sat around the airport waiting for orders and a military transport back to the war zone; nearly a full month had passed.

He would return rested but the relaxation part was quickly fading. It was replaced with anxiety, worry, and dread. When he reported to his first combat assignment he was a green kid thinking himself ready for anything. Now things were much different. This time he knew what to expect and the fear was eating him up inside. He would get himself together as always; he had to, what alternative was there? There were fifteen more missions to fly and he had to fly them all, one at a time.

The C47 transport plane hummed along at a hundred and sixty miles an hour on its way to an island designated simply as number 443. JD expected this island to be just like all of the other islands he had called home to this point. The only difference being that it would be closer to mainland Japan. JD's former group seemed to pull up stakes every few weeks to move north and west; ever closer to the Empire's home islands. The closer they got, the fiercer the resistance thrown up by the Japanese. Every mission seemed more dangerous than the one before. Each time he left the ground to face the enemy, the percentages in favor of a safe return decreased.

The transport plane was filled with boxes, crates, mail bags and two Army fliers, both hitching a one way ride to the same place. A head appeared between the pilot and copilot seats. The copilot's smiling face and a waving gesture brought JD to his feet. He made his way up to the cockpit. As he neared the threshold the copilot spoke over the roar of the two big Pratt & Whitney radial engines.

"Sir, we're about to make our approach. Your new home will be outside the port window when we start our turn. Thought you might want to get an advanced look. You know, sort of a bird's eye view."

"Thanks, thanks a lot, I appreciate it," JD yelled over the engine noise as he turned his attention to the window.

The sky was clear and JD got his first introduction to what was a rather large, tree covered patch of land in the middle of a group of several smaller islands. He could make out two runways crossing at a sixty degree angle. There were several planes parked near the east/west runway with a multitude of large hangers and buildings scattered around. Island 443 was a step up from the muddy insect infested places he had called home before his R&R. There was even a control tower. He began to relax.

"Like the New Zealanders say, this might be a bit of alright," he said out loud. By this time the other serviceman riding in the back with JD had made his way up to the front of the plane.

"Sorry Sir, were you talking to me?" the young flier asked.

JD turned away from the window and observed the look of excitement on the young man's face. "No, just talking out loud.

Here, take a look at your new home, Corporal." JD moved over to provide room for the corporal who immediately put his face up against the window.

Base headquarters were located just off the runway in a large building next to the control tower. JD found it without any trouble. He walked up the steps and entered the front door. A private sitting at the desk just inside the door lifted his head as JD entered.

"May I help you sir?"

Placing the heavy duffle bag down at his side JD addressed the clerk. "Yes, I'm First Lieutenant Joseph Dutton Jones Jr. reporting for duty." He handed the clerk his orders.

The clerk carefully looked over his orders, pulled a stamp from the left hand desk drawer then stamped and signed the orders before placing them in a basket at the corner of his desk.

"Very good sir, I have your new orders right here," and then he handed them to JD. "The Captain asked that you join him in the officer's mess as soon as you arrived. Most of the others are already here. Just go back out that door and straight across the path. It's that building right over there." He pointed over JD's shoulder.

JD turned and looked out the door behind him and saw a large Quonset hut directly across the way. Picking up his bag JD turned around and headed for the hut and an introduction to a new commander. Without another word the clerk put his head down and returned to his work.

As he came through the door, a Captain waved him over to a table. "You have the appearance of a guy just back from a vacation. I'm betting that you're Jones. Am I right?"

"Yes sir I'm Lieu..."

The officer spoke over JD's attempted introduction.

"Welcome Lieutenant and Merry Christmas. We've all been waiting for you. You're one of the last to arrive and we're scheduled to depart this afternoon. You almost missed out. I'm Captain Mason."

JD wished the Captain a Merry Christmas in return and then introduced himself. This time he was able to complete his response without interruption.

"Why don't you go over and join the party? We're right in the middle of it. Please get yourself something to eat then I'll take you around and introduce you to the rest of the group. We still have about an hour before assembly," Mason said with a smile.

"Where're we headed?" JD asked as he placed his bags on the floor next to the table.

"I wouldn't worry too much about that Lieutenant. When you've seen one of these islands you've seen them all. Wouldn't you agree?"

The Captain gave JD a sideways smile as he turned to his left, shifting his attention to one of the others at the table.

JD just nodded and returned the smile as he headed over to the chow line. *Well this was too good to be true. I'll bet money the next stop will be a downgrade from this place.* He grabbed a tray and took a spot in the chow line. The food looked pretty good. There was some sort of meat, mashed potatoes, lots of green vegetables, and a big sheet cake with yellow batter and white frosting. At least half of the cake was already gone, but he could see that someone had taken the time to decorate the top with a snowy Christmas scene. That someone had tried to make a Christmas in the tropics a bit more like home for a bunch of young guys. It was a good bet that nearly all were away from home at

Christmas for the very first time. JD thought it was a nice gesture and he appreciated the effort. He sliced off a big piece of the cake.

****

After a two and a half hour flight, the group arrived at the forward base which was to become their base of operation. There were no buildings yet, just a few tents set up back in the tree line. Out on one of the island's two runways the engineers were busily laying down steel Marston matting over the mud. This new invention was an engineering marvel. Marston matting was developed to overcome the effects heavy monsoon rains had on the hastily constructed dirt runways American engineers were building throughout the South Pacific. It was made from long strips of perforated steel which interlocked together and could be quickly assembled over a relatively level earthen runway to produce a solid surface able to support the weight of the largest bombers, in any weather. The forward airbase was obviously still very much a work in progress.

JD was assigned to a newly formed bomber group with a new crew and a new airplane. JD was still flying a B-25 but this one was a modified J version.

B-25s were being transformed to conduct low level strafing attacks. The B-25's original nose had been made of Plexiglas and fitted with a single machine gun. The new configuration housed eight forward firing fifty caliber machine guns in the nose.

The nature of the missions assigned to his new group was much different than he had experienced in the past. The traditional method of high level bombing called for the bombardier to acquire the target by observing through the Plexiglas nose. Once the target was in sight he would then use the top secret Norton bombsight to pinpoint the target before releasing his payload. High level bombing had not been entirely successful. Unpredictable winds aloft, combined with cloud cover over the target, anti-aircraft fire and fighter attacks, all contributed to poor bombing accuracy. High level bombing was now destined to be replaced by a new strategy; low level raids.

B-25s were being converted to support this new tactical approach. The original requirement called for a medium bomber with defensive armament. The new role as a low level raider demanded more offensive fire power. The eight new nose guns added to the four already mounted in blisters on each side of the fuselage, plus the two in the upper turret, could put fourteen forward firing guns on the target at the same time. This was serious fire power. JD thought that the newly configured B-25s seemed to be up to the new task, but only time would tell.

CHAPTER THREE
THE CREW

The strong winds and monsoon rains of the past few days had moved out of the area. There was no wind to speak of, just a light breeze which caused the sides of the tent to sway in and out ever so slightly. To a pilot in war time, awareness of wind and weather becomes second nature. Bad weather in the South Pacific could mean that he might get to live another day. The forecast predicted clear skies, with a light breeze to dead calm conditions. The mission planned for this morning would be a go. There was no chance that they would receive orders to stand down again.

****

JD sat up on his cot and pivoted his legs out over the side, feeling around in the darkness for the towel he kept on the dirt floor. His feet found it just as they had every morning for the nine weeks he had been stationed on this island paradise. The conditions on this little garden spot were either hot and dry or hot and wet. In any case, the floor was always dirty and the insects were always hungry. The worst part was that after each completed mission, fewer crews and aircraft returned. The group was down to seven full crews and ten operational aircraft, a mere twenty five percent of its original combat strength. The strategy of low level attacks on enemy targets had clearly improved results. There was no arguing the facts, but the cost in men and equipment was alarming.

He glanced down at his watch, it was nearly 0100 hours. The preflight briefing was set to begin in just ten minutes. There was no time to waste. He pulled on his socks, stood on the towel and began to dress. Regulations dictated that he be in full uniform, however out here, in the tropical heat and in the heat of battle, normal enforcement of such regulations had been less rigid. But, not under this commanding officer; when it came to the uniform, he insisted on following regulations to the tee. This meant that all crews would be in proper and complete uniform at the start of each mission which included tie, cover [hat], and flight jacket. Before every mission, JD couldn't help thinking of himself as a bit over dressed for the occasion.

With uniform on and regulations satisfied JD opened his foot locker and began to add his own personal touches. On his belt was the standard issue 1911 Colt .45 caliber automatic pistol with a full clip of eight rounds. JD added two additional clips stuffed in a pouch on the outside of his holster. He had fashioned the pouch from a piece of leather cut out of a discarded baseball glove. The previous owner's plane had not come back from a mission and somehow the glove hadn't been sent home with his other personal belongings. Also on his belt he attached a canteen of water, a small first aid kit, a compass and another pouch containing a silencer made to fit the Colt. He slipped his knife into the scabbard on the inside of his right boot and snapped the cover shut. Using a cut-down Army issue belt, he secured a second Colt .45 pistol with full clip against the inside of his left boot. Into both inside pockets of his flight jacket he wedged two boxes of "K" rations and in the outer pockets, four more. Some were for dinner and some breakfast. From his recollection of basic training, they had all tasted about the same. In one front pants pocket went a small can of gun oil, a can of lighter fluid and his Zippo. In the other pocket, more ammunition clips and two packs of Lucky Strikes. He had taken up smoking shortly after his first combat mission, which was quite nearly his last. It was a nervous habit that he planned to abandon just as soon as he stopped flying combat missions for a living.

This would be mission number forty-four, just one more to go after this one, and he wasn't taking any chances. JD had seen too much and heard about too many guys surviving a crash or ditching at sea only to be shot, or tragically die of thirst or starvation in an open raft. The way JD figured it, making the deal to eliminate fifteen opportunities of getting killed was risk management. Being properly prepared for any and all eventualities was also risk management. JD knew that he was a long way from Texas and like the Boy Scouts always say, "Be prepared." He was working the percentages, doing everything he could think of to improve his odds of returning safely.

JD turned and walked out of the tent into the hot, dark night. There were millions of stars overhead, but the moon wasn't visible. The sky reminded him of his home in the hills of Eastern Kentucky where there were no city lights to reflect upward and hide the stars. He had grown up staring out of his bedroom window on countless nights into a similar sky, wondering what he would become. These were the same star-filled heavens as back home, but he was not that same boy. He had imagined many possibilities for his future, but in his wildest dreams, a bomber pilot had never been one of them. Fighting a war had not come up either. Yet here he was, on an island in the middle of the biggest ocean on the planet. He was surrounded by young men just like himself. They came from all over the United States. All trained to do their part in killing people they had never met. Everyone here was about as far away from home as they could be.

These thoughts passed quickly. He knew why he was fighting and had no problem with any part of it. However, he had to admit to himself that there were times when he just wanted to go home. The stars had reminded him of home and in an instant, his mind had gone home. It seemed the shorter his time got the more he found himself thinking of home. His mind was back in the present now and so was he. JD told himself, "Two more to go. Just two more missions and you're out of here. Stay focused, no mistakes, just stay focused and survive to live another day."

Most of the crew members were already gathering inside the flight operations tent when JD arrived. Everyone appeared tired. No one spoke. There were just a few nods of recognition. JD grabbed a cup of coffee and sat down with his crew to wait for the officer in charge to enter and get the show on the road.

A moment after the last man sat down Captain Mason entered and walked up the makeshift aisle in the center of the folding wooden chairs with the assembled crews sitting on them. JD was aware that there were only twelve crewmen present this morning. This meant that three B-25s were scheduled to fly this mission. The Captain pinned a map on the board which rested on an easel at the front of the assembly. With a wooden pointer in his right hand he turned and addressed the group.

"Gentlemen this morning's target is an airfield, here," he said while pointing to an island on the map. "Aircraft from this airstrip must be neutralized before the Navy can attempt a landing here." He pointed to another island northwest of the target island. "The Navy has had a submarine stationed off the east coast of this morning's target for the past two weeks gathering intelligence to help us plan this raid."

He reached down and picked up a folder from the desk and began to read aloud from a summary of the Navy report. JD scanned around the room again as he listened. This time no one looked tired. Everyone was on the edge of their seats paying close attention to the Captain's every word. He had seen this same transformation many times before, especially from veteran crews. They were all keenly aware that from this point on, it was life or death. A mistake here and you increased the odds of never coming back. He could almost smell the adrenalin all around him.

In a clear monotone voice the Captain read:

"Shape: long and narrow. Area: seven thousand feet long by one thousand feet wide with a nearly flat topography. Features: sandy beaches on the east, north and southern coasts with approximately twenty-five feet of sand leading to the tree line. The western coast is rocky, giving way to thick corral just off shore. This corral extends beyond the western shore three thousand feet out to sea. Trees cover the entire island with the exception of a single east/west runway which runs straight down the center.

As many as twenty twin engine aircraft are parked along the south side of the runway hidden from view by the trees. These aircraft are located approximately sixty feet from the southern edge of the runway.

Along the north side of the runway, also under trees and large camouflage nets, there are several buildings which serve as barracks, fuel storage, base operations and repair facilities. These buildings are located approximately one hundred and ten feet from the northern edge of the runway. Troops and support personnel on the island are estimated by the Navy observers to number five hundred. Defenses consist of two five-inch naval guns mounted on turrets so they can cover all approaches. Range: five miles. These guns are positioned on what little high ground there is at each end of the runway along the southern shore. In addition to the five inch guns, there are four twin antiaircraft batteries, six heavy machine guns, and several light machine guns scattered throughout the island."

He paused to let the information sink in before asking for questions. Most were busy taking notes. Captain Mason waited until everyone stopped writing. Then he asked if there were any questions. There were none, so he continued with the briefing.

"The Navy has observed that every morning, at exactly ten minutes after sunrise, four patrol planes depart and take up early warning positions to the north, east, south and west of the island. Based on this information we have devised a plan that should provide us with the element of surprise."

He paused once again to make sure everyone was keeping up before continuing.

"The target island is located to the northwest of our location. To avoid giving away our intentions to possible enemy observers, you will depart to the northeast; climbing to five thousand feet. You are to maintain this course and altitude for thirty minutes. Then you will descend sharply to one hundred feet still maintaining the same course. Navigators will recalibrate your plane's altimeters before takeoff to insure they are giving an accurate reading. In the darkness, the water will be black so everyone keep your eyes on those altimeters. We don't want any of you taking a swim before you reach the target.

"After ten minutes you will alter course to a northwesterly direction maintaining the same altitude until you reach the Initial Point. At the IP, make your turn and start the final approach to the target from the east. This will put the sunrise at your back. Timing is vitally important. You must arrive at the target just as the sun appears above the horizon and before the patrol planes are airborne. You want the sun at your backs to blind the lookouts to your approach. Keep in mind that those patrol planes can't be allowed to get up and harass you during or after the raid. On final approach you are to climb to one thousand feet. At one mile out begin your dive. Approaching from the east you will make your run east to west."

He studied his notes.

"Your attack formation will be three abreast. *One For The Money*, on the left will target the parked aircraft. *Wildcat*, in the center will take the airstrip and those four patrol planes that should be on the runway readying for takeoff. *Barnyard Dog* who will be on the right, is to take out the buildings and troops inside. Jones in *Wildcat* is in the lead on this mission. Men, one pass is all you get, unless of course you want to circle around and take a second pass over the target. So make it count."

A few guys smiled at the Captain's last remark, but no one laughed. It would have been funnier if they weren't the guys who had to fly the mission. Nobody was going back for a second run over the target under any circumstances.

He waited for his last remark to sink in before finishing. "Come in fast with all forward guns firing. Drop your bombs from one hundred feet off the deck. The bombs that you'll be using this morning will be two hundred and fifty pounders. They will be fitted with parachutes so that you'll be away before they detonate. However, keep in mind the importance of a tight formation. If one of you is late over the target he will be flying low right through exploding ordinance. Keep it tight, and arrive together. All right, that's about all I have. Are there any questions?"

As the questions were asked and answered everyone paid close attention. The briefing continued for another twenty minutes until all instructions were given. Finally, the navigators were told to stay a few more minutes to go over routes and timing. All the others were dismissed to get some breakfast and study their detailed mission instructions. Takeoff would be in forty minutes. JD put his notebook and pencil in his shirt pocket and headed out of the tent while buttoning down the pocket as he walked.

After going over the mission instructions, JD filled a thermos with hot black coffee and took two sandwiches, stuffing them in a brown paper bag. He headed directly out to the flight line to walk around *Wildcat* for a thorough visual inspection. The ground crew always preformed this task. Although JD had never found anything wrong, he felt more comfortable if he did it again himself. This morning there was time so he instinctively went through the procedure. He had given his B-25 the name *Wildcat*, naming it after the University of Kentucky mascot. He was the first in his family to go to college but after completing just two semesters, he left school when his National Guard unit was activated. He planned to return to the university after the war and earn a degree in mechanical engineering. But today, that was the furthest thing from his mind.

Once his inspection was complete JD stepped into his main parachute pulling the straps over his shoulders. The backup emergency chute was then clipped to the shoulder straps across his chest. With both chutes on, and with coffee and sandwiches in hand, he climbed the ladder under the plane to take his place in the left-hand seat. The B-25 seats are designed to allow the main chute to act as the seat cushion. JD positioned the twelve inch square chute pack into the seat's framework and sat down. Sitting on his main chute he snapped the seat belt tight around his waist and shoulders.

JD began to go over the preflight checklist while he waited for the crew to arrive. The first one up the ladder was his copilot, Todd Kramer. This would be their sixth mission together. Todd was well qualified, having been the pilot on several missions before, joining this crew as copilot. Todd was slated to take over *Wildcat* as its pilot after JD finished his last two missions. JD liked and trusted Todd. He had proven himself to be rock solid under pressure and had a great since of humor which helped take the edge off when things got a little dicey. JD was confident that the plane and crew would be in good hands under Todd's leadership.

"Hey boss, you all set for an exciting morning?" Todd asked as he climbed in, finding his place in the right-hand seat. Todd settled in and secured his seat belt.

"I can't think of anything better than to get up early to watch the sun come up. It's just like being back home on the farm. Don't you think?"

Still focused on the checklist JD answered. "Now what would you know about being on the farm, anyway?"

Todd answered with a smile. "Nothing sir, I was asking you. I'm just a city slicker who wouldn't know one end of a cow from the other, you're the farm boy."

"That's for sure..."

But JD was interrupted when the third member of the crew poked his head between them. Without a word Jake Brunner the navigator, flight engineer and radio man offered both pilots a sucker, just as he had at the start of each mission. Not wanting to break with tradition, they each accepted his offer and stuffed the suckers in their pockets. Jake smiled and patted them both on the arm before retreating to his stool in front of the radio which sat atop the small navigation table located below and behind the cockpit.

Jake had joined this crew on the same day as JD. After completing his training, Jake arrived in the war zone on the same C47 as JD. His first and only combat experience was as a member of *Wildcat's* crew. Jake had been aboard *Wildcat* for all thirteen missions flown by JD since his return to the combat zone. Although they had flown together on thirteen combat missions, spread out over nine weeks, JD still felt that he knew very little about Jake, other than he was good at his job and he really liked suckers. Jake rarely spoke, generally keeping to himself. He just did his job and did it very well.

With the new aircraft configuration and switch to low level attacks the crew assignments on the B-25 had also undergone some modifications. The bombardier position was eliminated. Releasing the bombs was now done by the pilot or copilot who used buttons mounted to the steering control. At low levels there was no need to use the Norton bomb sight, or even to take it along on missions. This was a great relief to the officers back at command headquarters who constantly feared that the top secret device might fall into the hands of the enemy.

The fourth and final crew member was Nick Angelino, the waist gunner. Nick operated both the tail and waist machine guns located aft of the bomb bay. In the event of an attack, Jake would move up and take the top turret while the pilot and copilot operated the forward firing machine guns. Nick covered the rear as well as both sides of the plane. Normally, B-25 crews included a tail gunner as the fifth crewman. With the shortage of available crewmen in their group, on missions such as this one it was unlikely that opposing aircraft would be involved, so only a four man crew took to the air.

Nick had joined *Wildcat's* crew just a month earlier and this would be his fifth mission with this crew. He was very experienced with credit for twenty-eight completed missions. Nick had the second most completed missions among *Wildcat's* crew, topped only by JD's forty-three.

Nick was a replacement for Clay Hunter who had been badly burned when a fire broke out after *Wildcat* was hit by ground fire. A hydraulic line was severed and some rounds also struck an electrical box. The hydraulic oil caught fire and burned his face, neck and hands before he was able to bring the fire under control. His actions saved the plane.

Clay was transported out for treatment and that's the last anyone heard about him. Clay out, Nick in, that's all there was to it, the war goes on. With Nick's experience one had to say that he was an upgrade, hopefully better for all concerned, cold but true. That's how everyone learned to think about things, measuring situations and events against odds for survival.

Approaching the target at night meant that it was highly unlikely enemy planes would be up in the darkness to counter attack on the way to the target. Since this morning's target was the only known enemy airfield within several hundred miles, no attacks were expected during the journey back to base. When they reentered US controlled airspace fighter cover would be waiting to escort them on the final leg back to base. This mission had all the makings of a routine out and back. That is if they all arrived on time and with complete surprise.

Nick entered by the rear ladder which brought him up into the area of the plane located behind the bomb bay. He had a quick look around, checked his guns and proceeded to remove several candy bars from his pockets. As was his custom, he lined them up on a support brace. He would eat half the candy on the way to the target and the remainder during the return trip. This was a good luck routine from which he never wavered. Once the candy bars were all lined up Nick put on this head set. He spoke into the interphone using his throat mike.

"All set in back ladies, is everybody here?"

JD responded, "Glad you could make it this morning. Hey, by the way, got any candy bars back there?"

JD was part of the good luck ritual that had somehow gotten started with Nick's first mission aboard *Wildcat*. He would always ask the question and always received the same reply.

"I don't think so sir, but I might have some back in my foot locker. Did you want me to go back and take a look?"

"No, that's alright. We wouldn't want to be forced to leave on this mission without you. Tell you what, I'll wait. You can give me one when we get back." This was always JD's response.

"Yes sir... when we get back." And, this was always Nick's final word on the subject.

With this ritual out of the way, JD took command. "Alright everyone, report your status."

Each man officially announced his presence and reported that he was ready to go. When they finished their reports JD went over final instructions with his crew.

"We will maintain strict radio silence throughout the mission. Communications between aircraft will be via shielded signal light only. Interphone communications are fine, but let's all keep the chatter to a minimum. Keep focused on the mission.

"We're in the lead on this one. A yellow signal light has been attached to the bottom of our plane at the rear. It can only be seen from directly behind, so as to not give our presence away to anyone on the surface. The two trailing aircraft will maintain visual contact and follow our light. Jake, you'll have control of the light. One minute before each upcoming course or altitude change you are to flash the light for fifteen seconds. On final approach, when we start our climb to one thousand feet, the light is to be flashed continuously. When we start our dive to the target I want you to turn the light off."

JD and Todd completed the start-up procedure and both engines fired off immediately. Over the roar of the engines JD spoke to the crew through the interphone.

"Well men, we're ready to go. Good luck, stay on your toes and may God bless us."

CHAPTER FOUR
MISSION NUMBER FORTY-FOUR

The small group of B-25 bombers took off from their island runway on schedule. Within moments the sky began to consume the planes. In the darkness they soon vanished leaving behind only the popping sounds coming from their six 1,700 HP Wright R-2600-9 double cyclone, fourteen cylinder, air cooled radial engines. The familiar sound faded in the distance and soon the island was silent once more. They were on their way.

While all three planes climbed out, steadily heading for their assigned altitude JD was initially focused on his instruments but eventually looked up at the windscreen into the darkness beyond. *The moonless night sky seems even darker than usual.* He realized that he felt safe, hidden in the darkness five thousand feet above the ocean's surface.   The crew was busy for the first several minutes of the mission checking and rechecking all systems, confirming course, positioning extra cartridge belts for the machine guns, double checking everything. When *Wildcat* reached their assigned altitude JD turned the controls over to Todd which provided him with some time to think. He watched as Todd trimmed out the plane, checked the cylinder head temperature gauge and closed the cowl flaps. JD reached into his shirt pocket and retrieved the sucker. After removing the wax paper wrapping,

JD sat back and tried to enjoy the grape flavor of his little piece of candy. With the steady roar from *Wildcat's* two supercharged radial engines filling the cockpit he calmly played out the mission in his mind, rehearsing each step. The noise was nearly unbearable but the two pilots had grown used to it. After several minutes JD spoke into his interphone.

"Pilot to navigator, Jake, give me time and distance to the first course change."

Jake quickly answered back. "We will reach the first position in eight minutes and twenty six miles at our present speed sir. We'll maintain this course reducing altitude only at the first change."

So far everything is going well, nothing unusual. Once again, JD checked *Wildcat's* course.

"Pilot to gunner, Nick, do you have visual contact. Are they both still back there?"

"Yes sir, I can see their exhaust flames. They're both trailing about fifty yards back. One directly behind us, the other slightly above and behind but it's too dark to make out who's who."

Nick wasn't about to take his eyes off them. All three planes were essential if this mission was to have any chance of success. He didn't want anyone getting lost on the trip to the target. If tonight's mission didn't get the job done they would have to come back tomorrow or the next day and do it all over again. A second trip would not have the element of surprise and they would be sitting ducks for the island's defenders. So Nick was keeping a close watch.

JD spoke again, "Jake, be ready on that light when I give you the word, got it?"

"Yes sir I'm on it," he responded quickly.

"Jake, call it out to me at a minute and a half then count it down, Okay?"

Jake's response was clear and concise. "In roughly three minutes from now sir."

The remainder of the flight to the target was uneventful. All three bombers reached the Initial Point together. As they made their last scheduled turn and lined up for the final approach on the target, *One For The Money* and *Barnyard Dog* took up their positions alongside *Wildcat*. A very bright, red morning sun was just breaking the horizon behind the three planes. They were on time, so far, so good.

The three B-25s now flying in their prescribed side-by-side formation climbed in unison to one thousand feet. Within moments JD pushed the controls forward. In perfect formation the three bombers started their dive on the eastern end of the island. The landing strip came into view and the three planes opened up with all of their combined forty-two machine guns at once. Flames and smoke spit from every gun as each bullet left the barrels. Rounds from *Wildcat's* guns cut a nearly straight path along the center of the runway. The tracers quickly progressed in the direction of the four planes down at the far end, one of which had already begun its takeoff run. Their arrival was not a moment too soon. Trees began to splinter and branches flew in the air as the two planes astride *Wildcat* cut loose on their targets. With four hundred rounds per minute exploding from each gun, over twenty thousand shell casings were being ejected. Screaming overhead at tree top level with guns blazing, the planes expelled a wall of lead and spent brass which rained down on everything below.

It was all happening fast, but to the adrenaline filled flyers it seemed as though the attack was playing out in slow motion. Their concentration was so focused, they could smell the cordite from the guns as the rounds left the barrels. They clearly made out the smallest pieces of bark flying off the branches and they felt the hydraulic cylinders which operated the bomb bay doors thump to a stop signifying that the doors were now wide open.

Virtually wing tip to wing tip, the bombers roared low and fast over their targets. The noise and vibration coming from their six big, supercharged, radial engines screaming overhead sent panic through the Japanese below. The pilots of all three planes watched as soldiers ran in all directions seeking cover anywhere they could find it. Hundreds of birds left their perches atop the trees filling the sky in front of the planes. The bombs were released, slipping off their racks one after another. As they left the bomb bays the reduced weight caused the planes to immediately rise ten feet. The small parachutes opened just as planned and the bombs floated down to their targets.

The three planes reached the western end of the island within seconds. It was over in an instant. They had flown all this way for just seconds over the target, but the damage from a successful mission would mean that the threat from this island to American sailors, marines, and soldiers would be eliminated. Even before the bombs detonated, the four patrol planes were ablaze after hundreds of hits from *Wildcat's* machine guns which had raked them from end to end.

Nick quickly took his position at the tail gun. Jake had already climbed up to the top turret. The drowning sound of the hydraulic motor could barely be heard as it efficiently powered the rotating turret. Jake was searching the sky above *Wildcat* for targets. Both men were ready to return fire if need be, but there were no targets to be seen. The attack had been a total surprise with no damage inflicted by the enemy. The only thing close to a problem were some feathers that had been ruffled by the plane's propellers as they cut through the few birds that hadn't been fast enough to avoid the oncoming planes.

From his position looking out from the tail gunner's viewing window Nick watched as the bombs began to explode where they had fallen. Deep, jagged holes appeared along the length of the runway and the jungle on both sides burst into flames. From what he was seeing, all indications were that the mission was a complete success.

The three bombers cleared the western shore of the island at the same time, still flying in a tight, side-by-side formation. Moments after the beach passed under the planes they all began pulling up to gain altitude. JD looked to his left to see the copilot in *One For The Money* gave him a smile and a "thumbs up" signal. At that very moment JD watched as *One For The Money's* right wing exploded. The copilot's facial expression changed in an instant as he stared back at the severed wing and burning fuel streaming from the exposed wing tank. His smile was replaced with an expression of sheer terror. As JD continued to watch, helpless to affect the inevitable outcome, the wing ripped off and disappeared. A moment later *One For The Money* rolled over and went straight down, vanishing from JD's field of vision.

"What the heck," JD shouted out loud. "Where's this coming from?"

Shifting his view quickly to the right, JD watched as *Barnyard Dog*, trailing smoke from her right engine accelerated and rolled out hard to the right. The pilot was taking evasive action in an attempt to get out of harm's way.

Shells were exploding all around. The morning sky was on fire. JD and Todd saw tracers coming from below *Wildcat* and whizzing past the cockpit windows on both sides, heading straight up. The entire crew could hear rounds peppering the bottom of the plane. JD tightened his grip on the controls and pitched the left wing over until *Wildcat* was flying sideways through the air with the left wing pointing straight down.

With *Wildcat* now flying on her side, JD could see out his side window down at the sea below the plane. To his shock he saw that they were flying directly over a lagoon protected by coral reefs and filled with barges, patrol boats, small gun boats and several troop transports all at anchor. His mind was racing trying to make sense out of this unforeseen change of fortune. His thoughts kept coming back to the fact that the anchorage below had not been in the Navy report. He shook these thoughts off quickly and started thinking about how to get his plane and crew out of there.

Every vessel seemed to be firing up at them. Flying on its side, *Wildcat* made a smaller target so JD didn't attempt to level out immediately. Instead he pulled the controls tight to his chest changing their course to the left, away from the lagoon.

After clearing the reef, JD decided to level out and begin to climb. Todd was now pushing the throttles full forward with his left hand. The roar from the straining engines was unbearable. JD kicked *Wildcat* back to level flight with a hard turn of the controls to the right. Now as both wing tips came level with the horizon, *Wildcat* began climbing without losing precious air speed. Both pilots were desperate to put distance between themselves and the island.

Then it happened. The impact was terrific. Something hit with incredible force directly into the wheel well just behind and below the right engine. The wheel and shredded tire dropped out of the wheel well. After a short pause they simply fell away, leaving behind only mangled struts and hydraulic cylinders hanging precariously below the wing. The right engine, still running at full speed, was now loose on its mounting. The huge propeller blades were completely out of balance as they continued to spin at maximum revolutions. This caused the right wing to flap up and down with every revolution of the powerful engine. The uncontrollable motion was quickly transferred to the rest of the plane which was now warbling and vibrating badly. They had taken a direct hit and suffered serious damage but, unbelievably, there was no fire yet.

The Final Mission   Arnold D. Jones

Immediately, the left wing began to rise as the drag from the extended landing gear hardware and underperforming right engine were overtaken by the power of the left engine. JD turned the wheel full left which for the moment, kept the plane from rolling over right. Gradually, the plane settled back down nearly even with the horizon. At the same time, JD pushed hard against the left rudder pedal to stop a slow turn to the right which, if not corrected, would take them back over the lagoon. This problem too, was caused by the left engine overpowering the damaged one. He was straining with all he had to keep *Wildcat* in the air while preventing her from turning back over the deadly lagoon. Tracers were now coming from behind the plane but, as *Wildcat* continued away from the island the tracers were much fewer than before. Soon *Wildcat* was out of range of the island's guns altogether.

The B-25 is designed to fly with one engine at a minimum air speed of one hundred and forty miles per hour. They were already down to one hundred and fifty. JD was now thinking out loud, "With this added drag I'm not confident that our present air speed is fast enough to prevent a stall." He had no idea because this situation wasn't in the manual. "I didn't think she'll continue to fly unless we can reduce the drag or increased air speed."

JD called out to Todd. "We've got to get rid of some of this drag. Feather that engine then shut her down!"

Instinctively Todd was already hard at work trying his best to do exactly what was needed, but having no luck. Feathering the propellers on the damaged engine meant rotating the blades so they would no longer catch any air, thus reducing the wind resistance on the blades.

"It's not responding," shouted Todd.

"Okay, cut the fuel, just shut her down. The vibration is getting worse. We've got to stop it before it rips the wing off."

JD realized that he was now shouting too but he couldn't help it. Something had to be done soon or mission forty-four would come to a very bad ending. He decided he could find a way to deal with the drag of a pin wheeling propeller set at the wrong pitch but the vibration would doom them.

Todd screamed back in a tone that JD recognized as unadulterated fear. "No good, the emergency fuel supply shut-off valve is in the off position but she's still getting fuel, nothing's happening she's still running full out!"

An instant after Todd finished speaking the increased vibration proved to be too much for the damaged motor mount. Suddenly the big radial engine tore itself away from its mount. With the propeller still rotating at full speed the engine spun into the side of the cockpit. One of the three propeller blades came tearing down and through the Plexiglas window directly over Todd's head. The downward momentum sliced off his left arm just below the elbow. The huge blade continued its downward arc until it buried itself in the seat but, only after slicing through Todd's left leg. The blade was stopped by the armor plating located below the side window. It hung there suspended for just a moment before the engine fell down and away, pulling the propeller back up and out the window over Todd's head.

In the blink of an eye Todd's body went limp. He gently eased back into the seat and his head came to rest against the cockpit wall. His eyes slowly closed as he took one short gasp of air. Todd died right there, not ten inches from JD.

Blood was everywhere and JD was horrified. Even with the wind now screaming through the serrated hole in the window he couldn't get his breath and his heart was pounding at an incredible rate. JD felt sick to his stomach but held it in as best he could. He had never imagined such fear was possible. It took everything he had inside to keep from completely losing control.

In a panic JD reached to his left and hit the emergency horn, signaling the crew to bail out. He quickly returned both hands to the controls still forcing the wheel hard left. Letting go for just the time it took to sound the alarm had nearly allowed the plane to roll over. "I'll never be able to get out of here." He almost shouted. It was obvious that if he left the controls the plane would immediately roll and go out of control. Altitude is a pilot's best friend because it provides time to make corrections but *Wildcat* was no more than four hundred feet above the water. Only seconds separated *Wildcat* from total destruction. He had to stay at the controls.

"Think, think," he told himself out loud.

Months of training, plus endless hours of practice flying and forty-four combat missions began to pay off as his mind shut out the horror of the moment and focused on the problem. *With the right engine now gone the drag must be reduced. Maybe I could risk lowering the RPMs on the remaining engine to gain more control.* JD eased the throttle back ever so slightly reducing power. It worked. *Wildcat's* airspeed was reduced but he now had better control of the plane and the physical strain was significantly reduced.

He called to the crew through the interphone, but there was no response.

He was alone. Panic had caused him to hit the emergency horn. Now Nick and Jake were bobbing around in the Pacific Ocean praying that a U.S. Navy submarine spotted them before a Jap plane or patrol boat came along. He hoped they would make it. He prayed they would make it.

CHAPTER FIVE
DECISIONS

JD reached behind his seat groping around for his gloves. He found the right one. Using a gloved hand he wiped Todd's blood from the gauges in an attempt to assess the condition of the plane. Everything looked as it should with the exception of the fuel. Both the right and left wing tanks read nearly empty. He immediately switched over to the center tank located above the bomb bay, transferring fuel to the wing tanks. The center tank gauge indicated full. She was losing fuel from somewhere, but there was nothing that could be done about it. There was no direct connection to the engines from the center tank. The fuel could only reach the starving engine through the wing tanks. The transfer of fuel into these tanks meant that a good portion of the precious fuel would be lost before it could reach the engine, but there was no other choice.

At the reduced air speed *Wildcat* was slowly losing altitude. JD needed to make a decision. The choices were to try and gain some altitude then bail out while there was still an opportunity or try a water landing. Neither option held much appeal but he especially hated the thought of trying to jump out of the plane. With no good option he decided to continue on the present course for a while longer.

With no real plan, the crippled plane flew on as JD orchestrated a delicate balance between maintaining altitude and maintaining control. Raising the engine's RPMs allowed the plane to gain altitude but the controls were difficult to handle. On the other hand, lowering the RPMs restored control and reduced the physical strain but sacrificed altitude. He continued to switch from one to the other as *Wildcat* flew to the northwest. Home and safety were in the opposite direction but there was danger in changing course and risking going back near the island.

The weather was changing as clouds began to appear in the windscreen directly out in front of *Wildcat*. The clouds were dark and filled the sky from about five thousand feet above the ocean up to forty-five thousand. A storm was out there and *Wildcat* was headed directly for it.

The center tank fuel gauge now read less than a quarter full. He had lost track of the time but reasoned that *Wildcat* had been flying about thirty to forty minutes since switching to the center tank. At her present airspeed this would make *Wildcat's* position seventy or so miles from that morning's target. That's when he saw it. Out about fifteen miles and off to the left was an island. Closing the distance, soon a tree covered hill in the center of the island came into view. The island was covered by a thick forest which extended out on both sides of the hill forming the crescent shape of the islands land mass. The inner arc created a large bay. Waves were breaking far off shore against a protective reef. This outer reef left the water in the bay reasonably flat.

This was the spot. Instantly, JD made the decision to take a chance and put *Wildcat* down just off shore in the bay. Flying on only the left engine meant that the B-25 could not easily turn to the left. To avoid attempting such a risky maneuver JD continued past the island. He made sure the island was well behind the plane before starting a wide, slow one-hundred-eighty degree turn to the right. When the turn was completed he straightened her out. He was now back tracking. Soon the hill was visible out the right window as the plane passed by the island from the opposite direction. The plan was to continue on the same course and fly approximately five miles beyond the island before starting another wide, slow one-hundred-eighty degree right turn. When JD estimated that *Wildcat* was the proper distance past the island, he once again gently banked into the turn. As *Wildcat* completed this second and final turn the bay came into view out in front of the plane. He estimated that the approach would be about four miles, just right to get in good position for a touchdown in the bay.

With the bay now spread out before him, JD began to line up the struggling B-25 with his intended point of contact out on the surface of the bay. The fuel gauge now read nearly empty. This left no room for error. There would be only one chance to get the ditching right. There wouldn't be enough fuel to go around again.

Satisfied that the plane was properly lined up, JD detected a left-to-right cross wind as *Wildcat* started to descend from the south. A crosswind on approach meant that the plane would be drifting to the east away from the beach as it descended. This didn't matter now, he wasn't trying to hit a runway he was just trying to put her down in the bay. JD figured he couldn't miss it if he tried.

At fifty feet above the water JD feathered the propeller on the one remaining engine then eased the throttle full back, cutting power. Now gliding, he waited for the right moment before pulling the controls hard to his chest. *Wildcat's* nose came up as she neared the water. JD braced for impact.

The tail made contact first. The nose started to come down as the plane's belly cut the surface. JD was thrown forward as the bomber's speed was abruptly reduced. Then the left propeller and engine plowed the surface. This caused the bomber to pivot violently to the left a full ninety degrees. As she rotated, the right wing dipped down and cut an arcing path through the surface of the bay. Water sprayed up and poured in the cabin through the shattered window drenching everything inside. Then there was total stillness. To JD's relief she had held together. The left wing was pointing up and the right wing remained partially submerged. The sea came rushing in from below through the open bomb bay filling the cabin quickly. It was only then that JD realized they had forgotten to close the doors after releasing their bombs.

Then surprisingly, the water level stopped rising, *Wildcat* wasn't sinking. The plane was silent except for the sound of the surface of the bay gently lapping against the outside of the plane. In the stillness JD released his seat belt and climbed down to the area of the plane where Jake had been stationed just behind the cockpit and in front of the bomb bay. Standing in salt water up to his knees he could see rocks or maybe it was coral under the open bomb bay. She was hung up on whatever it was that lay just a few feet below the surface of the bay. This reprieve allowed JD to collect his thoughts. The good news was that he would have time to salvage anything that might be useful for survival on the island. The bad news was that *Wildcat* would undoubtedly be discovered by the Japanese.

Before there was time to develop a plan the peaceful silence was interrupted by the faint sound of a marine engine approaching from well out to sea. A quick glance through the window revealed a patrol boat, which he assumed was Japanese, approaching at a high rate of speed. The craft's motor sounded as though it was straining for all it was worth. As he continued to watch, the boat soon began to slow down as it reached the white water breaking over the coral reefs that lay just below the surface, about five hundred yards from the stranded plane.

The sea was quite rough outside of this natural protective barrier. It was apparent that the crew of the patrol boat was carefully searching for a safe passage through the reef line. JD turned his eyes away from the oncoming boat to the island. A quick assessment confirmed that he certainly wouldn't be able to make it to the island without being spotted. It was fight or flight time. He couldn't run and he was out numbered and out gunned. The situation was not good. *Wildcat* was now a trap.

Still watching out the window it appeared that the boat was working its way through the reefs and would soon be able to speed up again. Time was running out fast but remarkably JD's mind wasn't racing. He actually felt a calmness come over him. His view of the approaching boat was unobstructed because the right wing was submerged below the water, resulting from the centrifugal force generated when the plane had pivoted about the left engine.

Suddenly JD realized what to do. With both parachutes still on, he slipped down through the open bomb bay finding enough room between the bottom of the plane and the rocks. Once out, he made his way underneath the right wing, coming up inside the compartment located behind the missing motor and where the landing gear had been housed before being shot away. Grabbing hold of a group of hydraulic tubes that run along the inside wall of the compartment, he lifted both legs up and out of the water. Undetectable from the surface, the Japanese soldiers would have to swim under the wing to spot him. That is, if he could hold himself up inside the compartment.

Straining to keep from slipping back into the water, he waited. The weight of the two now waterlogged parachutes made the task that much more difficult. The patrol boat was alongside *Wildcat* now and the Japanese soldiers were yelling out in Japanese what seemed to be orders to whoever they thought might still be inside the downed plane. With both arms now strained beyond endurance he somehow managed to hold himself up out of the water.

The sound of automatic small arms fire filled the small enclosure. JD surmised that they must be shooting into the air because he didn't hear any rounds hitting the plane. Then movement could be detected inside the fuselage. It sounded like two people were entering the rear door with more yelling. After a moment, the yelling turned into conversation between the soldiers.

JD could hear the patrol boat slowly circling the plane in a clockwise pattern while the solders inside the plane continued to move about. He could hear the boat coming around until it was very close to his hiding place. He stayed perfectly still, holding on and lifting his legs as high as he could. He held his breath as the boat passed beyond the wing. After completing one circuit the boat come to a stop at the rear of the plane and several more soldiers entered the rear door. As they did so *Wildcat's* nose tilted slightly upwards from the extra weight now present inside the rear compartment. The movement allowed JD to get a better grip and to lock his heels over a flange that protruded from the edge of the wheel well. With both legs now supported, the strain was reduced significantly. The water was crystal clear and he would undoubtedly be detected if any portion of his body slipped out of the wheel well. He continued to hold on, pulling himself up inside the compartment as far as he could.

The conversation inside the cabin was muffled. However, JD recognized that the tone had changed. The previously aggressive tone was now replaced with a sort of I told you so banter between the soldiers. It was as if they had just cracked some secret code or found the solution to a difficult problem. At any rate, they were now exiting the plane, apparently satisfied.

After a few minutes the motor roared to life as it accelerated, pushing the patrol boat back toward open sea at a brisk speed.

JD stayed put for the next thirty minutes just in case a member of the boarding party had been left behind. Not detecting any sound or movement from inside the plane he slipped quietly down into the water. From handhold to handhold he made his way back along the bottom of the wing then under water coming up once more inside the bomb bay. Everything was as he had left it except that Todd's body was gone, as were the charts and maps from Jake's table.

By taking the parachutes JD had hoped to make it appear to a boarding party that Todd had brought the plane in alone before dying at the controls. The Japanese would reasonably conclude that the rest of the crew had bailed out somewhere far out to sea. He was confident that the Japanese soldiers would show Todd's body to their superiors. After which they would describe the scene while explaining that they had watched the plane go down. Because their boat had arrived on the scene mere moments after the crash, they could attest to the fact that no one had been observed bailing out of the plane. Everyone would be assured that Todd had been the only one in the plane when it came down. A story this straight forward would close the book on any further investigation. At least that's what JD hoped would be the outcome.

The sky was becoming much darker and soon it began to rain. Large droplets pounded the plane's aluminum skin. The sound of the rain against the fuselage made it seem to JD like he was inside a snare drum. He sat on Jake's table with his feet out of the water and unwrapped one of his sandwiches. The glass inner lining of the thermo that JD had brought along was unbroken so he poured a cup of coffee. It was still hot. There would be time to eat, gather up what would be useful on the island and then rest. Just in case there were people on the island, the trip to the beach wouldn't be attempted until it was dark.

The rain was coming down much harder when JD awakened, still sitting on Jakes navigation table. His head was all the way back against the large radio at an odd angle leaving him with a painful kink in the neck. It took a moment to get his bearings, but he soon remembered where he was and what had happened. He shook his head to clear away the cobwebs from the unintended nap. His neck still hurt. It wasn't like him to fall asleep so easily. He reasoned the strain from that morning's ordeal must have taken a lot out of him. He remembered finishing both sandwiches, drinking a little coffee and the next thing he knew, he was opening his eyes and feeling the pain in his neck.

It was now mid-afternoon. The rain continued and by this time the sky was very overcast. The combination of dark clouds and the pounding rain made it seem like the middle of the night. JD decided there was no reason to wait for nightfall. The heavy storm would be sufficient cover for the hundred and fifty yard trip to the beach. He stuffed the thermos bottle down the front of his jacket. It was time to go. He moved to the other side of the plane and pulled the life raft release located behind and above Todd's seat. Immediately, the container's cover swung down exposing the raft. He pulled it down tucking it under his left arm. Carefully, he made his way through the darkened interior easing down into the open bomb bay until his feet made contact with the rocks below the surface. Cautiously working his way across the rocks he eventually stepped up into the rear area of the plane where Nick had been stationed. To the left was an empty container where the waist gunner's life raft had once been housed. He had hoped that it would still be there because a second raft would have been useful in carrying equipment to the beach. His thoughts immediately shifted to Nick and Jake. JD knew their chances for survival were much greater now that it was confirmed that Nick had indeed taken the time to grab the raft.

As quickly as possible, he moved to one of the side waist gun openings and leaned out extending the raft outside the plane. He was holding onto the raft with one hand while pulling the cord with the other. Instantly the raft began to inflate giving off a loud hissing sound. The noise from the compressed gas rushing into the raft caused him to think for the first time about the possibility that there might be people on the island. If so, then most assuredly they would hear the noise. His arrival would hardly be a surprise now. There wasn't much to be done about it anyway. He couldn't stay where he was.

Using his neck tie he secured the raft to the plane and began gathering everything that he might need. He tossed in the large first aid kit, the fire axe, the emergency dinghy radio and antenna. He then took one of the waist machine guns, a thousand rounds of ammunition in two boxes, the binoculars, a couple of blankets and his thermo. He poked around for anything else useful and spotted the pyrotechnic pistol (flare gun) and two of Nick's candy bars still wedged in the support beam. These he also tossed in the raft. Checking his jacket pockets he confirmed eight boxes of rations, sun glasses and two ammunition clips. Then he took off his jacket, hat, parachutes, boots, pants and belt. All were carefully placed on top of the other items. He was ready to go.

As he worked to untie the raft he looked at the neck tie in his hands. *This thing's finally been useful for something.* He slipped out of the waist gun opening into the water. He positioned himself behind the raft and began to kick toward the beach. Progress was slow but steady, the rain was blinding but there was little wind and the bay was flat all the way to the beach. As he continued to kick he began to find a comfortable rhythm; and then he thought... *Could there be sharks in the water, possibly swimming all around me in the darkness?* He kicked harder.

-

CHAPTER SIX
A GUEST IN AMERICA

Max Slavina crossed the border into The United States a few weeks after JD ditched his plane in the bay just off the beach of the far away South Pacific Island.   Max's real name was Lieutenant Maki Itsagawa and he was an officer in the Japanese Imperial Navy.

Max had been a part of the Japanese force that had invaded and then occupied the island of Kiska in the Aleutian Island chain located west of Alaska. The Japanese high command ordered the invasion in an attempt to draw the U.S. Navy's attention away from the real objective which was Midway Island. The Americans ignored the invasion and kept their eyes on the more strategic outpost of Midway. This resulted in the first victory of the war by the U.S. Navy over the Japanese Navy.

After freezing in the far north for nearly a full year Maki was secretly removed from the island and deposited by submarine on the Canadian shore twenty or so miles north of Vancouver. Given the identity of a Panamanian national with the name Max Slavina he easily found war work in a factory that produced artillery shells. There he remained; working hard and living a solitary life while awaiting his assignment. Then, eight days ago word came. He was ordered to make his way to a small town in the Upper Peninsula of Michigan.

Max was a member of the Japanese military elite by way of his father and grandfather before him. He was well educated and had spent time in The United States as a diplomatic attaché during the late 1930s. His English was good, as was his Spanish. If his language ever betrayed him and as a result, he came under suspicion, he could always point to his Panamanian, Spanish speaking background as the reason for any English language difficulties. His appearance made him uniquely qualified for his assignment. He did not look Japanese, for that matter neither did he appear to be Asian. His facial features allowed him to pass for a native South American of Spanish and Indian ancestry.

Max boarded the east bound train in Vancouver and traveled as far as Winnipeg. From Winnipeg he moved south by bus. At the last rest stop before reaching the border with the United States he simply allowed the bus to depart without him. After watching the bus pull out he casually finished his soup and nursed the rest of his Coke.

The bus was gone, heading south toward the border with the United States. Max could relax now, so he leaned back. There was no reason to keep looking outside. After all, there was nothing out there but two gasoline pumps, a wire basket with six glass jars of bulk motor oil, a water hose for topping off radiators and the empty road beyond. He was really in the middle of nowhere. Another vehicle might not happen along for an hour or more.

He instead casually began to look over his surroundings. There were a few tables pre-set for four customers scattered around the room. Two truck drivers sat at one, eating their lunch and talking. They were the only other customers in the room. He sat at a small table sized for two people. It was positioned against the front wall under the last of three windows. From any of the windows a person could have watched as the bus pulled out but only from the window he had chosen could it be observed for more than a mile until it disappeared down the straight two lane highway. Across the room there was a counter with six red padded stools, each had a polished chrome pedestal. It was a nice place, clean but dusty, small but big enough. It was here to serve the busses, trucks and what few cars come this way.

Eventually he reached into his pocket for some change to leave a tip. Max considered his actions, "What is this tipping system all about? I don't understand it. In Japan we have no such custom. In Japan, people are paid by their employer. Requiring a customer to pay an employee directly is unheard of and somehow it seems disgraceful." After the appropriate time had passed he reluctantly left a tip, picked up the check, walked to the counter and paid the young lady behind the cash register. With a pleasant smile and a tip of his hat he walked out into the Canadian afternoon. There were several hours of daylight remaining and Max had a long walk ahead of him. Although he carried papers that would pass the most intense inspection he had no legitimate reason for being in Canada. His passport displayed an entry stamp but, if checked by the US side there would be no record on hand at his supposed point of entry. Max would walk across the border and avoid the issue all together.

As darkness approached he was nearing the end of his ten mile walk to the border. Max left the road moving east parallel with the border. A few yards off the road he simply disappeared into a farmer's field. He made his way steadily through rows of young corn that were only a few feet tall. To conceal his five-foot, eight-inch frame Max stayed crunched down as low as he could get. Continuing east, crossing into another field, then another, and yet another until he was confident that it was safe to turn south and cross over into the United States. He had been right, no one noticed.

Max walked south for two miles until he came to a road which he knew would be there. The two lanes of black top ran east and west. He came out of the woods and stepped onto the road at a location far from any intersecting north and south road. Anyone who happened upon him now would not immediately connect his presence with Canada. Max was safely across the border.

He thought to himself, *I'm back, and this time I will make a difference.*

While stationed in the United States he had traveled extensively, learning much about life in America. Life in the US was much less structured than in his country and he disliked it. He was from a homogeneous society where people fell into line, so to speak. To Max the Americans were disjointed, disorganized, and much too opinionated. To him, they were simply uncivilized.

More importantly, while in the United States he had visited the Naval base at San Diego where he observed the US Pacific fleet long before they were transferred to Pearl Harbor, Hawaii. There he took lots of pictures of the city with its expansive bay. The US Pacific fleet just happened to show up in every photograph. He was pleased that after the fleet was moved to Pearl Harbor his photography played a part in the planning for the Japanese attack of December seventh. He liked to think that it was a big and important part.

On a visit to Detroit, he traveled around the area and saw for himself the seemingly endless streets filled with factories, steel mills, forging plants, iron foundries and the vast proliferation of other automotive related suppliers. Cars and trucks were shipped by rail, by ship, and by hauling truck and trailer. The highways were packed with trucks moving materials from plant to plant.

In Cincinnati, he toured the many machine builders. They seemed to be everywhere, building lathes, boring mills, knee mills, presses, drills, and tooling of all sorts. Iron and steel came to Cincinnati daily from Pennsylvania by barge down the Ohio River. The river front was the busiest place he had seen in America. Max reported everything that he witnessed; sending back reports on a weekly basis for two years.

Max was comfortable navigating in America. He would have no problem accomplishing his assignment, the details of which he would soon learn from his contact in Menominee, Michigan.

CHAPTER SEVEN
SAFE

Jake and Nick sat warm, dry and comfortable in the little galley of a U.S. Navy submarine a hundred feet below the surface of the Pacific. The sub had plucked them out of the ocean just moments after they hit the water. Bailing out of *Wildcat* at less than four hundred feet above the surface barely provided enough time for their parachutes to deploy fully before reaching the water. Both men were uninjured but shaken from the experience. By the time they swam to each other and managed to inflate their raft the sub surfaced not ten yards away. They had been in the water less than twenty minutes.

"Now tell me again what happened, exactly?" Insisted the ship's Captain as he looked directly at Jake.

Jake started once more to share all that he could recall.

"Like I said before, I was up in the turret spinning slowly around scanning the sky for targets when we were hit. A shell came in from below the plane and struck behind the right engine. But there was no explosion or fire, just a tremendous jolt. Immediately upon impact the plane reacted violently and began to roll over, everything was shaking.

Within just a second or two, somehow JD and Todd regained control almost bringing the wings back level, but the whole plane was still vibrating badly. I kept one eye on the sky while sneaking a peek into the cockpit from time to time. The bomb bay was still open and the noise from the wind rushing by prevented me from making out what was being said, but I can tell you that both pilots were busy trying to maintain control. I didn't know what to do or how to react so I stayed at my gun." Jake paused.

"Yes, what happened next?" Probed the Captain, still determined to learn all there was to know about the mission.

"Well, after a short time, not even a minute, the whole engine came off and spun toward the side of the fuselage. That's when one of the propeller blades came crashing through the right side of the cockpit and struck Todd. Blood sprayed all over the place. Then I heard the horn and I was gone straight down and out the bomb bay." Jake sat back and took a deep breath.

"All right I understand. Let me ask you, did you see the plane after you got out?" The Captain asked, still focused on Jake.

Jake sat up, took a moment in thought, his hands on top of his head and elbows out to his sides. Then he responded.

"I didn't get a good look, but two things I know for sure. She was flying straight and level and fuel was spewing off the trailing edge of the wing that had been hit. There was a serious fuel leak."

"Thank you," said the Captain. Now the Captain turned his attention to Nick. "Do you have anything to add?"

Nick had been listening intently to Jake's account and was ready to add his perspective. The Captain had made Jake repeat his story several times so Nick wanted to make sure that he got his story correct and complete the first time.

"Well," Nick began, "just after the impact I stuck my head out the right waist gun opening to assess the damage for myself. There was no doubt that the shell hit the right wing. I didn't have any idea what had happened or if the pilots were still in control. All the way in the rear compartment you are isolated from the crew and I was trying to ascertain for myself how much trouble I was in for. That's when I saw a hydraulic cylinder hanging down from the wheel well. It was just dangling there and the wheel assembly that had been attached to it was gone. Fuel was flowing off the wing and I noticed that despite the fact that at the time we were flying straight and level, the right aileron was in the full up position. When I looked to the back of the plane I saw that the rudder was pushed hard left. To me this meant that JD and Todd were fighting to maintain control and at least one of them would need to stay at the controls. I know now that it had to have been JD because Todd had been seriously injured. Logically, JD couldn't leave the cockpit to bail out. If he had decided to release those controls at that time the plane would have simply rolled over and flown itself straight down, trapping us all inside. He saved our lives, that's for sure."

"Did you observe the plane after you bailed out?"

"Yes sir, I got a good look at the belly. When I followed Jake out the bomb bay I rolled face up. I was reaching for my rip cord with one hand and holding the raft with the other. I was having trouble getting a grip on the release handle. We were very close to the surface when we had to go, I didn't have any time to waste. When I couldn't get hold of that handle I let go of the raft straight away. I started grabbing for anything I could find with both hands. The moment I let go of that raft the wind turned me face up for a few seconds. The bottom of the plane was riddled with holes probably from machine gun and small arms fire. It was a miracle that one of us wasn't hit. Fuel was running off both wings leaving mist trails in the sky. I figure he couldn't have stayed up there very long after we jumped."

"Did either one of you see the plane after you hit the water?"

The two airmen looked at each other for a moment before Jake spoke up. "Yes we both did, and it was holding the same course and speed, flying away from us."

The Captain quickly followed up. "Which direction was she headed? Can you estimate her speed?"

"We're sure that he was on a northwest heading, maintaining around four hundred feet and maybe a hundred and fifty miles an hour." Nick answered for both of them and Jake nodded his agreement.

"If you think of anything else to add to your reports come and see me. I'll have the information transmitted after dark when the radio antenna can be safely deployed." The Captain dismissed both men so he could be left to write his report. His report contained the details provided by the two crew members and fixed the recommended search area at a maximum range of thirty five miles north and west of the recovery point. Joseph Dutton Jones was officially reported to be missing in action and Todd Kramer was reported as missing in action and presumed dead. The families of both service men would have the news within two weeks.

"Sailor," called the Captain.

"Aye sir."

The Captain's aide stepped in the galley from his post in the companion way just outside the door. "Take this to the code room. Have it added to tonight's outgoing transmission."

"Aye aye sir," answered the aide.

He was out and gone down the narrow hallway with the report in hand. The Captain returned to his cabin, took the ship's log from the small shelf above his desk, and dutifully recorded the rescue with all the related facts.

CHAPTER EIGHT
THE ISLAND

Kicking from behind the raft, JD neared the shore. His view of the sandy beach was blocked by the raft which was directly in front of him. Unsure of the remaining distance to the beach, he judged that it must be getting close. Through the driving rain a large formation appeared in front of the raft. As it came into view the wall of rock loomed above the surface of the bay some fifteen feet. JD stopped kicking and came around to the side of the raft to have a better look. Even in the driving rain it was obvious from its craggily exterior that this formation was actually hardened lava from a long ago volcanic eruption. The lava mound protruded beyond the sand continuing several feet out into the water. It seemed to split the beach almost perfectly in half. About a mile or so of white sand extended on either side of the mound. Choosing a course to the left while keeping close to the mound, he resumed kicking, guiding the raft the remaining few yards to shore. Soon, the bottom came up and JD was able to stand a few feet from the beach.

Cautiously stepping ashore, his bare feet left clear impressions in the sand. JD looked to the right. All he could see was the mound. Turning quickly to the left, there was nothing but sand. Squinting now, he stared straight ahead. Heavy foliage and the pounding rain made it impossible to see if anybody was lying in wait. Taking his chances, JD began to drag the raft over his footprints hoping to scrape them away. The raft, which had been light and maneuverable while in the water, was now heavy and cumbersome. The tree line was thirty feet inland. Although he was exhausted, the distance was covered quickly. After hiding the raft beneath a stand of small trees, he immediately headed back to the beach to obliterate any sign of his presence still remaining in the sand. As he approached he saw that the heavy rain had already washed all of the marks and footprints from the sand, restoring the beach's flawlessly smooth surface. JD wasted no time getting himself off the beach and back to the cover the trees provided. The rain was relentless, pounding down hard on everything. The large droplets were striking the branches, leaves and tall grass, creating a continuous symphony of sound that obscured any other noise that might sound the alarm of impending danger. His senses were on high alert in these new and unfamiliar surroundings. Anything or anybody could be approaching and there would be no warning and no time to organize a defense. He watched and waited, straining to pick up a sound, trying to be prepared for the unexpected. The downpour continued. The rain felt warm as it dripped from his head and shoulders, and the air temperature was at least ninety-eight degrees. JD was sticky and uncomfortable. Undeterred he maintained his vigil trying to listen for any noise besides the rain. Several uneventful hours passed and he finally began to relax.

As darkness mercifully began to fall, the rain remained constant with no letup in sight. JD was soaked from head to foot with salt water which added to his discomfort. Stripping off his underwear, he hung them over some nearby branches. *They probably won't dry anytime soon but the rain will hopefully rinse out the salt.* He stood for a moment in the open, allowing the driving rain to wash over his body, taking with it the salt from the bay.

Although tired and mentally fatigued, JD carefully disassembled both pistols rubbing them down with oil from the small container he had brought along. He found the silencer, placed it against his lips and blew it out until he was sure that it was clear. Very slowly, he screwed it onto the barrel of one of his pistols. In the darkness, he took care not to get it cross threaded. During basic training, countless times they had disassembled and reassembled their rifles while blindfolded. At the time this drill seemed a waste of time but it all made perfect sense now.

After making sure that they both were reloaded and in working order he rubbed a little oil on his knife. Then he took all of his clothes out of the raft and hung them alongside his underwear. Spreading out his reserve chute on the ground, he placed the remaining equipment taken from the plane on one side of the silk sheet leaving enough room to lie down alongside. Once settled, he flipped the raft upside down using it to cover his body, the sheet and equipment. With a Colt in one hand and the knife in the other he was in for the night.

"Dear Lord, thank you for bringing me this far and please give comfort to momma and dad when they learn the news. Please be with me tomorrow."

The rain eventually subsided, and he fell off to sleep that first night on the island; but his rest was interrupted repeatedly throughout the night by the unfamiliar sounds all around him.

At sun-up the following day, JD found his clothes to be reasonably dry and sufficiently free from salt. After dressing, he set out to explore the southern half of the island. His little camp was located to the left or on the southern side of the hill in the center of the island. He followed the tree line, staying off the sand and out of view of the bay. The temperature was already nearing ninety degrees despite the fact that it was still very early. From the rustlings in the tops of some of the taller trees JD knew that there was a westerly breeze but it wasn't getting through the trees to the beach on his side of the island. He was hot and low on fresh water. JD planned to keep an eye open for puddles of rain water as he scouted the island.

The air was still and the bay was dead flat. JD turned his gaze seaward as he made his way through the thick grass and tall vegetation. There, out in the bay, was *Wildcat* setting up on the surface seemingly as proud as a peacock, unmoved from the day before. He turned away and kept moving, paying attention for any sound and movement. There were no foot prints or any other signs that people had ever been on the island, at least not for a long time. As he walked along, to his left were the beach and the bay beyond, to the right the interior of the island. There were many mature palm trees everywhere but other fuller trees were in abundance as well. Some were twisted like so many stiff ropes woven together and extending skyward with branches protruding in all directions. The majority however, were dense stands of tall bamboo thickets. Although the bamboo was much taller, it reminded JD of the sugar cane which grew back home in Kentucky. The earth beneath his feet was mostly sand and covered by thick, very tall grass growing in clumps several feet in diameter. There was very little space between the clumps for walking. He continued on. It took two hours of slow deliberate exploration for JD to traverse roughly the one mile to the furthest point of the island which was the tip of the crescent shaped beach.

Sitting under a tree near the point JD could see the bay to his left, the ocean in front of him and to his right. There was nothing but open water out there; he was a long way from anywhere. He leaned back against the tree trunk and opened a box of his "K" rations, interrupting his expedition just long enough to have breakfast. When finished, he stuffed the chewing gum in his pocket, buried the paper, tin can and box, and then lit one of the four cigarettes that came with every meal. With the housekeeping done, he started back toward his camp, still chewing on the rock hard cereal bar which had been designed to be eaten slowly. As a pilot, he had always returned from his missions to regular Army chow. This was his first real experience with field rations and it made him wonder, *who on earth thought that this thing that I'm about to break a tooth on was a good idea?* He kept chewing and kept walking.

The return trip took him along the opposite shoreline. The wind on that side brought with it rough seas that pounded the backside of the island. There was no beach. Instead the shore was a flat rocky wall that progressively grew higher. As he moved back in the direction of the middle of the island the shore continued to follow the incline of the hill, taking him a little higher with every step. The wind kept the temperature about ten degrees cooler which made his task much more agreeable. At first the beach and the bay over to his right were still visible, however with every step the island continued to widen out. Soon the stands of Bamboo trees and thick foliage obscured his view of the opposite shore. The waves breaking heavily against the rocks and the rustling of the trees made it difficult to hear anything else. This put JD on edge. Carefully he took out the same pistol onto which he had attached the silencer the night before. He flipped off the safety, extended his arm down to his side and slowly continued in the same direction.

After traveling about a hundred yards, he decided to walk inland until he could again see the beach on the opposite shore. The foliage was thick and on several occasions his knife was needed to cut a path wide enough to maneuver through. He observed narrow paths of beaten down grass crisscrossing everywhere, obviously made by small animals of some kind. There was no way of knowing what type of animals populated the island because they were staying out of sight. When he spotted the beach through the trees he retraced his steps, returning to the opposite shore. Throughout the day JD continued the same pattern, moving up the far shore for a hundred yards or so then crossing back to the beach until he was confident that his reconnaissance effort had covered enough ground to insure there were no people around, enemy or otherwise.

As he neared his little makeshift camp loud grunting noises got his attention. Slowly he approached. There, rooting through his equipment and remaining K rations were three feral hogs. They were not very big, maybe fifty pounds, no more. In spite of their size, they immediately became agitated by his approach. As he studied his adversaries he thought, *these guys aren't going anywhere, they might even charge me if I'm not careful. They don't seem to have any fear of humans.*

One of the animals had discovered the K rations and was in the process of eating it entirely, wax coated cardboard box, tin can, wooden spoon and all.

"Hey, get out of here, hey!" JD yelled and waved his hands. The hogs just grew more agitated and aggressive. Suddenly, all three put their heads down and attacked at once, charging straight at him. One of the pigs took the lead while the others flanked their leader on both sides, only a half body length behind. The charging and snorting band of hogs were mere inches apart in a battering ram, flying wedge formation.

He instinctively dropped to one knee, giving no ground but his action didn't detour the chargers. JD raised his pistol and with a steady hand squeezed off three silenced but deadly shots in rapid succession.

Years of rabbit hunting with a .22 rifle in the hills around his home and the endless days of target practice on the range at Camp Gordon, Georgia had just paid dividends. All three hogs lay motionless at his feet. They had gotten very close.

JD searched around and picked up the three spent cartridges from the ground, not wanting to leave any unnecessary signs of his presence on the island for the Japanese to find.

He knew about hogs having been around them all of his life. On the farm, his family raised hogs, sold them for added income and slaughtered them for food. From time to time a hog would get loose and disappear in the hills near the farm and, within just a few months, it would revert back into a wild state transforming itself into a feral hog with protruding tusks and covered with hair. JD studied the dead hogs at his feet. He had no doubt that these hogs descended from domestic stock. People had definitely brought pigs to this island at one time. However, there was no telling how long ago.

He would eat well tonight. Tomorrow he would hang his belongings off the ground before setting out to explore the northern portion of the island. He had no salt or smoke house like they had back home, so most of today's kill would go uneaten. *What a waste.*

The next day's discoveries would prove to be much more substantial.

Access to the other end of the island was blocked by the steep slope of the hill, so JD walked back to the beach trying to find a way across. There he observed that the lava mound, which he passed while kicking the raft to shore two nights earlier, actually crossed over the beach and extended back up the hill. Clearly, the lava flow had originated high in the hill. From above, it had flowed down to the beach below before cooling off and piling up when it reached the water.   The path of the flow created a narrow ramp which gradually ascended some three hundred feet to a spot near the very top of the hill. He considered his options, "The hill can wait. I'll make my way up the ramp and explore the hill tomorrow. Today, I will stay with the plan and walk the northern end of the island."

The walk along the bay side started out very much the same as yesterday's, as did the walk back along the western shore. At first he observed nothing new. There were no signs of anything but an uninhabited island. However, on his fourth crossing back to the beach from the rocky western shore, JD came across a large pool of fresh, clear water. From one side to the other it was a little over a hundred feet across but, from end to end it was easily two hundred and fifty feet. He could see to the bottom and made it out to be three to four feet deep. The pool was fed by a small, but-free flowing waterfall which cascaded down the side of the hill. JD walked slowly along the perimeter of the pool trying to find a good place to kneel down and fill his canteen. This is when he discovered that he was not alone. There were boot prints in several places along the eastern bank of the pond. This was the bank nearest the bay. JD instantly dropped to the ground while arming himself. With gun at the ready, he found cover in the tall grass. Remaining absolutely still he listened and watched. Time passed slowly but, after several minutes, he was confident that no one was about. Now moving much more cautiously, he reached the southern end of the pond. Water was flowing down the hill in a steady stream just a few feet from where he now stood. Looking around he soon discovered a gasoline engine hidden in the brush. A closer examination of the surrounding area revealed hundreds of feet of hose, a large portable pump, and dozens of full five gallon gasoline cans. The pump assembly had Japanese writing on the gauge faces and instruction tags. Near the pump, off to one side, was a wooden box approximately three feet square and two feet high. JD unlatched the top and slowly opened the box. Inside were some hand tools, an assortment of spare parts, a few bottles of Saki, four brushes and several bars of soap.

It was apparent that the Japanese were retrieving fresh water from the pool. There was every indication that this was an ongoing enterprise. They would be back. Logic told JD that the Japanese probably returned after a heavy rain like the one on the night of his arrival. The Japanese surely realized that the rain water gathered up above and then flowed down the hill filling the pool. Following this reasoning, he surmised that they could be on their way to the island right now.

He immediately left the area moving to a well-concealed spot near the point on that side of the island. This location provided a clear view of the ocean and the bay. He took out the binoculars and scanned the approaches to the island. There was nothing out there. The visibility was unlimited and he saw only vast, open water all the way to the horizon.

Thinking out loud JD said. "They're not coming yet. I've got time."

Rushing back to the pool, JD quickly stripped off his clothes and took some soap and a brush from the box. He stepped down into the water and carefully made his way to the waterfall. As the water flowed over his body he tilted his head back and drank his fill. Using the brush and soap, he proceeded to scrub his body from head to foot. Once he was clean his clothes were next. He lathered his underwear, socks, pants and shirt. After rinsing his clothes under the waterfall, he filled his canteen.

A nearby tree trunk was used to bang the excess water from the brush. After which the brush was carefully returned to its place in the box. The lid was closed and the latch secured. JD kicked his heal into the sand and dropped the soap into the indentation before covering it up. He made a visual inventory of the area. Everything looked as it had before. With clothes in hand he headed back to the observation spot, out near the point.

While keeping a vigilant lookout, the wet clothes were hung out to dry. With help from the hot sun and a steady breeze, they dried in just a few minutes. He scanned the bay again. Nothing had changed. There was still no movement out to sea. Hours passed; he watched.

Eventually he put on clean, dry clothes over a freshly showered and scrubbed body. He felt great for the first time in days. With the exploring finished for the day JD found a nice spot with plenty of shade. The shade came from a lone tree just off the beach. This was a perfect place from which to keep watch while leaning his back up against the tree.

The island was a peaceful place, even a very beautiful place. Hours passed slowly as the day drifted away. There was no sign of anything manmade out on the surface of the ocean or in the sky above. However, there was life all around him. Just off shore on the sea side, opposite the bay, JD watched as several sharks patrolled the beach. Back and forth, up and down they swam. Their pattern never changed. They maintained the same leisurely pace throughout the afternoon. *Swimming in that beautiful blue water near the beach is now officially crossed off my list of future activities.* Eventually, the sun dropped behind the hill at JD's back casting a long shadow across the beach. He headed back to his camp while wondering, *How long will I be marooned on the island and just when will the Japanese return?*

The next day JD planned to set out early to explore the hill. Concerned that the Japanese might be coming soon, he took precautions. The pond lay on the opposite side of the hill from where he had made camp. Nevertheless, JD decided to move his camp further inland and away from the hill. The food and smaller supplies were buried while the larger pieces of equipment were carefully hidden in the undergrowth near the new camp's location.

On the morning of the third day JD had nearly reached the top of the ramp leading up the hill when he heard the boats coming toward the island from the bay. His position was concealed by the tops of some trees that grew on either side of the ramp. Their long heavy branches created a canopy that covered the ramp in shade and made it difficult to see from the bay or the beach.

He lay down flat right where he was and observed the arrival of two landing craft. They were riding high in the water although filled with large drums, apparently empty. Soon the boats pulled straight on the beach nearest the fresh water pond. Each boat carried a crew of three. The sailors immediately disembarked. Two headed directly to the pond while the remaining four set up a defensive perimeter. They each carried weapons and were watching both the island and the bay. Within a few minutes, one of the men reappeared from the tree line. He was holding a hose with his left hand as he struggled to drag it to the nearest boat. He agilely hopped on the deck and stuck the hose in the top of one of the drums. Then he blew a whistle.

The gasoline engine came to life in the distance and the filling process started. The task took nearly six hours to complete. During this time the four guards never left their posts. Rather, they continued unwaveringly to scan their surroundings while slowly walking up and down the beach to the right of the rocky mound. JD didn't move but, kept watching the watchers until the work was completed and the two boats were out of sight.

Dark clouds once again began to fill the sky. The sun which had shown brightly earlier in the day had now disappeared behind the gathering storm clouds. JD reached the top of the ramp and found himself on a plateau the size of a tennis court. The hill seemed more like a mountain from where he now stood. The plateau was surrounded by rocky cliffs in front and to his left and right. The cliff in the middle extended sixty feet above the plateau on which JD stood.

Out in the direction of the bay, the sea appeared to be very rough. Even the bay which had been flat during the last downpour was choppy. The rapidly deteriorating weather conditions gave every indication that this new storm would be a big one. He didn't want to attempt a climb back down a narrow, uneven and slippery ramp in bad weather. One misstep could be disastrous. It was nearly straight down on both sides and any fall would be over jagged volcanic stones.

The strong wind began to blow directly in from the bay with increasing intensity. Loose pebbles, small sticks and leaves were blown up by the powerful wind. Trapped by the cliff walls the debris was suspended in midair, swirling like little tornados all around JD. Rain began to fall. At first it was just a steady shower, then the clouds opened up and it began to hail. He rushed over to the tallest cliff face and nestled his body under a small overhang to protect against the marble sized ice which was pounding the ground all around and bouncing nearly a foot on impact.

As the lighting flashed overhead it also flashed inside the cliff face. At first JD thought that it might be some sort of reflection. Oddly he felt a cool breeze on his face even though he had it nearly pressing against the rock wall. Then, something even stranger happened. When the lighting flashed overhead it also lit up the inside of the mountain directly in front of his face. "Now what's going on here?" JD said out loud to no one.

He pushed in further, squeezing his body tightly into the ever narrowing opening under the overhang. Then it happened again, a bright flash of light. With his back to the storm and his eyes peering directly into the crevice just in front of his face, he saw the light flash through an opening between the rock walls.

There could be no mistake the flash was coming from inside the mountain.

CHAPTER NINE
THE MEETING

The city of Menominee, Michigan is located in the Upper Peninsula of Michigan just across the border from Marinette, Wisconsin. The two cities are separated by the river which runs between them to form a natural dividing line of the two States.

Max's bus deposited him in Marinette early Monday morning. From the bus depot he walked north and across the bridge into Michigan. Max continued into town until he spotted the courthouse. There, on the lawn in front of the building, right where he hoped it would be, he saw the town bulletin board. He scanned the various postings. There were posters for lost dogs, others for help wanted and things for sale or rent. It was all there.

After writing down a few of the rooms for rent and job offers his first priority was to find a place to stay. Within an hour he had secured a room at the home of an elderly widow who had started taking in boarders as her contribution to the war effort. The next day he went searching for work. Able-bodied young men were rare at this time so finding employment was not much of a challenge. Before day's end he had used a letter of recommendation from his former employer to secure a job at a local fish processing plant.

From his boarding house it was just a short walk to the river and new place of employment. The processing plant was located on the north bank not far from the mouth of the river. The fishermen could easily unload their catch at the plant before proceeding up the river to their docks which lined both sides of the river for nearly a mile upstream.

Each morning Max got up early and walked down to the plant. At the end of his ten hour shift he would return to his room where he cleaned up and then went out to dinner. He ate at the same restaurant every night. Not because he liked the food but because this was part of the instructions he had been given. He was told to be at the Uptown Café every evening between seven and seven thirty and wait to be contacted.

After maintaining the same schedule for three weeks Max had not yet made his planned contact. He was beginning to think about the possibility of having to spend extended time in this boring, uneventful place and he didn't like the prospect. He was after all, a man, and a man who hadn't been with a woman in over two years. He was lonely and in need of some female companionship. This is why he always asked for a booth in the same section of the restaurant. The waitress hadn't looked like much the first time he saw her or maybe he hadn't been paying attention. She was always nice to him and he found himself anticipating, with a good measure of excitement, seeing her each night. He considered, "It seemed to me that she's begun to fix herself up and has also been spending more and more of her free time at my booth. Maybe she too, is lonely. After all, I am one of the only young and healthy males in town. Why wouldn't she be interested? " Over the past few days Max had sensed that their short verbal exchanges were taking on a flirtatious tone. At first he had assumed that it was his imagination, but he started paying closer attention and eventually reached the conclusion that indeed she was acting differently somehow. She was flirting, he was almost sure of it.

Max walked through the front door of the Uptown Café as usual at around six forty-five and was waved to his booth. She immediately approached him appearing quite lovely, he thought.

"Hi, how are you doing tonight?" she asked with a smile.

"I'm fine as usual. I trust you will not find me too forward, but I must say that you do look beautiful tonight," he said sincerely. After all, he meant every word because she did look great. Better than ever.

"Why thank you; and I don't find you to be forward at all," she responded.

Her lovely blue eyes staring down seemed to cut right through him. She was interested, he could sense it. At that moment Max realized that they hadn't been introduced. While he had momentum he decided to remedy the situation.

"Please allow me to introduce myself. My name is Max, Max Slavina. What's yours?"

"Elsa Menzel, a pleasure to finally learn your name."

They both smiled; relieved to have gotten past this first step which had been much too long in coming. She took his order, still smiling. With an air of something that seemed to make her dance around the room she waited the various tables near his. He continued to watch her throughout dinner which was taking a long time because he was in no hurry. He realized, *Watching Elsa is addictive this evening, different and much better than ever before. But inevitably it has to end.* He watched as Elsa approached him with check in hand. *This is it. The evening will end and I can return to my room as always or I can speak. It seems simple enough, so why am I feeling such trepidation?* As she came closer he was unsure of himself, even nervous, but decided at the last moment to go for it.

"Thank you," he said taking the check from her hand.

Their fingers touched. He allowed his hand to linger on hers for just a moment while looking directly into her eyes. She held his gaze even after their hands separated. He took this as an invitation to make his move.

"What time do you get off?" he asked.

"At nine, why do you ask?"

"I was thinking. Maybe we could take a walk down by the river and watch the fishing boats coming in. It's always a pleasant sight, and it would be nice to share it with someone," he said; not able to think of anything better.

Elsa looked at him for a long moment before she finally spoke.

"I live upstairs in this building. It will take me about an hour to get ready. You could come for me at my room at say ten o'clock?"

Max was excited; at last someone to talk to. "That would be great. Oh, by the way how do I get there?" he asked.

"If you go out the front door and turn to your right there's a doorway on the front of the building at the very corner. Push the button twice and I'll buzz you inside. Take the stairs to the top. You'll find three doors at the top of the steps. Mine is the one in the middle. It will be open. Just let yourself in, all right?"

"That's fine, see you at ten."

He went straight back to his room to brush his teeth and make himself look as presentable as possible. When he had done all he could he headed out. At ten o'clock Max pushed the button as instructed. The electric buzzer sounded. After a short delay the door unlocked. He began to ascend the stairs. The stairwell was dark with only a lone light bulb glowing at the top of the staircase. The air was filled with the fragrance of powder and perfume. He was sure that no men lived in this building. As promised, the door was unlocked and slightly ajar. He let himself inside. The room was small but very clean and nicely furnished. He was standing in a combination sitting room and kitchenette.

"Hello," he called.

He heard Elsa call out from behind one of the two doors inside the apartment. "Max is that you?"

"Yes I'm here."

"Good. You're right on time. Please feel free to get a beer from the ice box if you'd like one. I'm almost ready. I'll be right with you. Just give me a few more minutes."

"That's fine, please take your time."

Max could sense the excitement in her voice and it was contagious. He was feeling pretty excited himself. He opened the ice box, took a beer, found the opener and then sat down. Once settled he took a deep breath and a slow draw from the bottle of beer. The beer was cold and it tasted good. He waited. At first very patiently, but soon he found himself overcome with anticipation. Making him wait was effective. His mind was all over the place. He told himself, *just take it easy and relax. Everything will be fine. You won't make a fool of yourself and she'll enjoy the evening.* On and on his thoughts went. He allowed thoughts to enter his brain of holding her hand or maybe, just maybe stealing a kiss if his timing was just right.

After waiting nearly fifteen minutes the door opened and she slowly entered the room. Her blond hair was down. Having always seen her with her hair up and covered with a hair net he hadn't realized it was so long and beautiful. Her face was absolutely gorgeous and her makeup looked like it had been applied by a Hollywood makeup artist. The nightgown was as white as freshly fallen snow but he looked right past it because her nude body was clearly visible through the shear fabric.

He stood as she approached him. When she got to within mere inches he realized that her cheeks were bright red. He was sure that the color wasn't the result of the makeup.

Elsa reached down and took both of his hands in hers. They looked into each other's eyes then she spoke. "I'm lonely and I couldn't help myself. I'm not like this. I mean I don't..."

Max released one hand raising it to her mouth and pressed two fingers to her lips. Carefully and very tenderly he wrapped both of his arms around her waist. Then he gently pulled her close.

"I understand. I'm lonely too. We're both lonely and I don't do this sort of thing either, but I'm so glad it's you, so very glad."

With a gentle kiss on the forehead he led her to the bedroom and closed the door behind them.

An hour and a half later they were sitting close together on the sofa, finishing off the last of a late night snack. Max was very comfortable and relaxed. He enjoyed their intimacy together. It had been truly unbelievable. He found himself totally content just to be with her, talking, eating, laughing and watching her. It was all so truly wonderful.

"We had better get started," Elsa said as she carried their dirty dishes to the sink.

"Where're we going?" Max asked.

"I'm your contact. We need to get going. It's a long way to Chicago."

"What?" Max was confused.

"I'm your contact and we need to get..."

"Wait just a minute please," Max said loudly. "You're my contact? How can that be? I mean I've been here for weeks. Why the long delay?" Max's questions flew out of his mouth like machine gun rounds.

Elsa took his hand, and then slowly explained.

"First, I had to confirm that it was you that I was waiting for. Then, I needed to be sure that no one was on to you, so I watched you when I wasn't working. Only when I was positive that you had arrived unnoticed and unattached could I risk making contact."

Max interrupted her. "You mean that tonight was just part of the plan?"

She did her best to explain, "Absolutely not, with you coming in every night for dinner and me following you every day, you began to grow on me. I started to realize how nice you were to people, not only me at the restaurant but around town, you know, wherever you went. I saw it and began to admire you a lot. I mean, you are very sweet and I fell for you. Is there something wrong with that?" Feeling he understood Max responded, "No of course not, it's just that, well, this is quite a shock. To find a girl like you, and to do what we just did, and then to find out that we are working together is a lot to take in at one time. I guess I can handle it... can you?"

"We'll just have to find out," she answered before kissing him long and hard.

At the boarding house, Max gathered up his few belongings and packed them into one small bag. He left a note for his landlady.

I regret that I must leave right away as I have just learned that my father is very sick. I must return home immediately to be with him. For your trouble, please keep the two week advance payment that I deposited with you and thank you very much for your kindness to me while I was in your home.
Max S.

From there, he went straight to the fish processing plant and left a similar note with the night guard asking him to give it to his boss in the morning.

A Ford sedan stood with its motor idling in the alley outside the rear of Elsa's building. She was waiting for him when he returned with his bag. In the dead of night they crossed the bridge into Wisconsin heading south, with Elsa at the wheel.

CHAPTER TEN
THE CAVERN

JD strained to see in the darkness. He reached into his pocket and retrieved his Zippo lighter. During the war the Zippo had become famous among GIs for lighting on the first try. It lived up to its reputation. By the glow of the tiny flame, JD could make out a very small opening a bit deeper in the crevice. He turned his body sideways and tried to fit through the narrow opening. Leading with his right shoulder, he held the lighter out in front with his right arm. It was difficult but he managed to push his way inward another three feet. Just then he began to panic. Thoughts of getting himself wedged and trapped forever flashed through his mind and sent a chill down his spine. Before he completely lost control the narrow slit widened out. He straightened and stood up at the entrance to a large cavern.

Outlined by the intermittent flashes of lighting, JD could make out an opening in the ceiling of the cavern some forty feet above his head. The shape of the hole was clearly outlined with each flash of lightning. It resembled a huge football. At the center its width was approximately twenty feet. He estimated its length at around forty feet. The back wall directly across from where JD stood was roughly a hundred feet away, and the room's length from left to right was at least twice that.

Outside, the hail had given way to rain and it was pouring down in sheets through the opening in the ceiling. A considerable space along the wall was protected by a large section of the ceiling that remained intact. Seeing that most of the floor was dry JD decided to find a place where he could comfortably sit and wait out the storm. The floor was sandy, and JD soon settled on a spot where he could lean back against the wall and relax.

After a while, his eyes became acclimated to the darkness and he was able to make out details of his surroundings. The wall from which he had entered and was now leaning against was nearly vertical. At the top it met the ceiling at a ninety degree angle. The back wall was concave in shape as was the wall to his right. They both followed the slope of the ceiling like the sides of a bowl, curving down, all the way to the floor. The remaining wall on the left was much different. Unlike the others which were bare rock, this wall was covered in vines. Thick, green, mature vegetation grew down from above extending all the way to the floor.

On the floor, directly below the football shaped opening in the ceiling laid a similarly shaped pile of rubble. JD concluded that the ceiling had collapsed all at once, crashing straight down to the floor of the cavern. There it had remained undisturbed for who knows how long.

Outside, the storm was now raging at full strength.   It looked as though it wouldn't let up any time soon. JD had little choice but to spend his third night on the island inside the cavern. Out of the elements, on a mountain top with limited access and totally hidden from view he felt safe for the first time since coming ashore. This night would provide JD with the first truly undisturbed and restful sleep he had experienced in the past several days.

The next morning he awakened to the sun shining brightly on the vine covered wall. He felt refreshed, well rested and his confidence was restored. JD took a deep breath and let it out slowly as he lifted his arm and pulled back his sleeve. He found his watch, it was already ten o'clock. Hunger pangs got his attention; yesterday he had eaten breakfast from one of the remaining boxes of field rations and that had been it. Twenty-six hours had passed since then. A quick inventory revealed two pieces of gum, the hard cereal bar uneaten from yesterday's breakfast, three cigarettes and a half full canteen of fresh water. The hard cereal bar now seemed like a blessing, he pulled back the wrapping and happily ate.

The morning sun shone brightly in every corner of the room. He was able to get his first clear look at the cavern. It appeared much the same as the night before but, he noticed additional features and a few surprises.

The first surprise was near the entrance. Something large lay on the floor. JD stepped over for a better look. Whatever it was, it had been constructed of bamboo poles tied together with small strips of vine, similar to those used in basket weaving. The flat framework panel was five feet by five feet in size and covered with some type of cloth. The panel had two legs, one of which was broken or rotted off. JD could clearly see two deep indentations in the floor where the panel legs had once stood. The two holes in the sand were located on either side of the entrance. He lifted the thing upright and immediately realized that it had once been used to block the passageway.

JD felt a chill run down his spine and quickly spun around checking to see if anyone was behind him, but no one was there. He was feeling a little spooked. Forcing himself to overcome his apprehension he continued the investigation. The material covering the framework appeared to be sail cloth. Upon closer inspection, he realized that the side which faced the opening had been stained with dirt, possibly to make it look more like the surrounding rock to anyone on the outside. *Someone tried to camouflage the entrance, but who, or why, but more importantly, when?*

Next he carefully examined the entryway. It was narrow, but apparently had been intentionally piled nearly full with stones and boulders in an attempt to close it up even more. JD surmised, "Whoever had taken the time to do this must have been small in stature if they had used it for a primary entrance. I wonder if there might be another way in and out of the cavern." He decided to be on the alert for another entrance.

JD felt like a detective analyzing clues. He knew that native people of this region were small and that could be the simple answer. However, the sail cloth made JD think that the builder of the framework structure could have been European, maybe even from a sailing vessel. *The material certainly looks like it could have once been a sail. That doesn't make a whole lot of sense because this island isn't even on any current Army maps that I've come across. It certainly could have been missed by the Europeans in the days of sailing vessels.*

JD leaned the panel against the entrance and shoved a rock under the missing leg to keep it in position. He continued to ponder. *If it had been a European who made the framework barricade, that might explain the presence of the hogs I encountered that first day on the island. It might have been a shipwreck. Survivors may have come ashore and who's to say that the pigs didn't swim ashore from the same ship?* At this point JD knew that his thoughts were merely conjecture. However, at the same time, he found the cavern and the discoveries so far to be both extraordinary and intriguing.

He continued to survey his surroundings, but now more intently, alert for any signs of the cavern's former occupants. As he walked around the perimeter he came to a pool of fresh water against the wall opposite the entrance. The source was back in the rocks behind the wall. The pool was dammed up at one end, trapping the water to a depth of about a foot. Water was gently flowing over a bamboo obstruction located at one end of the pool. The dam was obviously manmade. A steady stream of water ran over the top of the dam and along the floor, eventually disappearing into the cracks at the base of the wall to the right of the entrance. JD felt sure that this was the source that fed the pool down below which was now used by the Japanese. *Whoever it was that had been holed-up in here had plenty of fresh water. Construction of the dam was quite clever and very useful.*

Proceeding along the edge of the water in the direction of its source the pool soon began to narrow as it curved away and disappeared behind the back wall. JD took a few steps further along the back wall. When he reached the end he turned and continued walking slowly along the vine covered wall. Carefully, he searched for anything out of the ordinary.

JD had nearly reached the end when his eyes were drawn to the floor. Protruding from underneath the vines which grew down to the floor he could see two pieces of bamboo. Bending down he picked up one of the lengths of bamboo and held it in his hand. It was two feet long and two inches in diameter and unusually heavy for such a small piece. Bamboo is a hollow material and should have been light to the touch. Instead it felt more like a baseball bat, or even a club. The first four inches of the outside surface was smooth as if it had been polished or sanded. In contrast the rest of its length was worn and scratched. A close examination of the end revealed that several progressively smaller diameter pieces of bamboo had been pounded down, each through the center of the next larger piece, creating a very strong laminated construction. The shaft was nearly solid with no space between the pieces.

JD pondered its use. As a weapon, it seemed much too short to be useful. *There must be an altogether different use, but nothing comes to mind.* Kicking around on the floor under the vines, two additional and nearly identical shafts appeared. All four bamboo shafts had the same, smooth four inch section at one end as well as the same wear pattern along the remainder of their lengths. Each was reinforced in the same manner as the first one he had examined. Progressively smaller pieces of bamboo pounded one into the other. *Clever, yes; but for what were they used?*

With his dad away from home nearly every day, working on the railroad most of the farm work had been left to JD and his brothers. JD was familiar with building and repairing all manner of things around the farm. Carpentry was one of his strengths. In his experience, the only time you sanded or polished a round shaft was to bring it to size. After which you fit it into a hole. Wooden dowels were common in the barn. They could be used for hanging bridals, harnesses, and yokes on the posts outside the stalls. To him, these bamboo shafts were very similar to the wooden dowels he made and used back home. JD worked through the possibilities. *If my assumption is correct then there should be some two inch diameter holes somewhere in the cavern. If these are dowels and holes do exist why were all these shafts on the floor and not sticking out of the walls?* It was a mystery. Unable to think of a better scenario he decided to search around for some holes in the walls.

Retracing his steps, JD again walked the perimeter. This time he studied the walls very carefully looking for round holes. After having had no luck locating any holes he found himself back at the vine covered wall. Once again JD paused for a moment to think. *If any holes do exist, then they must be behind those vines.*

He started the search directly above the spot where the first two shafts had been found. A little to the right and only two feet from the floor, he found a nearly round hole long hidden under the thick vegetation. JD wasn't surprised when the shaft fit perfectly and stopped after it reached a depth of four inches.

He knew he was getting close but his mind was still processing, "There is no doubt. The shafts were made for this hole but it's still unclear to me why someone would have wanted to hang something so low to the ground and what could it have been? Well, I've got three more shafts in my hands I need to find three more holes." Not finding another low to the ground, he moved up the wall, continuing to search behind the thick vegetation. The second hole was twelve inches to the left of the first one and twelve inches higher up the wall. Mathematics had always come easily to JD. He promptly calculated the position of the next hole. He was confident that he knew where it would be and he thought that he might now even know the purpose for the holes. He would soon find out if he was correct.

It was there, a foot up and a foot over, three holes in a row climbing the wall on a forty-five degree angle. If his assumption was correct, then this would be the cleverest of all the discoveries he had made so far. He inserted three of the shafts in the holes. Taking the remaining shaft in his right hand he carefully placed his left foot on the lowest shaft, then his right onto the next shaft. With each step he used his left hand to steady himself against the wall while inserting the shaft from his right hand into the next higher hole. Holes continued to materialize exactly where he knew they would be. He removed the lowest shaft and stepped up on the next shaft. Repeating the process again and again he ascended the stairs leaving no trace behind. He made steady progress toward a ledge protruding from the back wall above the area where the pool had disappeared. The ledge was approximately ten feet below the ceiling of the cavern. Eventually, he stepped up on the ledge and removed the remaining shafts. *A disappearing staircase, very impressive.*

The terrace on which he now stood was high above the floor of the cavern. It was small, just a few feet in all directions. As he stood facing the back wall and with the vine covered wall to his left, he saw two torches lying at his feet. Beside the torches stood a wooden bucket half full of something that bore a close resemblance to tar and smelled disgusting. The revolting substance was some type of oil, but it was much thicker than he would have expected. He figured that over time the oil had lost most of its moisture, turning it into the thick substance now remaining in the bucket. A length of hemp rope lay stretched across the terrace floor. One end was tied off to a boulder and the other attached to a wooden block and tackle. The block and tackle was laced with another rope which was rolled neatly on the floor. A large canvas bag was attached to one end of this rope. The canvas was the same material as the sailcloth used on the barricade. The block and tackle and the hemp rope were both very old. Everything JD saw in front of him had all come from a sailing vessel. He was sure of it.

The disappearing ladder did not provide a method for carrying anything up to the terrace unless you were a gifted acrobat. The bag and pulley system was undoubtedly the method used for hoisting supplies up to this level. The only thing remaining to investigate was an arched opening at the back of the terrace. JD had not found a second passageway into the cavern but thought a second entrance might be located on the other side of this crude doorway.

Starting in, he realized the purpose for the torches. It was very dark inside so he retreated back out where the touches lay. He pushed one of the torches down in the bucket of gooey oil. It found its way through the thick upper layer that had formed, protecting what oil remained in the bucket from the air. With the Zippo he lit the torch which instantly cast a bright but very smoky glow. Stepping through the little doorway the space immediately opened up to reveal someone's living quarters.

There was a bed fashioned from bamboo and vines, apparently the same construction method as was used to build the barricade. Studying the bed JD couldn't help but think that this guy was prolific when it came to finding creative uses for the nearly limitless supply of bamboo found all over the island. The bed was crisscrossed with rope that supported a straw-filled mattress. The rope and mattress were rotted and partially collapsed, however the bed frame itself seemed solid. Next to the bed sat a large sea chest adjacent to a lantern hanging on the wall. JD checked the lantern, it seemed it be in working order. When he put his lighter to the wick of the old lantern it took to the flame of his Zippo like it had been waiting for that moment forever. The room brightened, allowing JD to snuff out the smoky torch against the dirt floor. In one corner was an area which had been used as a hearth. Two flat stones, a small cast iron skillet and a few handmade wooden spoons and forks were the only pieces of cookware in view. Above the fireplace dark smoke stains could be seen. A crack in the ceiling above the fireplace appeared to be a natural vent. The smoke from the torch was trapped against the ceiling. It was steadily migrating in the direction of the crack where it vanished. Just to one side lay a small pile of lead fragments, a musket ball mold and about fifty cast musket balls. *The fireplace was an important part of this room and this guy's life, whoever he had been. The fire was used for light, for cooking, for warmth, even though I haven't been cold during my stay on the island, and for manufacturing ammunition.*

An ample supply of dry sticks and larger pieces of kindling were neatly stacked on the floor near the fireplace. Off to one side of the bed, away from the fireplace, were five kegs of gunpowder. Only one keg had its seal removed. There were no firearms in sight, but a well-rusted dagger rested on a wooden box near the bed. An inventory of the room's contents included a drinking cup, a bowl, an old hat, a ship's bell, dried up ink in a small glass container, several well-used quills with ink on the tips, a few other odds and ends, and a book.

JD grabbed the book and headed out the doorway in search of better light. Out on the terrace once again, he leaned against a wall in such a way as to allow the sun to shine on the leather cover.

CHAPTER ELEVEN
THE ASSIGNMENT

Max stood on the sidewalk overlooking Navy Pier on Chicago's waterfront staring in disbelief at the *USS Wolverine* as she slowly made her way out to sea. Black plumes of smoke billowed from the four smokestacks which ran along the starboard side of her flight deck as the aircraft carrier's powerful, coal fired boilers pushed the five hundred foot vessel away from the dock.

The *Wolverine* was following close behind her sister ship, the *USS Sable*, which had left her moorings at Navy Pier only moments earlier. The two carriers followed the same routine every morning on their way out to Lake Michigan. After cruising a few miles from shore they would head north to a position just off the mouth of Milwaukee's harbor, then turn around and work their way back to Chicago. Traveling side-by-side at a separation distance of three miles, they repeated the process over and over, day after day. From bases on shore planes came, flown by novice pilots attempting their first carrier landings and takeoffs.

Protected from Japanese subs off the west coast of the United States and German U boats lying in wait on the east coast, the training of Navy pilots could here proceed without menace from the enemy. Hundreds upon hundreds of pilots were being qualified for duty in the Pacific as the US continued to bring the war ever closer to Japan's doorstep.

The *USS Wolverine* had been commissioned into the Navy fleet on August 12, 1942. The *USS Sable* was commissioned nine months later on May 8, 1943. Both had outstanding records of uninterrupted service.

Max hadn't known for sure why he had been told to come to Navy Pier this morning. Now however, he knew that his assignment would be somehow connected to these ships. It was obvious that this training oasis had to be eliminated. Max was sure that he was about to be given his chance to heroically serve the Emperor.

As it was a beautiful summer morning with plenty of sunshine accompanied by a cool northerly breeze, Max decided to walk to the meeting place. As the two carriers faded to specks on the eastern horizon Max turned around and casually walked away. The meeting place was north of Navy Pier. He first crossed Shore Line Drive and proceeded west up Wacker Drive. He established a relaxed pace as he made his way to Michigan Avenue where he turned north. Max crossed over the bridge still maintaining a leisurely tempo. It was a thirteen block walk to his destination. He was a little early and saw no reason to hurry. Instead, he would enjoy the perfect weather and just take his time, after all this might be his last chance.

His mind was filled with conflicting thoughts. A week ago this assignment would have been a dream come true. But now, after Elsa, he was thinking more about how to stay alive as opposed to doing his part in the plan that would soon be revealed. This couldn't be right. Putting personal concerns on an equal footing with the Emperor was wrong. After all, the Emperor was his god and the god of all Japanese people. But, he had experienced something very special with Elsa that first night. It made him think about life in a completely different way. His family had existed for generations with the sole purpose of serving the Emperor in battle.

Now, in the time of the empire's greatest need, he was thinking of himself and her.

Turning onto Walton Place, the Drake Hotel, tall and imposing, came into view. The doorman, who was decked out in a burgundy colored top hat and tails, held the door open with one hand welcoming his newest guest. The beautiful Drake Hotel was one of Chicago's finest. Max was impressed by the building's opulent exterior; however his mind remained conflicted. He managed to return a nod of thanks. He saw the doorman's other hand held out with palm up. Max withheld a tip, he didn't slow his pace and he still didn't like tipping. The doorman closed his hand, dropped his arm to his side turning his attention once more in the direction of the sidewalk and his next prospect.

The door opened onto an elegant lobby bustling with activity and noise. The large room was filled with people busily milling about. Some were checking out, others checking in. At least twenty-five were queued up, waiting to enter taxi cabs which only occasionally rolled up the hotel's horseshoe-shaped driveway. Others were standing around in small groups talking or reading the morning paper and many were just waiting for something or somebody. Max had no idea what these people were waiting for nor did he care. His mind was clearing now as he shifted his thoughts to what would happen next. To Max, the lobby was a madhouse that had nothing at all to do with him.

Max looked around searching for the elevators. He spotted a bank of elevators located all the way across the lobby on the far wall. He headed in that direction, working his way through the people and around or over luggage which was stacked wherever room could be found.

Reaching the other side of the room, Max found himself standing with several others in front of four ornately decorated, brass elevator doors. As nonchalantly as possible he worked his way to the front. After only a short wait the bell sounded and the door to the first car opened. Several people exited the car. Max and about a third of the waiting crowd quickly squeezed inside. The elevator operator, a middle aged woman in a burgundy uniform similar to the doorman's, however not nearly as fancy, sat on a small stool in front of her operator panel. She pulled the lever closing the door and without looking up she asked. "Floor please?"

The passengers started calling out their floors. Max heard his floor called, so he said nothing. The door closed. In due course it opened on the sixth floor. Exiting the elevator car, Max spotted the information sign posted on the opposite wall. It sent him to the right. He knocked on the door to room 620. It opened almost instantly.

"Please come in," said the tall dark haired German who answered the door. "Won't you take a seat?"

Max sat down in a high back winged chair and the German sat across from him in a matching chair.

"Well did you see them?" he asked.

"Yes I watched as they left the pier. It was quite an impressive sight," answered Max.

Before responding further the German poured them each a cup of coffee then leaned back in his chair.

"You know it is amazing that these Americans have the resources to build not one, but two aircraft carriers for the sole purpose of training pilots. I mean it's truly amazing."

He paused to let Max take in his comments but Max remained silent, so the German continued.

"We can't stop them from building planes. I'm told they produce a hundred thousand a year. That works out to two thousand a week or three hundred a day. That's hard to imagine.

Did you know that at the start of the war they only had eight carriers? To date they have added twenty big Essex class carriers and countless escort carriers. At last count, they have over a hundred carriers in the Pacific alone. All of that has been accomplished in just three years. It's unheard of in the history of warfare."

Max had known that the war wasn't going well for his country. Hearing the numbers from a third party and fellow conspirator for the first time struck him very hard. It seemed hopeless. For the first time he thought about the real possibility of actually losing the war. Fear rose up inside him.

"What can be done?" he asked almost desperately.

The German leaned forward and peered straight into Max's eyes. "All the carriers and all the planes on their decks and in their hangers are useless without pilots who can take off and land safely from those decks. We will deprive the Americans of those pilots by destroying the *Wolverine* and the *Sable* right here in the middle of the United States. Your assignment is to bring the war home to the United States by winning the next decisive sea battle of the war, the battle of Lake Michigan."

"I don't mean to sound defensive but how do you plan to accomplish this?" asked Max.

"We have a plan and it is already progressing on schedule. You are one piece, albeit a very important piece, but nonetheless just one piece. Let me tell you what we have in place so far. A boat will be used to deliver two torpedoes within range of the carriers. A friend has identified a commercial fishing boat that we will secure when the time is right. The boat works out of Port Washington which is the next port north of Milwaukee just a few miles up the coast. This type of vessel is very common on the lake and they all look so similar that it's nearly impossible to tell one from another. These boats fish alone, never in pairs or fleets. They stay out on the lake for days at a time. She won't be missed for several days. By the time they go searching for her it will be too late."

The German continued to proudly pour out the details of his plan. "We will stow away on board. Once out to sea we will overpower the two man crew, weigh down their bodies and throw them overboard. Then the boat will be taken to a workshop down an isolated inlet which has already been prepared for our purpose. There, it will be fitted-out to accept the two torpedoes. They will be mounted on either side of the hull above the gunnels and hidden under false side boards."

When the German paused to sip his coffee Max took the opportunity to speak. "That all sounds very good, but may I ask where and how we acquire the torpedoes?"

"Excellent question; did you know that there is a ship builder in Manitowoc Wisconsin who is building submarines for the U.S. Navy?"

"No," said Max and then asked. "How do they get to the ocean?"

"They are placed on barges and floated down the Mississippi River to New Orleans. To answer your first question, every sub takes a shakedown cruise right here on the lake. Part of the shakedown includes the firing of live torpedoes with dummy war heads. Several are fired by each sub to insure that all eight tubes and outer doors function properly. The torpedoes are fired at stationary wooden targets which are set up near shore. Nets are hung behind the targets to capture the torpedoes after they pass through the targets so that they can be salvaged and reused. All torpedoes are fired toward a break wall. A few penetrate the net or miss it altogether and hit the wall. Those that do are sent out for repair. On occasion, a torpedo is so badly damaged that it cannot be repaired. When this is the case it is designated as unusable scrap. We arranged to have two perfectly good torpedoes designated as scrap. They are now in our possession. No one will be looking for them. Both have had their motors recharged. All that remains is to arm them with high explosives and detonators."

The German then boastfully added, "I smuggled the explosives into the country myself. So you see, much has already been accomplished."

Max now knew what his role would be in this scheme. He had training in explosives and was considered an expert in the field. "So I am to arm the weapons, is that right?" he volunteered.

Yes that is true," answered the German. "However the plan also requires that you construct two contact detonators to be installed just before the torpedoes are rolled off the side of the boat. We can't risk having the explosives in the torpedoes triggered prematurely. It may be necessary to have the boat at sea, presumably fishing, for days before the opportunity to strike presents itself. You will be on board as part of a two man crew. I will handle the boat and you will be responsible for arming and launching the torpedoes."

"When?" asked Max.

"We have not received the go ahead as yet, but soon. We have information that in the near future both carriers will take part in an exercise involving the test launching and recovery of unmanned drone aircraft. It has been confirmed that this exercise will take place off the coast of Grand Traverse Bay, Michigan which is at the far northern end of the lake, approximately two hundred miles north of Chicago. These are secret tests of new advanced radio controlled aircraft. The tests are to be conducted away from any major population center."

"Why wait? Why not attack between Milwaukee and Chicago and get it over with? After all, with every day that goes by more and more pilots are qualified." challenged Max.

The German took his time as he explained. "Your enthusiasm is commendable. Japan's need for immediate relief is obvious to all involved. Being Japanese it would seem to you to be particularly urgent. It is a very big lake but the southern end, specifically along the daily route of the two carriers has very tight security. All ships planning to travel below Milwaukee must port first and be searched by the Coast Guard before heading south. All ships cleared to sail below Milwaukee are required to take on a Coast Guard pilot. Commercial fishing in the southern section of the lake is banned completely anytime the carriers are present. So you see, we must wait for an opportunity which will take the carriers out of the security zone."

Max realized that he was enthusiastic. He had made his choice without knowing it. He would do his part. He could be counted on by his Emperor. This was not the only reason or even the most important one. He would do it because it must be done. His naval training taught him that throughout Japan's history, victory always came after a decisive sea battle. This might be the decisive sea battle that would lead to victory. He could not turn his back on destiny.

CHAPTER TWELVE
THE JOURNAL

The cover was made of heavy brown leather with a solid binding. A leather strap with a hole near one end was hand stitched to the back cover. The strap was long enough to wrap around to the front where it was fastened over a small brass pin protruding from the front cover. The hole in the strap fit snuggly over the pin to secure the contents. The book was approximately three inches thick. The pages were around fourteen inches from top to bottom and roughly ten inches from side-to-side.

JD gently pulled on the strap, it released from the pin. He lifted the cover gingerly to reveal the inside pages which were yellowed from age but, the writing was as clear as the day it had been laid down with quill and ink. The pages seemed at first glance, to be made from a combination of pulp and linen but he couldn't be certain. He wasn't at all sure that such a combination was even possible. In any case, they were thick and seemed to be holding up well against the years. Nevertheless, JD exercised great care as he leafed through the pages hoping they wouldn't turn to dust and crumble in his hands. To his relief, he found the pages to be in nearly pristine condition.

Written on the inside of the front cover near the top was the date April 8, 1862. Below the date a signature was written on a diagonal. The signature was bold and dark, and read Thomas Johnston.   This was a personal journal, written some eighty-two years earlier.

Opposite the inside cover, the first page was filled with very neat writing. The spacing was good and the letters of each word were on the same gentle angle. Each letter was fully formed and written in a flowing style. As he began to read, JD's first thought was, *Thomas Johnston must have received high marks in penmanship.*

Page one, "This is the journal of Thomas Johnston a seaman aboard the *Randall* a privateer in service to Her Majesty, Queen Victoria of England."

JD knew that a privateer was nothing more than a pirate with a commission from the Queen to steal whatever he could from anyone other than an English ship. Whatever prize was taken would be shared with the Queen in the proportions outlined in the commission document. To all other countries, these were pirates plain and simple; and the *Randall* had been, without a doubt, a pirate ship.

At the time, England and Spain had been peacefully coexisting for many years. However, it seemed that the British Royal Court and the Queen herself were not above intrigue. Spain had been making herself wealthy at the expense of her colonial possessions. One of which was the Philippines. The Philippine Islands were being plundered. Unimaginable riches were being sent back to Spain in what to Queen Victoria must have seemed a continuous convoy of treasure ships. Resurrecting the long abandoned policy of secretly commissioning private ships such as the *Randall* to attempt to divert some of the fortune to London must have seemed worth the risk.

There was a blank space after which the writing continued. "We set sail from Portsmouth harbor with seventy souls on board in the early morning of this the eighth day of April in the year of our Lord 1862. We are without waving crowds to bid us success. Rather, we slipped out of port without fanfare or notice. Our voyage is to take us south to Cape Town then east around the Cape and on to the Indian Sea. From there we head for the Pacific where we intend to capture Spanish treasure. I depart on this adventure having left no kin behind. Alone in the world, this crew is my only family and I am filled with anticipation of our most certain future success. After which, I will return to England a man of means, God willing."

This concluded the first day's entry. JD consumed page after page and found that most entries were usually no more than one page in length. Many times, Johnston recorded several days on a single page. On such occasions the author would record the weather and the ship's approximate position and course. He would conclude each entry with a brief description of an uneventful day. The journal was much like an informal ship's log. Through the first forty pages the *Randall* had been at sea for ninety-one days. JD began to skip over the short entries and focus on dates that filled at least a full page. He was interested to learn how and why Thomas Johnston had come to be marooned on the island.

JD continued reading the journal, finding a long entry, reading it, and then going back through previously skipped pages to fill in facts and events relating to the information from the pages he had read. After two hours, JD was able to piece together a reasonably clear picture of the major events that had transpired during the long-ago voyage of the *Randall*.

It seemed that the *Randall* made the voyage to Cape Town in a rather routine manner. She arrived at Cape Town harbor as planned, where she took on provisions and made minor repairs in preparation for the next leg of the voyage. When the time came to depart, several crew members, including both of the ship's carpenters, were nowhere to be found. After delaying the ship's scheduled departure for two weeks in order to conduct a search for

the missing crewmen, the *Randall's* Captain was forced to depart
Cape Town harbor shorthanded and without a carpenter among his
crew. No actual details relating to the reason for the sudden
disappearance of the men was recorded. Instead, conjecture that
the men had likely been enticed by stories of diamonds in the
inland hills of southern Africa.

Sixty-two able-bodied men were aboard the *Randall* the day
she departed Cape Town harbor. According to Thomas Johnston,
this would be enough if no one came down with fever or suffered a
serious injury.

The established sea lanes of the day would have had the
Randall sail southeast from Cape Town past the Cape of Good
Hope. Once beyond the Cape she would steer north following the
eastern coast of the African continent. After sailing through the
straits between the continent and the massive island of
Madagascar, she would turn due east and cross the Indian Sea from
a position north of the island.

After departing Cape Town the *Randall* sailed past The Cape
of Good Hope and followed the coastline as normal. However,
before reaching the southern end of Madagascar she changed
course and headed due east from a position south of the island.
This track would keep her latitude several hundred miles south of
the sea routes taken by most other ships. As the *Randall* crossed
the Indian Sea she did experience some bad weather and for
several days they were caught in the doldrums with little to no
wind. For the most part however, the trip was uneventful and no
other ships were seen and none saw her.

She continued on an easterly course eventually passing
through the Timor Sea north of Australia. The *Randall's* Captain
skillfully navigated his ship between the hundreds of islands which
lie to the north of Australia until finally reaching the Pacific Ocean
off the eastern coast of the Philippines.

When the *Randall* sailed into the Pacific Ocean the skies were clear with a steady westerly wind blowing every day. Nights were clear with calm seas. The crew took these as good omens. Soon after reaching the Pacific and somewhere off the coast of the Philippines, the *Randall* encountered a lone Spanish vessel and took her without firing a shoot. She was riding low in the water, slowed by the weight of her heavy cargo of gold. Unable to outrun her pursuer, she raised the white flag in surrender. The Spanish crew was treated humanely by the *Randall's* Captain. In honor of the white flag displayed by the Spanish Captain, he and his crew were allowed to board the long boats. They were given food and water for the two day journey to shore. The crew of the *Randall* was in good spirits after such a quick and profitable success. The *Randall's* Captain however was concerned. It was highly unusual for a treasure ship to be sailing without escort. He posted extra lookouts.

According to Thomas Johnston; "Eight days later in the early afternoon I was the first to report that three Spanish man of war were off our port bow and heading directly for our ship and our prize. The treasure ship was slow, and if we were to stay with her there would be a fight; one the *Randall* couldn't win." The three, cannon laden, Spanish man of war caught up with the captured treasure ship in the late afternoon. The *Randall* had been taking on water for several weeks which under normal circumstances is expected. However, with the loss of our two carpenters the problem could not be properly addressed while the ship was underway. "Our pumps were keeping up with the water level below decks so there was no real danger of losing our ship. The absence of a carpenter and the constant leaking were an influence on the Captain's earlier decision to transfer only a sample of our captured booty to the *Randall*. The vast majority remained aboard the Spanish ship which the Captain manned with officers and crew from the *Randall*. This decision proved to be both costly in gold but also fortuitous because we could still make good speed in a light wind. Low in the water and unable to make any real speed, the Spanish war ships easily caught up with their treasure ship and recaptured her. Through his telescope, the Captain watched helplessly as the Spaniards slaughtered the officers and crewmen he had assigned to sail the treasure ship back to England. Outnumbered and out gunned, we were pursued by two of the Spanish ships and decided to make a run for it. Throughout the remainder of the day the chase continued as our crew of able-bodied seamen worked to put up every inch of sail available. The Spanish ships were closing the distance ever so slowly. As night fell they were only a half mile off the *Randall's* stern. They began to fire off shots from their small swivel guns which were mounted to the upper deck rails along the bows of both ships. The crew of one of the Spanish ships had somehow been able to muscle a larger cannon up to the bow and fire it over the rail. But, their efforts were to no avail as the *Randall* remained just out of range. The captain, the helmsman and I all stared out over the aft rail as cannon balls splashed harmlessly not thirty feet off our stern. Night was falling and a light overcast hid the stars, it was quite dark and the *Randall* showed no lights. The Spanish ships, on the other hand, with what appeared to be every lantern they had aboard hanging from their bowsprits, remained in hot pursuit. Sometime during the night hidden in the darkness, the Captain ordered a hard turn to port. We were able to change course without being detected. At dawn the Spanish lookouts must have been amazed when they could find no sign of their prey. The *Randall* had vanished."

During the next few weeks it was clear that things aboard the *Randall* were going from bad to worse. With the loss of their fortune the crew was in a foul mood and the leaking had become much worse. The pumps could no longer keep pace with the volume of water rising in the bilge. As a result, the Captain ordered the crew to form a bucket brigade to supplement the pumps. The constant work was backbreaking with no letup in sight. One day, the *Randall* sailed within sight of this island. She was beached out on the point where the crew attempted to make repairs to the damaged hull. Fishing was good and there was an abundance of fruit and fresh water. Animals from on board were taken off the ship and placed in large containment pens which were haphazardly constructed by the crew. Several of the pigs dug their way out and not all were recaptured. The goats that escaped were easily rounded up and placed back in the enclosures. The crew worked in shifts which provided an abundance of free time. It seemed that all would be well as the repairs advanced in good order. Some members of the crew had their doubts. The experienced crewmen knew without being told that the *Randall* could not be repaired properly without a stay in the shipyard. This fact combined with the reality that the *Randall* was seriously undermanned surely would mean that once the temporary repairs were completed the *Randall* would return to England. There would be no further opportunity to capture Spanish treasure. For the crew, this meant returning to England as poor as the day they had left. This was not acceptable to many of them. Whispered rumors carried the bad news to the rest of the crew in short order. Soon a plot was hatched. The crew would seize the ship, kill the officers and then sail to the small British penal colony located in Australia. The English courts had sent convicts to Australia as a convenient way of emptying their prisons while at the same time populating the far off continent. This was not a place where any right thinking Englishman wanted to be but, it would suit the mutineer's purpose. Upon reaching the coast of Australia they would send a party ashore at a remote location to hide the treasure. The band of cutthroats calculated that its value split among their small group of mutineers would do them all fine. That is, as long as they did not have to provide the Queen her tribute. After the treasure was safely hidden away they would sail into port. There they would tell a revised story of the recapture of the treasure ship. Their version of the story would include the loss of the Captain and other officers at the hands of the Spanish. Later, they would retrieve the treasure and divide it up. Every man, now well off, would be free to make his own arrangements to return to England or to go wherever he pleased.

During the initial plotting Thomas Johnston was isolated from his shipmates. Thomas was the Captain's most trusted lookout so the moment they landed he was instructed to find a good location from which to stand watch for any ship that might sail close on to the island. Thomas climbed to the top of the island's only hill where he discovered the plateau. With minimal repositioning this location provided a three hundred and sixty degree panoramic view. From this position he could see every approach to the island.

He was ordered to stay on the plateau and keep a vigilant watch so he gathered the supplies, equipment and personal belongings needed for an extended stay atop the hill. At this time he had not yet discovered the cavern so he made use of sailcloth to fashion a tent out on the plateau. A large brass bell would be used to signal the Captain and crew if a ship was spotted. Sometime after Thomas had been stationed on the plateau, out of boredom most likely, he discovered the cavern and the water supply inside. For some reason, he kept this discovery to himself. As it turned out this would prove to be a very wise decision.

Thomas Johnston did eventually hear of the plan. Being a loyal seaman he immediately took the news to the Captain. After hearing of the intended plot the Captain enlisted Thomas and a select group of trusted officers to take the treasure off the ship and hide it on the island. They accomplished their assignment in secret, burying it during the night on the beach in several locations near the ship. On orders from the Captain, Thomas returned to his post where he waited to see what would happen.

According to the Journal: On the day that the *Randall* was successfully refloated the mutineers struck. The depleted group of loyal officers and crew were easily overpowered and killed. "I was at my usual post as lookout up on the mountain when the attack commenced. I witnessed the savagery with no means by which to offer assistance. I had discovered the cavern earlier and out of fear used it to conceal myself from the mutineers. After searching the island for the treasure without success the cutthroats climbed the hill looking for me. I stayed hidden for some time. I dared not show myself for many days. When I did eventually venture outside it was always in the dead of night. One morning two weeks after the mutiny the *Randall* was gone. She had sailed away from the island in the middle of the night. Now I was alone. Over the next several months I retrieved the bags of gold coins from their many hiding places beneath the sand and carried them to my cavern home."

Thomas faithfully continued to journal during his time alone on the island. His writing stopped abruptly after the final entry on the third of August 1865 without providing any clue as to why.

JD stood on the terrace looking down at the floor of the cavern as he ran through in his mind the story that he had just read. He felt that he knew Thomas Johnston or at least understood him. His writings were those of a man with principles and standards and at least some education. JD realized that he liked Thomas Johnston. JD had learned how Thomas had come to be marooned here but now he wondered what happened to him after enduring nearly three years of total isolation on this island. He tried not to think about his own fate but it was difficult to muster that much self-discipline. *How long will I be marooned here?*

The Final Mission

CHAPTER THIRTEEN
THE CAVE-IN

Several weeks had passed since the discovery of the journal. The cavern and the room on the terrace were now JD's home. After moving in his meager belongings he restrung the bed with nylon line from his parachute then fashioned a mattress and pillow from the silk parachute cloth. He stuffed them with anything soft that could be found around the island. With the two blankets from the plane for covering and silk sheets made from his parachute, the new bed and home were now really quite comfortable.

The first thing JD had done was remove the rotten portion of the bed so he could assess the framework. Using his knife he started at the head of the bed and began cutting away the old hemp rope that had been used to support the mattress. Cutting and pulling, the mattress started to fall away one section at a time. JD worked his way along both sides and the foot of the bed, cutting the remaining sections still attached to the frame. Once this was finished he returned to the head and tried to remove the mattress in one piece but it crumbled in his hands. He was forced to take it away one handful at a time tossing the debris into the fireplace. After removing just a small section he noticed that there was something beneath the bed. Under the decaying mattress were twenty leather sacks tied off at the top with leather pull strings. It was the treasure he had read about in Thomas Johnston's journal. The sacks had been simply shoved under the bed, hidden almost in plain sight. Each bag had no less than three hundred coins, some contained a few more. While pulling each bag out where he could have a better look JD estimated the weight to be fifty pounds per bag. The total weight came to approximately one thousand pounds. Basing his calculations on the 1940s fixed rate of $32 per ounce he estimated the total value at somewhere around $500,000. JD felt like a guy who was all dressed up with no place to go.

When rescue came, hopefully soon, the gold would remain his secret. Someday after the war he would return to retrieve it from the place where he had carefully hidden it. For now, JD had removed ten coins from one of the bags. These he would take with him as evidence of his discovery.

JD decided. *If I can find a way to survive the war I'm confident a way can also be found to return to the island for the gold. My desire to stay alive is more than enough motivation to keep going. Any thought of becoming financially secure after the war is no more than something to dream about.*

JD took it upon himself to continue Thomas Johnston's journal for as long as he could using only the one lead pencil he had with him. Writing about how he came to be on the island, and describing the discovery of the cavern and journal kept his mind sharp. As for discovering the gold, no mention was made.

The Japanese were regular visitors to the island in the weeks that followed. Shortly after a hard rain JD would anticipate their arrival and most of the time he would be right. Sometimes they arrived in two boats as they had on the first visit he observed but on other occasions only one boat came. The routine of the Japanese was always the same as that first time with one exception. From time to time the guards on the beach didn't restrict their movement as much as on that first visit. Sometimes they would casually wander down the beach as far as the rocky outcropping.

However, none had ventured beyond that point to the other side of the beach.

Strangely, he began to look forward to their visits. He even gave them names based on their physical appearance or his observations of their behavior. There was "Toad" who had a stocky build and a flat face. "Shorty" was a little guy who looked to be no more than twelve years old. "Slim" normally filled the barrels. "Charlie Chan" worked at the pump and had a long mustache which hung below his chin. "Lefty" always carried the hose to Slim using his left hand. The few times they failed to show when he expected them JD felt disappointed. His feelings toward the Japanese visitors were confusing after all they were his enemy. With no other reasonable explanation he attributed his disappointment to his ever growing loneliness.

Weeks, then months went by and JD found himself settling into a daily routine. Mornings were spent picking fruit from the abundant vegetation found all over the island. Snare traps were set out in places where evidence of small animals could be seen. So far, he hadn't had any luck snaring the kind of animals he had hoped to catch; instead the occasional sea bird would be waiting in the trap.

The afternoons found him down at the beach fishing from the calm waters of the bay. The fishing started out as a waste of time. But lately he was beginning to get the hang of it. The fish proved much more filling than fruit or skinny sea birds which tasted like spoiled fish, so he stayed with it. Fishing turned out to be a learning process and from time to time he would be rewarded with one or more good sized fish. The more he did it, the better he became. Days without fish to eat soon became few and far between.

The pigs, for the most part, stayed out of sight but fish guts proved to be excellent bait for drawing them out where he could get a good shot.

JD was now an expert at sun drying meat and fish on the hot rocks near the beach. The cavern was well stocked with fruit, dried meat and fish. Food, water and shelter are the basics of life. It demanded hard work and a disciplined schedule to insure these needs were met.

JD would go over to the pond and take a small piece of soap after each visit the Japanese made. He had enough stockpiled in the cavern to last for months, even if he took a bath every day. Late afternoon was the time for washing out clothes and trying to mend the holes in his uniform. After the sun went down darkness became a problem. Domestic work such as food preparation by fire light, dinner and clean up occupied the time before sleep. JD had been reduced to a hunter and gatherer much like the cavemen he had learned about in school. Now he felt qualified to teach the class.

On one such ordinary day with fruit gathered and snares checked JD returned to the cavern. There he stored the morning's fruit before heading out to the plateau to write in the journal and scan the approaches to the island just in case rescue was near.

It was an exceptionally hot and bright day. The glare streaming down through the open roof of the cavern was difficult to take without the use of sunglasses which he had left outside on the plateau right next to the journal and binoculars. With bamboo shafts in hand he was ready to descend the disappearing staircase. The sun was at high noon shining straight down on the floor of the cavern. Something reflected from the floor into JD's eyes. He squinted as he searched for the uppermost hole in the wall into which the first shaft would need to be placed. There it was again, something very shiny was in the rubble down near the center of the cavern floor. He stepped back and focused his eyes down to the floor but couldn't see anything. When he moved toward the edge, there it was again. JD moved his head ever so slightly until he once again found the exact spot where his eyes were lined up precisely with the reflection. He had it. He found the spot, the reflection shown on his face. Something was down there. Not sure what it might be, he concentrated his focus right at the thing that had caused the shimmering reflection.

Then to his utter disbelief he saw him. He was right there. Thomas Johnston was so close that JD could clearly see the brass buttons on his coat gleaming in the sunlight. He had been there for nearly eighty years.

JD grabbed the bamboo shafts and began to descend the staircase keeping an eye on Thomas as he made his way to the floor of the cavern. He placed the lengths of bamboo down on the floor and slowly approached the large pile of rubble that he was now certain had fallen from the roof on August 4th 1865, the day after Thomas Johnston's final journal entry. JD climbed through the rubble stopping next to the journal's author. Lying undisturbed for nearly eighty years he looked down upon the body of Thomas Johnston. He began to remove the rocks and earth from the marooned seaman. Carefully and respectfully he unearthed the body. Two blunderbusses hung on leather straps from the nineteenth century seaman's neck and tucked in his belt was a third. All were cocked and loaded. An ivory handled dagger and a smashed spyglass lay near the remains. His waist coat was blue with two rows of big brass buttons. The skeleton appeared to be that of a man no more than about five feet five or six inches tall. Long, shaggy, red hair extended below the tan bandana which he wore around his head.

"Hello my good friend; a pleasure to meet you," said JD.

That evening inside the cavern he got to work. With the proper respect due the marooned sailor, JD dug a grave and carefully lowered the body of Thomas Johnston down inside. JD sat quietly while dutifully recording the funeral in Thomas's journal. The circumstances of his untimely demise due to the cave-in of the cavern's roof were recorded along with the location of the grave. JD knew the twenty-third Psalm by heart so he spoke it over the grave with tears in his eyes and a lump in his throat.

"The Lord is my shepherd; I shall not want. He maketh me lie down in green pastures; He leadeth me beside the still waters. He restoreth my soul: He leadeth me in the paths of righteousness for his names' sake. Yea, though I walk through the valley of the shadow of death, I will fear no evil: For thou art with me; Thy rod and thy staff, they comfort me. Thou preparest a table before me In the presence of mine enemies; Thou anointest my head with oil; My cup runneth over. Surely goodness and mercy shall follow me all the days of my life, and I will dwell in the house of the Lord forever."

He covered the grave with the sandy, loose dirt he had dug from the floor of the cavern; afterwards he packed it down as best he could. He placed a large rock in position as a headstone. JD stood next to the grave and took a moment to think about the life of Thomas Johnston, the life he had read about in the Journal of a good man turned pirate. He would think more about Thomas in the days to come, this man from an earlier time, but with whom JD now held a common bond.

CHAPTER FOURTEEN
THE UNEXPECTED CATCH

About a week after the funeral JD awakened early as had become his routine since learning how best to catch fish in the light surf off the beach. Most evenings he would set four lines about thirty feet out in the bay near the large lava mound that protruded from the beach. For bait he used pig intestines taken from the occasional hog that he was able to track and kill or fish heads from the previous day's catch. In the morning there would be a fish on each of the four lines. It rarely failed. However, if the catch wasn't pulled out of the water shortly after the sun came up there was a good chance that larger fish or even a turtle would strip his lines clean. After adding a good measure of fish to his diet, JD could feel himself gaining more and more strength. Getting to the beach early was essential to having the protein from the fish that he needed to remain strong and healthy.

Emerging from the cavern he was greeted by another warm and dry day. Looking out at the bay there was *Wildcat* now almost completely submerged. The only thing still visible was a portion of her left wing rising out of the water and pointing skyward. He wondered how many more days until she was gone, leaving no trace. He knew that it didn't matter but her presence out there somehow provided him with a sense of security. When she eventually did give up the ghost he would be alone. At least that's the way he felt.

When JD casually turned his head to the left he was stunned to see a single Japanese landing craft resting on the beach. Like all the others that had visited the island to pump fresh water from the pond, it too was full of empty barrels. The weather had been dry for over a week. On previous visits the Japanese had always arrived just after a rain when the pond was full of fresh rain water. He had been careful after each rain to make sure that no trace of his presence anywhere on the island could be found by the visiting soldiers.

Why are they here now, it hasn't rained? He quickly shifted his train of thought and refocused. *What difference does it make? What matters right now is that my four fishing lines are in the water.* The homemade bamboo poles were in plain sight, wedged into the rocks of the mount. The landing craft was beached on the opposite side of the mound about two hundred yards away from the fishing poles. As long as the Japanese stayed on their side of the mound the poles were out of their line of sight. If however, one of them took a stroll down the beach, like he had seen them do on other occasions, there was no doubt that the poles would be discovered. He knew the Japanese would not stop until they found the owner of the fishing poles and that couldn't be allowed to happen. JD had to get down there fast and somehow get those poles out of sight. While thinking about what must be done he was quietly making his way down the hill, careful to stay out of sight.

The whistle blew and the gasoline engine came to life in the distance while JD observed, he spoke under his breath; "Okay, let's see, one of the soldiers is up on the boat filling the barrels. If I'm correct there are three soldiers on the island. One must be at the pump and the other is pulling guard duty on the beach."

The only one not occupied was the guard and unbelievably; he was now casually making his way up the beach toward the mound. JD's heart was racing as he descended toward the beach all the while carefully studying the guard. He identified him as Lefty. Still on the sloping lava path that leads down the hill, JD allowed himself to slip down the side away from the soldiers and boat. The slope was covered with vegetation which provided a buffer between JD's body and the sharp volcanic rocks. In spite of the thick covering the vegetation provided he could feel the rocks cutting at his chest and hip as he neared the ground. With both feet safely planted on solid ground he crouched down and stopped for just a moment to take out one of his pistols and attach the silencer. Still crouched out of sight, he gently pulled back the slide loading a cartridge in the chamber. He clicked off the safety. With his free hand he reached for his knife and placed it between his teeth. Crab walking and crawling he worked his way to the beach along the base of the mound keeping low behind the hardened lava flow. Lefty was out of his sight now, somewhere on the beach on the opposite side of the mound. JD had no idea how close he might be.

JD's mind was racing as he formulated his plan. *I've got to get out to those poles, cut the lines, grab the poles and beat it back to the high grass and trees. It will be a race to get to the bamboo poles ahead of Lefty.*

Reaching up he took hold of the first bamboo pole, cut the line and laid the pole down on the ground. The second pole was dispatched in like manner. He reached out and grabbed the third pole. In the air, out in front of the mound, attracted to the disturbance in the water an ever increasing number of gulls were gathering. The birds circled and swooped while screeching noisily. Each time a line was cut the fish on the other end began to flutter and stir. At this the squawking became ever more piercing. JD hadn't anticipated the problem the gulls were causing. Very suddenly a number of gulls began to dive in the water attempting to catch the weakened fish. Undaunted but now extremely anxious JD kept at it. He managed to retrieve the third pole. Now there was just one more to go. As he began to cut the line on the fourth and final pole one of the divers come up with a fish in its mouth. Unfortunately, the fish was attached to the line on the last pole. The pole slipped through JD's fingers and went sailing a few feet out in the water just in front of the mound. The unforeseen weight of the bamboo pole caused the gull to release the fish and fly away empty handed. But, it was too late for JD. Lefty, alerted by the noise was already coming around the mound to investigate. Wading chest deep in the water Lefty appeared. He was face to face with JD and he was ready. He quickly steadied himself while simultaneously attempting to aim and fire his rifle. The two were only feet apart. JD was staring into Lefty's dark eyes. Lefty was glaring back at him with an expression that combined surprise, fear and determination. His rifle was up and pointed directly at JD's chest. In an instant JD, who was already raising his right hand, aimed and fired one silenced shot from his .45 automatic. The bullet struck Lefty in the center of his forehead passing straight through, ripping off his hat along with a large portion of the back of his head. The rifle fell from his hands and immediately sank in the surf. Lefty's knees bent causing him to drop face first at JD's feet, revealing the gaping hole in the back of his head. As blood mixed with salt water, a crimson halo quickly spread on the surface at JD's feet.

They had been only a few feet apart. It had been close, just like the shooting of the pigs. *Why am I thinking about that at a time like this?* He got that thought out of his head and without a moment's hesitation, pulled the body around to his side of the mound and dragged it up on the beach. Focused now, he concluded; *There's no reason to waste time by attempting to hide this body. Clearly the other two soldiers must be killed before they discovered their comrade is missing and come after me.*

Leaving the body face down in the sand JD scrambled to a spot several feet further inland where he could remain concealed while taking a look over the lava wall that divided the beach. The second soldier was busy filling a barrel. He gave no indication that he had any idea what had just transpired. JD continued to watch until the soldier filling the barrels had his back facing the mound. JD climbed over to the other side and silently disappeared into the trees. He advanced the two hundred yards through the underbrush and trees until directly in line with the bow of the landing craft. There he slipped the knife back into his boot and waited until the soldier topped off one barrel and began to fill another. With the sound of the waves rolling onto the beach, the wind in the trees and the pump motor running in the distance, JD rushed out of the woods sprinting the thirty yards straight toward the boat. His boots dug into the sand slowing his progress. It was as if he was moving in slow motion. JD kept his eyes fixed on the soldier's back, if the soldier turned around JD would be in the open with no place to hide. The soldier surely had a weapon and if he saw a wild looking man rushing him, JD would be forced to start firing from long range with a pistol. The chances of hitting anything would be anyone's guess. But, the filler never heard or saw him. He didn't respond at all.

Two shots to the back of the head, just like that. He wasn't thinking, just moving fast, that's all; moving fast on auto pilot. He leapt up on the bow in one long stride. With his left hand JD seized the dead soldier by the collar and flung him off the boat onto the sand. He saw the face of his second victim for the first time, it was Shorty. JD jumped down and dragged Shorty's lifeless body into the trees.

Stopping beside a thick clump of large bushes he knelt down and popped the clip out of the pistol. It wasn't empty but it wasn't full either. He reloaded with a full clip and double checked to confirm that a round was in the chamber. Finding it hard to breathe JD realized, *I've got to calm down, I must maintain control.* After taking several deep breaths and slowly exhaling he started toward the pond. JD had realized what must be done the moment he came face to face with Lefty, he stayed focused. There was no thinking, just doing. Keenly familiar with every inch of the island after walking it for the past several months no time was lost in reaching the pond.

The gasoline engine was running. The pump was pumping but the Japanese pump operator was nowhere to be seen. He asked himself, *Could it be possible that there are only two soldiers and not three?* Then he remembered; *Oh yes, the gasoline engine had started when Lefty and Shorty were in plain sight. A third soldier started that engine. He's here somewhere.* JD took cover behind a patch of tall grass. He surveyed the entire area but saw nothing and heard only the sound of the pump motor chugging away. *Where is that guy?* His mind was now racing at a fever pitch.

Suddenly it hit him like a lightning bolt. *The boat, I must get to the boat immediately.* The boat was the place where the remaining soldier would eventually need to go. If by chance he had seen what had happened to Lefty or Shorty he would try to escape. JD turned and quickly retraced his steps as he rushed to a concealed location in the trees with an unobstructed view of the landing craft. Shorty's body lay just a few feet away. He waited and watched. All day he remained motionless, eyes scanning around but he saw nothing. He sat crouched, out of sight, hour after hour. It didn't bother him at all. This was life or death. He had never been so focused.

The gasoline engine ran out of gas well before noon. The island became instantly quiet and still. The wind was down now so the normal rustling of the trees and action of the waves against the beach were nonexistent. JD remained motionless listening, watching, and smelling, all of his senses intensified.

As night began to fall, shielded by the gathering darkness, JD detected something over to his right, not very far from his position, just a faint sound at first then he saw something. His senses were on high alert as he remained frozen. Yes, movement, there he was; just to the right not thirty feet away bent down, slowly sneaking toward the boat. JD fired a shot. It missed but the third soldier must have heard the bullet zip past his head because he instantly broke into a run heading directly toward the beach. JD was after him within a split second but his legs were stiff from lack of movement. He stumbled then quickly regained his balance. He willed his legs to move and they responded. JD's target appeared from the trees first and then jumped on the bow of the boat. JD was only ten yards behind, but being on the run and using a handgun on a moving target made for a difficult shot.

He dropped to the ground, automatically assuming the prone position just like in basic training. Legs spread, boots dug in the sand for leverage and with both hands steadying his weapon he fired off five rapid shots. His target dove into the boat. JD was not altogether sure that any of the rounds had hit their target. He hurriedly got to his feet and without any hesitation charged right after him. JD leapt up on the bow screaming like a wild animal while firing in the direction of where the target should have landed. The slide stopped, the gun was empty. He raised the butt of the gun and took a firm grip on its handle ready for hand to hand combat.

His target was there, right where he had expected him to be, lying face down between the barrels. He was bleeding from several bullet holes in his back and legs. JD figured that at least three shots out of the first five, plus perhaps one more from his wild charge had found their mark. The guy wasn't moving. JD took hold of the soldier's left shoulder with one hand and rolled him face up while raising the pistol in the other. JD was ready to beat him to death if need be. The mustached face of Charlie Chan stared skyward through lifeless eyes. JD turned away and dropped to his knees on the foreword deck of the boat, his heart beating out of his chest all the time struggling to catch his breath. Feeling completely exhausted he took a moment to settle down and think about what to do next. JD's head was spinning, "My God, I've just killed three men in close combat. This is terrible, and so different than dropping bombs from high above the target." The events of this day were so unanticipated that his mind was having a difficult time catching up with the reality of what he had done. Within a few moments JD was able to regain a measure of composure which allowed his mind to refocus.

Within thirty minutes the bodies of Lefty, Shorty and Charlie Chan were securely tied to the floorboards of the boat. JD threw the cargo netting over the drums and three bodies. Then he tied the nets down securing his cargo. Finding several of the drums empty, he proceeded to unscrew the plugs and toss them aside. To prevent air pockets he reloaded and shot a few holes near the bottom of the empty barrels.

In the darkness, JD was especially careful navigating around the reef. Once out beyond it he opened the sea cocks and a steady stream of sea water rushed in from one and then the other.

The boat already had several inches of water covering the floor. The pump at the pond had run for over an hour until it was out of gas. Fresh water had overflowed one of the barrels covering the bottom of the boat.

The next fifteen minutes were spent steering in circles in open water near the point opposite the bay side. From this entirely different perspective, and with the glow from a half moon glimmering off the water, the island appeared alluring like pictures of tropical paradises in National Geographic Magazine. JD's eyes were drawn to a section of the beach just in from the point. He realized that this was more than likely the very spot where the *Randall* had been beached those many years ago. He had wondered how her crew had been able to free such a large and heavy ship from the sand. From this perspective it was easy to imagine lifting the sails during a strong westerly wind and letting the wind simply blow her back out to the deep water just off shore.

With the motor running at full speed, JD brought the little boat past the point and as near to it as he could safely maneuver. With the boat on a southerly heading which would take it straight out to sea, and with the steering wheel lashed down so as to maintain that course, he dove off the transom and swam the short distance to shore. Standing on the shore at the very end of the island in only his threadbare undershorts he watched the landing craft's progress until it eventually traveled far enough away from the island that it faded from sight.

The engine would fail when the water raised high enough to drown it out. Out there somewhere in the vastness of the Pacific Ocean it would sink, leaving no connection to the island. Daylight wouldn't come for another seven or maybe eight hours. Long before that the boat and its cargo would be gone forever. No one would see a thing.

He turned away and began the mile long walk back down the beach to retrieve his clothes, weapons and other belongings. Then he would pick up the hose, and put it away, fill the gas tank on the pump motor, police the areas around the pumping station, the two killing scenes and the beach. As he worked he thought; *After this I'll go to bed. I might even fall asleep if the pounding in my chest ever stops and I can find a way to calm down. If I allow myself to take the time now to think about what has happened I just might go mad.* He walked on a while and then realized, *Tomorrow promises to be an intense day. They will come, I know it. What a mess, what an absolute mess.* Then an odd thought came into his head, *I better not set out the fishing poles tonight.*

The Final Mission Arnold D. Jones

CHAPTER FIFTEEN
A CHANGE IN PLANS

The following morning, well before the sun appeared on the eastern horizon JD was already busily preparing for the return of the Japanese. Their next visit wouldn't be for water alone. The Japanese would thoroughly search the island from one end to the other in hopes of finding any sign of their missing landing craft and crew.

The first task was to clean and ready the machine gun brought from the plane. The two boxes of ammunition contained one thousand rounds. At a firing rate of four hundred rounds per minute he could put up a heck of a fight for all of two and a half minutes, not very long.

The pile of rubble, which lay on the floor of the cavern directly opposite the entrance, would provide excellent cover for a gun position. JD went to work positioning the .50 caliber Browning behind the rocks and debris. It was pointed directly at the entrance. He smoothed out the ground to the side of the gun. He then set the two ammunition boxes on the prepared surface and opened their lids. After lifting the top of the receiver he pulled out the end of one of the ammunition belts and set it in place. When the receiver was closed he pulled back the slide, cocking the gun. He then repositioned the second box and pulled the end of the belt out where it could be reached easily. When the first belt was spent he would be ready for a quick changeover to the second belt. There would be no time to free the belt if it were to get hung up. He double checked his work before moving on to the next task. This would be his first line of defense against a frontal attack. The old kegs of gun power were brought down from the terrace and placed near the entrance. They would be his second line of defense. If the soldiers made it inside a few bullets fired into the kegs should blow them into the afterlife. After which he was out of ideas and would be out of luck.

If the Japanese found the entrance and made it through the opening, which he planned to fill with boulders and rocks, he knew that defending the entrance was his best option. They would need to be persistent and even lucky to discover the cavern so he might only need to wait out the search. There was enough food on hand, if he watched it, to last for maybe two weeks and the water supply was endless. If his luck held they would never know he existed.

Hopefully they would just go away.

JD remained hunkered down for several days. Leaving just enough room to squeeze through the opening he kept watch from out on the plateau. Using the binoculars day after day he scanned the sea in all directions but saw nothing accept an empty ocean. On the fourth day of his watch it began to rain and visibility was reduced significantly. The clouds were so thick and dark that on several occasions throughout the day *Wildcat's* wing could not be seen from JDs perch atop the hill. At these times the entire Japanese Imperial fleet could have been anchored just off the beach and JD wouldn't have known a thing about it.

A steady downpour persisted for nearly a week without letup. As a result, the water flowing down from the hill filled the pond below to overflowing. JD anticipated that the Japanese would return shortly after the rain stopped. Remaining on alert for several days with such poor visibility had turned him into a nervous wreck.

Surprisingly, several days following a letup in the rain the clear skies hadn't coaxed the Japanese to return to the island. The sound of planes passing in the distance could be heard once the weather had cleared. However, they were too far away to be seen even through the binoculars. The engine noise sounded like American planes but he couldn't be sure. They were just too far away.

JD had plenty of time to think and he used a good portion of it dreaming up different scenarios as to why the Japanese still had not materialized. The one he liked the best was that the war was over and the Japanese had surrendered. The most likely seemed to be that they had pulled back from whatever nearby island they had been occupying and taken up a position too far away to allow them access to his island's water source. If the planes were American that would support his assumption. Whatever the true reason he couldn't be sure, but he thought it very strange that they had not returned.

JD was determined to remain vigilant and stick with the present course of action. The observation position atop the hill offered the best vantage point on the island. Until the food ran short he would stay right there. For now, he would watch and wait.

A few more uneventful days passed. Then, one evening at around seven with the sun still above the western horizon, a speck appeared far out to sea. Although the sound of planes overhead had become a daily occurrence nothing had been visible approaching from the sea until now. Staring through the binoculars he locked his gaze on the little dot as it gradually grew larger. Eventually, it came close enough to clearly make out that it was indeed a ship. A large and very fast moving vessel was steadily closing the distance between itself and the island. The ship was bow on as it approached, which made determining the type nearly impossible. He continued to observe as it remained on a heading directly toward the island. After some time the vessel was close enough that the silhouetted shape identified it as a war ship with sleek lines. JD Kept the glasses fixed on the ship, the shape was unmistakable. *It's a naval destroyer and she's coming straight on. The question is whose ship is it, friend or foe?*

He continued to observe until absolutely sure. There, high above the smoke stack, waving boldly from her superstructure were the stars and stripes of a well-worn and tattered American flag.

It was an American destroyer and there was no doubt that it would come very close to the island. Without pause he pushed and squeezed through the entrance of the cavern to retrieve the flare gun and all five flares. By the time he returned to the plateau the sun was low on the horizon and he was sure that the ship's lookouts would see his signal flares against the darkening sky. Originating from high atop the hill, and with no obstructions between the flare and the ship, his confidence was high.

The first flare shone brightly in the twilight sky. *A blind man couldn't miss seeing that.* He waited for a response, nothing. The flare burned out as it disappeared in the trees near the beach. He reloaded and fired a second flare. This one caught the wind and hung in the sky for a long time as it traveled all the way to the bay where the water snuffed it out. Again there was no response from the destroyer which was now even closer to the island.

I'll use them all, I don't care. This is the best chance I'll ever have. As he pulled the trigger on flare number three he began to pray, "Dear God, please help me." At that very moment the signal horn from the destroyer began its whooping blast. They had seen his signal.

Every good feeling he could ever have imagined came over him at the same time. He was momentarily overcome with emotion. Involuntary tears of joy filled his eyes and started to spill out and run down his face. He was getting off this prison, he was free, and he would have a chance at life. He had hoped for rescue every day but maybe he hadn't really allowed himself to believe it would actually come. Now it was here, he was overwhelmed. He just stood where he was and watched the ship.

On the ship, the lookout had reported the first flare to the bridge just seconds after it appeared in the sky. His rescue was assured from that moment. The Captain had ordered the lookouts to confirm their sighting while at the same time giving orders to prepare an armed shore party.

As the destroyer came within a mile of the island it slowed and turned to show its port side. The three twin gun turrets rotated and all six big, five-inch guns zeroed in on the island. The ship's launch was smartly lowered to the sea. Smoke billowed from the destroyer's stack as she immediately got back underway. It was dangerous for a war ship to stay in one place for too long making itself a target for unseen enemy submarines or planes. The destroyer maintained her distance from the shore as she began to circle around. The turret motors wined as the main guns stayed locked on their target during the circling maneuver.

The launch approached the bay, but in the gathering darkness, wisely did not attempt to navigate the outer reefs. Instead the helmsman steered the boat toward a landing out on the point. Soon, the small craft was in the surf and then beached on the sand. The shore party quickly jumped over the sides and began to fan out taking up positions twenty feet in front of the beached craft. Two sailors with rifles at the ready slowly advanced up the beach.

By this time JD had composed himself and had grabbed the journal. He was already on the beach by the time the launch had made its landing. The two members of the shore party continued to make their way cautiously up the beach toward the middle of the island while in contrast, JD ran for all he was worth toward his would-be rescuers.

Both sailors spotted him at the same time. Running directly toward them was a long-haired creature in tattered clothes with a very long full beard covering his face. One of the sailors fired a warning shot in the air and yelled out.

"Halt and identify yourself."

JD froze in his tracks, stunned by the sudden and unexpected discharge of the rifle and the stern command. He was so excited that he had forgotten about how on edge the sailors must be in this situation.

Gathering himself, he spoke to another human being for the first time in months, "First Lieutenant Joseph Dutton Jones Jr., United States Army Air Corps."

"Okay Lieutenant, don't move and show your hands," said the sailor in charge as he advanced alone toward JD, leaving his partner behind with his gun trained on the wild looking stranger.

JD dropped the journal on the sand and stood motionless, both hands out in front of him with palms up. The sailor stepped forward stopping when he was no more than two feet away. The two young men stood face to face. One was cautious and careful; the other furious, upset and angry. The click of the flash light brought forth a bright beam which the sailor shined into JD's eyes as he examined the face behind the beard. The blue eyes staring back told him that the man who stood before him was not happy, to say the least. He reached for JD's dog tags. While doing so JD didn't flinch but continued the stare into the sailor's eyes with a look so intense that the young sailor was unnerved by the experience.

Something snapped inside JD when they fired the shot and trained the rifles on him. To him it was clear, "How could anyone mistake a six foot two inch white man for a Jap? Furthermore, the enemy wouldn't have fired flares in the night and then come running toward an armed shore party on an open beach without a weapon. This feeling I've got is different, maybe it's because they've robbed me of the joy I was feeling about finally being rescued. I've been worrying and waiting for such a long time. I've fought for my country without question and even killed three men in combat."

Suddenly, JD understood his feelings. He hated killing. He hated the very thought of it. Being put in a position that necessitated killing and then being challenged and having to prove to this kid that he was worthy of rescue had rubbed him the wrong way. He felt as though he could rip this guy's heart out if given the slightest provocation.

The young sailor before him was on edge but he managed to find and read the dog tags around JD's neck. "Sir, welcome back," the young sailor said as he pointed the light toward the ground and out of JD's eyes.

Still unable to give up the anger bubbling inside his head JD looked past the young sailor. He picked up the journal at his feet and began to walk away in the direction of the launch.

"Let's get out of here, sailor." He led the sailors out to the point and into the launch. The destroyer was coming around heading for a rendezvous with the launch.

JD turned back to take one more look at the island. "I'm so glad to be putting this place behind me." At that instant the treasure flashed across his mind, "Well, putting it behind me for a while, I hope one day to come back and finish with the island once and for all."

CHAPTER SIXTEEN
RETURN TO DUTY

The deck crew hustled the hauling lines down to the launch even before anyone had an opportunity to start up the boarding net. Two of the sailors grabbed the bottom of the net steadying it and motioned JD to start climbing. He stuffed the journal down the front of his trousers and made his ascent to the deck of the destroyer with the boarding party following close behind. An electric winch began to lift the launch from the sea. The moment the smaller craft's keel cleared the water the destroyer was underway. Within a minute or two she was making good speed in the darkness that had now completely concealed the island.

An officer motioned for JD to step inside a nearby companionway. He did so and the officer followed. When they were both inside and out of the wind and noise the officer spoke.

"It's good to have you aboard Lieutenant. I wanted to get you off the deck so we don't need to yell to be heard. Are you okay? Any health issues that need immediate attention, anything at all?

"No I'm in good health I think, nothing hurts, and nothing's broken."

"That's good. How about food, are you hungry, could you eat something?"

"Yes, I am hungry," JD replied as he noticed his clothes and for the first time realizing just what he must look like to those around him. "Would it be alright if I got myself cleaned up first?"

"You'll bunk in with me. I'll take you to our quarters where you can clean up and borrow some clothes. Meanwhile, I'll round up the barber. You could use a haircut and a shave. After you're squared away we'll go to the galley together."

"Thanks, that sounds great. It'll be good to wash off that island."

As they started down the passageway toward the room, the officer turned to JD. "By the way, I'm Jess."

"They just call me JD," he hesitated a moment before adding. "You know something Jess? I don't think you'll ever appreciate how good it is to meet you."

"Listen JD, I forgot to mention that the Captain would like for you to meet with him after you've eaten. Questions, I guess. I'll take you to him after dinner."

"Sounds fine, and thanks for everything. I was pretty uptight back on the island when I was rescued but I feel much better now."

When he finished, Jess patted him on the back as they reached the room.

The barber proved to be quite skilled as he made short work of the task before him. When he was all done JD splashed on some of Jess's Old Spice and felt a sting that rivaled being stung by a dozen bumble bees all at the same time. A look in the mirror confirmed that his face had not the slightest cut or even scratch, just a very close shave and a flawless haircut. Decked out in a Marine uniform supplied by the ship's laundry he felt fantastic and now a little hungry.

Dinner consisted of mashed potatoes, green beans, corn, fresh rolls and a large steak. JD liked the food very much. However, his island diet had caused his stomach to shrink and there was no way he could consume all of his food. The clothes he was wearing were two sizes smaller than normal but fit him with room to spare. He hadn't been on a scale but he figured to be down about thirty-five pounds. Feeling so good, he decided right then and there to keep the weight off from then on.

A few moments later he thought about his contrasting circumstances. *Over these last several months I've been on a constant hunt for food wherever I could find it. Now I'm thinking about how to restrict my eating habits in order to prevent gaining weight.* Suddenly over taken by emotion, tears welled up in his eyes and streamed down his cheeks. Closing his eyes right there at the table, and thanked God for his rescue.

After a while, a sailor entered the galley from the passageway and stepped over to the table where JD and Jess were talking over coffee. He handed Jess a note.

Jess read it quickly then turning to JD said, "The Captain will be delayed and has asked that you use the time to let the doctor check you out."

"Fine with me, I feel so content that I'll even stand still for a shot if the doc wants to give me one."

The sick bay had eight empty cots. Apparently JD was among a crew of very healthy sailors. The doctor was no more than twenty-five or twenty-six years of age but quickly proved to be well qualified. He spent the next thirty minutes poking, prodding, and listening to JD's chest. After completing his examination, for good measure he administered two shots as a precaution against anything that JD might have contracted on the island. JD was declared fit and healthy, and sent to the Captain with his medical report in hand.

The door to the Captain's quarters was open. Jess cleared his throat while standing in the passageway just outside of the open door. The Captain was sitting at a small desk writing something when he heard the noise.

"Come in gentlemen," he said with a gracious tone in his voice. The two young officers entered and stood at attention in the center of the small room.

The Captain turned in his seat to face them before speaking. "Please, relax and won't you both sit down?"

As they found chairs he continued, "Jess I would like you to stay and take notes of this interview." Then he turned to JD.

"Let me get right to it. We had no idea that you were on that island. It was very fortuitous that you were rescued. Our original plans had not included going anywhere near there. We first learned of the island from the interrogation of a Japanese sailor who was taken off a small boat by one of our ships on patrol. The Japanese craft just happened to be filled with empty barrels. He told his interrogators that the barrels were intended for fresh water and eventually revealed the source of the water which just happened to be where you were. That island is not charted. We had no idea that it existed. You might never have been discovered. Fresh water out here is an extremely valuable commodity so we were dispatched to check out his story. We arrived too late in the day to begin a search of the island. Let me ask you. Is there really fresh water on that island?"

"Yes sir there is a generous supply which runs off the hill into a large pond. The Japanese made several trips to the island for water while I was there."

"That leads me to another question. The prisoner said that the last boat to make the trip for water before they evacuated never returned. A check of navel records around that time doesn't indicate any action in the waters near that location, so we have no explanation for why that boat didn't return. Do you know anything about it?"

Reluctantly, JD told the story. When he was finished the Captain was silent for a few moments. Then he spoke.

"Son that's amazing. You killed all of them single handed; that's gruesome but it had to be done. They might have come searching for their comrades and if they had found you I hate to think of what would have been done to you in retaliation. You should thank God that events worked out the way they did."

JD looked up and spoke very introspectively. "I already have sir, I already have."

Then the Captain added the most interesting fact. "Under the pressure of advancing elements of our Navy, the Japanese garrison stationed on a nearby island to yours was forced to evacuate without an adequate supply of water. They moved north and took up a defensive position on an island thirty miles away but soon depleted their water supply. The Japanese sailors that you encountered had been sent to retrieve drinking water for the garrison prior to the pull-out. When they failed to return, the garrison was forced to move out without the needed water. By the time the Marines launched their invasion they were met with very weak resistance from the Japanese. It was a walkover. Hundreds of Marines were spared injury or death in part because of your action against the Japanese team sent to resupply their troops with water. Obviously you had no idea of the positive consequences that would result from your bravery but I'm here to tell you it made a difference to a lot of Americans. The boat that was intercepted by the Navy and led to your rescue had been sent from the northern island which was much further away. The boat was out of fuel when discovered. They were just too far away to make it. They said that there was gasoline on the island. Their intention was to refuel for the return trip once they reached their destination."

JD didn't know what to say but eventually found some words. "I had no idea, I was just fighting to stay alive another day. That's all there was to it, sir."

They both just looked at each other for a moment neither knowing what to say next. Then the Captain changed subjects. "What did the Doc say? Is that his report you have there?" asked the Captain while for the first time noticing the papers in JD's hand.

"He gave me a clean bill of health." JD handed the medical report over to the captain.

The Captain took the report and said, "I was just filling out my report on your rescue. We'll get word to your family just as soon as possible. That should take a heavy load off their minds."

This prompted JD to speak. "Sir, I want to thank you for saving my life. You specifically, as well as every member of your crew, from the bottom of my heart, thank you."

"Let me tell you Lieutenant, your rescue is a rare but positive episode in this war. As you well know, war is mostly hell on Earth. Let me assure you, this crew is overjoyed to have been a part of getting you safely off that island."

The Captain's words made JD think about the many responsibilities thrust upon the Captain of a war ship and he thought that he would be proud to serve under a man like this.

Using the notes taken by Jess the Captain carefully added all that had been said to his report, signed it then folded the paper in half. "Jess when you leave would you give this to the radio room. It's the report on our Lieutenant here. Have it sent to Pearl at the earliest. Would you do that?"

"Aye aye sir, nothing would please me more," Jess answered with an expression of pride on his face.

JD liked these guys a lot. He felt like his old self again for the first time in over five months. Things were good.

On the fourth day aboard ship the Captain asked all officers to join him in the ward room for breakfast. JD was invited to join the meeting where he had an opportunity to meet the rest of the destroyer's officers. He learned that the ship had been at sea this trip for almost six months and had seen its share of action. The group around the table was highly competent and mostly young, in their mid-twenties with one exception, the chief engineer. He was in his late thirties maybe even forty and didn't have much to say. It was clear to JD that he held personal power within the group. Everyone showed him respect, including the Captain. What they received in return was a soft spoken gentleman who exuded confidence, knowledge and mentoring skills. But, most impressive was that he seemed to have absolutely no ego. He was like a coach on the field to assist, advise and teach. This was a well-oiled machine, this United States Navy Destroyer.

Some of the officers present were coming off duty and would head for their bunks after breakfast while the others would take up the daytime duties of commanding the ship. Just before they were about to disperse the Captain addressed the group.

"Early this morning we received orders to steam directly back to Pearl. It seems that someone thinks that we might need a little break. JD, we won't be able to get rid of you so you'll return with the ship to Pearl."

The response to this news was a spontaneous outpouring of joy and relief mixed with smiles and pats on the back all around. JD was no exception. These were some happy guys. The Captain raised his hands to settle down the group then he spoke.

"I intend to get this crew home safely, so we cannot lose focus. Inform the crew if they don't already know that we will be returning to Pearl. Then inform them that we'll be at general quarters all the way back. I want every man to be on alert and at the ready. This ship is taking zero chances. Remind everyone that we are still in a war zone. Set a zigzag course and maintain it right up to the mouth of the harbor. Gentlemen you have your orders."

With that the room emptied until only JD and the Captain remained. The Captain looked at JD and finally spoke. "Son, I have some bad news for you so I'll just say it. Your father passed away while you were on that island. I'm very sorry. I was given no further details so for now, that is all the information available. Again, I am very sorry to have to bring you such bad news." This was a blow. JD didn't have words, he couldn't form thoughts, and he just stood there. The Captain disturbed a long silence with a question spoken with authority. "How did you sleep last night?"

"I slept well," JD answered like a zombie without the slightest expression.

"Good, then you won't need to return to your quarters. You will accompany me to the bridge and spend the day there. You can perform lookout duty from the bridge while I command the ship. Let's go."

The seas were calm and the sky was clear during the cruise back to Pearl Harbor. Zigzagging to protect against submarine attack served to extend the duration of the voyage but after several days they reached the harbor and were tied up at the dock.

During the trip, JD had gotten to know several of the crew and most of the officers on a first name basis. They were a good bunch of guys who proved to be easy to talk to. Their companionship had helped him come to grips with his father's passing. He felt better by the time the ship reached port. As the crew disembarked, JD stood at the gangway and said his goodbyes to all the sailors and officers that he had met.

Finally, it was his turn to leave the ship. Now back in his Army uniform which had been expertly patched and mended by the ships laundry, he walked down the gangway and made his way over to Hickam Field and Army Air Corps Headquarters. JD was officially returning to duty.

The Final Mission Arnold D. Jones

CHAPTER SEVENTEEN
GOOD NEWS AND BAD

General Clayton Davis and two Colonels were already in the large conference room when JD entered. The General returned JD's salute and they all took seats at one end of a long dark mahogany conference table which stood in the center of the room. The General sat at the end of the table with JD and one of the Colonels on his right and the other Colonel across from JD. As soon as they were comfortable the General started the conversation.

"Well, Lieutenant please allow me to say that we are delighted to see you safe and in good health."

"Thank you sir, it's good to be back." JD said.

"Have you been enjoying your time here in Hawaii?"

"Yes sir," answered JD cautiously. After all this was a General and JD couldn't remember ever speaking to a General before so he decided to keep his answers short and to the point. He was operating on the premise that the less said the less chance he had to make a mistake.

"Let's see, you've been here what, ten days, is that right?"

JD thought for a moment then answered. "Actually, twelve days, if you count today; sir."

"Quite right, if you count today. Have you had an opportunity to contact your family?"

"Oh yes sir, I sent a telegram the moment we docked in port and have received a return telegram from my mother," answered JD.

"I'm sure that she was relieved to hear from you. I understand that you recently lost your father. Hopefully, your mother is doing well after her loss," the General said with a questioning tone to his comment.

JD responded, "I'm sure that she's doing the best that she can under the circumstances. I still have a little sister at home so she is busy caring for her. That sort of keeps her mind off what happened."

"We sent her our best. These are difficult times for many families." The General paused before changing the subject to the real purpose of the meeting. "We've read your report. Thank you for such a detailed and complete transcript. It truly is very well done."

"Thank you, I did have plenty of free time while a guest of the Navy. I used the available time during the cruise back to Pearl to work on the report. I did my best to recall as much detail as possible. After all, it's been a long time since the day of the mission and much has transpired in between," explained JD.

"The three of us here today have spent several hours over the past few days discussing your report and have just a few questions for you. But first, you will be happy to learn that your two crew members were rescued shortly after hitting the water."

JD's mind was in overdrive. "Why are a General and two other high ranking officers taking up their obviously valuable time on such a routine matter? This makes no sense, something else must be going on here." Unsure of just what it could be he found himself once again waiting for the other shoe to drop.

The General began once more. "The crew's account of the mission agrees with yours. Naturally their recall was from a different perspective but essentially their reports match your account almost exactly. Lieutenant, we would be very interested to learn if you consider your actions as heroic at any time during the mission and during your time on the island?"

"I am relieved and extremely happy to learn that Nick and Jake both made it. That's great news, thank you so much. As for heroic actions, nothing like that took place. I was simply trying to regain control of the plane until the crew could get out safely. In truth, I may have been premature with the alarm. After all, I did manage to regain control and fly for nearly a full hour after they bailed out."

"Could you have left the controls and joined your crew to bail out when they did?" asked one of the Colonels.

"Well, I don't think it would have been impossible but it would have been very difficult, that's for sure. Better put, at the time I didn't think that was my best option," JD answered as he relived in his mind those tense moments back on that terrible day.

Speaking with unbridled enthusiasm the General interrupted. "Son, what you did was heroic. You saved the lives of two men at the real and likely risk of losing your own. You know and we know that your crew would have never made it out if you had decided to abandon the plane at that moment. Hell, that's the very definition of a hero if I've ever heard it. The fact that you had the good fortune to save yourself after the others were safely away just adds to it."

The room grew quiet for a long while but it wasn't an uncomfortable silence. The four men sat calmly thinking about the events described in JD's report.

The Colonel sitting directly across from JD, and who had been silent up until then, looked at JD and spoke. "Lieutenant, you are what is known as a reluctant hero and we here in this room want you to know that they are the best kind."

General Davis picked up the conversation. "We have carefully evaluated the reports from everyone concerned. After meeting you and hearing your thoughts on the episode we are all in agreement that your actions indicate that you acted with uncommon valor putting the lives of your crew first before your own welfare. Further, by continuing to press the enemy while on the island, untold lives were saved in the invasion. Because of your heroic actions on both occasions countless men are alive today who might very well not be. I have the honor to inform you that you are being recommended to receive an Air Medal for your actions in the plane and for your actions while on the island, the Silver Star."

JD felt overwhelmed and somewhat embarrassed by the General's declaration and he couldn't help letting it show on his face. Maybe he had acted heroically but he alone knew that all he did was the job he was trained to do. To JD, the real heroes were the guys who trained him. He found himself wondering if they ever received medals.

"According to your file, it appears that you have one more mission remaining in order to complete the full sixty necessary and reach your combat limit. Is that correct?" said the Colonel who sat across from JD.

"Yes that is correct, sir; one more to go," said JD.

The General broke in once more. "Well you're not going to fly it here, son. As far as I'm concerned, you've already done enough. Hell son, even a cat's only got nine lives. You're going back to the States. It just so happens that we can kill two birds with one stone. I have recently received a request for a pilot with combat experience in B-25s for duty back in the States. You fit the bill, so pack your bags and report for duty in Milwaukee, Wisconsin. We'll issue your orders and make arrangements for air transportation back to the west coast. It will take a few days, so consider yourself on leave until your orders come through. Just check in here every couple of days."

JD stood in anticipation of being dismissed when the General added, "By the way, that shoe box over there on the other end of the table contains all the mail that's been held for you since you went missing. I had it rounded up and delivered here; thought you might like to catch up on your reading while waiting for orders."

JD walked to the end of the table to retrieve the letter box which was filled to the top. "Thank you very much sir," JD said as he reached over and picked it up nestling it under his arm.

The three officers stood and walked over to JD each shaking his hand while offering their congratulations and wishing him well when the General spoke. "There's one last thing that I almost forgot. Take this voucher to the paymaster and collect your back pay. I'm sure you're a little short of cash." He smiled as he handed the voucher to JD. He took the voucher from the General and stuffed it into his right pocket alongside five of the gold coins that he had held out of the treasure before burying it on the island. The other five were in his left pocket.

"That's very thoughtful of you sir. You're right, I could use it. Thanks very much." JD thought about it for an instant and realized that he was actually happy. This was the end of a long and dangerous road.

Addressing the General, he said. "Again, I want to thank all of you for the great news, but could you tell me anything about my new assignment?"

The general took a piece of paper from the table in front of him, scanning over it before he answered. After a moment he looked up and spoke.

"This is interesting. It says here that the two training aircraft carriers currently on duty in Lake Michigan will be taking a goodwill cruise that will require air support. That's what you'll be doing Lieutenant, flying your final mission over Lake Michigan. Good duty if you can get it, and you've got it."

After being dismissed, JD left the building and went straight over to a small park-like area not far from the building's entrance. There, he selected a bench shaded by a stand of mature Palm trees and sat down. Taking off his cap and placing it next to him on the bench he then positioned the letter box squarely on his lap.

The telegram received two days earlier from Momma had provided the details of dad's passing. Dad had suffered a massive stroke while at the throttle of his railroad engine. The firemen who shared the engine's cab with Dad, stoking the firebox with coal, took control immediately and as quickly as possible stopped the train. However, by the time he was able to reach him dad was unresponsive. He laid in a coma for several days before dying peacefully in his bed. JD felt that he could put the other letters from the family aside for a few minutes. He would have an opportunity later to take his time and read them all. Now however, he was looking for a letter from Susan.

After his letter informing her of the deal that would delay his return home was received by Susan things had changed. Their correspondence beforehand had been almost daily. Afterwards, letters came weekly and soon even less frequently. He was hoping for the best but was prepared for the worst. He began to rummage through the box which contained at least twenty-five letters. It was beginning to look like he wouldn't find anything from Susan, but after sorting through nearly all of the letters, there it was. The post mark indicated that it had been mailed around the same time as his forty-fourth mission. This was an old letter. He sorted the remaining few letters but there were no others from Susan, this was it.

In order to speed up mail for military personnel the government had created a special design for all such mail. It was called Victory Mail. There was no envelope; instead the paper had the address layout preprinted on one side. The sender would write on the opposite side then fold the four corners inward and seal it. Address information would be written on the outside using the form provided. This made all address information uniform throughout the postal system thus speeding up the sorting process. JD carefully opened the four flaps and began to read the letter.

> *Dear Joe,*
> *When you wrote to me of your decision not to come home I was heartbroken. I missed you so much. I just couldn't understand such a selfish decision for the life of me. My disappointment was inconsolable for a very long time. I kept thinking, how could you do this to me. But eventually, I came to realize that you did not mean all of those things you said to me when we were together. I have met someone who truly loves me and would never be as self-centered as you. We are to be married next month. He is from North Texas and has an important job working on his father's ranch. He is supplying beef and oil to the war effort. His work is vital to our nation's struggle for victory over the enemy. He needs me to support him in this all important work. So I am saying goodbye to you Joe. I am getting on with doing my part for the war effort. I wish you well.*
> *Susan*

He didn't think himself a fool. She had distanced herself in the last few letters. This had certainly been clear so this wasn't a complete shock. After reading her take on his decision he couldn't help feeling just a little bit lucky that it was over now instead of later. He admitted to himself that it did hurt but surprisingly not as much as he thought it would. Still, the finality of it all turned his stomach.

As the morning drifted into afternoon the letters from the box had all been read. Letters from Momma, brothers, sisters, aunts, his dad, a few friends, and even the minister all were uplifting and informative.

The one from Dad however, was special. As always, Dad had talked of plans for JD's future. He had a way about him, always alert to potential opportunities for after the war was over. It was all good stuff but mostly, Dad's objective was to provide hope for the future by offering momentary relief from the worries that come with war. JD was going to miss him but he was blessed to have the memories and the life lessons that his father had instilled in him through the years. His father not only taught with words but more importantly, by action. People knew him as a man of principle just by observation. He knew what he stood for and he lived it every day. Sitting there on that bench on the base far from home, JD determined that he would do his best to emulate his father.

Losing *Wildcat*, becoming marooned on the island, the discovery of Thomas Johnston and his journal, hand-to-hand combat with the Japanese, the rescue, Dad's passing, the recommendation for medals, Susan's letter and the treasure were all on JD's mind when he picked up the box and walked away.

As he passed a trash barrel he looked down at Susan's letter in his hand, wadded it up and tossed it in with the garbage. Just as he released the little ball of paper he said out loud, "That's one less thing to think about."

CHAPTER EIGHTEEN
CHICAGO

"Union Station, last stop, Union Station, last stop, Union Station." The shouts of the conductor awakened First Lieutenant JD Jones.

He tipped up the bill of his officer's cap which had been covering his eyes, keeping out the world around him. With eyes slowly opening, he took a quick inventory; duffel bag under his legs, flight bag securely on his lap, leather flight jacket covering his chest and arms with the wool collar pulled up under his chin. JD estimated that he had been asleep for at least five hours, maybe more.

As the conductor passed by his seat JD asked, "Conductor, excuse me, are we on time?"

The conductor stopped in the aisle and answered, "No sir, not this trip, we'll be arriving one hour and twenty minutes late. I truly am sorry;" then he added, "Sir is you comin or is you goin?"

JD answered thoughtfully, "I've been there. So I guess you could say I'm comin."

The conductor tipped his hat to JD and said, "Welcome home Lieutenant, good to have you back in these here United States."

The trip had begun in San Diego, California six days earlier. A place on the express had been impossible to get so JD was relegated to the local which stopped at seemingly every whistle stop all the way to Chicago. As the train pulled into the south end of Chicago's Union Station JD pulled his legs and feet in close to clear the way for his fellow passengers to move by. He waited until the train was nearly empty before picking up his belongings and entering the men's room at the far end of the car. There, he would get himself squared away before leaving the train. He found his shaving kit near the top of his duffle, splashed some water on his face and went to work.

He took his time. *There's no need to hurry now. The connection to Milwaukee is already long gone and that was the last train of the day. The next train north isn't scheduled to depart from Chicago until seven o'clock in the morning. The only thing to do now is to clean up, stow my gear in a locker and take a cab downtown.* He looked at his watch. *I've got seven hours to kill so there isn't any reason to miss a night on the town, especially when the town is Chicago.*

In the summer time, in the middle of a world war, Chicago was open for business twenty-four hours a day, seven days a week. Looking in the mirror, he was satisfied with his efforts. Confidently, he stepped off the train and made his way into the station, anticipating his first visit to the windy city.

He went to the stand of lockers to stow his duffle. As he turned the key on the locker door he was ready. The plan was simple, go up the stairs and out onto Jackson Street. Find the taxi stand and ten minutes later he would be downtown. That's when he caught a glimpse of her. She moved through his line of vision from left to right. Just that quickly, she was there then she was gone. The station was packed with people, most in uniform, moving in all directions at once. *So how is it that she stood out in the mob?* JD went right. Jackson Street was to the left. His focus was on getting another look at that girl. As the faceless mob closed in on all sides the reality that she was gone hit him. A feeling of anxiety rose up in the pit of his stomach.

He looked about as good as a twenty-three year old officer could look in uniform. Standing six feet two inches tall, one hundred eighty-five pounds, sun bleached blond hair and a fresh South Pacific tan, all of which were topped off by a set of wings. But, looks can be deceiving; on the inside his stomach was a mess. *What's going on here? She's just a girl, heck, one of many. Come to think of it I didn't even get a clear look at her.*

He stood there with the face of a golden retriever who had lost his best friend. Five minutes later the "dog" was still wandering around the grand hall of Union Station with no best friend in sight.

"Snap to!" he said out loud. It helped. The sounds and smells came back into focus. The aroma of fresh coffee turned his attention to the USO counter. JD walked over and sat down on the nearest unoccupied stool. A pleasant young woman served him coffee, a ham and cheese sandwich and a smile. He was starting to feel a little better as the two struck up a light conversation. Her name tag read Darlene so JD told her his.

"Hi, my name's JD," he said with a smile, "Thanks for the sandwich. I hadn`t realized how long it's been since I'd eaten."

"When did you eat last?" she asked as she placed her elbows on the counter and nestled her very cute little face in her hands.

"Oh let's see, it was somewhere outside of St. Louis, probably ten hours ago. The train stopped for water and I went inside the station to the USO counter there."

"Do you like USO food, Lieutenant?"

"Sure it's fresh, free and always served with a smile," he responded while still smiling.

He thought she was nice, but as the counter became busier Darlene moved away out of necessity, she was intending to work her way back to the big, handsome young flier, but business was too good.

He felt better, calmer, more like himself as he slipped down off the stool. The crowd had thinned out and now he could actually see across the huge room. Many people were still there but had begun to settle in for the night. Clusters of servicemen were huddled in corners, on the benches and on the floor, everywhere.

GIs and their equipment littered the grand hall. It was a typical ending to a typical wartime day. This same scene would be duplicated in every bus station, train station and airport throughout the country tonight and every night for the duration. They were all in it together. Somehow it was exciting, quite an adventure, everyone busy doing something important. All were making their individual contributions to the general good. He was glad to be back.

There at the magazine counter, she stood, directly across the aisle, with no one and nothing between them. "What am I going to do now? I can't allow her to get away again. Alright, get a hold of yourself and think of something." He made his decision, so with a deep breath and a steady gate; he walked the fifteen feet to the magazine rack.

JD came to a stop behind and slightly to her left. Peering over her shoulder just inches from her neck he saw that she was scanning the pages of Look Magazine. He could see the top of her hat. He estimated her to be somewhere between five six and five eight in heels. Her thick, brown hair fell just to the top of her perfectly shaped shoulders. JD could smell her perfume as he stood silently wanting to speak but reluctant to risk upsetting the moment, fearing it would end before he could get it started.

A sudden booming sound interrupted his timing when a luggage wagon pulled by an overworked Red Cap dropped a large trunk from a stack of luggage. It struck the marble floor directly in front of the two strangers. The sound immediately drew her eyes from the magazine to the hapless luggage handler and the massive trunk at his feet. JD turned to investigate at the same time. As if by magic, several Red Caps appeared and began muscling the trunk back up on the wagon.

In unison, the two strangers turned back at precisely the same moment and eye contact was made for the first time.

In mid-turn she was stopped by his eyes. At that moment her mind emptied, sounds faded to complete silence leaving only the hammer beat of her heart pounding out a sound that could be heard, she supposed, by everyone within a hundred feet. She tried to come to grips with what she was feeling, "I've never before felt this sensation. Nature has been hiding this one. If just seeing him can do this, what else is in store? My God is he good looking, but what if he just walks away?" Her mind searched for a situation extending reaction. She was saved from further anxiety by his words.

"Hello. May I introduce myself?" he asked softly.

She nodded affirmatively, displaying the best self-confident, yet slightly apathetic, but equally interested look that she could conjure up, under the circumstances.

"I'm Joseph Jones but everyone calls me JD," he offered his introduction with an accompanying smile.

"It's a pleasure to make your acquaintance. I'm Ann Marie Collins but please, call me Annie won't you, Lieutenant?" She never looked away from his deep blue eyes as she spoke.

While she responded, he was able to get his first good look at her face. *She's lovely. She has the prettiest green eyes I've ever seen and her face is just right. I didn't know how to describe her except to say that she is absolutely beautiful.*

She waited for him to respond and she could see that he was concentrating very hard. She enjoyed the look of his face at that moment and decided to keep the conversation going.

"What does the D stand for in JD?"

"Dutton, my full name is First Lieutenant Joseph Dutton Jones Jr., named after my dad. Everyone just called him Dutt and so the family started calling me JD, less confusion that way I guess," he answered.

"Well I'm not easily confused so I'll call you Joseph; would that be alright?" she asked with a cute grin; then added. "Was your dad a First Lieutenant too?"

"No what I meant was that..."

"I was kidding," she said with a laugh.

He liked her; this girl was obviously beautiful but she was fun too.

"That's just fine Annie. I would be pleased to have you call me Joseph. Just having you talk to me is great," he said sincerely.

"Well Joseph, what brings you to Chicago? I mean where are you headed?"

"I'm headed for Milwaukee, Wisconsin but my train arrived late and I've missed the connection. The next train isn't scheduled to leave until seven in the morning so I thought that I might as well see the city. I've never been to Chicago; in fact the biggest city I've been to is Auckland, New Zealand and there I just hung around the base waiting for a plane back to the Pacific Theater. I didn't see much at all."

He added the extra information because he wanted her to know that he was home from the war and hopefully she wouldn't worry about getting close to a guy who was going off to war. The experience with Susan had some influence on his decision to add the extra information.

She just looked at him for a moment and then spoke. "You're just coming back from the war is that right? Are you on leave or something?"

She didn't fully understand and wanted more information. He took this as a good sign. "Tell you what, do you have some time to say, have a cup of coffee and I can tell you about it?" JD asked while liking the fact that she was showing this much interest.

"Well, I'm headed back to Detroit, that's where I live, but I was bumped off my train. Without priority I don't even have a valid ticket now. I'm on a waiting list for tomorrow but there's no guarantee that I'll get out then. I may have to wait another day."

She wasn't sure why she was sharing all of that information but somehow she wanted him to know that she had the time. Then she added. "I would be happy to have a cup of coffee with you First Lieutenant Joseph Dutton Jones Jr."

He couldn't take her to the USO counter because that was strictly for military personnel and besides, it wouldn't fit the occasion. *Things are progressing pretty well to this point, and there is no reason to screw it up.* The problem was that he was totally unfamiliar with Union Station and had no idea where to find a nice place.

Annie could see his dilemma. His face was like an open book. She decided to help him out.

"The restaurants are on the second floor, this way." She pointed to the staircase just to the left of the magazine stand.

"Sorry I've never been here before," JD felt a little embarrassed.

She eased her arm around and under his and started him in the direction of the staircase. He reached over with his available hand and patted the arm that she had placed around his.

"Thanks, I'm following you, lead on."

Annie squeezed his arm tightly while looking up into his eyes with a reassuring smiled as they climbed the stairs that lead to the upper level.

There were far fewer people on the second floor and several of the restaurants were closed for the night. They spotted a nice place with tables out in the aisle, giving them the appearance of being out on the sidewalk like pictures he had seen of Paris restaurants. JD liked it and asked, "How's this one?"

"Looks fine to me let's go in," Annie said as they walked up to the young lady standing out front with menus in her hand.

The outside tables were nearly full of people, some eating, others having coffee and a few just killing time. Inside, the room was nearly empty. Booths lined the back wall and continued along the adjoining wall with tables arranged in the center of the room. JD spotted the booth in the far corner where the booths along the back and side wall intersected. Over the booth there was no overhead light only a small table lamp. The corner booth looked like a romantic getaway, the kind you see in the movies. He thought it would be the perfect place to have some privacy while getting to know each other better.

Annie saw it too and pulled on JD's arm which she was still holding.

"Joseph, what do you think about that booth over there in the corner? Do you think that would be a nice place to talk?"

"We'll take the booth in the corner if it's available," he told the young lady.

"That would be just fine," she said as she led them to the far corner of the room then waited while the young couple made themselves comfortable.

Once they were seated she handed each a menu, Annie first then JD. When this was completed she stepped back a half step and said, "I must say that when I saw you two walk up I hoped that you'd select this booth. You know this is the most popular spot in the restaurant. It's really quit cozy back here," she paused before asking. "Can I bring you something to drink while you read the menus?"

JD looked at Annie and she quickly ordered her drink. "I would like a Cherry Coke please," she said while looking at JD.

He gave her a quizzical glance before eventually ordering coffee for himself. Annie watched his face and just smiled.

When the young lady walked away, Annie placed her menu to one side so she could see JD and leaned in across the table. She spoke softly. "I never drink coffee, but at the time, sharing that small fact with you didn't seem to be my best option."

JD was enjoying the way this girl approached life so he decided to try and see what else he could get out of her. "Best option, what did you mean by your best option? Your best option for what exactly?"

Annie was still leaning across the table as she answered, "Would it shock you if I said that you are the best looking man I've ever seen in my life? The very moment I saw you I hoped you'd speak to me. When you introduced yourself I was relieved and excited. I didn't want to mess it up by saying no thank you to your offer. I was prepared to learn to drink coffee and even say I liked it no matter what it tasted like, if that's what it would've taken to have a chance to spend more time with you." She spoke as frankly as she had ever spoken to anyone, and it surprised her that she had done so. "We don't have unlimited time, so I thought that I'd save us a lot of back and forth and honestly tell you what I was thinking when I said, 'my best option.' She relaxed and eased herself back to her side of the booth.

JD sat motionless for just a second or two. He was having some trouble taking in and processing what he had just heard. A compliment yes, but this girl was unlike any he had ever experienced. She was honest and confident, that was for sure. He felt he could tell her anything without putting a damper on the moment. JD had dated his share of high school girls, as well as Susan, but this level of openness was all new to him. He decided it was safe to match her frankness.

"You know Annie, you're absolutely right. I agree we don't have unlimited time. So I will lay it out for you from my side as best I can. I caught a glimpse of you nearly an hour before I introduced myself. You were passing in the crowd and just that quickly you disappeared. I spent some time searching for you, but I had nearly given up when you reappeared at the magazine stand. I had to meet you. I didn't know why, but I just had to. Is that honest enough for you?"

"I would say so. What do you think is going on here Joseph? I mean what is this? In the middle of a world war in a station jammed with people, two complete strangers find each other in a mass of humanity and are instantly attracted to each other. Is this fate or are we just messing around because we are both alone in a strange city? Somehow it doesn't make complete sense."

Annie had a look of confusion on her face when she finished talking. JD had no idea her heart was beating at an accelerated rate and she could feel her own chest moving in and out with every beat of her heart.

The waiter soon returned with the drinks and took their orders. Annie sipped her Cherry Coke through two small paper straws from a distinctively shaped Coca-Cola glass. JD added some cream, lifted his cup from the saucer and began to slowly drink the hot coffee.

"Let's see if we are just fooling around or is it fate," JD offered.

"How do you suggest we do that?" Annie asked.

"I suggest that we do what we intended to do from the start. We can sit here, relax, talk and learn more about each other. What do you say?" he asked cheerfully.

Annie looked at him across the table and began. "Well let's start with you. After all, you got me up here with a promise to tell me more about what you are doing. I guess that would include what you have been doing in the war. Would you agree?"

"My story is a long one and you already know a portion of it but I know nothing about you," JD responded. "Won't you tell me about yourself, please? I'm dying to know more than that you are lovely, sweet, witty, very helpful and extremely smart; and oh, you smell good too."

She laughed and said, "What else is there to tell?"

They were both laughing now. Annie felt at ease with this stranger, this attractive First Lieutenant who was definitely turning out to be both an officer and a gentlemen. After taking a moment to regain her composure she began.

"There's not much to tell, but here goes. I was born and raised in Detroit. I'm twenty-three, live with my parents and have a job working in a small factory just outside the city. My job is inspecting gun turret parts that are shipped to the tank plant just a few miles up the road from our plant. I work six days a week, as many hours as I can stand. I use my Sundays to go to church where I sing in the choir. Monday morning it starts over again."

JD asked. "What about your family?"

"Mom and Dad are wonderful. I'm very close to them both, but Mom and I are the closest. I enjoy helping her around the house mainly to just be with her. She's a lot of fun, making a game or contest out of everything that we do. I have a little brother. Actually, he's not a baby anymore. Matter of fact, I came to Chicago to visit him. He's stationed at The Great Lakes Naval Training Center north of Chicago. He's a mechanic working on the Navy training ships deployed out on the lake."

"You didn't mention dating. Do you have someone special that I should know about?" JD asked.

"Sure, I enjoy dating but, with my schedule there hasn't been much time for that lately. To be totally open with you, there has never been anyone special. I'm not sure why, I don't consider myself that picky. It's just that the right guy hasn't come along yet, I guess. Come to think of it, I've had sort of a dry spell lately when it comes to dates."

JD thought, *We can change that.* But he didn't think he should say anything right then. "What's your brother's name?" asked JD. "I may have a chance to look him up."

"Brad, actually its Bradley Collins. He's very nice," she answered. "I think you would like him."

JD kept listening as she gradually opened up more and more throughout dinner. He sensed she didn't like talking about herself but had grown more comfortable as the evening progressed. To JD, her life seemed very sweet and it was clear that she was a nice girl from a solid family. Church and God had come through as an important part of her daily life and that of her parents.

He liked that because he was raised to put God first. God was taking a back seat in his life. God had become sort of a safety valve to JD. He called on God only when the pressure became too much to handle alone. In his heart, he was keenly aware that this was not the best approach. It did seem that God was hanging around close by, sort of watching over him, stepping in when called upon. Maybe meeting Annie in such a unique way was God getting more involved. He had no idea but, his mother had told him many times that God would guide his steps. Her exact words were, "Rejoice for the steps of a righteous man are ordered of God." He knew she was quoting the Holy Bible but he wasn't sure which book or passage it came from. He made a mental note to look it up later. After learning about her beliefs and background JD decided that meeting Annie might have divine providence written all over it and a little bible study might be in order.

"What do you say we take a cab ride down to the waterfront? There is something down there that I would like to show you."

"I thought you have never been to Chicago?" Annie said inquiringly.

"That's true I haven't, but what I want to show you goes along with my story, which by the way, I'll share with you when we get there."

The Final Mission

CHAPTER NINETEEN
THE FIRST LOOK

At two fifteen in the morning, hand in hand, Annie and JD stepped out the door of Union Station on the Jackson Street side. Several taxis were parked at the curb in the designated passenger pickup lane which was only a few yards away and directly in front of the young couple as they exited the building. The evening was clear, with temperatures in the high sixties and falling. Cabbies stood around, some talking, some smoking, others reading the evening paper. They were all anxious to grab a fare on a very slow early morning. Annie changed her mind, now thinking that it was a perfect evening for walking and talking.

As they approached the long row of taxis the cabbies took notice. The driver of the first cab in line flipped his cigarette to the sidewalk. He started for the rear door of his cab and with a fluid motion pivoted on the ball of his left foot snuffing out the butt while reaching for the door handle.

Annie squeezed JD's hand to gain his attention. When she had it she said. "I'd like to walk awhile. Do you mind?"

He smiled, "that would be just fine. As they walked past the open rear door of the first cab in line he added, "But, which way to the lake?"

She pointed to the right. "We just cross that bridge and walk straight down Jackson Street. It's about ten blocks or so to the lake." The cab driver closed the door and returned to his buddies to resume his conversation.

As they casually strolled east on Jackson Street, JD described his family and their small town life. She seemed very interested, asking questions about the mules, horses, cows, pigs, chickens, even the dog and barn cats. JD thought that she might be acting like her mother, making it fun, and putting him at ease. They were enjoying each other's company very much.

By the time they reached the sidewalk that stretched along the shore of Lake Michigan he had advanced his story, taking her up to the week before his forty-fourth mission. JD had been careful to focus on the guys, the officers, the planes and life out in the Pacific, while steering clear of the horrors of actual combat. JD had no intention of exposing this lovely young girl to the details that would only fuel her nightmares. She seemed much too sweet and innocent to deal with such things.

Standing on the sidewalk JD looked north then looked south, turning to Annie he asked. "Which way do we go to get to Navy Pier?"

"North," Annie answered. "It's about a mile. Why what's at Navy Pier?"

"Something I've never seen before. We'll see it for the first time together then I'll finish my story."

They began walking north along the shore in silence, still holding each other's hand.

She liked holding his hand. It seemed that somehow they were communicating by touch. She could sense his emotions and she was transmitting her deepest feeling back to him. Annie felt sure he was feeling something similar. Her attraction was intensifying with each breath, each step, and each gentle squeeze of his hand on hers. She wanted desperately to kiss him but wouldn't dare be so forward. *I know that taking his arm and holding on to it in the station was a bold move, but so far it has worked out. Kissing him first is just too much. My modesty won't allow it. What might he think of me if I were to do such a thing?*

JD was experiencing similar feelings. *I've had about all I can stand. If I don't take her in my arms and kiss her right now I'll explode.* Nearly out of control, new and unfamiliar feelings were overpowering his normally logical thought process. *Waiting is no longer possible. The time for taking chances is now, this very moment.* Stopping on the sidewalk, he turned to Annie and without a word put both arms around her waist, slowly pulling her close. For a moment they stood there without a word being spoken. She was looking up into his eyes and he was gazing down into hers. Her eyes were saying yes. Without a word, he kissed her and she responded with a tenderness he could not have imagined possible. Under a clear starlit sky they kissed for a very long time.

Annie felt like she couldn't get close enough to JD. *I love the way he's holding me so tight; but oh how I wish he could squeeze me tighter and pull me in even closer.* She was his at that moment. *Nothing has ever been like this for me and nothing will ever be the same again.*

JD was in another world or better said he was lost in this world. He was so captivated by Annie's embrace and kiss that for a moment in time he was completely oblivious to everything around him. JD's mind was coming around. *She's so soft and warm, and I can feel her heart beating from her chest to mine. I had no idea what a kiss could be.*

Eventually they regained control and were able to continue their walk to Navy Pier. Annie now with her head on his shoulder and JD with his arm around her waist, slowly they neared the guard rail which separated passersby from the Pier. They didn't speak; there was no need.

As they approached the Pier, the two aircraft carriers were lit up brightly by flood lights as work crews made repairs, preparing the big ships for tomorrow's assignment. Further down the sidewalk another couple was leaning on the rail also passing the time by looking out at the two ships while talking softly to each other. They too had come to the Pier in the early morning hours specifically to give the young lady her first look at the carriers.

"What did you want to show me?" asked Annie when they had come to a stop in front of the two large ships.

"Those carriers right there. They're why I'm here. My assignment is to fly air support for those two aircraft carriers."

"Really?" said Annie. "Why on earth would they need air support on Lake Michigan?"

"Now that seems to be the question of the day. I have no idea, but that's my assignment."

Just a few feet down the railing, Elsa looked over at the young Army Flyer and his well-dressed companion thinking, "They make a lovely couple." She returned her attention back to Max.

"They are big. Are you sure that just one torpedo each will be enough?" she said at a whisper.

Max responded in a low whisper, "Well that's what the German has planned and I agree. One hit will do the job. These carriers don't have armor plating or torpedo blisters. Actually, they have no protection at all. The real challenge my dear, is getting close enough to insure that the torpedoes hit amidships where they are sure to do the most damage."

Elsa thought about his explanation and about the assignment. She wasn't at all comfortable with what she knew so far and it troubled her. They stood there for just a moment longer before turning away.

"I'm pleased that you were able to join me. I've missed you," Max said as they crossed Shoreline Drive heading back to the parking lot and Elsa's car. "Did you have any problems leaving your job?"

"No not at all. I told everyone that I was moving back to Iowa where I have a job waiting for me. You know the usual, more money, and closer to the family. They even threw me a small going away party on my last day. It was nice."

"That's good... very good," Max said as they neared the car. "We don't need any complications. Time is growing short. We will be called upon soon. Until this is over we must make sure not to draw any undue attention to ourselves."

Elsa pulled out the hand choke about halfway then turned the key before mashing the starter button. The car's engine came to life. "You're right of course. We need to become almost invisible." After a pause she continued as the engine warmed up allowing her to reset the choke, "How are you set up?"

"I have a room. Actually, it's a flat above a hardware store right on the main street in Port Washington. A man named Mr. Dolans is the landlord and proprietor of the hardware store. He's a nice enough elderly widower who has two sons. Both are off fighting the war. When I told him that I needed a job he offered me one in his store. With both sons gone he's shorthanded and I was just what he needed. He takes the rent straight off the top of my wages. It's a great setup and no taxes on the income. It's a good deal for him and for me."

"What about me?" Elsa asked.

"We're all set there. I said that my wife might be joining me if I found a job," Max explained. "I told him that's why I needed a full flat and not just a room. I think he wanted to help and that's why he offered the job so quickly. He didn't even check my references."

She stared at him for a long time. He thought he knew what she was thinking.

"Listen Elsa, I understand and I respect you. There is a bedroom for you and a large divan where I can sleep. I give you my word. I am not taking anything for granted."

"I know. It's just that I really don't do that. You know, I mean, it was wonderful and I think the world of you but…"

Max interrupted her, "Please say no more. If it happens again it happens. If not, so be it, but I will respect your privacy no matter what. You have my word."

"Thank you Max you are very understanding and still just as sweet." She smiled with relief as she turned on the head lights before pulling out headed north toward Port Washington and the flat above the hardware store.

Annie and JD gave merely a passing glance to the other couple as they walked away. Annie was still anxious to hear the rest of JD's story. The temperature had fallen nearly ten degrees when they neared the lake. Only now was Annie beginning to feel the chill in the air. She squeezed in closer to JD as he held her around the waist. A shiver passed through her body and JD instantly responded by taking off his coat.

"Here let me put this around you." She stood still as he placed her arms in the sleeves and buttoned up the coat. It was huge and hung halfway down her thighs and her hands were lost in the sleeves. JD took his time rolling up both sleeves until her hands reappeared. "There, I want you to be cozy warm but I still want to be able to hold your hand," JD said with a clear tone of satisfaction.

They had begun to walk back toward Union Station when Annie said, "I was promised the rest of your story if I let you show me those ships, how about it?"

"I am enjoying myself so much that I completely forgot."

"Well I didn't. That's not to say I haven't been enjoying myself. It's just that I truly am very interested to hear all about you. I mean it."

JD gave her the highlights of his last mission, again steering clear of the events that could upset her. She seemed most interested in the part about the island and Thomas Johnston.

"Joseph that is most interesting. What an adventure you must have had. Weren't you thrilled at so many exciting discoveries and mysteries?"

"At the time I was actually nervous and scared," JD answered. "Telling it just now made it seem even to me like a story in a book and not something real."

"I don't know what's wrong with me, of course you were scared," she said. "Hearing the story afterwards is one thing. Living it in the moment is something different altogether. I'm so sorry."

JD wondered if she really understood. If so, this girl was something special. He stopped and kissed her again with the same result as the first time. *She is very special in more ways than one.*

Annie brought him back to his story. "If I've got it right, you still had one more mission to fly in order to finish up, is that right?"

"Yes that's correct."

"Well what happened on that one? Why didn't you tell me about it?' she inquired.

"I can't tell you because I haven't flown it yet. Let me explain. I was transferred here to do my last mission over the lake. They told me that I had done enough out there. They had a request for a pilot with my experience for a mission back in the States. So they sent me here to fly number forty-five," JD continued. "Once I complete this one my combat requirement will be fulfilled. Then I have a thirty-day leave coming. I was planning on going home to see Momma and the family. If you don't mind, I would like to use some of my time to come to Detroit and see you, if you think that would be alright."

"Please don't take time away from your mother. She would be so disappointed if you short changed her after all that she's been through." Annie said this because it was the right thing to say. What she wanted to say was that she would be counting the seconds until their next meeting and nothing would please her more than for him to come to her.

"Annie, I believe that I can work it out to allow me to do both. If so, can I come see you?"

She stopped walking and slowly turned to look at him, when she had his total attention she said, "Please come."

With a sigh of relief JD smiled and said, "Annie, you can count on it."

"I will do just that but please go home and see your mother first. Will you promise me that, please?"

"May I be perfectly open with you?" he asked.

"Joseph, I thought we were being honest, I know I have been."

JD said, "Of course we have, what I am trying to say is that at this moment I would promise you anything. That's not how I am normally. Something is drastically different and it has been since the moment that I saw you in the station. Annie, I have never told a girl this before but I must tell you now. It just seems right. If this is not love then I cannot imagine what love could be. Annie, I'm sure that I am in love with you. I can't help it but it's true. Please don't think me childish or silly but, I love you."

Annie looked at him for a very long time. He was serious, she knew that for sure. She finally spoke, "we're being honest here so I owe it to you to tell you the truth." She paused to select the right words then continued. "I had no idea what love was until tonight and maybe I still don't. What I do know is that if what I feel for you is not love then I'll take it anyway. Joseph, I love your eyes, you thoughtfulness, I love everything about you. Joseph, I love you too. I can't help it either."

JD was pleased and exhausted from worrying about how she would react to his pronouncement. "Well," he said. "That's a relief. I'm new at this. So what do you think we should do now?"

She responded, "We have planted a seed. What we do now and forever is nurture that seed every moment of our lives to insure that it grows strong and healthy."

JD just looked at her. She was someone very special.

They embraced and held each other for a long time before making their way slowly back toward Union Station and the departing trains that would separate this couple so young and so much in love.

Annie and JD retrieved their bags from the lockers where they had been stored and spent their remaining time together sitting in the small waiting area at the south end of Union Station. Trains traveling south, east and west depart from the south end of the building. JD's train was heading north. He would need to run the length of the building to catch his train. No matter, time spent with Annie was too precious to let running through a crowded terminal be a hindrance.

The train to Detroit was announced over the loud speaker. The time to separate was near. It had come too quickly for them both. After exchanging addresses and promising to write, JD and Annie reluctantly said goodbye. He had her phone number written down in three separate places as insurance against misplacing it. Annie didn't have his phone number because he didn't have one. But, he promised to call her with the number just as soon as he could find out what it was. Their goodbye embrace was long and tender. Naturally, they wished the moment could be extended but surprisingly it was not a sad occasion. In truth, the two young people were both filled with great expectations.

Annie was able to find room on the morning train to Detroit. Soon, she was safely aboard. Although weighed down by his bags JD sprinted to the opposite end of the station to board the train to Milwaukee. Both were headed back to their individual lives each with new and unexpected hopes for a brighter tomorrow.

CHAPTER TWENTY
BACK TO WORK

JD's destination was Mitchell Field, located on the shores of Lake Michigan just a few miles south of downtown Milwaukee. The field was named after Army General Billy Mitchell who was originally from the area. Mitchell was an early proponent and vocal advocate for the expansion of military airpower. However, between the two World Wars, military budgets were small. The vast majority of resources were allocated to the Navy to support the fleet. The Army was forced to operate on a very limited budget. The General took on the Navy by professing that a bomb dropped from an Army airplane could sink a Navy battleship.

If this bold statement could be demonstrated then the future value of the battleship in warfare would be in question. The Navy brass was determined to protect the reputation of their battleships which were the pride of the fleet. The appropriations that traditionally flowed to the Navy had much to do with the prevailing wisdom of the time. Most world powers held to the belief that the country that possessed the most battleships would naturally control international affairs.

General Mitchell proved his assertion by sinking a captured German World War I battleship with bombs dropped from his planes. However, the Navy was able to disgrace him which led to his eventual courts-martial. He was discharged from the United States Army. Later, when it became obvious to everyone that he had been right all along, his reputation was restored. The airfield at Milwaukee and the B-25 Mitchell medium bomber were named in his honor.

The main door of the hanger was wide open and the newly assigned First Lieutenant walked straight inside. This is where the Officer of the Day had said his plane could be found. There was only one plane in the oversized hanger and it wasn't what he had expected to find.

"What is this thing?" asked JD. "Is this what I'm to fly, I mean they have got to be kidding!"

A sergeant in mechanic's clothes stood next to his tool box and the obsolete aircraft inside the main hanger at Mitchell Field. He was a little disappointed with the reception being given to his pride and joy by this new hot-shot pilot.

"Sir, what's wrong with it? Don't you realize that what you have here is a very fine example of the Douglas B-18 Bolo Bomber?" he said with pride.

JD was quick on the uptake. He instantly recognized that for the sergeant standing before him this was a sensitive subject, even personal. An adjustment in his approach would be needed to avoid offending this guy.

"Allow me to start over, if I might. I do know what it is sergeant and it may interest you to know that I trained in one of these, way back in 1942. With all due respect to this very fine example and to you, it was obsolete back then. Now I'm not saying that this plane is not in good condition; after all it appears to be so clean a guy could eat off the landing gear."

"That's right and she's in perfect mechanical condition inside and out," the sergeant was on a roll. "I've put my life into this plane. She's ready to do her part, I promise you that. She deserves a chance and if she ever gets it, lookout."

"From her appearance alone I'd have to agree with you. However, I was selected for this duty assignment based on my combat experience in B-25 Mitchell bombers not in B-18s. This plane here was a surprise that's all. I was expecting a B-25."

So he isn't a ninety-day wonder, fresh out of some academy, after all, thought the sergeant. "You've seen combat sir?" asked the sergeant with interest.

JD recognized a significant change in the sergeant's tone. "Yes, I've seen enough to make me the most careful flyer you'll ever meet," JD responded with a pat on the shoulder for the sergeant.

"What are you doing here? What I mean to say is, we had twenty of these with crews and support personnel, the whole works; but they're all gone now, except this one of course. Then out of the blue, you show up."

"What happened to them?" asked JD.

"Oh they're gone. The planes were sold to Brazil for their air force I guess, and the personnel were all reassigned to combat stations in Europe."

"When did they all leave?"

The sergeant thought about it for a moment before answering. "Four weeks, yes that's right; four weeks ago this past Saturday matter of fact."

"Please forgive me for asking, but why did you remain behind and why keep the one plane here without a pilot?" asked JD.

"Hell sir I don't have the foggiest idea why I'm still here. I joined up to fight and here I sit. As for the reason why this one plane remains, I have no idea, absolutely none. But, I'll tell you what; I decided to make lemonade out of lemons. During the past few weeks I've put my life into this plane and she's the best she can be. I promise you that. I mean, what was I supposed to do just sit around moping and complaining? Who'd listen anyway?"

"I see your point," JD said. "I take it from your response to hearing that I've seen combat that you have not. Am I correct?

"Yes sir you are correct." The words came out as though the sergeant had just bitten into a sour apple. He didn't elaborate but instead, sort of clammed up after having to admit that he hadn't seen combat.

JD tried to find a way to put some ointment on what was apparently a sore spot for the sergeant. "Well sergeant I wouldn't let it bother you too much. We all have our jobs to do and everyone is equally important to the war effort."

"With all due respect, I just don't see it that way at all. I'm a qualified pilot same as you and all I have been able to do is taxi this plane from the hanger around the field and back again. It just isn't right in my book."

Knowing the serious need for combat pilots, JD was sure that there was more to the sergeant's story than he was telling. He decided to find out. "What's your name sergeant?" asked JD.

"Don Rogers, sir."

"Well Don, tell me what happened? If you are a qualified pilot then tell me straight. Why haven't you been assigned?" JD asked the question as an officer speaking to a subordinate and Don caught the change in demeanor immediately.

"Sir, I completed flight training and received my wings. Afterwards, I qualified in bombers and the very next day I screwed up."

"What did you do?"

"Well, the following morning our squadron went up early to practice formation flying. When we returned to the field I decided to buzz the tower. You know, the new wings and everything. Well I got pretty close, made a lot of noise. I had no idea that a General was on the base, let alone that he just happened to be in the tower at the time. That was my undoing. He was very upset by what he called 'a complete lack of discipline'."

"He gave orders to ground that 'so-and-so, hot-shot pilot', meaning me. So I got grounded right then and there. We all thought it would be a temporary thing, you know, a lot of bluster. But it turned out to be much more because no one ever rescinded that order. Eventually, they took away my wings and busted me to sergeant. I was a certified airplane mechanic before I qualified for flight training. I guess that's why they transferred me here. Well, I've been right here for nearly a year working on the B-18s. That is until they went away. When transfer orders came down for everyone else my name wasn't on the list. Within a few weeks the unit packed up and pulled out, including the commanding officer. It's like they all just forgot about me. Yeah... that's me... the forgotten man."

"Did you get in contact with anyone to ask questions about being left behind?"

"Sure," said the sergeant. "But that's the funny thing about it. I was ordered to just sit tight. I was told that they'd look into it and get back to me. No one called, no letter, nothing. I tried two more times; same result. I gave up. I guess if they need me they know where to find me."

"What about pay, I mean they must know you're still in the Army. Do you get paid?"

"Actually that too, is a bit strange. I get paid but at the same rate as before, Lieutenant grade." Don had a sheepish grin on his face now.

JD was puzzled. "You mean that you haven't told anyone about the mix up?"

"Sir, you can't be serious?" Don immediately replied.

JD decided to let that issue go for now and changed the subject. "What type of plane were you flying?" he asked.

Don lifted his head. His chin had been nearly touching his chest as he told his story. Obviously he wasn't very proud of his situation. The sergeant was now standing almost at full attention. "I qualified in a B-25 Mitchell medium bomber sir," he proudly answered.

Their conversation gradually shifted back to the B-18 Bolo. Don took JD through the plane in great detail including time in the cockpit sitting side-by-side with JD in the left seat and Don in the right. This is where they were when a staff car pulled into the hanger stopping a few feet from the nose of the plane. A Major exited the back seat through the door held open by his driver. She stayed by the car as the Major approached the plane.

He yelled up to the two men in the cockpit, "gentlemen may I have a word with you?"

They both yelled back, "Yes sir."

Then JD called out from the side window, "we'll be right down sir."

In short order they were out and standing at attention before the Major and saluting. "Please, as you were gentlemen," the Major said as he returned their salutes.

Both men relaxed and waited for him to speak. Neither had ever seen the officer who stood before them. "Lieutenant Jones?" JD stepped forward. "I am Major Brock."

They shook hands as the Major then turned to Don, "I was told that I could find Lieutenant Rogers here. Do you know where he might be sergeant?"

"Sir, are you looking for Lieutenant Don Rogers?"

"That's correct, any idea where he is at this moment?"

Hesitantly, he answered the Major; "sir, I'm Don Rogers."

Major Brock looked at Don studying him up and down. "You're out of uniform Lieutenant," the Major barked back.

"Well sir..."

JD took advantage of Don's hesitation. "Sir, I think what he is trying to say is, that there has been what might be sort of a snafu."

"Excuse me Lieutenant, exactly what are you saying?" the Major asked.

"Well sir you know snafu, 'situation normal all fouled up'."

"I was under the impression that you arrived today. How is it that you are involved with this man's uniform?" Brock asked while staring coldly. JD felt himself slipping into the abyss. This was not a good start from his side but he also felt that the Major was coming on pretty hard.

The Major turned his attention back to Rogers. "Rogers, I know all about your situation." Brock said with a very serious tone in his voice. "You were never busted and you still have your wings. I have heard that some people feel that a pencil pushing Pentagon, excuse of a General had no right to pull what he did on you. Personally, I have no opinion on the subject. However, it could be said that you wouldn't be much of a pilot if you hadn't buzzed that tower. Heck we've all done it. I'm sure you noticed that your pay remained unchanged. Nothing related to the incident was ever entered in your record. Whatever was done was necessary in order to protect a good pilot, who just happens to have very poor timing. It took a little longer to blow over than expected but the threat is now gone. So the next time I see you Lieutenant, be in the proper uniform. Is that clear?"

Rogers was still confused and wanted to ask the Major to elaborate but let that thought dissipate. All he could manage was to say, "Yes sir."

Major Brock checked over his shoulder and around the area before speaking again. "Let's not talk here. Come, get in the car. We'll take a little drive," Major Brock said as he turned back toward his car.

JD went around to the passenger's front door, let himself inside and turned his shoulders and head so that he could join in the conversation when it started. The driver held the rear door behind her seat for Major Brock while Don went around to the other side and found his place on the back seat next to Brock. The staff car left the airfield and headed south along the lakeshore toward Racine. Major Brock sat in silence for a few minutes then told the driver not to listen to the conversation that was about to take place.

"Jones, I understand you've been given some general knowledge of your assignment. Am I correct?"

"Yes sir."

"What have you been told, exactly?" Major Brock asked. JD didn't know much. But he did pause to gather his thoughts before giving his answer.

"Well sir, I was told to report here to complete one more combat mission which will fulfill my sixty mission requirement. I was also told that I would be flying air cover for the two aircraft carriers which sail Lake Michigan." Then he added a little more that he had just remembered, "Oh yes, I was also told that B-25 combat experience was a requirement for this mission. That's all I know about the mission, sir."

"I wouldn't hang my hat on your combat experience if I were you Lieutenant," Brock said in a dismissive tone.

JD said nothing but thought, *What have I done to this guy?*

Brock turned in his seat to face Don Rogers then asked him what knowledge he had regarding the mission. Don's answer was straight forward. He told Brock that it was all news to him. He had no knowledge at all. The car followed the road with the lake on their left and the morning sun on their right.

Arnold D. Jones

CHAPTER TWENTY-ONE
PREPARATIONS

The olive green staff car continued south along the western shore of Lake Michigan. The sun was bright against a nearly cloudless blue sky. Even though the calendar said it was summer the air felt like fall. The trees still had all of their leaves but high in the tops of the tallest trees the leaves were already turning from green to yellow or red. Under a bright sun the lake was the most beautiful deep, dark blue, imaginable.

JD had never seen the Great Lakes in daylight and was enjoying the view very much. The lake was to his left which meant that he had to look through the driver's side window. No one spoke for a while as the car gently swerved to the right then back to the left as the road followed the shoreline south.

A turnout appeared just ahead prompting the Major to call out to his driver. "Corporal, pull in just ahead there to the left and stop." Her head nodded once as she began to slow down. Traffic was extremely light with only an occasional car heading north and no cars were following them south. JD thought that the sparse traffic was due either to gasoline rationing or from the look of it; this road might just lead to nowhere.

The staff car pulled into a clearing cut into the thick tree line. The tires made a crunching sound as the car rolled on to a small gravel-covered parking lot with only a handful of spaces. JD spotted a fifty-five gallon barrel painted green with the word "trash" stenciled in black letters on its side. His mind went back to the island and the Japanese soldiers he had killed. He shook his head and tried to get the memory out of his mind. The barrel was placed between two unpainted wooden picnic tables set back under the trees. These were the only manmade objects visible in the small park setting. The picnic tables were positioned so as to offer their users shade and a clear view of the sandy beach and blue water just beyond. The driver chose a parking place in the center of the empty lot and turned off the motor. This time, Major Brock didn't wait for his driver to open the door; instead he got out and motioned for his two passengers to follow him. The driver was half way out of her door when Brock gave her instructions to stay with the car and to sound the horn if anyone approached the car while they were away. She got back in the car and closed the door without a word.

"Gentlemen, what say we take a walk?" Brock said in a way that sounded both like a question and an order.   Without a word the two men followed as he led them down to the beach. The wind was out of the west and the surface of the water was nearly flat. The beach was protected from the wind by the trees but the temperature near the water was much cooler than at the airfield. "Do you feel that?" Brock asked as they walked slowly along the water's edge. "The water never warms up. It's too deep for the sun to have much of an effect no matter how hot the air temperature might get."

JD looked out on the lake. He couldn't see the other side. The native American Indian word "Michigan" means big water. It was easy to image what the inland tribes must have thought when they first broke through the thick forests of Wisconsin to gaze upon this sight for the first time. Their frame of reference would have been the thousands of small lakes and rivers that cover Minnesota and Wisconsin. As the trees parted, suddenly before them stood this vast body of water unlike anything they had ever seen. Someone must have blurted out; "big water." The name has stuck to this day.

To JD it looked like the ocean. The only difference was the smell. This was fresh water; absent was the smell of salty sea air associated with oceans. In its place was nothing. It was more like the absence of smell rather than a difference in smell. He was sure that anyone who had been to the ocean could never mistake the two.

When the three men had covered about a hundred yards, Major Brock stopped and turned around to face his two Lieutenants. "This is far enough. What I tell you from this point on is top secret. Nothing said will be shared by you in any form to anyone ever. Is that clear?"

Rogers responded first. "Sir, I understand completely and you have my word on it."

"What about you Jones?" Brock asked.

"You have my word sir, what is said here will remain secret."

Major Brock appeared to be satisfied. "Okay, pull up a rock and sit down." Brock had led them to a spot on the beach where several large boulders protruded from the sand. They each sat down on one of three large boulders forming a small tight circle. Their knees were nearly touching one another's.

Major Brock started, "The Army and Navy have been working on a joint project. The objective is to develop radio controlled pilotless aircraft. The purpose of this project is to use the aircraft as controlled flight bombs. The idea is to pack the planes with high explosives for concentrated attacks on very specific and well-defended enemy targets. High-level carpet bombing has proven to be ineffective on the type of targets we have in mind for these new radio controlled planes. The targets are so well defended that any attempt to approach from lower levels is pure suicide."

Brock paused seemingly to focus on what he had to say next. Both men waited patiently for him to continue. They each had questions but knew that this was not the time to speak.

Major Brock gathered his thoughts and continued. "Have you heard of something called television?"

Rogers answered first once again. "Isn't that something about sending a moving picture through the air and displaying it using a tube at the receiving end?"

Brock smiled, pleased with the answer. "An over simplification maybe but essentially correct Lieutenant," he said.

Brock turned to JD. "What about you Jones, ever hear of it?"

"Sir, I know less than he does." JD shrugged his shoulders as he answered, sure that this was strike two. Things still weren't going well.

JD was not surprised by Brock's disappointed expression in his direction and wag of the head.

"Then let me explain. The idea is to fly the airplane using radio control from a second plane which will stand off, well away from the flying bomb and the intended target. A television camera mounted in the nose of the flying bomb will transmit a clear picture of the view in front of that plane; just like the actual view from the cockpit that a real pilot would have if he were at the controls. This picture will be used by the control plane to guide the flying bomb directly to the target. But in this case, there is no pilot in the cockpit. The intended result is to deliver the maximum payload exactly on the bull's eye with no risk for loss of life. Do you men follow what I have just said? Do you have any questions? If so, I will do my best to answer them before we discuss your part in the project."

JD was first to respond this time. "Sir what type of targets do you have in mind?"

Brock seemed taken aback by JD's question. "I meant questions related to the technology Lieutenant, not the targets."

Brock's continuously degrading tone did not suit JD at all. He decided that it was time to speak his mind and live with the consequences. "May I speak freely sir?" asked JD.

Major Brock didn't like where this was going but reluctantly answered. "Yes Lieutenant, speak freely."

"You asked for questions, and I clearly heard you say that you would do your best to answer them, sir. Further, you did not limit the subject of the questions that we might ask. So I asked a question for which I would like an answer. If you didn't know the answer you just needed to say so. Anything beyond that could be construed as nothing more than a case of over inflated ego, sir. At this point in my Army career I don't need to be belittled. If you have a problem with me I suggest that you tell me straight out, sir."

JD was hot and he was ready to continue if given the slightest provocation. The three men were still sitting in very close proximity to each other. That, plus JD's unflinching glare into Brocks face which was less than a foot in front of his own, made the tension unbearable for both Brock and Rogers.

Brock composed himself before challenging JD. "Jones, do you want to return to the Pacific to fly your final mission?"

Without hesitation JD came right back at him. "That's not a problem for me at all, sir. I didn't ask to be sent back to the States. I was told that I would be going back. In the Pacific, our commanding officers answer our questions honestly out of respect for the risks we were taking. I will take that over this any day of the week. At least out there I knew what I was up against. It's your call, not mine, so send me back if that is your preference, sir"

Brock studied JD. What he saw was a big guy who was feeling belittled and who was making it clear in every way he could that he didn't intend to take any more. Brock had read JD's personnel folder which was filled with one positive report after another. It contained no negative comments. Up to and until this moment, JD had been a model soldier. This caused Brock to rethink his approach and quickly conclude that the guy might be justified in his reaction. He had come highly recommended and was the perfect fit for this assignment. It would be hard to explain to his superiors the need to replace a pilot with those credentials at such a late date. Brock concluded that compromise was best.

"Alright son, you might have a point. My approach could have been different and it probably should have been. I recommend that we start over. What do you say Lieutenant, fair enough?"

"Yes sir, fair enough," JD gave his answer while maintaining his focus.

JD had not been seeking a victory. Rather, he had determined to put an end to Brock's abuse and let the chips fall where they may. He had been raised to be respectful to those in authority over him and to also respect his elders. On the other hand, he had also been raised with the understanding that he should never allow anyone to take advantage of him. Now it seemed as though he might have gotten a victory. Time would tell if that was good or bad. Officers tended to have long memories and eventually the chips would fall somewhere that was for sure. JD didn't respect or trust this officer.

"Alright, let me have a try at answering your question; several targets have been identified. When the invasion of Japan comes there are several highly defended military targets that must be destroyed ahead of our troops coming ashore. Hundreds of drone aircraft will be launched from carriers to take out these targets which up 'til now, have been impregnable. However, our first priority is the underground manufacturing facilities that house the German V-2 rocket assembly. The invasion of Europe is in its infancy and we are making progress. However, the Germans continue to launch their V-2 rockets any time the weather is favorable. Their target all along has been London. We must eliminate this threat before they figure out that a more beneficial use would be to target our troops, equipment and supplies. We have no defense against this weapon; therefore, our only option is to attack the source."

The wind had shifted during their discussion. It was now out of the north causing a chop to appear on the lake and the temperature was falling steadily. Impervious to the chill in the air Brock continued.

"Both carriers will soon temporarily interrupt their pilot training activities to take part in a planned test of the radio controlled and television guided flying bomb project. The testing is top secret so it will be conducted well away from prying eyes. The location selected is at the far northern end of the lake, off the coast of Michigan, out from Grand Traverse Bay. The area is sparsely populated and the roads around there are well inland with dense woods along the shore. This makes it unlikely that passersby will get a look at the activity taking place out on the lake from the shore. The technology is still under development. By conducting these tests over water and well away from shore any mishaps will occur in the lake, thus avoiding the need for an elaborate cover story."

JD asked, "Sir, what part do we play in the project?"

"I was getting around to that," answered Brock.

Rogers chimed in with a question of his own. "Sir, what's the timing. What I mean, when is the testing to take place?"

"The timing has not been released yet but we have every reason to believe that it will be announced soon. Your job will be to fly above the radio controlled test planes. If control is lost you are to shoot them down preventing a crash over land."

JD asked, "Are we to use the B-18 to accomplish this mission?"

"You are to fly the B-18 over to Willow Run airport which is just west of Detroit. Leave it there and take command of a new B-25 that is currently being specially prepared for this mission." At the mention of Detroit JD's thoughts immediately shifted to Annie.

Rogers was thinking of his B-18 when he asked. "What is to happen to the B-18, sir?"

Brock didn't understand Don's attachment to the plane however in the spirit of what was now good communication he answered the question. "She will remain at the same facility where the new B-25 is presently undergoing modifications. She is scheduled to be converted for submarine detection. When complete, she will be sent off to Greenland for antisubmarine patrol duty. When the tests are completed the plan is for you to pick up a crew and fly her to Greenland. You will remain in Greenland as her pilot."

"When should we leave for Willow Run?" JD asked the question trying to sound deeply committed, which he was. But his motivation was twofold. The prospect of seeing Annie once again also had much to do with his request. Then he offered an explanation.

"I'd like to have as much time as possible with the new plane and special equipment. Don is a mechanic; he should look everything over in detail and I'll need training with the new equipment. We may be of more use there than here."

"You may be right Lieutenant," Brock answered thoughtfully. "I'll see to it at once."

The Final Mission   Arnold D. Jones

CHAPTER TWENTY-TWO
THE ARSENAL OF DEMOCRACY

Detroit was nick-named the Arsenal of Democracy because of the military hardware that flowed to all corners of the globe from its factories during the war. The automotive manufacturing infrastructure in place at the start of the war had been converted to war time production in record time. Tanks, planes, jeeps, trucks, all manner of weapons and equipment poured out of Detroit night and day throughout the war. The output of these factories overwhelmed the best efforts of the enemy to keep pace.

JD and Don Rogers were headed to Willow Run. Their destination was thirty five miles west of downtown Detroit.

Willow Run was the home of Ford Motor Company's huge Willow Run Assembly Plant. Four engine B24 Liberator long-range bombers were coming off the automotive-style production line at the rate of one an hour. By war's end nearly eight thousand would be produced there. Army flight crews just out of training would be assigned planes as they were completed and then fly them directly to their assigned theater of war. The vast runways were always busy with non-stop departures.

The Army Air Corps maintained a top secret facility at the Willow Run site where specialized modifications to all types and models of aircraft took place. This modification center was JD and Don's destination.

They departed Mitchell Field before seven in the morning for the one-hour flight that would take them across Lake Michigan then southeast to Willow Run. JD was in the left hand seat with Rogers, his copilot, in the right seat. Rogers had been right; the B-18 Lobo was in great shape. She was a little sluggish in her response to pilot input. This was one of the reasons she had been replaced by newer models. This particular plane did have the short comings of her design but she performed at the very top of her design capabilities. Both pilots were impressed.

The weather conditions were good with a westerly tail wind of ten knots. The skies were partly cloudy with visibility of ten miles. The flight across the lake and over western Michigan proved to be routine. After takeoff, JD handed the controls over to Don and he flew his pride and joy with perfect execution all the way to Willow Run. As JD observed his copilot, he concluded that Rogers was a capable man to have at the controls. To be sure, he would allow Don to line up and make the landing on his own.   JD called through the interphone, "You take her in."

"You know a lot of time has passed since my last landing," he responded. "I'm a little rusty, but here it goes."

The large assembly building came into view first. The giant structure was at least a mile long with dozens of Liberators parked between it and the runway. The massive adjoining parking lots were filled to capacity with cars in all colors and shapes.

After receiving instructions from the tower Don lined up for a landing out of the east directly into the ten knot head wind. At two miles out Don began calling out orders to JD like a professional, "Air speed one-twenty-five, flaps down, landing gear down."

JD confirmed each step as the plane seemed to glide down under the steady hand of its pilot. JD was impressed by the natural control that Don was demonstrating as he continued to bleed off air speed and then ease the plane onto the long runway. They touched down with the two main wheels first. Don continued to fly the bomber until the tail wheel made contact with the surface. This was the most near-flawless touchdown that JD had ever witnessed. Every step was smooth. Don hadn't landed the plane as much as he had flown it all the way down, using up just a fraction of the runway's length. *Text book from start to finish.*

Tower to B-18, well done skipper, take the first turn off to your left. You are cleared to taxi straight to the tower. You must show your orders and report in there. Again, nice landing, we see all kinds in a day. Thanks for showing us how it's done."

After reporting in and showing their orders, JD wanted to go find a phone. Annie would be at work but he thought her mother would surely be home to receive his call. He couldn't wait to see Annie again. "Hey Don you got change for the phone?" JD asked as he counted out the loose change from his own pocket.

"What do you need?" Don responded now reaching into his pocket.

"I have, let's see…" JD counted the change in his hand. "Four quarters, three dimes and a nickel, you think it's enough?" He didn't mention that he also had ten solid gold coins, one or two in every one of his pockets.

Don handed over the few coins he had on him and said, "Take this just in case, but give back what you don't use. Payday is a long way off."

"No that's okay, please take this. I want to hold on to the change; I may need it later and thanks," JD said as he handed Don a dollar bill.

"See you later; I'm going to try and locate our plane," Don made his comment as he started to walk away toward the nearest building.

JD spotted a row of phone booths out by the fence. Walking in that direction he squeezed the change in his left hand and started digging through his pockets hunting for Annie's phone number with his right. It was somewhere, he was sure he had written it down.

CHAPTER TWENTY-THREE
COMPLICATIONS

The German had hastily called for an emergency meeting. He had been brief and to the point, no details just a time and place to meet. It didn't feel right to Max. He speculated that this could be it. Either the schedule was now set or something was wrong. He couldn't be sure but over the phone the German had sounded different somehow. The self-control he demonstrated when they first met had given way to a less confident tone. Max thought he even detected a flicker of anxiety.

Elsa and Max sat in her Ford outside of a small bar fifteen miles west of Port Washington. They found themselves far out in the country with nothing but a few farms, lots of trees and this little bar. They were in the middle of nowhere. The wind had died down making the night air as still as a graveyard and it was pitch black. They had driven out under an overcast, gray, afternoon sky. Now that same blanket of clouds concealed the moon and stars, cloaking the area in total blackness. Max couldn't see his hand in front of his face. He switched on the dome light and looked at his watch. It was nearly ten. Two hours had passed since their arrival. The German was an hour and a half late. He switched the light off. Very few cars had passed by but when one did Elsa and Max could hear it long before its headlights came into view. Each time a car approached it would continue past, disappearing down the road leaving them in silence once again. They had arrived at the designated meeting place well before eight-thirty. Max had not wanted the German to arrive first and be forced to wait for them. But, there was still no sign of the German. Elsa was beginning to worry. "Do you think something has gone wrong?" she asked.

"No, don't worry," Max answered, still looking out in the direction from which the German should appear. "We'll wait until eleven. If he doesn't arrive by then we simply drive·back to the apartment and wait to be contacted again."

A part of Max hoped the German wouldn't show and that they would never hear from him again. Recently, he was thinking more and more about a life with Elsa and less and less about the war and his mission. A life in the United States or Canada with Elsa was the object of his daydreams and he seemed to be dreaming more of late. She had been true to her word not allowing them to become intimate again. As time passed they were growing closer and dearer to each other. Playing at being a married couple was like practice for the real thing. He enjoyed spending time learning her mannerisms and getting to know her likes and dislikes. Max was fighting the urge to fall in love with Elsa but, it was a losing battle.

They both heard it at the same time, the faint sound of car in the distance. Max turned the light on and checked his watch once more. It was nearly eleven and the approaching car would soon be in sight. He turned off the light. If this car just drove by he would call it off and return to Port Washington. They had time to make the drive back and still get some sleep before the start of another work day.

The car's headlights came into view and the couple watched them grow larger and brighter. The car slowed and turned into the parking lot. The German from the Drake Hotel had arrived and he wasn't alone. Another man was in the passenger's seat. The big black, four-door sedan parked alongside the Ford. The German and his companion exited the car and casually walked over and climbed in the back seat of Elsa's car.

The German was the first to speak. "Sorry for the delay, we had to make sure we weren't being followed. I chose an indirect route to get here and we become lost for a time. I hadn't realized it would take this long. I truly am sorry and I trust you didn't worry."

"We were beginning to become concerned," Elsa answered for them both. "But no matter, you're here now so everything is as it should be."

The German smiled, pleased with the control Elsa was displaying. She gave no hint of the panic she had felt during the long wait.

"Max," said the German. "I think it best if you pull out and drive west. This road is rather deserted the farther you go in that direction. We can talk and drive at the same time, safer that way."

Max eased out onto the two lane asphalt covered road and headed west traveling at the posted speed of thirty-five miles an hour. The road was nearly straight with no sharp curves or hills, just a ribbon in front of the headlights. He turned on the high beams and wondered, "Why all the precautions. What is really going on and who is this stranger with the German?"

The German waited until they were a mile or so away from the bar then looked out the rear window. Seeing nothing he addressed his comments to both Max and Elsa. "A problem has developed so we must alter the plan. Max, do you remember I told you we had identified a fishing boat that would be used to transport the weapons?"

Max answered, "Of course, I remember. I also remember that during our time together you never told me your name."

The German smiled, "Please forgive me, my name is Rinehart, and please allow me to explain why we called for this meeting, It seems that the owner and captain of that boat suffered an unfortunate accident and as a result has become incapacitated. We have confirmed that he is not able to work and therefore his boat will not leave port for the rest of this fishing season. This situation has resulted In our immediate need for a suitable replacement craft. Just this morning information was received confirming that the carriers will be moving north soon."

Elsa spoke up; "How soon?"

The other man reached out and put a hand on Rinehart's arm stopping him from answering Elsa's question. "Please allow me to answer that," he interjected. "But first, my name is John and it is a pleasure to meet you Elsa and you as well Max." He nodded his head while offering a very slight smile in their direction. They both nodded waiting for his answer to Elsa's question while wondering who he was.

"The exact time remains uncertain but we have learned that the equipment to be used in the test departed Cincinnati by truck this morning. It is heading for northern Michigan. Based on what we know this means at the earliest, preparations could be complete in two weeks."

Max thought about what he had just heard. "But I take it you think the start of the testing will be later than say two weeks, is that right?"

"That's correct. Still missing are the four drone test aircraft which are currently being modified to receive the equipment. Also the B17 which will actually be responsible for controlling the four drone aircraft has yet to depart. All five remain in California but work is nearly complete. When they are ready we will need to be in position to move. This is why a replacement fishing boat must be secured without delay and taken to the workshop to be fitted out with the weapons." As the newcomer, John finished talking and he released Rinehart's arm and sat back in the seat.

Elsa, who had attentively listened to John's explanation, asked another question. "Do you have an alternative plan in mind for a replacement?"

This time John remained silent allowing Rinehart to take over. "Actually we have identified three separate boats that fit our purpose. All that is necessary now is to target one of the remaining two. One is out in the lake as we speak and we can't be certain when it will return. For now, it will remain under surveillance. If it does happen to return in time we will know. That leaves us with the remaining target which returned to port this morning. This boat, the *Mary Jo* unloaded her catch today and will head back out on the lake in the early morning, day after tomorrow. In twenty-six hours you Max and I will stow away on board the *Mary Jo*. We will seize the boat about one hour out of port and deliver her to the workshop. The weapons, explosives, equipment and materials needed are already there. Max and I will make the modifications to the boat; load the torpedoes and other weapons on board. This work will take several days to complete. When the boat is ready the three of us have nothing more to do but wait for the signal to move."

Elsa and Max did not respond, instead they were both thinking about what had just been revealed to them. This sudden major change in plans had shaken their trust in the German's competence. Such changes so late in the day could spell disaster. There also remained the unspoken motive behind all the cloak and dagger associated with this meeting. Max decided to speak up and ask some questions.

"Gentlemen I have a few questions," Max started right in while watching both the road ahead and the rearview mirror. "First, why did you have us come all the way out here to meet and why did you take the long way to get to this meeting. What have you not told us?"

Elsa had been thinking those exact thoughts therefore she was pleased that her concerns were out on the table. But, as she looked at Rinehart and John, if these were really their names, she didn't like what she saw. Their individual reactions to Max's questions were exactly the same. Both men were flustered, neither responded right away. It was as though Max's challenge to their story was totally unexpected and equally unappreciated. Then Rinehart looked at John and it was at that moment that all pretense regarding who was in charge disappeared. Rinehart was waiting for a signal from his boss, this newcomer John. Elsa realized that they had not expected questions and therefore had not prepared answers in advance. Comprehending that their lack of preparation made them vulnerable Elsa decided to press the issue.

"I feel that we deserve answers to these questions and any others we have for you. If indeed we are all in this together, there can be no harm in full disclosure of the risks. Everything you know that is even slightly related to this mission must be shared with us now. If you hold back anything, I for one, am out right now."

Elsa sat with her back to the passenger's door looking back at the two men. Neither Max nor the two rear seat passengers had any idea that in her right hand, concealed under her unbuttoned coat was a semiautomatic pistol aimed directly at John's chest through the back of her seat. Tension was thick as the car continued west along the dark road where there would be no witnesses if she killed them both. She thought about it.

"Perhaps you are right, both of you," John began. "We are in this together; you should be told exactly what you are up against."

Everyone waited and Elsa felt her finger tensing against the trigger.

John looked over at his partner and addressed him, "Rinehart, go ahead tell them what has happened."

Rinehart looked at John for a moment just to confirm that he understood. John's expression confirmed he had the green light to proceed. Now confident that he was free to disclose all the details, Rinehart turned his attention to Max and Elsa. He took a deep breath, before beginning.

"We don't know what it means, but the Army Air Corps has been called in to fly air cover over the carriers during the tests. It seems that this had not been a routine decision because the pilot selected has been transferred from combat duty in the Pacific specifically for this assignment. From what we can gather, he is a top man with extensive combat experience. He has been recommended for numerous medals for heroism in the line of duty. For all we know he might be their version of The Red Baron, Manfred Von Richthofen, our immortal fighter pilot and ace from The First War. Even more disturbing, the Army has prepared a special airplane just for this mission and we understand it has been painted red. It will soon be seen over the lake. This has us concerned. Despite all of our precautions and planning the Navy must be expecting something. Why else would they go to such extreme measures to protect two carriers operating in the middle of their own country?"

Max pressed the two Germans with another question, "What else?"

The German, whose name they now knew to be Rinehart took on the answer. "Look, this accident that has taken away our first choice in fishing boats seems to be much too convenient. I question the timing. There is no real solid reason to question the legitimacy of the accident but it is suspect in my mind. These two things added together have caused us to make significant last minute changes in our plans and that is never good. So you see, we are just as concerned as you two and that is why we selected a meeting place far from prying eyes or ears."

Max was satisfied by what he considered to be a reasonable explanation. He looked over in Elsa's direction and for the first time caught a glimpse of the gun as she returned it to her coat pocket. He took that as a sign that she too was satisfied with the German's explanation.

He felt a shiver run down his spine. Although they had been living together for some time, he had no idea that she even owned a gun. Seeing it in her hand, combined with the look on her face, convinced him that she knew how to handle it and undoubtedly, would have used it if she had not been satisfied. This changed everything. Although he hated to think about it, Max thought he might have reason to fear everyone in the car.

Then Elsa asked, "Okay; what do we do now?"

CHAPTER TWENTY-FOUR
PUTTING THE PLAN IN MOTION

Rinehart passed a sheet of paper over the seat to Elsa. She took it from his hand. In the darkness, Elsa could see that something was hand-written on the paper. The interior of the car was just too dark to make out exactly what it said.

Rinehart began to relate the plan, "We will turn around and head back to the bar shortly. From there I want you both to go straight to your flat. Gather all of your belongings, making sure you leave nothing behind. Then drive away. Say nothing, just go. You are to proceed without delay. It is imperative that you be gone before morning. Please be very careful, and watch for anyone who might be observing your movements. If you suspect that you're being observed or followed find a way to get them off your trail. Elsa, on that sheet of paper in your hand there are two addresses. The first is the location where you are to deliver Max, along with the time he will need to arrive. I will already be there waiting. Max and I will stow away on the boat. Elsa, for the time being you will keep all of Max's belongings with you. The second address is the location of the workshop. This is where you are to go after Max is dropped off." He reached over the seat a second time. This time he handed her an envelope. "Please, look inside," said Rinehart as he waited for her to open the envelope.

She lifted the flap revealing a thick stack of bills. There were twenties, tens and fives. It looked like a lot of money, but again, it was too dark to make an accurate count. Next to the currency she found three war ration books filled with food and other ration stamps. In addition, there was an "A" window sticker for the car's windshield. The "A" sticker indicated that a car had priority status and could travel long distances without restriction or fear of being challenged. The sticker also would allow for the purchase of unlimited amounts of gasoline. The last item in the envelope was a key. She took it and held it out to get a good look.

"That's the key to the side door of the workshop," Rinehart offered before continuing. "After delivering Max, return to the highway and proceed north. Go to the workshop. Once there, enter the cabin through the side door. When you are safely inside, make your way to the garage and open the door from the inside. Pull the car in the garage out of sight and close the door. Make yourself at home and wait; we'll be along. Use the money and ration stamps to purchase gas and enough groceries to last the three of us for four weeks. No one has seen that many ration stamps in one person's possession so be very careful. Keep them out of sight. Don't buy all the food and supplies at one store. Stop along the way at four or five different places. We can't have your grocery purchase raising suspicion near where we will be staying." Elsa nodded her understanding and stuffed everything in her purse.

John interjected, "Memorize the information and destroy that paper before returning to your flat."

Elsa indicated she understood and would do as instructed by a nod of her head while Max turned the car around and drove back to the bar parking lot. Upon arriving at the bar, John and Rinehart simply said goodbye and then left immediately in the big black car.

Max and Elsa waited before leaving. Well after the two Germans had driven away, Max pulled the Ford out of the parking lot and drove back on the same road that had brought them to the meeting. This time however, they were heading east, back toward Port Washington and the flat above the hardware store. The Ford trailed the big black car by ten minutes or so leaving about an eight mile gap between the two cars. By the time Max pulled out of the parking lot the German should have already turned onto the road heading south, back toward Chicago. The delay was intended to make sure that both cars wouldn't be on the same road at the same time. Max didn't know if this maneuver would help if, by chance, they were being observed. Elsa had suggested it so Max went along with her. He didn't want to be disagreeable as he was still unnerved by the fact that she had a gun and apparently knew how to use it.

On the way back to town Elsa sat with her back against her door from where she had a good view of the road ahead, as well as behind. Max would handle the road ahead while her focus was on the road already traveled. This far out in the country street lights were few and far between. The headlights of Elsa's Ford cut a path through the night but behind the car there was nothing but blackness. This bolstered the couple's confidence that they were not being followed. To make sure, Max pulled off the road into an all-night filling station and restaurant used mainly by over-the-road truckers. The filling station was located on the northeast corner of an intersection with the main north/south highway.

Several trucks were parked at the gas pumps as well as all around the building. Some of the trucks had enclosed trailers while others had fixed beds mounted behind the cabs. Nearly all of the fixed beds had wooden sides with canvas tarps covering their loads. Max eased in between two of the trucks making it impossible for the Ford to be seen by a car approaching from the direction of the bar where their meeting had taken place. Max stayed in the car to watch the traffic while Elsa went inside to the ladies room. For nearly ten minutes, he watched the road through a space between the cab and the trailer of the truck parked next to Elsa's Ford. No traffic came down the road from that direction. Elsa had not returned either. He continued to watch and wait.

Elsa entered one of the two stalls in the ladies room and locked the door behind her. She removed the money from her purse and carefully counted out two thousand dollars. She returned the money to the purse and took out the note and began to read. Max was to be taken to the city of Sheboygan which is on the coast of Lake Michigan north of Port Washington. The drop-off location was at the corner of Indiana Street and South 20th Street. The spot was just south of the Sheboygan River. She surmised that the *Mary Jo* must be moored somewhere along the river near there. The trip would take no more than three hours. Max was to arrive at five in the afternoon, a full seventeen hours from now.

She continued to read. Her second destination was a bay situated southeast of a town named Rapid River, Michigan. From the map drawn out on the paper before her, she saw that the workshop occupied a spot near a bay on one of many small inlets dotting the bay's jagged shoreline. The population was sparse in that area of Michigan's Upper Peninsula and there were so many little rivers and inlets that it looked to her like the perfect place. A boat could motor down the bay and then enter the lake through the passage between Rock Island to the south and Saint Martin Island to the north. From there, it was a reasonably straight shot across the lake to the area where the carriers would be cruising.

With the instructions burned into her mind, Elsa proceeded to tear the paper into several small pieces. She carefully dropped every piece in the toilet bowl and pulled the handle flushing them away. After washing her hands and making a quick check of her makeup, Elsa turned and casually walked out of the restroom. Before returning to the car she purchased a pack of double edge safety razor blades and slipped them in her purse.

The door of the Ford opened and Elsa slid onto the seat next to Max holding her purse in her lap. "See anything?" she asked.

"Nothing, not one car or truck has come from the direction of the bar." He said while not turning to look her way.

"What do you think?" Elsa asked as she too stared out at the road then back to Max.

"I don't know, but it appears we're safe, for now anyway," Max answered, still not looking in her direction.

"What's wrong? You're acting like something's wrong. What is it?" she asked while attempting to surreptitiously remove one of the razor blades from its protective case.

Max turned and looked at her before answering. "What's the gun for?"

"Protection Max, what do you think it's for? Its protection for us both, I don't trust those guys." A look of bewilderment came across her face as she gave the answer to Max's question.

"It would have been nice to know that we might kill somebody tonight. You know Elsa; it's not a little thing. It could have happened. What were you thinking by not telling me what you had in mind?" Max's question was delivered with a seriousness that left no doubt that he was deeply concerned.

"Listen Max, you need to know something and I might as well get it out in the open right now. I have good reason to fear those men and you should too." Now Elsa was even more serious than Max.

Max turned toward Elsa. "Alright you have my attention, please, go on."

"I'm German, they're German, and you're Japanese. The war in Europe is going poorly for Germany. Much more poorly then has been reported by either side. It is critical to Germany that Japan stay in the war. If Japan surrenders the entire might of the Allied combined forces will be free to come down against Germany. If that becomes a reality the war is lost. Germany will be overrun by vastly superior numbers of men and equipment. Germany needs time. This is the only reason for Germany's involvement in this sabotage plan. If things get out of hand and they find themselves in danger the plan will be aborted and you will be eliminated. It's that simple Max. I have gotten too close to you and they know it. Killing me along with you would be necessary in their twisted minds. They would do it without a second thought. Believe what I am saying. Have no doubt in your mind that I am telling you the absolute truth."

Max had a lot to think about. Her explanation seemed plausible, but he had a question rolling around in his mind. He struggled to put together the right words, not wanting to make her believe that he doubted her word. "That's fine; I understand but if they kill me how could it be done without jeopardizing their objective of keeping Japan in the war?"

"It might work to their advantage. They could say that we were stopped for something unrelated and tried to fight our way out and were killed by the police. The Japanese government would be led to believe that the plan had not been compromised, just delayed until someone else could be brought in to take your place. If I were killed with you it would make the story that much more believable. So you see Max it could be done. I don't trust them. For goodness sake Max we're spies, all of us."

Her final words hit home. He had not come to grips until that moment with the very real fact that he was a saboteur; yes, a spy. He was no longer an officer in the Japanese Army. If caught, he would be taken as a spy and shot. If this was the measuring stick which determines who was and who wasn't a spy, he was definitely a spy. He knew that from this moment on he had better start thinking and acting like a spy. "I believe you. You're right, I am a spy who has a well-defined mission which clearly holds more importance to me and my country than it does to anyone else in the conspiracy."

Elsa took his hand in hers before speaking. She was still holding the pack of razor blades in her other hand. "You mean more to me than the mission. I would have killed two of my fellow countrymen to protect you from harm. I love you Max. Let's find a way to get this done without being killed ourselves, and then we can disappear together."

Max wanted to believe her. "Alright, it's just you and me... Now give me that gun."

She smiled, let go of Max's hand and confidently reached in her pocket handing over the gun. When he had taken the gun she casually added. "I have another one you know."

Without losing a beat Max said, "That's fine, now we both have one."

Elsa gripped the razor blade which by this time, she had carefully maneuvered out of the pack. Max didn't see it in her hand. Elsa raised her arm and pushed the blade firmly against the windshield using it to remove the gas ration sticker from the inside of the glass. Then she replaced it with the new "A" sticker from the envelope.

"Pull around to that empty pump. Let's fill up here then we start our first and final mission," she said as she pointed toward one of the pumps.

The Final Mission

CHAPTER TWENTY-FIVE
TOGETHER AGAIN

The phone rang twice before JD heard a female voice on the other end greet him.

"Hello, Collins residence." The voice wasn't Annie's but it did sound a little like her. JD didn't remember Annie speaking of a sister so he assumed this must be her mother.

"Excuse me but are you Mrs. Collins?"

"Yes, may I help you?"

"Yes I hope so. My name is Joseph..."

"Are you calling for Ann Marie?"

"Yes ma'am I am. By chance is she home?"

"No she's at work. The bus won't drop her off until around six-thirty. Are you the boy she met in Chicago?"

"Yes, I sure am and right now I happen to be out near Ann Arbor. I believe I'll be here for a few days, but should know more about my schedule tomorrow. Well anyway, I was wondering if you might consent to me calling on your daughter this evening at your home."

"She has spoken to me about you. From what she said, I'm certain she'd be pleased if you called on her this evening."

Annie had indeed spoken to her mother about the young officer from Union Station. In fact, he was all she had been talking about since returning home. Her mother knew that Annie was smitten and she was anxious to meet the young man herself.

"May I ask you to let her know that I'll be there at seven? If you don't think that's too late."

"Could you arrange to be here at say, six-thirty? You could meet her at the bus stop."

"Yes ma'am that sounds like a great idea." JD liked the thought of seeing Annie's reaction when she stepped off the bus and saw him standing there. It sounded like fun. "Excuse me, but where's the bus stop?" asked JD.

"It's on the corner of Six Mile and Van Dyke. Do you think you can find it alright? You can have dinner with us when you get here. Now be sure to bring her straight home. No dilly-dallying. We'll all be hungry and her father won't want to wait," said Mrs. Collins.

"I'll be looking forward to meeting you and Mr. Collins, and thanks for the invitation to dinner. I haven't had a home cooked meal in over a year," JD said with excitement in his voice.

"Well now don't get your hopes up we're just having leftovers tonight. After all, there's a war on, you know," she said while thinking that she might have enough sugar saved up to bake a cake.

"Anything will be fine with me, don't you worry. See you shortly after six-thirty."

JD thanked Mrs. Collins again before hanging up the phone. He turned away and decided to look for Don. He was easy to find. JD spotted him walking toward the row of phone booths.

"Did you get hold of her?" Don asked as he approached.

"No but I talked to her mother and got an invitation to dinner tonight," JD answered proudly.

"Sounds good, how you going to get there?" asked Don.

"First things first, I have the invitation taken care of, now I can start to work on the logistics."

"I've been busy too, you know. I found the plane. We can see it tomorrow. They told me it will be complete late today if we don't bother them," said Don.

"Well done, my boy. So what do we do today?" said a very pleased JD.

Don was full of information. "We're being housed off base, there's no room here. This place is packed with outside contractors and with crews waiting for planes. They take priority for the available bunks. I have a map to a local home. It's being used as a bed and breakfast sort of arrangement. The place is about three miles east of here. I got our bags out of the plane and tossed them in that Jeep over there," Don said as he pointed across the tarmac toward a lone Jeep parked near the gate.

"How'd you manage a Jeep?" JD asked as they started toward the gate. "This solves my transportation problem."

"Well, I figured you were going to Detroit no matter what, so you would need transportation. I told the desk sergeant what you were up to and she was more than accommodating. Just return it the way you found it," Don said as they climbed in the front seats.

"Thanks man I appreciate you looking out for me."

Don didn't say anything in response until he was settled behind the wheel of the Jeep and had it headed in the direction of their lodging. "I have to admit that my efforts on your behalf were spurred on by my desire to get a date for tonight myself." JD smiled as he looked over at Don.

"Well, how'd it work out?" asked JD.

"You are aware that as an officer I can't fraternize with noncoms. Therefore, I agreed to meet her this evening to discuss her interest in applying for Officer's Candidate School."

JD quickly responded, "So she's interested in becoming an officer is she?"

Don didn't look away from the road as he answered. "She has no interest at all, as far as I know."

They drove in the open air with the windshield folded down against the hood. The wind was blowing in their faces and all around. JD felt relaxed and carefree as he thought about Don. The more he learned about him the better he liked him. He put his head back and said, "I guess you have been busy today."

"Yes, but in a good way; and the day's not over yet. In my immediate future I envision very good things, if you know what I mean," Don responded in a jubilant tone.

"I get your drift, if you know what I mean," JD was laughing as he spoke.

The big old home was on a lovely tree-covered block with similar houses on both sides of the street. The two fliers were met at the door by a lady who appeared to be around sixty. She was short, with gray hair pulled away from her face and rolled up on the top of her head. She was pleasant enough, showing them to the small second floor bedroom they were to share. It was spotlessly clean but that's all that could be said for it. She handed them both a key before offering them instructions.

"Those are keys to the backdoor. If you come in late use the backstairs and be quiet; I have other guests. Breakfast is at six o'clock, kitchen closes at six-fifteen. See you at breakfast." She walked down the hall and disappeared down the steps.

"We have the whole afternoon to kill; got any ideas?" asked JD. Don opened his bag and tossed two thick manuals on one of the beds. "We have some studying to do before they'll check the plane out to us."

JD picked up one of the books and read the cover. It read 'Weapons Manual for B-25 Chase Plane.' "What's this?" he asked as he flipped through the first few pages.

Don picked up the other manual and turned to answer JD's question. "I had a few minutes to look these over while you were off hunting for a phone. This plane is configured with missiles, one cannon, something called hedgehogs, radar; all kinds of new equipment. We need to be up to speed on this stuff before we start training tomorrow."

"You're right. What do you say we go back to that restaurant we passed about a mile back and grab some carryout? I need to stop by a filling station to get a map of Detroit. Then we can find a tree to sit under where we can eat and study outside for a couple hours," offered JD.

Don grabbed his hat and started out the door with the manuals in his other hand. "Let's go then, I'm hungry."

They spent the better part of the afternoon studying the manuals. A significant portion was familiar to them both so they breezed through those topics without much effort. JD possessed more hands on experience than Don. His assistance on several topics accelerated Don's comprehension. On the areas covering the new equipment they worked through the details together.

Eventually, JD put down the manual in favor of a map of the Detroit metropolitan area. After figuring out the most direct route to the bus stop, he decided it was time. He took Don back to the boarding house, cleaned up, put on a fresh uniform and made his way to the bus stop. He chose a path that would take him north for a short distance, then east on Eight Mile road to avoid the downtown area and its rush hour traffic.

JD parked the Jeep in a drug store parking lot situated directly in front of the bus stop. The lot was hidden from the view of anyone walking along the sidewalk or passing along Van Dyke Avenue in a car. A person would need to be almost to the end of the drug store's facade before he would notice that there was an empty lot between the drug store and the next building. Both buildings were two stories tall and the walls which faced the parking lot showed their exposed, unpainted red brick construction.

People were everywhere, some just walking along the sidewalk, with others entering and exiting the various businesses along the avenue. Several people were gathered at the stop waiting for the next bus to appear and take them away. A newsboy was doing a brisk business selling the afternoon edition of the Detroit Times at a nickel a copy. The whole area was bustling with activity.

JD was lucky to have found an empty parking place. He got out of the Jeep and walked toward the bus stop a few yards from the corner. Looking up Van Dyke Avenue to the north, he could see bumper-to-bumper traffic making its way slowly across Six Mile Road heading toward downtown. He took up a position in front of the bus stop near the curb in order to have an unobstructed view of the oncoming traffic. He checked his watch; it was six twenty-eight. He had just made it on time. He waited.

Ten minutes into his wait the roof of a bus could be seen slowly making its way south. The lighted sign above the windshield read "Jefferson Ave". The red and tan bus was in the curb lane and he figured that this was the one carrying Annie. Several people waiting at the bus stop began to fumble in their pockets and purses for change. Their actions reassured him that this bus would stop. He hoped Annie would be on it.

Annie was busy in conversation with the girls seated around her as they all filled the time talking about anything and everything, the same way they did each evening on the trip home. One of the girls in a seat near the front was the first to notice the officer standing on the sidewalk just ahead as the bus neared the next appointed stop. "Would you look at that?" she said to those around her.

Annie and several others looked up from their conversation to see what she was talking about. Annie couldn't believe her eyes. Instantly, she couldn't catch her breath and she felt the blood rushing to her face. She quickly recovered enough to smile and instantaneously start to inspect her appearance.

Annie turned to the girl next to her. "How do I look? How's my hair? What about my make up?"

The girl looked quizzically at her. "Do you know him? Come on tell me, who is that guy?"

Annie couldn't help feeling a sense of pride as she listened to all of the comments being uttered by the bus load of gawking females. "Well out with it, who is he?" asked the girl again as others turned in their direction to catch Annie's response.

"He's a friend, a very, very, good friend."

Normally, in such a situation JD would be trying to figure out just the right approach to use as she exited the bus, but not this time. He was so very excited to see her face, to look at her, to be with her that he had not rehearsed his next move. Although they had only met the one time he was past that kind of thinking. He was crazy about her and he was fine just going with events as they developed.

Annie walked down the center of the now silent bus with every eye on her. Heads and eyes followed as Annie passed. Everyone held their gaze even after she was out the door and on the sidewalk.

She stood before her handsome young officer with a large purse hanging off one shoulder by the strap and a battered old lunch box in her hand. The bus waited with the door standing wide open. Everyone's attention was riveted on the couple. Even those who were preparing to get on waited to capture a glimpse of what would happen next. They weren't disappointed. Watching her step off the bus, JD was sure that she was the most beautiful woman in the world. Dressed in her pants and blouse she really did look cute. At that moment, he remembered something that his father had said about his mother.

"Son, your mother would look good to me if all she was wearing was a burlap bag." He felt exactly the same about Annie at that moment.

Without a word being spoken he reached out and took the lunch box from her hand while putting his other arm around her waist. In one continuous fluid motion, as natural as anything, Annie eased over next to him snuggling in tight seemingly melting to his side. He bent down and tenderly kissed her lips as they walked away together, completely unaware of anyone else.

A collective sigh could be heard aboard the bus, after which the newcomers climbed on board. The driver finally closed the door and pulled away into traffic. The bus was quiet.

"Surprised?" he asked while assisting her into the jeep.

"Yes, very pleasantly surprised. I am so happy to see you."

"Which way is it to your house? I'm invited to dinner and your mother instructed me to bring you straight home. I believe, 'no dilly-dallying', were her exact words."

Annie pointed the way. "No dilly-dallying you say. Well if you did dilly-dally for just a moment or two I don't think she would know."

He found a place to pull over and immediately brought the Jeep to the curb. He turned off the engine and just looked at her. She had that same look in her eyes that he had seen just before he kissed her for the first time. This time instead of a kiss they held each other tightly for a long time. When they separated Annie spoke first.

"I've been dreaming about this moment. I think about you nearly all the time. You made my dreams come true today. Seeing you there waiting for me was such a wonderful present, better than any Christmas in my whole life." Then she kissed him as before.

He restarted the Jeep, put it in gear and posed a question. "Do you think that this is what your mother meant by 'no dilly-dallying'?"

Annie answered, "Joseph, that's exactly what she meant."

CHAPTER TWENY-SIX
MEETING THE FAMILY

The Collins' home was located on the eastern edge of Detroit. It was situated midway along a residential street lined with overarching mature trees. The trees shrouded the street in shade, converting the rows of the two story red brick homes on either side into a cozy neighborhood. Each house had a large front porch covered by a substantial looking roof with large pillars at the corners to support its weight. Annie's porch was rather high and needed a set of five steps to reach it. All of the houses were very close together. There was parking on the street but no driveways. Without driveways the homes could be squeezed tightly together allowing for more to be built on each block. The garages were located at the back of the lots with their doors facing an alley.

With the houses arranged in this fashion people came out on their front porches in the evening to escape the summer heat and to speak to their neighbors. Many of the homes on Annie's block displayed banners in their front windows with a red star for every serviceman from the home currently serving in the armed forces of the United States. Annie's home was no exception. Proudly displayed in one of the front windows was a banner with one red star for her brother Brad.

As JD and Annie walked up the sidewalk toward her front steps most of the neighbors were already out on the nearby porches. Several waved and a few greeted Annie but most just watched the young girl and her tall Army officer as they made their way to the front door. All would have something new and interesting to talk about on this late summer evening.

Inside, to the left of the entryway, was a large living room with the dining room directly behind it. Over to the right was a staircase leading to what JD supposed were the bedrooms on the second floor. Behind the staircase were the stairs which led down to the basement. As Annie led him further down the hall he saw the kitchen, a large pantry, a bathroom and what looked to be an all-purpose room. In this room there was an upright piano, a sewing machine, a desk and a table with a partially completed puzzle laid out waiting for someone to return to the unfinished task.

Annie's mother made JD feel almost as welcome as if he had been in his own mother's kitchen. The meal was perfect as was the homemade chocolate cake with chocolate icing. He thanked her over and over again for the wonderful meal. After dinner, Annie and her mother retreated to the kitchen busily cleaning up the dinner dishes while JD and Mr. Collins went outside to the front porch. Mr. Collins sat back on a glider built for two while JD made himself comfortable in a wooden rocking chair.

Mr. Collins was the first to speak, "I like to come out here almost every evening. To me, it's very relaxing. When the Tigers have a night game scheduled I keep the radio on in the background, loud enough so as to hear what's going on but not so loud that it disturbs my thinking. Annie's mother joins me most nights. Sometimes we talk, but sometimes we just enjoy each other's company without saying much at all. Do you know what I'm talking about son? Life and love is more than, you know..."

"Sir, I wonder, could your question have to do with how Annie and I feel about one another?"

"I have to admit; yes, that's exactly what I was talking about," Mr. Collins responded while the glider moved back and forth.

"If I get your meaning, you're telling me that love is much more than the attraction that Annie feels for me and that I feel for her. I know that sir, and I give you my word of honor as an officer and a gentleman, you and Mrs. Collins have nothing to worry about in that regard from my side. But honestly, I am so deeply in love with your daughter that I couldn't possibly be completely sure that I understand all I should about such things. I give you my word that I have the best of intentions when it comes to my relationship with Annie and my feelings for her."

Mr. Collins rocked a while in the glider thinking about young people, recalling in his mind that powerful attraction which brings a man and a woman together for the first time. He felt himself smiling as he thought about the first time he saw Annie's mother. *You can't fight love, it's just too powerful. Besides, I really like this young man and there is no denying Annie is head over heels in love with him.* He brought himself back before responding.

"Joseph, I have told you what I thought you should know and from your answer it's clear to me you understand my meaning. That's all I have to say on that subject. As for you personally, I like you son, and I can see what Annie sees in you, besides that uniform. I've heard so much about you this past week I feel like I've known you for years. Let me say that I'm sorry to hear that you recently lost your father. If I can help in any way in the future, not to replace him obviously, but you know, with a little fatherly advice, I'm here for you."

JD was touched. This was a nice guy. "Thank you very much. I'll keep that in mind."

Eventually, the ladies joined the men on the porch. They all talked and laughed about everything but the war. JD loved listening to Annie's family and watching them interact with each other. Escaping from a soldier's life, if only for one evening, was much needed medicine. He pushed the war well back in his mind and allowed the evening to give him a bit of hope. He dared to imagine a time when war would no longer consume every aspect of his life. Just like all of the men in uniform during WW II, JD was signed on for the duration. There were no discharge dates, so making firm plans for the future was impossible. This night was a preview of a day when war and every bad thing that came with it would be gone from his life forever.

It was getting late and JD didn't ever want it to end, but he knew that Annie and her father needed to get off to bed soon so he decided to do the right thing and take his leave. "I want to thank you for one of the best evenings I've ever had; but it's late and I must be heading back to the base."

Annie looked stunned. She hadn't realized how late the hour had become. Mr. Collins pulled out his watch and announced that the hour was indeed late and he needed to call it a night.

Annie got up. "Let me get your hat, I'll just be a minute." She went into the house with her mother trailing close behind.

JD and Mr. Collins were exchanging handshakes when Annie and her mother returned. Annie had JD's hat and Mrs. Collins was carrying a large brown paper bag. "You take this food with you. I'm sure your buddies will enjoy it. I cut you off half of that cake for your ride home." Mrs. Collins handing JD the bag and gave him a warm hug.

"Well ma'am now I know that God answers prayer."

"Whatever do you mean?"

"I was praying for another piece of that cake but I was embarrassed to ask. After all, I had two big pieces after dinner," JD said, knowing it was true but hoping also that she would be pleased that he liked the cake.

Mr. Collins turned to JD. "Joseph, what do you say we ask God for something much more important than cake?"

JD felt a kind of quietness come over him.

"That would be fine sir." The four of them took hands as Mr. Collins led them in prayer.

"Dear heavenly Father at the end of another day, a day that you have given us, we come to you with our request. Please keep your hand of protection on this young man as you have to this point in his life. He faced danger every moment and your mercy and grace are needed if he is to survive. We ask you knowing that you are able to keep him safe if it be your will. We are asking that it indeed be your will. We praise you and worship you, being ever careful to give you all the glory. In the name of your Son and our Savior Jesus Christ we ask these mercies. Amen." They all added their own Amen.

Annie reached up and pushed JD's hat down firmly on his head. "Let's go soldier. Come on, I'll walk you out to that fancy car of yours." They stood beside the Jeep holding hands for a few minutes before JD could find the right words. "That was wonderful. Please thank your dad for doing that."

"I was surprised that it took him that long. We have been praying for you as a family every night since I told them that I loved you and that I intended to be your wife."

"When did you tell them that piece of news?"

"The day I got home from Chicago." JD smiled and just looked at her while thinking that he just might be the most blessed man alive.

"Listen Annie, tomorrow I should find out how long I can expect to be in Michigan. I'll call you just as soon as I can confirm my schedule, hopefully tomorrow. We can make plans to see each other again before I need to go back to Milwaukee."

"The sooner the better," Annie answered. "I may be able to come out to where you are on Sunday afternoon if that would work out better."

"It sounds like we'll be together soon, one way or the other," JD said as their time together this day was coming to an end.

Their parting was tender but too short for them both. JD placed the bag on the floor in front of the passenger's seat, well out of his reach. Finally, he headed the Jeep back to the boarding house and Don. He couldn't wait to offer a piece of that cake to Don. His decision to place the bag out of easy reach was the best way to keep his hands out of it. If it were any closer the cake may not survive the journey.

What a wonderful evening, he thought as he put the miles behind him. *Happiness, yes this must be what makes up true happiness; being with good people, talking about good things, just enjoying being alive. It doesn't hurt that I'm also deeply in love and anticipating with joy every look and gesture that Annie makes.*

At two-twenty-five in the morning he used the back stairs without making a sound and slipped ever so quietly into his room. JD closed the door behind him, switched on the light and put the bag of food on the table. Don was nowhere to be found. *Don was right; he is having a very busy day, and apparently it isn't over yet.*

With thoughts of the wonderful evening spent with Annie and her family still rolling around in his head JD pulled the sheet up under his chin and closed his eyes. He was pleased with how well things had gone at the Collins home but he missed Annie already.

CHAPTER TWENTY-SEVEN
THE NEW AIRPLANE

At six the following morning Don was already up and eager to get going. He was making enough noise to wake the dead causing JD to slowly open his eyes. He knew that Don couldn't have gotten to bed until well after three in the morning, so JD guessed he was still high with the euphoria from the previous evening's date. Taking a cue from his energetic roommate JD scrambled out of bed making every effort to catch up. While walking past the table on the way to the bathroom, he looked down and noticed Mrs. Collin's bag of food lay empty. Only a few chocolate cake crumbs remained on the top of the table.

After a hardy breakfast of ham, eggs, toast and hot, strong, coffee the two fliers were out the boarding house door and on their way to Willow Run. JD was amazed by how well Don had eaten at breakfast on top of all that food from the bag and the half of the cake.

Showing their IDs at the gate, JD and Don were cleared to enter the facility. Don made a right turn and headed directly for the group of out buildings. Don parked in front of the building where the previous day he had located the plane. The new B-25 was already outside standing tall on the tarmac just beyond the open hanger doors. There were no people out on the tarmac as the two fliers walked up to the plane, but several could be seen busily going about their work inside the hanger.

"Wow, she's beautiful," Don exclaimed as they walked toward the plane. "Would you look at those bright red markings?"

The plane's aluminum skin was mostly unpainted. The polished aluminum was far different from the drab green color JD had grown so accustomed to back in the Pacific. A bright morning sun reflected brilliantly off the plane's polished surface. She seemed to sparkle like a diamond. Along each side of the fuselage there were wide red stripes which gracefully narrowed as they neared both the nose and tail. The two engine cowlings were red as were the propeller hubs and tail rudders. The first ten inches of each propeller blade was painted a bold yellow, as were the tips of the eight .50 caliber machine gun barrels protruding from the nose and the four on the side blisters.

"We definitely aren't going to hide from anyone in this baby," Don observed.

JD gave her a good walk around inspection then commented. "Look at this Don, she has no waist or tail guns and the upper turret is gone. She's certainly not configured to fend off attacks from fighters. All the fire power's in the front."

Don was looking at the pods mounted under the wings. "What about those rockets? Did you have those back in the Pacific?"

Five rockets were mounted under each wing outboard of the engines and beyond the swing radius of the propellers. There wasn't much room out near the ends of the wings but the engineers had done a masterful job of fitting the rockets in the limited space available. "No, we didn't have any rockets but on many occasions we sure could've made good use of them. You know Don, I thought you mentioned a cannon. I don't see it, do you?"

Don was quick to answer, "You remember there was an entire section pertaining to the operation of the cannon in the manual. Besides, the guys working on the plane yesterday mentioned it as well. Come to think about it, I saw it on the floor next to the plane. "JD walked under the wing and up to the nose of the plane. There he noticed a patch that had been riveted over a hole in the aluminum skin. It was just below and to the right of the machine guns. "Don look at this. Apparently they planned to put it right here," JD said and pointed out the patch to Don.

Don stepped back to get a better prospective of the plane, and then spoke. "Come to think of it, that cannon did look mighty big. I bet they scrapped the idea because it didn't fit. That's my guess." JD hadn't seen the cannon but Don's description as to the size of the thing was good enough for him. "I can't disagree with you. I guess the thing just wouldn't fit."

Both men continued their inspection of the exterior of the plane. She looked exceptionally nice to JD. Although essentially the same in overall design as the B-25's used in combat, the new nose and the absence of the top turret and other guns gave this plane a much sleeker appearance.

Don and JD were nearly finished with their observations and inspection when the activity inside the hanger shifted to the tarmac and the new plane. Most of the personnel now gathering around the plane were civilian. Two men wheeled a cart carrying a large fire extinguisher out of the hanger, stopping near the right engine. A fuel truck came up alongside and the hose was passed up to someone on the wing. He immediately began filling the tanks.

JD and Don were still standing near the nose wheel when two men approached. One was a civilian with a clip board the other an Army sergeant. "Good morning gentlemen I'm Glen Kelly and this is Sergeant Gary Waters."

JD handled the introductions as the four men shook hands with each other. Glen Kelly waited for the introductions before he spoke. "The plan this morning is to familiarize you men with the weapons systems aboard this plane. I understand that both of you have ample experience in B-25s, is that right?"

They both nodded in the affirmative, while waiting to learn more about who this civilian was.

"Good, that's just fine. I'm from Stanford University. I'm a member of the team that has been working for some time on the guidance system which will soon be tested over Lake Michigan. This plane has been configured to serve as the safeguard against any test plane leaving the designated test area if, by chance, the guidance system happens to fail. If ordered to do so, your job is to shoot down any out-of-control test plane before it reaches land. Naturally, this will prevent property damage and loss of life. Just as important however, the equipment inside the test planes cannot fall into the hands of our enemy. All evidence is to go to the bottom of the lake."

JD and Don listened as Kelly continued. "The sergeant here has been training to act as radio operator, navigator and flight engineer. He is to be the third and final member of your crew."

Sergeant Waters stepped forward and addressed the officer. "Gentlemen it is an honor to have been selected to join this crew and I hope to perform my duties well."

"I'm sure we'll get on just fine sergeant, welcome aboard." JD wanted some background on young Gary Waters. "Do you have any actual flight experience prior to this assignment?"

Waters answered without hesitation. "No sir, but I have been training for the past six months for this assignment and feel that I'm ready for anything."

Don looked at JD and JD looked at Waters while thinking back to the time when he was first assigned to the Pacific. He had felt the same way, full of spit and vinegar, just exactly the same as Waters was feeling right now. "I hope so son, I truly hope so." That was all that JD could think to say at that moment. He would find out soon enough if Waters was up to the task. If not, he would wash him out. It was that simple.

Waters looked like he was trying to think of something more to say in response to JD's comment when his eyes brightened. "Sir, I was told that you have an outstanding war record and were selected for this assignment because you are the very best. I am confident in my preparation and in you sir."

Don shook his head then plunged in. "Isn't this a fine state of affairs? I have no experience; Waters like me is also a rookie. The only one who has any idea of what to do is the First Lieutenant," he pointed to JD as he spoke. "I'm not sure after hearing from our young sergeant whether he is just trying to suck up to the boss or if he means what he said. Either way, we have a lot of work to do if we're going to make a first class crew out of our little band of misfits."

Kelly was listening but showed no outward sign that he even cared about the subject being discussed. He seemed focused on the preparations which were nearly complete. JD noticed Kelly's focus.

Taking charge, JD began to give orders. "Don, round up your equipment. You too Waters, and find your places aboard the plane. We will take her up for a shakedown flight. Let's see how ready we all are to work together as a crew. Kelly, I expect that you plan to accompany us on this flight. Is that right?"

"Yes I do," Kelly answered.

"Good, round up some gear and climb aboard. I want you on the step between Don and me, and bring that clipboard. We're ready to start training." JD said as he began to step into one of the parachutes that a worker had pulled out of a cart and laid on the concrete near the group.

It took a full twenty minutes for JD to complete his visual inspection of the new plane. He confirmed the noise wheel locking pin was in place then used the ladder to climb up on the wing. He checked the fuel level in all tanks as well as the oil level in both engines. Everything checked out as required. Inside he and Don slowly and carefully completed the preflight check list.

At the end of the runway the B-25's big radial engines roared as the RPM's were increased to takeoff power. He held them at takeoff power for more than the usual time frame. The engines were smooth, no sign of a miss or roughness of any kind. He asked for permission to take off and was cleared to go.

With the ten rockets mounted under the wings JD expected that the additional drag would translate into more runway length required to lift the plane into the sky. To his surprise this was not the case. The plane reached takeoff speed very quickly and was airborne just as they passed the first turn off.

"Kelly, what did you do to these engines?" JD hollered as the plane lifted off the ground.

"Bigger, more powerful superchargers, they were developed as part of the B29 super fortress project. We tried them on these engines with larger coolant lines and the results have been outstanding; more power and speed. What do you think?" JD was impressed. Even with so much weight being removed with the elimination of the guns, upper turret assembly, and an empty bomb bay *Wildcat* could never have matched the power of this new design.

After reaching an altitude of five thousand feet, Don who was taking his turn at the controls, made a wide turn over Lake Erie and headed north following the Detroit River toward the city of Detroit. They flew directly over Grosse Ile, a large island just up river from the mouth of Lake Erie. Soon, the plane turned slightly east and north still following the river until they could see the city below. Briggs Stadium, the home field of the Detroit Tigers Baseball Club, was just beginning to fill with early arriving fans preparing to take in batting practice and a late season day game. JD had heard somewhere that the Tiger's owners provided free admission to servicemen in uniform and their dates for all games. Seating was in the lower grandstands out in right field. As he eyed the scene below he thought that it might be a good idea to take Annie to a game, if he could work it into his schedule.

They continued out over Lake St. Clair leaving behind Detroit and the neighboring city of Windsor, Ontario Canada located just across the Detroit River. Lake St. Clair is only twenty miles long and they covered the distance quickly. At the north end of the lake the St. Clair River leads up to Lake Huron. With the two engines purring in perfect synchronization the Blue Water Bridge linking Port Huron, Michigan and Sarnia, Ontario Canada eventually came into view at the mouth of Lake Huron.

JD called out through the interphone, "Waters, do you read me?"

Waters responded. "Yes sir, I'm here."

"Good, plot a course back to the field."

Don started a slow turn to the left heading west then south west using dead reckoning to estimate the location of the base. "I can get us back no problem." JD gave him a stern look and Don instantly realized that this wasn't about finding the way back but rather about finding out if Waters could plot a course that would get them back.

After a few minutes Waters came back. "It's two hundred and twenty-three degrees to the southwest. At our present speed we should reach the field in twenty-six minutes, sir."

JD and Don both looked at the compass, they were on the same course. JD smiled as he called out to Waters. "Good job sergeant, we'll fly your course."

Don turned to Kelly who was standing on the ladder his face between the two pilots. "What happened to the cannon?"

"Too big, wouldn't fit without removing the copilot's position. We decided that you were more important to this mission than that oversized artillery piece. I trust you agree."

Don turned to look at JD. He had a look on his face that said, "I told you so". JD just nodded.

Waters came on the interphone. "You should have the field in sight. Do you see it yet?"

With the clear sky JD had spotted it several minutes earlier but didn't want to destroy the kid's confidence. "Yes there it is. We can take it from here." JD asked, "Don, do you see it, can you make it out?"

Don had been looking at the base for several minutes himself but went along with his pilot. "Yes there it is. I see it. Not bad Waters, well done."

For the next seven days they continued training. The first thing to be addressed was the alignment of the eight .50 caliber nose guns. The angle of fire was adjusted to bunch the rounds from all eight guns so that they merged together at four hundred yards out. The overriding consideration being that the test planes would be flying much slower than their chase plane and they wouldn't be taking evasive action. Therefore, any shooting at the target would be from a close distance. If called upon to shoot down one of the test planes they would literally be shooting at a sitting duck. In this type of situation the main objective would be to put enough rounds in the target to provide the best chance of destroying it. Unlike combat where hits could take an enemy plane out of action without necessarily bringing it down, complete destruction of the test planes was essential to the success of the mission. Concentrated fire would be the key. However, just in case something unforeseen happened, the blister guns mounted in pairs on either side of the fuselage were aimed nearly straight ahead with only the slightest inward alignment. This insured a wider field of fire would still be available at close range.

JD had no experience with rockets and considered them as a safety valve to be used only if the guns were to jam or if they ran short of ammunition. The decision was made to keep all ten rockets aimed straight ahead. Rockets were effective out to a half mile or more, much further than the range of machine guns. From that range everyone felt comfortable with a wide field of fire. JD was thinking in terms of point and shoot. They were bound to get a hit with at least one of the ten.

On the afternoon of the seventh straight day of training Glen Kelly, who they were now calling The Professor, Gary Waters, Don Rogers and JD were all sitting together inside the hanger eating a late lunch of sandwiches, potato chips and coffee. They had all been working long hours since that first day together. The new crew had logged several hours in the air and were beginning to feel comfortable with each other. In between air time and The Professor's ground instruction classes the crew also preformed all critiquing of the planes systems. This was JD's idea. He knew from experience that if the crew did the work this would increase their knowledge and familiarity with all of the systems aboard the new plane.

Don tossed the wrapper from his second sandwich in the trash drum ten feet away. "Perfect shot," he said. Then he finished the last swig of coffee before tossing the cup in after the paper. Looking over to The Professor and asked, "What's next?"

"Well," began The Professor. "We're about done. There's just one more item to go over, and that would be the hedgehogs."

JD spoke up, "I was wondering about those. I understand they are used for submarine killing. Are we expecting subs on this mission?"

"Of course not Lieutenant," the Professor answered with a grin. "Let me explain. As you know, depth charges are normally used to hunt and destroy subs under water. They are set to explode after reaching the selected depth below the surface. You don't need to hit the sub to damage it. You need only to explode the depth charge close to the sub and the damage it can cause could be devastating to any sub nearby.

"The hedgehog, on the other hand, is dropped in the water and detonates on contact with metal. They were developed by the British and are dropped directly onto submarines as they are trying to submerge after being surprised by British patrol planes. The pilots can clearly see the sub as it starts to dive. In this type of situation depth charges are not effective so the Brits came up with the hedgehog for just such occasions."

"That's good to know, but how are we to make use of them on this mission?" JD asked.

The Professor waited until he had everyone's full attention. "If you down a test plane we assume that it will sink. Agreed?" The three men nodded their heads in the affirmative, still listening. "The hedgehogs are for the plane that doesn't sink right away.

"Lieutenant Jones, you are an experienced combat bomber pilot selected for this mission because you have the experience and skills necessary to manage the plane, the pressure and the crew. You also have proven that you can drop ordinance on the target.

You are to make absolutely sure that the test planes sink. There will be several targets mounted on top of steel barges positioned out in the lake into which the test plane will be flown. Make sure that the targets and the planes disappear forever."

"Got it," said JD.

"Good, then let's go drop some hedgehogs and see how accurate you are," said the Professor as he got up and motioned the crew to follow. The remainder of the afternoon was spent dropping hedgehogs filled with flour on targets painted on the ground between the runways of Willow Run. The Professor had been right; JD could indeed drop ordinance on the target. The plane, equipment and crew were finally ready. Training was over. It was time for the real thing.

That same afternoon JD placed a call to Major Brock back at Mitchell Field. He was connected to the Major right away.

"Yes Lieutenant, good to hear from you. How is the training progressing?" Brock asked.

"Very good sir, we have completed our training and are ready to perform the mission."

"Well done Lieutenant. We have received word that operation Eagle Eye will begin in ten days. Everything is moving on schedule. The Navy will break off pilot training and free the carriers to sail up the lake to Traverse City a couple days ahead of the start date. The cover story for the voyage is a goodwill visit to the city for the purpose of stimulating naval recruitment," Brock reported.

JD was anxious to put this final mission behind him. His thoughts turned to his upcoming thirty-day leave. The news that the schedule for the tests was now firm was received with excitement. He could start to plan the rest of his life. "What are our orders, sir?" JD asked.

Brock couldn't help but be pleased with the progress that his two young fliers had made in such a short time. He had been receiving daily telegrams from JD as well as from the Stanford professor. The professor's reports were glowing endorsements of the crew's effort, skill and overall commitment. The reports rang with professionalism on all counts.

"Jones, are you sure we're ready?" Brock probed.

"Yes sir, without a doubt," JD answered.

"Alright then, you men take a forty-eight hour pass this weekend. After which you are to bring that plane over here to Mitchell Field and be ready to do some serious flying for your country. Do you understand JD?"

JD thought he did understand. The old man had said 'well done' and now he was adding substance to his words by offering a weekend pass. "Yes sir I understand, and thank you sir. We'll see you on Monday; and thank you again sir."

"You two stay out of trouble, and keep an eye on your young navigator too. We can't have any complications at this late date, and bring that new plane over here in one piece. Tell Don he better think twice about buzzing this tower."

CHAPTER TWENTY-EIGHT
THE FIRST MISSTEP

FBI Special agent Ted Holbrooke was at the wheel as the car circled the block for a second time. Then a pickup truck began to pull out from a parking spot just a few spaces south of a little hardware store.

Main Street in the small coastal town of Port Washington, Wisconsin was paved, with a single lane of traffic in either direction. There was additional room on both sides for parking. Green parking meters sprouted from the sidewalk in front of each space. The town was busy this morning. The sidewalk was bustling as customers made their way between the numerous stores, offices, and other small businesses that lined both sides of the street. The hardware store was on the west side of the street. It faced a freshly swept sidewalk shaded by a large awning attached to the front of the store. The surface of Lake Michigan's deep blue water could be seen just beyond the buildings across from the hardware store. The bright sun glimmering off the surface of the water added to the picturesque little town. He pulled the car into the vacated parking spot.

His partner was Bob Thorsten. The two had been together for nearly a year working out of the FBI field office located in the Chicago Federal Building. They were assigned to the Midwest

Division of Internal Security. This was a fancy name for chasing down leads on suspected subversive activity that could threaten national security. The two had followed up on hundreds of leads from the public covering a host of topics. Until today not one lead had resulted in anything real. Rather, they had turned out to be merely well intentioned concerns that led to innocent conclusions. Today's road trip had all the ingredients of another exercise along those same lines. So far their efforts hadn't paid many dividends but this was the work the two agents were being paid to do. This was a new case, a fresh start, and who knows, this time they might be able to do some good.

A local resident named Dolans had called the FBI regarding his concern over the sudden disappearance of one of his employees and the employee's wife. There was a twist to his story which drew the attention of the Agent in Charge so he decided to assign his two hardest working agents to interview Mr. Dolans.

Ted felt the front tire nudge the curb. He turned off the ignition. With his left hand he pulled up on the handle setting the parking brake. "Hey Bob, you got any change for the meter?" Ted asked.

Bob was halfway out his door and reaching in his pocket for the change. "Sure, it's my treat."

The two men entered the store and heard the bell over the door announce their presence. An older gentleman with an apron covering his white shirt as well as the upper half of his black trousers came from the other side of a long wooden counter to greet them. The two men were dressed in dark suits which were in stark contrast to the dress of the locals. The man now approaching them was in fact the best dressed person they had seen since leaving the main road and entering the small town.

"Good morning gentlemen, I'm Willard Dolans. How can I help you?"

"I'm Special Agent Ted Holbrook and this is Special Agent Bob Thorsten." They both displayed their FBI credentials.

Mr. Dolans studied the ID with interest. He had never seen an FBI agent before and was impressed that the FBI had come to his little hardware store. "Thank you for coming out so soon. I hope I'm not wasting your time. I know it's a long drive up here."

Bob spoke up first. "Please sir, there's no reason whatever to apologize. This is our job and you were correct in reporting your concerns. Is there somewhere we might talk privately?"

Mr. Dolans started for the door.

"It's nearly lunch time and I was about to close for the noon hour anyway. Let me just put the sign on the door and we can talk here."

He hung the "closed for lunch" sign on the front door, locked it and then turned back toward the agents. He motioned them to a small area at the rear of the store which was also out of view to passersby. The three men found themselves in a makeshift break area with a few wooden barrels arranged around a well-worn card table. A small potbellied stove stood in the corner with a pot of coffee warming on top.

Mr. Dolans grabbed the pot and began to pour coffee into three mismatched cups. "There's sugar right over there and the cream is in the icebox underneath. Make it the way you like it." He pointed to a small counter top just to Ted's right.

"Thank you Mr. Dolans, coffee sounds great." They moved over to the little counter where the sugar bowl was sitting out.

"Please call me Will and find yourselves a seat around the table there." The men fixed the coffee to their liking and all three sat down around the table.

Ted started the interview. "Will, would you mind just repeating your observations and the conclusions you've drawn from them?"

"Well, this young man came in the store several weeks ago. I own this building and for years my family and I lived above the store. We were able to move into a home a few blocks from here about ten years ago. Ever since then I have rented out the space up there for extra income. Well this guy came in, like I said, a few weeks ago in response to the posting for a flat to rent that I had placed that very morning on the public billboard at the courthouse. He said he needed a flat because once he found work his wife would be able to join him and they needed more than just a small apartment. He was a very likeable young man and I took to him right off. As he was explaining his situation I got to thinking that I might be able to help him while at the same time helping myself. You see, my sons who had been working here in the store are both in the service now and as a result, the store is understaffed. I proposed an arrangement whereby I would provide the flat and a small salary in exchange for his help around the store. After all, he needed a place to live and a job. The arrangement fit us both so we agreed."

The two agents had been listening quietly without interrupting Will as he told the story but he seemed to be running out of gas so Bob spoke up. "Will, what is his name?"

"Oh, forgive me, Max, Max Slavina."

"Did he say where he was from?" Bob asked.

"He didn't say because I didn't think to ask at first but, as we began to work together it came out. When I realized they had up and vanished I took a look around the flat and then went to my file to check for clues as to where they might have gone. I still had the list of references Max provided the day I hired him. It had all gone so fast that I never checked him out."

Bob continued asking the questions Ted was now taking notes. "Can we have a look at those references Will?"

"Just a minute, let me see here." He reached his right hand down into his apron pocket and came out with a piece of folded paper. "Here you are agent. This is the sheet he provided."

Bob took the paper and held it so that both he and Ted could see what was written on it.

After taking a minute or two to examine the letter Bob spoke. "It looks like he was working up north in Menominee, Michigan at a fish packing plant of some sort. Before that he worked in Western Canada. Will, do you know if he was an American?"

Will paused as if thinking about his answer. "Well that's part of the issue. He said he was a Panamanian citizen but a couple of locals didn't believe him."

Bob asked, "Why so?"

"It seems that these guys had been down in Panama working on the canal a few years back and had lots of knowledge about the place. When they heard Max was Panamanian they came by to swap stories with him; you know, talk about the place. They told me to be careful with Max because he didn't know the lay of the land, so to speak. Simple things like where particular cities and landmarks were located. They said half the time he didn't have any idea what they were talking about." Will said.

Bob posed another question. His interest was beginning to peak. "Did you challenge Max about their doubts?"

"Sure, but he said they were confused and he didn't find it appropriate to argue with the customers so he just went along with them. I let it go at the time but now it has me thinking."

Bob continued to gently press Will for more. "Can you provide the names of the two men you are referring to and possibly where we might find them?"

"Yes, sure, they both live right up the street very near each other. I've known them for years. They have reputations for being pretty heavy drinkers. I kind of figured that into my original conclusion."

Ted jotted down the names and approximate locations of the two men's residents. The agents would interview them on the way out of town, just to make sure.

Bob continued the interview for several more minutes and learned that Max was a good worker and according to Will, a real asset to the company. The wife was German. This fact was obvious to everyone because of her lingering accent. Being German in Port Washington was as common as a pair of old shoes. Half the population was of German descent. So the wife's German background might not indicate anything sinister. More likely it meant absolutely nothing.

Will told them that on several occasions she too had helped out in the store. She was good with the female customers. More and more had begun coming in on the days when she was scheduled to work. The old man liked her and enjoyed having her around. By his account, she was good looking and carried herself with poise and a good measure of dignity. Ted kept writing, taking down her complete description.

"What was her name?" Bob asked.

"Elsa was her first name but she slipped and told me her last name was Menzel but quickly corrected herself. She made the excuse that getting used to her married name was taking more time than it should." Will's tone gave the impression that he questioned her explanation.

Bob wanted to return to the reason Will had concerns. "So tell me Will, just what raised your concerns anyway? I mean, besides that question of Max possibly not being a Panamanian?"

"Like I said before, I let myself into their flat and had a look around. You know, looking for clues about what happened to them and maybe finding out where they might have gone. When I got in there the whole place was as neat as a pin. I mean it was like nobody ever lived there. However, they had rearranged the furniture to their liking. I went back the next day to put things back the way they had been before. When I repositioned the sofa I found this underneath the corner below where the small end table had been." Will handed Bob a second piece of paper.

It was letter size with the name of a hotel printed at the top. It read, The Drake Hotel Chicago, Illinois. Written on it, in a mixture of English and possibly Chinese or Japanese, were some notes. Bob studied the writing but the only thing he could read was the English. He passed the sheet to Ted.

Ted looked it over and didn't have any better luck. The words he could read were sprinkled throughout the character writing. It was as if the characters necessary to describe the English words didn't exist so the author just plugged in the English words. Ted saw the words "pier", "Greater Buffalo", "Seeondbee", "Navy", "top", "Chicago", "flat", and "teaching". The words were scattered throughout the writing but neither Bob nor Ted could connect any meaning to what they saw.

"What did you make of this Will when you first saw it?" asked Ted.

"Well, Max was a little guy, about five feet, eight inches tall, I'd say a hundred and thirty-five pounds and he looked Mongolian with straight black hair. I think the guy was Japanese."

Will then pointed down at the writing on the piece of paper. "And I bet you, that there is Japanese writing. I'm sure that the English words have something to do with the two old passenger ships that the Navy converted to aircraft carriers."

Both Bob and Ted had knowledge of the USS *Wolverine* and the USS *Sable* but they were unsure as to how the sheet of notes before them translated into a concern about the two carriers. "Will, just how exactly did you make that connection," asked a confused but interested Ted.

"Boys, I thought it would be obvious to the FBI." Will said with a grin that exposed his perfect teeth.

Bob interrupted.

"Come on now Will. We can put together Navy Pier and work out flat top but that's far from a solid connection. Could you fill in the dots for us, please?"

Will's demeanor turned serious before speaking. "Boys, those carriers came right past this shore, and real close-in so all the people could have a look at them when they made their first voyages down the lake to Chicago. The first one came by this way, then about six months later the second one steamed past. Everyone in town went down to the shore to get a look. Heck, we all got pictures. It was a big deal for all the towns on this side of the lake. Don't you see, when they came our way they were newly commissioned. They had been given new names but we knew them by their old names, the *Greater Buffalo* and the *Seeondbee*. They were in these waters for years under their original names. Shoot, most people don't even know the new names now. The other English word in that note is "teaching". Those carriers are for teaching pilots to land and take off from an aircraft carrier at sea. So there you have it. That's why I called the FBI." Will sat back and waited for a response from the agents.

Ted looked over at Bob while not trying to give anything away. Bob didn't look his way instead he asked Will another question. "You didn't happen to check out those references did you?"

Will remained serious as he answered. "Yes sir I did. At both the packing plant and the Canadian company Max left in a hurry. He didn't give notice and he left no forwarding address either. In each case he took off pretty fast. At the packing plant he left a note with the night watchmen."

Ted thought that this time they had something but exactly what, he wasn't sure. He wanted to end the interview and confer with his partner so he decided to ask a closing question. "Will, just one more question for now. Do you have anything to add to what you've told us? You know, maybe something we might have forgotten to ask."

"I don't think those two were married and I'll tell you why I say that. First, she used the wrong name, like I told you before. Then there's the way they were around each other. They weren't like newlyweds, no touching, no cute looks, no spark.

"When I looked in the flat it sure looked to me like someone had been sleeping on the sofa. It was all matted down in the shape of a person's body. One side of the bed was settled while the other side was still full and fluffy. That is the same bed that my wife and I shared for years. I know how that bed is. I'm telling you only one person slept in that bed. If that isn't enough, the guy I talked to at the packing plant told me Max's employment papers said he was single. He started working for me just three days after he left that job and two of those days were the weekend. When would he have had time to get married?"

Before leaving, the two agents asked Mr. Dolans to keep the interview and his concerns a secret. He promised not to discuss the matter with anyone until given the okay from the FBI. Mr. Dolans reopened the store for the afternoon as he let the two agents out the door, promising to remain silent.

Ted pulled the car out onto Main Street heading north. A few blocks up the street a huge church sat atop a hill. The massive structure with its location high above the town dwarfed the other buildings on the street. A set of stone steps led from the sidewalk up to the church. There were at least fifty steps. *A person would need to be in good shape to attend this church.* He turned right just in front of the church onto a side street that led down to the lake. The car slowed and came to a stop along the curb with a view of the water. Ted set the brake and turned the engine off before turning toward his partner.

Bob was the first to speak. "What do you make of his story Ted?

"Well I don't like it at all. If there's any truth to what Will has put together then we have a lot of work to do, and we may not have a whole lot of time in which to do it."

"Yes that's true alright, but what do you think?" Bob rephrased his question. "What I mean is, do you find it plausible, and do you agree with his conclusions?"

"I'm not sure. I would feel better if I knew absolutely that we are looking at Japanese and not Chinese on this note. I think it would send a cold chill down my spine if it were indeed Japanese. It would be almost a certainty that we have a Japanese spy focused on those carriers and maybe the Germans are involved, too."

Bob had an idea. "Start the car. I think I know a way to find out fast if that's Chinese or not. Head back toward that street we were on when we came into town. Just before we made the turn on Main Street, I remember seeing a Chinese restaurant."

Bob turned out to be right. The Chinese restaurant was just off the corner of Main Street and down three buildings. They parked and went inside. Each ordered lunch. Throughout the meal Ted engaged the Chinese waiter in small talk. When he brought the check to the table Ted asked him to look at the characters on the sheet of paper. Ted folded it in such a way as to prevent him from seeing the entire message. The waiter immediately confirmed that the writing was Japanese.

Back in the car, Ted offered a plan of action. "Bob you take the train back to Chicago and I'll stay around and interview the two guys that expressed concerns about Max's claim that he was from Panama. When you get back to the office contact immigrations to see what they can come up with on Max Slavina and Elsa Menzel. Let's find out if there are any records under those names. Check income tax records with the IRS and also compare the names against the list of people of interest that the Director has compiled back in Washington. Contact the Canadians and ask them to interview Max's former employer out in Vancouver. We need to accumulate everything we can dig up and see if we can put together a picture that makes some sense. You better send up a team to go over that flat for fingerprints and anything else they can find. Here, take this note with you and have it translated. Let's find out what was so important that they needed to write it down.

"When finished here, I'll head north to see what I can find out up in Menominee. We'll keep in contact by phone."

The agents agreed on the division of work then Ted drove Bob back down to Milwaukee to catch the train to Chicago. The two agents separated at the train station, each heading in opposite directions.

CHAPTER TWENTY-NINE
INQUIRES

After returning to Port Washington to interview the two former canal workers FBI Special agent Ted Holbrook headed north. The two men had told convincing stories that led him to believe their assessment of Max. Ted concluded that it was likely that Max wasn't from Panama. However, nothing the two men said in any way indicated a Japanese connection.

The agent reached the outskirts of Marinette, Wisconsin just past one o'clock in the morning. Several small motor lodges dotted the highway as he approached the town so he decided to spend the night on the Wisconsin side of the Menominee River and cross over into Michigan the next morning. It had been a very long day and he was tired. A good night's sleep would rejuvenate his mind. He wanted to be at his best for the work ahead. Throughout the long drive north his mind had been in overdrive thinking and rethinking about Max and Elsa. He was tormented by the need to know who they were and what they were up too.

Ted had been a Special agent with the FBI for five years, and before that a police detective with the Gary, Indiana Police Department. All of his training and experience told him there was something to this case. Worry was creeping into his mind. If he wasn't successful in running down Max and Elsa the results would be bad, very bad. The interviews planned for the next day had to draw out information that would be useful in finding the two suspects. Yes, he had come to the conclusion that they were indeed suspects. He suspected them of planning espionage against the United States of America; now he had to prove it. More importantly, he had to find them.

The motel room was small but as clean as his mother's house. After folding his clothes over the only chair in the room he rested his head on the pillow and was asleep before he knew it.

****

By the cover of darkness, Rinehart and Max slipped off the dock and down onto the aft deck of the *Mary Jo* without making a sound or causing the slightest ripple on the surface of the water. The aft deck was only two feet long from the transom to the back of the pilot house. A large doorway nearly as wide as the boat's twelve-foot beam stood open and the men slipped inside, out of view. The fishing boat was approximately forty feet long with all but the aft two feet of its deck covered entirely by a wooden cabin. The pilot house, where they now stood, was high enough for a good-sized man to stand completely erect. There was a lone porthole on each side of the cabin. Each was about a foot in diameter without glass, just openings. The only other windows were at the front of this tall section of cabin. The windows extended from the ceiling eighteen inches down to where they met the ceiling of the forward cabin. The much lower forward cabin covered the remaining length of the boat. It extended from the bulkhead, which separated the pilot house from the forward cabin, all the way to the bow. The helm was mounted on the bulkhead. Through the windows the helmsmen had a good view of the water out over the bow and to both sides.

Sliding the door open, the two men could see that the forward cabin was used for storage. Fishing nets and other equipment filled the long room. Ducking down, they entered the forward cabin, closing the door after them. Concealing themselves as best they could under the nets which covered the floor they prepared for the crew to arrive. The bilge was awash with ten inches of cold, fishy-smelling water. Max felt the icy muck soaking through his pants and shoes. Neither man spoke. They waited in the darkness, each clutching a semi-automatic pistol.

****

Elsa had been in Marinette earlier that day where she stopped to purchase groceries. This had been her second stop after delivering Max to his drop-off location. After crossing the river she drove straight through Menominee, not wanting to risk being seen by someone she had once known. Now she was settled in for the night just a few miles north of her former home, in an overnight tourist camp cabin. In the morning, while continuing the trip north, she would stop two or three more times to complete the necessary shopping; then it would be on to Rapid River. She planned to arrive by early afternoon to insure that enough daylight remained to allow her to locate Rinehart's workshop in the remote Michigan Upper Peninsula wilderness.

The two man crew of the *Mary Jo* came on board at three in the morning and efficiently got the *Mary Jo* underway. Rinehart's plan was to overpower the crew and seize the boat several miles outside of the harbor where their deed would be concealed by darkness and miles of open water. While still motoring down the river the door to the forward cabin slid open. The overhead light was switched on and the first mate stepped inside carrying additional nets. As he started to place the nets in with the rest he was startled to see the two men lying partially exposed among the nets on the floor of the cabin. He quickly recovered.

"What are you doing in here?" He demanded.

Max was nearest to the crewman and he was first to speak. "We've had a few too many beers tonight and..." He was talking as he made his way to his feet.

The first mate took one step back and Max raised his gun while immediately stepping forward while closing the distance between the two. Max tried to take control of the situation. "Don't move and don't make a sound."

With the barrel of the pistol touching the center of his forehead the first mate did as he was told. Rinehart was up on his feet now and quickly stepped past Max and the first mate as he burst into the aft cabin. The captain was at the helm guiding the small fishing boat down the river. Rinehart leveled his gun on the captain and with his other hand reached up and placed a finger to his lips indicating that he didn't want to hear a word out of the captain's mouth.

"Get us out of here. You are taking us across the lake to the Michigan side and we don't expect any trouble out of you two or I promise bad things will happen." Rinehart's statement was meant to make the two men think there would be a happy ending to this frightening situation. It seemed to work. The captain nodded and continued to navigate toward the mouth of the river and the lake beyond.

****

The next morning, Ted Holbrook stopped by the fish packing plant that Max had listed as a reference. There, he learned that Max had been on the job for only a few weeks and by all accounts he was a good employee. According to the paperwork contained in his file, he was single and lived in town. His attendance was excellent and nothing negative had been noted in his file. The letter of resignation left with the night watchmen was there along with a reference letter from the same Canadian company Max had given to Mr. Dolans at the hardware store in Port Washington. Ted asked if he could take the letter of resignation with him and the office manager obliged, eager to help the FBI. Max's personnel file provided his home address. Ted made this his next stop. From Max's former landlady Ted was not able to learn much more of value about Max. He did learn that Max paid in advance, kept to himself, and was neat and very polite. He also took his meals each night at the Up Town Café. Max's room was already occupied by another tenant so going over the room would be fruitless. Ted headed over to the Café.

As Ted entered he could see that the restaurant was very old and the décor was dated. The brass pipes once used to carry natural gas for lighting, before electricity, still crisscrossed the ceiling above the main dining room. The newest thing he could see in the room was a framed portrait of President Roosevelt, Teddy not Franklin. The Agent wondered if this was a political statement of some kind or just an oversight. However, in spite of these observations The Uptown Café appeared to be a very nice establishment, seating about thirty people in wooden unpadded booths as well as at tables all of which were covered with red and white checked table clothes. When Ted arrived it was lunchtime and the place was busy. He took a seat in a booth near the front door and ordered one of the daily specials he had seen written in chalk on a blackboard positioned out front on the sidewalk near the restaurant's entrance.

After finishing his meal, Ted ordered coffee and was now nursing it, stalling until the lunch patrons cleared out of the restaurant. Eventually, the room emptied, leaving two waitresses who were cleaning up and preparing the room for the evening dinner crowd. He got a glimpse of the cook out back in the kitchen. A lady of fifty or so who looked to be the manager was at the cash register going over the receipts from lunch.

Ted stood up next to his booth and in a loud but polite voice said. "Ladies, ladies, could I have your attention?" All three looked up from their work to see Ted holding out his FBI identification.

"I'm Special agent Ted Holbrook with the FBI. May I please have just a few moments to ask you a few questions? I promise it won't take too much of your time."

The room wasn't very large so all four people were just a few feet from each other. The three ladies were drawn to Ted's booth out of curiosity more than anything else. An FBI Agent was something one might read about in detective magazines but actually seeing an FBI agent in such a small out of the way place was extraordinarily rare. The small group gathered around Agent Holbrook while carefully looking him over.

"Ladies, I'm making inquiries about a man named Max Slavina. Do any of you recognize that name?"

They all shook their heads indicating they had never heard the name before. "I understand that he used to come in here regularly to have his dinner nearly every evening for several weeks. That is, until a few weeks ago when he left town."

"What does he look like?" The manager asked.

"Approximately five feet, eight inches tall with dark hair, he's in his late twenties to early thirties. Ring any bells?"

The younger of the two waitresses responded to the description. "That sure sounds like that guy who always sat over there." She pointed in the direction of the booths and tables near the kitchen door. "Come to think of it, I never really waited on him. He always sat in Elsa's section."

"Sure I remember the guy." The other waitress seemed to be concentrating on the booth the younger waitress had pointed out. "He was nice looking but never said much. He would come in every night around the same time and have his dinner. He never seemed to be in a hurry though. Some nights he would hang around for hours drinking tea, keeping to himself. It was like he had nowhere else to go."

The younger waitress offered a different take on the other waitress's observation. "You know, to me it was more like he was waiting for someone to join him but sadly, no one ever did or at least no one I ever saw."

Ted was having a hard time maintaining his concentration. The moment the name Elsa had been mentioned he knew he was on to something. He was trying his best to listen to what was being said while at the same time formulating his follow up questions. A tie in to Elsa right here in the restaurant was important and he needed to be careful.

The ladies continued talking to each other as if he were not around. They were debating if the lonely young man was waiting for someone or just hanging out to be among people for just a little longer before returning to his sad, dark, lonely room. To Ted it appeared that the speculation between the three women might never end, so he eased himself back into the fray.

"This war has been difficult on many relationships, what with so many people being separated. Loneliness is almost as big an enemy as the armies we're fighting against. It's such a shame."

The manager responded. "You are so right. We should be more sensitive to the people around us. I for one, am going to take what you said to heart."

Ted said, "See, some good can come out of this war. We can all do better, you know, try harder to show a little more compassion toward one another." The young waitress felt a tingle move down her spine as she looked at the attractive FBI Agent who was the most sensitive man she had come across in her young life. And, he wasn't wearing a wedding ring either. "You know," continued Ted. "I would really like to meet Elsa maybe she could help me understand Max a little better. When does she come in to work? I would love to meet her and talk about her impressions of Max."

The Manager responded. "Elsa quit her job here and went home."

"Really, when was that?"

The manager answered, "Four weeks, maybe six at the most. I can look it up if you wish."

"That's probably a good idea. I should get the exact date for my report," Ted said in response to her offer and then added. "Where's home, I mean where was she headed?"

The manager thought about it for moment while the others too, seemed to be trying to remember. Soon the manager answered. "Iowa I think, yes I'm sure she said she was returning to Iowa."

"Thank you; that could help. I wonder, did she leave before Max stopped coming in for dinner or afterwards." Ted asked as carefully as he could. The ladies didn't know he was also looking for Elsa and Ted didn't want to let on that he had any prior knowledge of Elsa or her tie in with Max Slavina.

"Let me see, I think he stopped coming in before Elsa quit," the manager said thoughtfully.

The young waitress confirmed the manager's recollection. "That's right, Elsa was here lots of nights after that guy, Max you said, stopped coming around."

The other waitress looked thoughtful before speaking. "That's funny, now that you mention it, she did say she was going back home."

Ted asked, "What's funny about that Miss?"

"Well, I saw her this morning. I was over the river in Marinette. I needed to drop off my other pair of work shoes for heels at the shoe shop. My father knows the shoemaker over there so I take my stuff to him. Well anyway, I was coming out of the shop when I saw her driving through town. I waved but she didn't see me. I had forgotten she was moving back home until you reminded me just now."

"You sure the person you saw was Elsa? I mean, could you have been mistaken. Could it have been just someone who looked like her?" Ted prodded.

"No, it was her alright, same car, and definitely her."

"Which way was she headed, north or south?" Ted asked.

"North, across the bridge, I had to walk north myself and I watched as she crossed the bridge and then turned right. I don't know for sure but it looked like she might be passing through. The main road north is the next light up from where she made the right turn and there's not much out that way except the road leading on into the Upper Peninsula."

"I wonder, can you recall what kind of car Elsa drives?" Ted was beside himself. He couldn't believe Elsa was so close.

"Oh sure, it was a Ford, same car she's always had."

Ted was interested in more but continued his gentle approach. "Just to confirm you weren't mistaken can you describe her car, you know color and style, things like that, anything you can remember?"

"Well, that's easy, its bright blue. I love that color, and all I can add is that it has four doors with a white pin strip along the side. It looks really nice. I always liked it."

Ted followed up. "Did the car have any scratches or scrapes, marks of any kind?"

"No, not that I ever noticed, she always kept it nice and clean. It was a pretty car."

Ted turned to the manager. "Are you in charge of the restaurant ma'am?"

"Yes, my husband and I own the place. He volunteered for the Army as a cook and even though he is nearly too old, they took him. He's a cook at Fort Bragg, loves it. I'm keeping things going while he's away," she answered with a note of pride in her voice.

"That's fantastic. You are to be commended, and your husband. What a great story," Ted responded then asked. "I wonder, could you tell me where Elsa lived."

"No problem there. She rented a room upstairs above the restaurant right next to Lillie's room."

"Who's Lilly?" Ted asked.

"I'm Lilly, Lilly Adams," said the young waitress. "There are three small apartments upstairs. Elsa was in the middle one and I'm in the one on the right. Mrs. Hammond has the other one." She pointed to the manager as Mrs. Hammond.

"Oh, I see, forgive me I didn't allow you ladies to introduce yourselves. I know two of your names now but I don't yet know yours," he said addressing his comments to the remaining waitress.

"My name is Jane Walters and my husband is in Europe. I think France but I'm not sure. I haven't heard from him in three weeks." She was beginning to tear up as Mrs. Hammond reached over and put an arm around her.

Mrs. Hammond came in close and said. "Now don't let yourself start worrying again. Everything will be just fine, trust me, you'll see."

Earlier in the conversation Ted had been trying to play on the women's emotions when he referred to the stress the war had caused among so many Americans. Now he was seeing firsthand that he couldn't have been more accurate. "Jane, if you would like, I could try to find out about your husband. After all, I have some connections in the government. Please let me try," Ted offered warmly.

She composed herself and gave Ted her husband's name, rank and serial number. Ted took down the information promising to do his best to get word to her as soon as possible. "I want to thank you all for being so helpful. I believe I can leave you to your work now and please, forgive me for taking up so much of your valuable time. Mrs. Hammond, might I impose on you to walk me to the door?"

The two waitresses went back to their work as Mrs. Hammond and Agent Holbrook exited the building. Outside, Ted stopped and addressed Mrs. Hammond. "Ma'am, I want to ask you to counsel Lilly and Jane. This is a matter of national security. Nothing said in there can be repeated to anyone ever. Please, I am counting on you to express to the others that they must remain silent about this matter and the fact that I was even here. It is imperative that if any of you come in contact with Max or Elsa the FBI must be contacted immediately. No hint can be given to either one that they are the subject of an FBI inquiry. Can you promise me this?"

"Do I understand you to say that Elsa is somehow involved in whatever it is you're investigating?"

"Yes, that's right. I didn't feel comfortable exposing this information in front of the others but we have good reason to believe that Elsa is involved somehow with what we are investigating. She must not be alerted to our concerns. Can you do this for me and for our country?" Ted was imploring her and she understood his meaning.

"I know that if you could tell me what this is all about you would. But I guess you have your reasons for being so vague. Yes, I will do as you ask and don't worry. If the cat gets out of the bag it will not be because of one of us. I can assure you of that." Mrs. Hammond spoke with conviction and a good measure of resolve.

Ted thought about one more thing. "If I get word on Jane's husband good or bad, I would appreciate it if I could pass what I find to you and you could tell Jane. I'm not good at those types of things."

"Special agent, you are good at such things, believe me. No need to fret I will be glad to tell Jane. If the news is good we can rejoice together. On the other hand, if necessary, who better to comfort her in her time of need?"

Ted had one more question. "By chance, might Elsa's room still be vacant?"

"No, it was rented the very next day after she left. I'm sorry."

CHAPTER THIRTY
THE CHASE

After leaving The Uptown Café, Special agent Ted Holbrook found a pay phone and placed a call to his partner. On the second ring the phone was answered at the Chicago FBI field office. The operator put him through right away.

"Hello, Special agent Thorsten speaking. How may I help you?"

"Bob, its Ted, I'm about finished here. Have you found out anything on your end?"

"Yes I have quite a bit to report," answered Bob.

"Anything interesting that we can use?" asked Ted.

"I think so. Let me go over what I have. Okay let's see...." He fumbled through the papers on his desk before locating the one he wanted. "The Canadians have no record of a Panamanian citizen by the name Max or Maxwell Slavina or anyone with the last name of Slavina entering their country. However, the Mounties, interestingly, were able to confirm that he did indeed work in Vancouver. That part checks out. Some good news, the company he worked for is a military contractor so all employees are required to wear a photo ID. Max was photographed. They're sending us a copy of his picture. It should get here in a few days. I put a rush on it so we'll see how that goes. "They're sending an investigator out to the company to interview anyone who had contact with Max. We'll have a preliminary report tomorrow."

Ted responded, "They probably won't learn much. From what I found out he keeps to himself, not giving much away to anyone."

Bob continued, "Same result with US Immigrations; they have no record of him crossing into the US. So we know for certain that he's in this country illegally. I put out an all-points bulletin two hours ago. We can add the photo to the description we have now when it comes in. "The Panamanians did a quick check and found several males with the name M. Slavina. They're running them all down now. Might take some time to confirm whether or not he's from Panama but I'll stay on it. The last thing I have on Max is that the IRS has never heard of him."

"What about Elsa?" Ted asked.

"She's a US citizen by birth. There's a lot on her. Born in nineteen sixteen, that makes her twenty-eight years old. At the end of the First World War the parents, who are German citizens, were working at the German embassy in Washington DC. According to the information they were registered as domestic help but they could have been anything. In the two years leading up to the war Elsa traveled extensively; going back and forth between the two countries, sharing about the same amount of time in each. At the start of the war the parents returned to Germany but she stayed here."

"There is a social security number issued to an Elsa Menzel. The IRS has her filing taxes for the past three years. Very little income reported, low paying jobs. She's had jobs in Illinois, Wisconsin, and Michigan. I dispatched a team to interview the employers listed on her tax filings. We'll see what they come up with."

"Bob, do you have the names of the employers?"

"Sure, got it right here." This time he found the paper right away.

"Is the Uptown Café on the list?"

Bob read through the list of employers. It was the last one listed. "Yes, here it is."

"She worked there Bob, it's our Elsa alright. That's where she met Max."

"Well now how about that? This is getting interesting." Bob was intrigued and now he could feel his interest beginning to peak.

Ted continued to ask questions from his mental checklist. "What about the list they have in Washington? Does either name appear on that list?"

"No, I just got off the phone with Washington. Neither name appears on the list so as it stands now both are unknown. The team you asked for is on the way up to Port Washington to go over the flat. Hopefully, we can find some prints and match them to someone we have on file but that could take some time. The file contains hundreds of thousands of print cards."

"Have them narrow it down by age. Let's assume Max to be mid-twenties to early thirties and we know Elsa is twenty-eight."

Bob was quick to respond, "Already being done. The boys in Washington are way ahead of us. They're compiling both lists now and pulling the cards. If we get lucky and the team finds some prints we get first priority but it could still take some time."

"Is there anything else Bob? Has anyone been able to translate the note yet?"

"Yes, and it looks bad. That guy Dolans was right on the mark. The note contained information relating specifically to the two carriers. It lists when they depart, which carrier moves out first, when they return, the docking procedure and where they go. There also is a lot of detail on the recent activity taking place at night when they are moored at Navy Pier. Max is all over those ships. People here are convinced that something's up."

Ted was thinking about all of this new information when he asked. "You have anything else of interest?"

"I checked with the Department of Motor Vehicles in Michigan, Illinois, and Wisconsin for any vehicles that might be registered under Max Slavina or Elsa Menzel. We got a hit in Michigan for Elsa. She owns a Ford. I have an APB out on the car."

"Good work Bob. I have solid information that the car and Elsa were spotted this morning heading north out of Menominee. It's a Ford alright, bright blue, four door sedan with a white pin stripe running down the side. Add that to your broadcast."

"Ted, that's a real break in the case, the first one. What else did you find out up there?" Bob asked with the first sign of excitement in his voice.

Ted spent the next few minutes filling Bob in on all the details of his interviews that day. When he had finished they both agreed that Ted would follow Elsa's car and head north in the morning, checking hotels, restaurants, stores, any place that she might have been seen.   Bob would call the police and all ferry boat operators in Mackinaw putting them on alert for the car and Elsa. Ted planned to inform the police in Menominee to be on the lookout for her if she tried to leave the state via Wisconsin. For now, his plan was to catch her himself or trap her in the Upper

Peninsula of Michigan. Bob would follow up on the information coming in from the various inquires he had underway. They agreed to talk by phone again at noon the next day.

Ted made one final request of Bob. "I have some information on a soldier fighting in Europe. His wife hasn't had any word from him in several weeks. The poor thing is out of her mind with worry. Could you check him out for me? I gave my word to make the effort."

"Not a problem, I'll get right on it. Give me what you have on him."

"Thanks Bob I appreciate it." He passed the details to Bob after which he headed over to the police station to arrange for someone to monitor the bridge leading south into Wisconsin.

Ted was up early the following morning. He traveled north along the two lane road that took him into the Upper Peninsula of Michigan. Summer cottages dotted the shoreline. The occasional gas station, general store, seasonal motel and restaurants were the only other evidence of human habitation. This made Ted's job much easier. He was able to stop at every business establishment with a degree of confidence that none would be overlooked.

It wasn't long before he picked up Elsa's trail. She had spent the night in a tourist cabin which overlooked the lake. It was no more than ten miles north of the border. Elsa was already long gone by the time Ted arrived. She had paid for the room when checking-in and no one remembered seeing her leave. To his disappointment, the room had already been cleaned. It was likely that any clues left behind by Elsa had been removed or wiped away. He took the key anyway and carefully looked over the room but there was nothing of interest inside. He returned the key, got in his car and headed north. Although frustrated that she was gone he was encouraged by the fact that Elsa couldn't be too far ahead of him.

Ted had no idea how much of a lead Elsa actually had but it appeared to be just a few hours. He moved north, stopping at several businesses, but no one remembered seeing the car or the girl. He continued traveling for about twelve miles. The road turned to the northeast as the pursuit continued. Thick forests of birch trees grew out of the sandy soil lining both sides of the road. There were no intersecting roads, nothing but trees and more trees. As the road curved a small restaurant appeared on his right. He rolled to a stop and went inside where he got his second hit. The waitress confirmed that a woman matching Elsa's general description had been in for breakfast. The waitress reported that Elsa was wearing blue slacks with a light blue blouse, and carrying a large black purse. Also, she said that the lady hadn't eaten very much, leaving most of the food on her plate. No one had gotten a look at the car. Nonetheless, Ted was confident that it had been Elsa. According to the waitress she spent about thirty minutes having her breakfast before leaving, still heading northeast. Based on the approximate time of her departure Ted estimated that Elsa had a three hour lead on him.

Just a few miles up the road from the restaurant Ted pulled into the parking lot of a small general store. There, to his surprise, the clerk reported that a woman matching Elsa's description, right down to the large black purse, had been in the store. After spending a half hour shopping she left with four bags of groceries and a box containing household cleaning supplies, bug killer, candles and stick matches.

"Can you remember anything else about her, description of the car, anything like that?" Ted asked the clerk before getting back on the road after Elsa.

The clerk was a man around fifty or so and didn't need to think about Ted's question very long.

"It was a blue Ford. I carried her bags out to put them in her trunk. There wasn't much room left in the trunk so two of the bags had to go on the back seat. That car was already stuffed with grocery bags before I put mine in there."   Ted thanked the clerk for his help and again headed north, now only two and a half hours behind his prey. Ted gave back the thirty minutes with stops at the next five establishments he came to. None of the people at these businesses reported seeing Elsa or the car. Ted quickly got back on the road after each interview.

A few miles outside of the small community of Escanaba Ted pulled in to purchase gas, and ask around about Elsa. The gas station attendant remembered her. She had purchased gas and asked to use the ladies room. Ted showed his FBI identification; in return, he was handed the key to the ladies room. A careful look around the small very neat room indicated nothing of interest. He dumped the trash can out in the sink and rummaged through papers of all kinds, candy wrappers, paper cups, two soda bottles and a few unmentionables but without discovering any clues.

Ted approached the attendant handing him back the key. "Sir, I need you to keep the door to the ladies room locked. Don't let anyone in there, and don't you go in either. I'm conducting a government investigation. We will be sending up a team to go over that room. You can give the key to them."

"When will this happen, I mean, how long will it be locked up?" asked the attendant.

"I hope to get them up here as early as tonight. They're close by on another assignment. We'll do everything we can to make it fast." answered Ted.

"You want to use my phone to call and arrange it?" offered the attendant.

"Thanks, if you don't mind, that would be a big help. Say, by the way is my watch right? I have one forty-five, what do you have?"

The attendant pulled out his pocket watch and flipped it open. "You're close enough, I got one forty-seven."

The attendant directed Ted to the phone. Ted placed his noon call to Bob, albeit a little late. After expressing his concern over the lateness of the call Bob took down the location of the gas station and agreed to make arrangements for the team to proceed directly to this new location after finishing with the flat in Port Washington. Bob was excited to learn that Ted was hot on the trail and didn't keep him on the phone very long.

Ted pulled out heading northeast. From the attendant he learned that Elsa spent over an hour going back and forth from her car to the ladies room. When returning the key she inquired where the nearest drug store could be found. The attendant confirmed that the lady seemed a bit under the weather.

The drug store was ten miles away in the small downtown shopping district of Escanaba. Ted headed straight there without stopping at the businesses in between the gas station and the drug store. He was taking a calculated risk operating under the assumption that Elsa wasn't feeling well and would seek relief before anything else.

Sure enough, Ted was proven right when the pharmacist confirmed that Elsa had been in the drug store less than an hour ahead of Ted's arrival. The pharmacist had waited on Elsa and was able to tell Ted that she had a severely upset stomach with cramping and a painful head ache. His diagnosis was female problems. He prepared the medicine he felt would solve the problem and she went on her way.

"About when did she leave the store?" asked Ted.

"Oh, I'd say not more than forty-five minutes ago," responded the pharmacist.

Ted was back on the road without a moment's delay, this time on a hot trail. On a hunch that she would have no reason for stopping in Escanaba, Ted drove through town without stopping. Ted reasoned that since Elsa hadn't known where to find a drug store it followed that she didn't have prior knowledge of the area. By following that logic she wasn't headed for Escanaba; more likely she was driving through, going somewhere else.

He continued to analyze what he knew so far from his day of tracking Elsa. It was obvious that she had no idea that she was being followed. After all, she was leaving a trail of breadcrumbs that a child would have no trouble following. She had a destination; that was for sure. Based on her purchases the place needed to be cleaned and there were bugs. That could mean the woods, a cabin in the woods that hadn't seen a woman in a long time. But the whole area was nothing but woods for hundreds of miles in all directions. Small isolated cabins were everywhere. He tried to remain positive. The food was interesting. From what he could tell, she had enough food for one person to hole-up for months. Two or three or even four could hole-up for weeks. It was mid-afternoon with four or five hours of daylight remaining. Ted decided to drive through the next small population center, the town of Gladstone, Michigan. Sticking with his train of thought, Elsa would have no need to stop, but he was wrong. He gambled that she would drive right on by and continue northeast. In Gladstone, Ted drove through town slowly, not stopping but searching for the car, just in case. But the blue Ford with a white pinstripe wasn't there. He slowly made his way along Main Street looking in all directions for the blue Ford. He had no way of knowing that Elsa was at the far end of town tipping the bag boy after he placed the last of her grocery purchases in the car. Soon, she was back on the highway, now no more than three or four miles ahead of her pursuer.

Ted decided to continue driving until five o'clock. At that point he would start checking restaurants, motels and tourist camps again. By then, she would be hungry or too sick to continue. He had been driving very fast since leaving Gladstone and should be no more than a half hour behind. He would find her; maybe even tonight. He had no way of knowing that she was just a few minutes ahead of him.

Following the map she had memorized two nights earlier in the truck stop restroom Elsa turned off the highway and headed southeast. She was working her way to the eastern shore of the large bay south of Rapid River. The road turned from pavement to asphalt but soon the asphalt ended and only dirt remained beneath the tires of Elsa's Ford. The car rolled steadily but slowly on toward a second turnoff which would take her even deeper into the uninhabited woods. After covering more than six miles Elsa spotted the next turnoff. This much narrower road was no more than a wide path with only two tire ruts. High weeds grew between the ruts and rubbed the undercarriage of the car creating an eerie sound, breaking the stillness around her. Tall trees lined both sides of the road growing just inches from either side. The branches overhead obscured the sun, turning the road into a dark, cold tunnel. Slowing down now to less than five miles an hour, she kept a careful lookout for the landmarks indicated on the map etched in her mind. She checked them off one by one as they passed. The first one she came to was a culvert which carried water from a brook guiding it safely under the road. Then the second landmark came into view. A long abandoned and nearly dilapidated farm house stood on the left with a maple tree growing through the front porch roof. The white paint which covered the wooden siding of the building's exterior had long ago given way to the elements. Greenish-gray mold now took its place and the gutters along the massive porch's roof had all manner of vegetation sprouting from them. It was just as she had pictured it. She drove on even slower. *I'm close now, yes there's the final landmark.* Elsa's concentration intensified. What little sunshine remained was now nearly gone. *It seems as though nightfall is coming much too soon. I must find that entrance.* Her mind was permeated with thoughts of what she would do if she missed the entrance. Then Elsa saw it on the right. Filled with relief, she eased the car on and then up the long neglected and nearly invisible driveway.

At a little past five, Elsa parked the car in front of the garage, stopping several feet from its double-hung doors. She left the motor running, took the car out of gear and set the parking brake. Stepping from the car with the door key from the envelope in one hand and a box of matches in the other, she walked along the side of the broken down cabin until reaching the side door. The woods were quiet. The only sounds being the Ford's motor smoothly idling behind her and a few birds chirping in the nearby trees. She slipped the key into the old padlock. It fit the lock and turned easily.

Taking off the lock and swinging the hasp out of the way she pushed the door open and stepped inside. The interior of the cabin was dark. Elsa lit one of her long wooden matches. Holding the match above her head a large room came into view. She stepped inside further until she was standing in the large room. Beyond the far end of the room in which she now stood the garage was faintly visible by the light of the match. Carefully, she moved forward in the direction of the garage. There was no doorway into the garage. It was more like a continuation of the big room. Elsa walked slowly toward the garage then stepped down onto its dirt floor. The garage was completely empty. There were no tools hanging on the walls, no work bench, absolutely nothing was in there. Elsa headed for the big double doors. Standing just in front of the doors she lit a second match. The light revealed a long, thick wooden beam running across both doors. It was held in place by four support brackets which were mounted to the doors. These brackets held the beam in place, which in turn kept the doors tightly closed. She carefully took hold of the massive wooden beam and tried to lift it. It was very heavy, causing her to struggle but she managed to get it off the brackets and on the floor. She dragged it over and left it against the side wall. Elsa returned once again to the doors and leaned her shoulder firmly against one of the doors. She began to push as hard as she could. It grudgingly began to swing out, flattening the tall grass on the other side as it went.

Light filled the room. Cobwebs hung from the rafters and clung to the doors and walls. The place was filthy. Grass had grown high and thick along the outside of the cabin and now it was wedging the bottom of the door. No matter how hard she pushed it refused to budge any further. Elsa squeezed her way through the small opening between the doors. Now standing outside she took hold of the edge of the door with both hands and struggled to pull it open. Yanking and pulling all the way, the door finally stood open. She moved to the other door and did likewise. This one was even more difficult to budge but it eventually began to move. In her weakened condition it had taken nearly all of her strength to force the doors open wide enough to allow the car to pass through.

Soon, the car was safely concealed inside the building with the doors closed and the beam back in its place. Elsa took the time to return to the driveway and kick the tall grass in front of the doors back up as straight as she could in an effort to erase any trace of her presence. She entered the cabin, again from the side door, closing it behind her and bolting it from the inside. By the light of another long match she made her way back to the garage.

Confident that no one had been following, Elsa felt safe. The medicine wasn't helping. She craved rest but the cabin was absolutely filthy. Elsa climbed back in the car and lay down on the front seat. Tonight she would sleep in the car. Tomorrow she would deal with the dirt. When Elsa closed her eyes, she was asleep.

Unknowingly, Ted drove past the road which only moments before Elsa had taken south. He continued on the main highway which by this time had turned due east toward the Straights. At five o'clock he began stopping at the various business, checking for Elsa. By seven-thirty it became apparent that Elsa might have driven straight through toward Mackinaw or more likely, she turned off somewhere back along the road behind him. He retraced his path checking at every business along his back trail until he stopped at a small store on the northeastern end of Gladstone. The store was closed but lights were on inside. He banged hard and loudly on the door until a young man took notice and walked over to the door.

"We're closed!"

Ted placed his FBI credentials up against the glass. "Open the door, official government business."

"What? The store is closed. I'm just cleaning up, can't sell you anything tonight. You'll have to come back in the morning.

"FBI, open that door now!" Ted yelled through the glass.

"Yes sir." The young man promptly swung the door open and stepped out of Ted's way.

Ted was inside standing close to a tall, thin, high school-aged boy. "I'm looking for an attractive woman, mid-twenties, blond hair, blue slacks and blue blouse with a nice figure."

"Really... me too." The kid responded as if he had been waiting his whole life for just such an opportunity to use that line. Ted had to give it to the kid, he was quick and his response made Ted almost laugh out loud.

"Well funny man, have you seen her?" The kid began to laugh and so did Ted. Ted composed himself. "Well, have you?"

"Yes, she was here."

Ted couldn't believe it. Maybe he still had a chance to find her. "Alright, that's good. When was this, what time?" Ted asked.

"We close at six. I'd say about two hours before closing time, maybe four maybe four-fifteen. Yeah, right about then, no sooner that's for sure."

"Help me out here, how is it that you're so sure it wasn't any earlier?" Ted followed up.

"I start at four but today I got here a little before starting time so I went out on the floor to bag groceries. I wanted to pick up some extra tip money. I was bagging for Mrs. Fairchild and Mrs. Erickson when I saw the good looking blond get in line to check out. I took her bags out to the car and she gave me fifty cents. She had it all, good looks, nice personality and money, hard to forget her."

"Thanks, I wonder what you can tell me about the car."

"Ford, four door, and blue I think."

"Was there anything about the car that you noticed; you know, anything that stood out, anything in the car?"

"The car was full. I mean full of food and supplies, lots of grocery bags."

"Did she say anything to you? Was she in good spirits?"

The young man took a moment before responding. "She thanked me and said that it was a big help because she wasn't feeling all that well. She really appreciated my help, things like that. Then she gave me the half dollar and said, 'see you later'."

"Which way did she go?" Ted asked.

"She went straight out of town, that way." He pointed northeast.

"Anything else you can remember?"

"She had blue eyes."

"Thanks for your help. Sorry I had to disturb your work. Your information has been useful thanks again."

Standing in the parking lot of the small store Ted was coming to grips with the fact that he had lost her. "She's got to be somewhere between here and the spot where I turned around. But where is she? "

   With nothing more to be done that night a discouraged Ted Holbrook got in his car, drove a block down the road to the nearest motel and rented a room. It was late and he was tired. In the morning he would call in and report the bad news.

CHAPTER THIRTY-ONE
THE CALM BEFORE THE STORM

At JD's insistence, Gary Waters reluctantly agreed to tag along with JD, Don and Sandy Granger. Sandy was Don's date and she still had no interest in becoming an officer. Her interest, it would soon be discovered, was in having fun; and she was good at it. Sandy was from Oklahoma and had joined the Army a year earlier looking for adventure. Until now she hadn't found much but being with an officer like Don on a forty-eight hour weekend pass was exactly what she had had in mind.

The little group pulled up in front of Annie's home at eight o'clock Saturday morning. Annie was ready and waiting on the front porch when the Jeep came down the Street. With a spring in her step, a big smile on her face and carrying a basket of food in her right hand, she stepped down from the porch heading for the Jeep parked at the curb. Watching as she approached, both Don and Gary were impressed.

Don was the first to speak. "Man she's a real dish, you've got good taste buddy."

Gary didn't say anything; instead he just watched Annie as he vacated the passenger's seat to squeeze in the back with Sandy and Don. JD hopped out of the driver's seat and came around the other side of the Jeep. With a kiss and a smile he helped her get in the front seat.

"Good morning," said JD in a gentle voice.

"Good morning to you Joseph. I have towels and blankets for everyone on the porch."

"I got it," Gary said.

He jumped out of the back and retrieved the pile from the stoop then climbed back in the Jeep.

"Here, can you find a place for this?" Annie passed her large picnic basket to JD.

"No problem," JD said.

He wasn't sure where to put it. The Jeep was small with barely room for the passengers. But Jeeps were innovative little warriors. JD found room on the back bumper next to the spare gas can. He rested the basket on the bumper and tied it on between the gas can and Sandy's basket which had made the ride from Willow Run intact.

When everyone was settled JD made the introductions then started the engine and put the transmission in gear. "Which way do I go to get there?" JD asked.

"Belle Isle is south, straight down Van Dyke till you reach Jefferson Avenue but we need to make a stop first. Go straight and turn right at the first street." Annie answered while pointing up the street.

JD asked Annie where they were going but he already knew. When Annie was told that Gary would be coming along she immediately decided that he needed a date. JD thought that this was a great idea but with Gary being so young JD made the decision to spring it on him at the last minute, to prevent him from making an excuse and ducking out on the day's activity.

JD had been given a direct order to keep Gary out of trouble. This he couldn't do if Gary and he were separated; and nothing was going to prevent him from spending as much time with Annie as he could manage. He wasn't heartless so he made Annie promise to select a date based on all the right criteria to insure that Gary would be thankful for his decision, even with the deception.

The Jeep turned right and then left before Annie directed JD to stop in front of a home just a few blocks over from Annie's.

"What's here?" Don asked.

JD answered Don's question while turning to look at Gary. "Gary, your companion for the day lives here."

Gary said, "Really?" But he didn't seem upset or even that surprised. Gary got out and asked, "What's her name?"

Everyone looked at Annie. "Her name's Tiffany, Tiffany Marino. I went to school with her from first grade all the way through high school. She's a dear friend, and very sweet."

"Great," said Gary. "Any friend of yours is fine with me." Gary started to walk up to Tiffany's door without as much as a moment's hesitation. He turned and said. "Here goes, I hope she likes me."

JD looked at Don and stated more than asked, "You told him didn't you? Nobody's that cool under fire."

"I had to sir. He needed to know, but don't worry. He told me he's had a date... once."

Annie started to laugh, JD smiled, Don seemed relieved and Sandy said. "Don't worry he's as cute as a button. She'll love him."

Don thought, *I wasn't worried about her I was worried about him;* but he let it go.

Gary was in the house for a few minutes before he and Tiffany came out the front door smiling and making small talk. She was five feet two with a petite figure and a very pretty face.

Gary escorted her to the Jeep where he introduced her to the group. "You know Annie of course. Say hi to Don and this is Sandy. She's with Don and this is our leader JD."

"Hello everyone; thanks for inviting me along. I haven't been to the beach all summer. This is so nice of all of you. If you like, you can call me Tiff." Everyone greeted her warmly, relieved that she and Gary had gotten off to such a positive start. Tiff seemed like a nice girl and she and Gary appeared to be equally pleased with each other.

With Tiffany's basket tied to the front fender and the three borrowed beach umbrellas secured to the side of the Jeep, the band of fun seekers were off for a day at the beach. The three young couples were packed in tight for the half hour drive to Belle Isle.

The island is located in the middle of the Detroit River and can be reached by the bridge that connects it to the mainland. The entire island had long ago been transformed into a vast city park. JD couldn't believe his eyes as they crossed the bridge and followed the road to the right. The first thing he saw was a very large fountain with water spewing up and cascading down in all directions. People were already out en masse enjoying the warm summer morning. Everywhere he looked the grounds were manicured like the gardens of an English estate with flowers of all kinds and colors. Driving past the fountain the Jeep followed the road in a gentle arc leading them across the middle of the island's western end. Winsor, Ontario, Canada could be seen across the river. They continued driving past the Casino building which housed a large combination dance floor and roller rink. Next, the glass covered conservatory with even more gardens came into view. Numerous memorial statues dotted the landscape. Next, they drove past a large indoor aquarium. Just a short distance beyond the aquarium was the entrance to the zoo.

The road curved around, taking them back in an easterly direction along the southern shoreline. There were streams and ponds on both sides of the road with couples and families leisurely paddling rented canoes through the labyrinth of scenic canals. In the nearby woods, people could be seen riding horses or walking the paths that honeycomb the interior of the island like a giant spider web. There were handball and tennis courts, baseball and cricket fields, picnic grounds and even a golf course.

The group tried to take in as many of the island's attractions and its scenic beauty as they could. Eventually, they reached the eastern end of the island. The road turned to follow the northern shoreline with a view of downtown Detroit ahead on their right. Soon they would be at the beach.

Tiffany and Sandy saw the deer at the same time and both let out a scream. "Look, look, see that?" yelled Sandy.

They all quickly looked to their left to see a small herd of about twenty deer standing in a clearing near the road. The largest buck had a huge, fully developed twelve-point rack. A rack of that size is rare but the most astounding thing was that he was an albino. As the rest of the herd was brown, the leader was pure white with big pink eyes.

Annie was the first to speak. "You know for years we've heard a rumor that there was an albino buck on Belle Isle but no one has ever been able to get a picture of him.

Don reached down between his legs and pulled the draw string on his bag revealing a Kodak Brownie box camera. "Stop the

Jeep. Today we make history." Don aimed the camera, holding it steady for a moment then he pressed the lever and heard the shutter click. "Got it, just a moment, stay right here and I'll take one more for good measure." He turned the crank on the side of the camera advancing the film then looked through the view finder. "There, got him again." Don said obviously pleased with himself.

Everyone was excited about the start to their day. Annie speculated, "I bet that picture would make the papers if Don wanted to share it."

Tiffany said, "I kind of feel like it might be better if the pictures were never made known. After all the speculation about the white deer would end once the pictures get published. The legend which is so much a part of Detroit's local folklore would be gone forever."

Sandy offered," I think that people really don't want to know the truth. Most people just enjoy talking about things like this more than proving them."

And so the conversation continued until they reached the parking lot at the beach. They were all having fun, being together, laughing, and enjoying the start of a lovely day. The war seemed so far away that they had forgotten about it if just for a little while.

The girls found a picnic table in the shade of a large elm tree. They immediately staked their claim covering it with a table cloth and placing the baskets on top. With this done, they headed for the large stone bathhouse to change.

Meanwhile, the guys headed straight for the beach where they found a sunny and secluded section of sand. They drove the umbrella poles deep in the sand and spread the blankets and towels under each. With their work done for the day it was off to the bathhouse.

Don, Gary and JD stood outside the bathhouse having changed into their government issued swim trunks with numbered keys to their rented baskets attached to their wrists. At the end of the day their clothes and valuables would be waiting for them safe and sound stored in the baskets inside of the bathhouse.

Annie was the first to exit the ladies side. She was in a one piece white bathing suit. JD got his first look at her legs. They were long and slender. He was more than pleased with the image he saw before him. Sandy and Tiff followed right behind. Both were stunning in their swim suits as well. Sandy had on a dark blue strapless number that accentuated her broad, slender shoulders and Tiff looked like a little doll in her yellow suit with a black stripe down one side. The three couples paired up and headed for the beach.

Annie held JD's hand as they walked toward the sand. The Detroit River showed only a slight chop and the waves were no more than two or three inches high as they lazily rolled ashore. JD's thoughts shifted to his Pacific island where he had spent endless days looking out at *Wildcat* and the beach with its breaking surf.

"You know Annie, I was thinking of the island out there in the Pacific and the rolling surf I saw every day. This is so much nicer. Having you by my side, holding your hand and feeling so carefree is like a dream come true. What I mean is, that island in the Pacific was a beautiful place, difficult under the circumstances yes, but beautiful. But you make this the most wonderful place in the world... I just wanted you to know that." JD said.

She let go of his hand and put her arm under his arm just the way she had at the train station the first time they met; but this time she nestled in close to his side. "I was thinking too. Don and Gary are nice guys and I am enjoying this day with all of us together more than you can imagine. I've been to Belle Isle many times but being here with you somehow has me feeling like this is really the first time I've truly seen this place. My time with you makes me feel that way. It's like I started really living the moment I saw you for the first time." Annie said.

The day started just like that. It couldn't have been better.

Gary and Tiff didn't stop talking all morning. They were getting to know each other in an easy sort of way. Don was doing all he could to keep up with Sandy. She was the first in the water and the last out. Her energy level was much higher than that of the others. JD and Annie were in love.

By noon they all had too much sun so they took a break for lunch in the shade of the mature elm tree which towered high above the picnic table.

The girls enthusiastically began opening their baskets and proudly arranged the food on the table. There was fried chicken, hot dogs, potato salad, baked beans, sliced tomatoes, potato chips and ice cold Coca-Cola. Sandy brought candy and apple pie.

The group agreed that it would be best to stay out of the sun for a while. They all went back to the bathhouse where the girls retrieved shorts, tops and sandals. The guys put on their olive green undershirts and shoes. Hand in hand the three couples crossed the street and found themselves in a meadow that led to the trees.

Soon Don was alone. Sandy had wondered off in the woods and Don's calls to her went unanswered. "Where's Sandy?" Tiff asked when Don appeared from out of the woods all alone.

"I don't know. She was there then she was gone. I called to her but she didn't answer." Don looked bewildered and confused.

They all started for the woods spreading out to cover more ground. After fifteen minutes of searching JD was starting to get worried. He had orders to stay out of trouble but it seemed that trouble had found him. Then they heard hoof beats that sounded like the Seventh Calvary was coming toward them. Sandy burst out of the woods at a full gallop atop a large black horse with a white patch down the center of its face. She held the reins in her left hand and with her right she held a tight grip on the reins of five more horses.

"I got us some horses. Come on, we can see more of the island on horseback then on foot. The big white one's yours JD. He's the boss just like you. Don you take the red one he's the fastest one they had. Gary, I found that beautiful Quarter Horse for you. Tiff and Annie, I brought you guys the two little Pintos. Now hurry up, take them. They nearly pulled my arm off." Sandy said nearly out of breath.

Don just shook his head. "She's from Oklahoma."

"Thanks Sandy but for the love of Mike girl, we were all worried that something happened to you." JD said.

"There's no reason to worry about me. I've been riding horses all my life. I can handle any horse you can put a saddle on." Sandy responded while flipping her head back sending her lovely red hair out of her face and back to its natural position flowing over her shoulders and down her back.

JD was speechless. He was astonished that Sandy had no idea what he was talking about. He and Sandy were on two completely different subjects. He looked to Don for help.

Don was fixated on Sandy sitting atop her horse. *Man, she's absolutely the most beautiful thing I have ever seen. With that gorgeous face all flushed and those big eyes literally sparkling; all I can think about is that she is fascinating in a wild sort of way, and I feel pretty darn good about it.* He soon noticed that JD was looking at him.

"Come on man. Don't look at me like that. Heck I just met her, but isn't she something?"

Tiff spoke up as she mounted her little Pinto. "Are you sure we can take these horses off the bridle path; after all, nobody else can."

Sandy smiled. "Don't worry about a thing. I showed the stable hand my dog tags and told him I was with two Generals from the Calvary who wanted to ride around the island on horseback. He gave them to me, so I wouldn't worry about it."

"Which of us are the generals?" JD asked sarcastically as he adjusted himself in the saddle of the big white Stallion.

Sandy laughed out loud. "Don't be silly, Tiff and Annie of course."

JD and Sandy were experienced riders but the rest of the group had never been in a saddle and it showed. But soon they all had a good feel for the horses and were riding like the experienced horsemen they were supposed to be. Sandy had been right. Exploring the island's attractions on horseback proved to be a memorable experience. Everywhere they went, the Zoo, the conservatory, the fountain, they would tie the horses out front. Children and adults alike came over to pet the animals or take pictures beside them. It was fun and exciting. The presence of the horses seemed to bring out the best of everyone while adding something special to the day's activities for all involved.

By five o'clock the horses were tired and hungry so the girls returned them to the stable after which the three couples found themselves back at the picnic table. Everyone was hungry so it was time to take a second run at the baskets of food. This meal was far less formal than lunch had been. Instead of the girls setting the table and serving the guys, this time they all stood around the table peeking in the various baskets taking this and that; talking, laughing, and eating. The girls had packed more than enough food for everyone to relieve their hunger and then some. With all satisfied, the guys repacked the Jeep while the girls retreated to the bathhouse to shower and dress. Don, JD and Gary cleaned up and once again were outside waiting for the girls to appear. The sun was setting over the city when all three couples were finally reunited outside the bathhouse.

Tiff was walking between Sandy and Annie as they exited the bathhouse with her eyes on the three young men in uniform standing together about fifty feet down the sidewalk. "Sandy, Annie, please stop for a minute." They all come to a stop on the sidewalk, Sandy and Annie both looked to Tiff.

Tiff spoke in a low voice. "Look at those guys. They are so gorgeous in those uniforms and they have been so sweet. I can't describe how I feel except to say that I love this day. Do you know what I'm trying to say?"

Annie took a stab at a response. "No doubt, I've never seen anything that looks as good as JD does right now. I'm sure you two feel the same way about Don and Gary, as you should. After all, they have been tender and kind every moment they're with us. It doesn't hurt that they're all so doggone good looking too. You know girls; the war has forced us all to grow up faster than we might have under more normal circumstances. Somehow we need to find a way to understand the responsibility thrust upon young men like our three. They are away from home, in the military, and being asked to fight and die for an idea. They have to live in the now because they might not have a future. It could be taken from them at any moment. I am in love with JD. I wasn't looking for love. It wasn't a priority for me. Actually it was the furthest thing from my mind. Nevertheless the moment I saw him I knew. Isn't it strange how that could happen?"

Sandy said, "I played up to Don because he is an officer and I was looking for excitement but I sure got more than I was bargaining for. What a guy he turned out to be. No matter what I say, and I can say some things that don't come out the way I intended, he never lets it bother him. He is the kindest man I have ever known."

"That's what I was trying to say," said Tiff. "Gary is different somehow, like being with a man not a boy, yet he's so young. War causes us to grow up, see things in the now for what they are right now with little thought for the future. God help me but this has been the best day of my life. I feel grown up."

Coming from the Casino building the sound of big band music lofted overhead. The evening's dance party was already starting. JD said, "I'm not much of a dancer but that music sounds inviting what say we go dancing?"

"You bet," said Sandy. "That's for me, let's do."

They all piled in the little Jeep and headed for the music.

CHAPTER THIRTY-TWO
SUNDAY

Autumn was beginning to show signs that it would soon replace summer in the Upper Peninsula. The morning dew was thick and there was a cold breeze blowing in from the north. Elsa stood outside in the high weeds. *"Once upon a time this surely had been a lovely yard leading from the cabin down to the water.* She shifted her gaze to the still water of the bay while sipping a mug of hot tea. *I wish this tea could settle my stomach. The queasiness has stayed far longer this time than during past episodes. The cramping is nearly gone but I'm not completely over the sickness. This whole trip to this filthy, God forsaken, hellhole of a place has drained all my strength.* As she took in her complete surroundings a final thought entered her mind. *Perhaps under different circumstances I would have enjoyed time away from the world I know and I might have even found something nice about this place... but I doubt it.*

Max and Rinehart had delivered the *Mary Jo* just hours earlier and the boat was now safely tucked away in the boathouse with the door lowered behind it. In the darkness, they had found the inlet along the shoreline by the light of the blue lantern Elsa had hung atop the pole which had been positioned at the mouth of the slit for that very purpose.

The two men were asleep now and Elsa wouldn't bother them until nightfall. The work would begin in earnest tonight and she wanted to be able to do her part, but she still felt weak all over. She would spend her Sunday trying to rest and gather strength for the work ahead.

Looking out at the bay, she was thankful for the impossibility of seeing anything below the surface because under the water, out in the vastness of the lake, was the crew of the *Mary Jo*. When she closed her eyes they were there. Elsa needed rest but how could she, she was living a nightmare. The pain in her stomach was worse now. The cup in her hand turned bottom up. The remaining tea emptying onto the weeds at her feet, she turned and walked back to the cabin.

****

At ten o'clock Sunday morning at FBI headquarters in Chicago, Agents Ted Holbrooke and Bob Thorsten sat on one side of a long conference table. Across from them were two more agents and the Agent in Charge of the Chicago office. Ted gave his report first. The group listened without interruption. Next Bob shared the results of his portion of the investigation. Again everyone just listened. This was the first time any of the three newcomers to the case had had an opportunity to learn the details of Ted and Bob's activity. When they both finished the Agent in Charge spoke up.

"Thanks for coming in on Sunday gentlemen. I know you've all been working long shifts but I've got a sense that we have cause for concern on this one and time is of the essence," said Barry Coil the Agent in Charge.

The four agents took in what he said without responding verbally. There was really not much to be said. To a man they were in agreement that Max and Elsa were an obvious threat. Their task today would be to lay out a plan of attack.

Barry Coil turned to one of the agents he'd invited to the meeting. "Ernie, please tell the group what you have going on from up there in Sheboygan, Wisconsin."

"Well I received a report that by itself is very puzzling. If we combine it with what you guys have developed on this case a possible connection could be made. It seems that a commercial fishing boat named the *Mary Jo* regularly sails out of the port there in Sheboygan. The captain has been fishing out of that port for more than fifteen years. All the locals know him and his family. He and his first mate went out a few nights ago just like they've been doing all summer but this time something strange happened. The morning following the *Mary Jo's* departure on what was supposed to be a routine fishing trip, a local businessman named Zack Leonard stopped by the captain's home. He inquired after the *Mary Jo* and when told that she was out on the lake fishing he made a startling revelation. Mr. Leonard operates a small repair shop along the river and it so happens that he had repaired the *Mary Jo's* outriggers; did some welding I believe. Anyway, the captain asked him to leave the repaired outriggers on the dock outside the repair shop from where he intended to retrieve them on his way out to the lake in the early morning. The captain never picked them up so Leonard came by to inquire about what the captain wanted done with them. The wife contacted the local authorities who in turn contacted the Coast Guard. The Coast Guard attempted to raise the *Mary Jo* on the Marine radio but didn't get a response. Several other boats heard the call and are on alert. The entire fishing fleet is monitoring the emergency channel but there haven't been any distress calls and none of the other commercial fishing boats have reported seeing any sign of the *Mary Jo*. It appears that the *Mary Jo* has vanished. Needless to say, the family is frantic. Everyone knows that you can't deploy fishing nets without outriggers. So the question is, why go out on the lake fishing if you can't fish?"

Bob asked, "Ernie, did the captain have a second set of outriggers?"

"That's the first thing I checked and the answer is no. From what I could gather I am confident that he didn't borrow any either. So you see, the situation is troubling to say the least."

"In the context of your case it moves from troubling to alarming. It's not beyond the realm of possibility that your suspects took the boat. If they are after those carriers they could have a plan that requires the use of a boat. Don't you think?"

Bob said, "Barry, assuming that the disappearance of the *Mary Jo* is somehow connected to Max and Elsa could be a stretch. It's a possibility of course but only one of several explanations that could explain what happened."

"Obviously you're right Bob. However, for my money this is something that we can't afford to dismiss." Barry Coil interjected.

Ted spoke up. "Okay, for the moment let's go with it. Assuming they have the boat, what are they going to do with it?" Ernie had a bit more information to share with the group. "I read in the newspaper that the carriers will make a goodwill trip up to Traverse City to promote naval recruiting. This will take the ships out of the restricted navigation zone enforced at the southern end of the lake. They would be more vulnerable to some sort of attack in open, unprotected waters."

Fred Taft, the other agent at the meeting cleared his throat loudly to gain everyone's attention before speaking. "I've spent some time up that way over the years. I think I can add some background to this discussion. There are several docks along the shoreline in Traverse City but only one that is big enough to moor ships as large as those carriers. The dock is wide open to the downtown district with no barricades or fences. There's really nothing to prevent someone from walking within feet of any ship docked there. The street runs right along the dock. Heck, just driving down the street you could throw a rock on the deck of a docked ship from a moving car. It seems to me that if I were

The Final Mission   Arnold D. Jones

planning some sort of attack I would keep it simple and do it right there. I wouldn't need a boat."

At this point the others began to chime in with all sorts of contradicting statements. Barry Coil raised his hands bringing the discussion down from the increasing level of intensity. Everyone took a breath and Barry addressed the group.

"Alright men let's take a pragmatic look at what we have so far. From what Ted and Bob have been able to find out we can safely say that up 'til now the activity of our suspects has been confined to the Illinois and Wisconsin side of the lake. Agreed?" Everyone agreed and Barry continued.

"We can assume with some degree of certainty that Elsa is still in Michigan's Upper Peninsula. We have people watching the Mackinaw ferry boat piers and the bridge which crosses back into Wisconsin. Neither the car nor the girl has appeared. Every local policeman, fire fighter, public works employee, telephone company employee, along with gas stations, drug stores, motels, restaurants and grocers, are all on the lookout. We have nine agents pulled from this office and the Detroit field office in the Upper Peninsula searching for her right now. They have interviewed hundreds of people along the main road as well as on many of the side roads and they report no one has seen Elsa or the car since the night Ted lost her trail. So we've got to believe that she's holed-up somewhere. If she was moving there's no way she or the car wouldn't have been spotted. From what we have learned from Ted's interviews of people who did see her it's clear that she's just too good looking to go unnoticed for this long. If she went to ground the night of Ted's chase we can further assume that she is holed-up somewhere near Rapid River, Michigan. The food and supplies that she had in the car confirms that she was headed somewhere she intended to stay for a while."

Fred Taft burst everyone's bubble with his next observation. "You know, she may have just run out on the whole thing. Just look at what we know about her. She was alone and she was sick. Maybe the plan got to her. She couldn't take it and ran. This would explain the supplies and the drive into the wilderness. Elsa is an American citizen after all. She has lived in this country for her entire life with the exception of a few visits back to Germany to see relatives. Tracking her could be useful in finding out how deep the spy ring has penetrated our intelligence but it may not prevent an attack on the carriers. Our best course of action may be to concentrate our efforts on this guy Max Slavina and the other collaborators, if there are any. We know that Elsa wasn't with Max when Max took the boat, if indeed he did take it. He surely would have needed help. That means there's at least one other person involved."

Barry didn't agree with Fred's assessment although he could be right. He knew that it was important to allow everyone the freedom to express any and all ideas no matter what was said. Barry felt that things were progressing well. Everyone was thinking and contributing. But he thought that this might be a good time to take a break. "Let's break for lunch. There's a little hamburger stand around the corner that stays open on Sunday. We can walk over together and be back in under an hour."

As the agents walked down the hall toward the bank of elevators Barry purposely trailed a few paces behind the others. They were talking amongst themselves about the case. He knew that no time would be lost during the break. It was possible more would be accomplished in the less formal setting of the restaurant.

****

Church let out at twelve-thirty. JD, Annie, Don, Sandy, Gary and Tiff all attended. After returning from the day at Belle Isle, Sandy spent the night at Tiff's home while Gary and Don slept in Annie's brother's room. JD slept on the couch in a sleeping bag that belonged to Annie's brother.

They all met up at the Collin's house for breakfast then walked the four blocks to church. The three young men in uniform caused quite a stir in the little church. The pastor asked them to introduce themselves and everyone welcomed them warmly. At the end of the service JD, Don, Gary and Sandy were called to the platform and the pastor led the congregation in a special prayer just for them. It was a blessing for them all. JD saw a tear at the corner of Don's eye and Gary had tears freely running down both cheeks.

JD had been to countless church services during his life; not necessarily because he wanted to be there but because his parents made sure he was there. After JD's experiences of the past two years he felt good about being back in God's house especially without being told he had to be there. He actually wanted to be there. Adding to the experience was the fact that the girl he loved also wanted to be there.

On the walk back to the Collin's home they were all talking and telling stories. JD held Annie's hand in his and thought that it couldn't get much better than this. He leaned down and whispered in Annie's ear. "I was surprised you came down to the living room last night after everyone was asleep. But I was glad too."

"I had such a wonderful time I thought that you deserved a good night kiss," she said.

Annie had slipped out of her room and joined JD on the couch where they kissed and held each other for over an hour. She lay down beside him and they held each other and did all the things young people in love do. But through it all JD was inside the sleeping bag and she was outside. Every attempt he made to free himself from the cocoon was met with Annie's words.

"If you manage to get yourself out of there I'm headed straight back up those stairs; so settle down big boy. Just hold and kiss me, alright?"

JD would readily agree and go back to kissing for a while but soon he was at it again, and once more she would straighten him out. This was repeated over and over until JD was almost happy when Annie did say goodnight and headed back to her room. Not to be misunderstood, he wanted her to stay all night but he was so worked up that when she did finally leave he was able to regain some measure of control. However, getting to sleep proved to be much more difficult. His mind was racing and his emotions were slow to relax. Thankfully, the day had been an active one and his body was tired. Sleep eventually won the night.

****

The FBI agents returned from lunch and worked throughout the afternoon. The sun was now shining on the windows which faced west. There were long shadows from the tall buildings of downtown Chicago. With an hour of sunlight remaining the small FBI taskforce was putting the final touches on the plan they had developed. When it was all finished Barry Coil handed the document to Ted Holbrook. "Ted, why don't you take us through it one last time?"

Ted scanned the first page and then began to read aloud.

"Step one. Maintain the search for Elsa and the blue Ford at present level of manpower.

Step two. In addition bring in the Michigan State Police, expanding the search to include all connecting roads north and south of the main road on which she was last seen.

Step three. Dispatch ten more agents to interview all persons who reported seeing Elsa. Draw out additional information wherever possible. Check all hospitals, doctor's offices and any other medical facilities in case Elsa sought more serious medical attention.

Step four. Station agents at each ferry boat pier; do likewise at the bridge in Menominee. Around the clock coverage is to be given at both locations.

Step five. Assume that Max has the boat. Alert the coast guard to be on the lookout for the Mary Jo. If located, board and secure the vessel.

Step six. Determine the maximum range of the Mary Jo based on the estimated fuel on board. Create a search grid based on the boat's maximum range. Assume the boat was taken north. Contain the initial search to that part of the lake, islands and shoreline.

Step seven. Inform the Navy of the situation and the threat. Set up a command center to funnel all incoming information and updates. Special agent Bob Thorsten will be in charge of the command center. The command center will be located in the Chicago FBI building.

Step eight. Enlist the services of the Civil Air Patrol. The volunteer civilian pilots will be called upon to overfly the search grid looking for the Mary Jo or debris from the possible sinking of the vessel.

Step nine. Issue an APB in all states which border the Great Lakes, include the boat, Elsa's Ford, Max and Elsa; also include all vital information and descriptions.

Step ten. Maintain strict confidentiality regarding the potential threat to the carriers. As a matter of national security no mention of the carriers is to be included in any written communications outside the FBI, the United States Navy and Coast Guard."

When Ted finished reciting the outline of their ten step plan, Barry Coil spoke up. "Alright men that's enough for today. I will assign each of you the steps that best suit your expertise. In the morning we will meet right here and get started. You can go now. I will stay and put in a few calls to the Navy and the Coast Guard. We need to bring them in on this now. The rest will have to wait until the morning." After a short pause he added. "The public must never learn about this threat so deep inside our country. The damage this could cause would surely aid and comfort the enemies of this country. This is top secret men. Take it to your grave. Understand?"

They all understood and acknowledged the fact before heading out.

The agents took the elevator down to the lobby and left the building on their way to a good night's sleep in their own homes. They would come to work early the next morning resolved to break the case at any cost.

****

JD and his crew left the Collins home after a full day of socializing with Mr. and Mrs. Collins and a few neighbors. Sunday was coming to an end, but what a wonderful day it had turned out to be.

JD had been a hit when he sat down at the piano to play some old gospel tunes his mother had taught him over the years. He never thought anyone would like what he considered to be old uninteresting songs. To his surprise, everyone gathered around the piano enjoying the atmosphere created by the sound of his music. As it turned out, both Mrs. Collins and Annie were very good singers. They took to the songs quickly. Soon they were leading a sing-along. JD smiled when it became apparent that Don knew some of the words by heart. After just a few times through even Sandy, Tiff and Gary were making a joyful noise right along with everyone else. It was so much fun.

JD even kissed Annie goodbye in full view of her parents and she kissed him back. The outward show of affection seemed to fit the whole weekend. Annie's mom and dad hugged everyone as they said their goodbyes. JD realized that he had been right, "It just doesn't get much better than this."

****

Elsa covered the windows of the boathouse with some old blankets to conceal the activity that would begin when the sun went down. Sunday was just beginning for the three conspirators. It would be a very long night.

CHAPTER THIRTY-THREE
REASSIGNMENTS

It was late on Sunday night when JD and his crew returned to Willow Run. After dropping Sandy and Gary off at their quarters on base JD and Don drove straight to their boarding house. As they were getting out of the Jeep the door of an Army staff car parked across the street opened and a soldier came over to the two officers. He offered a salute which JD promptly returned.

"Good evening sirs, I have a message for First Lieutenant Jones," said the soldier.

"I'm Jones."

"Please sign here sir."

JD took the soldier's clipboard and pen and stepped over under a street lamp to read what was written on the paper clipped to the board. "What is this?" JD asked.

"Sealed orders, you'll need to sign for them first, sir."

JD found the signature line near the bottom of the page and wrote his name before returning it and the pen to the soldier who was waiting patiently beside JD. The soldier took the clipboard, checked the signature then handed JD a sealed envelope. He brought himself to attention and saluted the two officers again. They returned his salute and he immediately turned and walked back to his car then drove away.

"I wonder how long he was waiting." Don said in a pondering tone that indicated he really wanted to know.

By the time the car's engine started JD had opened the envelope and was reading. He hadn't responded to Don's comment so Don waited quietly as JD read the sealed orders in his hand. JD's facial expression slowly began to change. Annie had been right. JD's face was an open book. He was clearly perplexed by what he was reading. When he finished JD handed the orders to Don.

"Read these orders Don and tell me what you make of them." JD looked even more puzzled.

Don moved closer to the glow of the street lamp and began to read. When he finished JD could tell that he was concentrating very hard. Don returned the orders to JD then spoke. "Well it says the Eagle Eye mission has changed. It was top secret before, I got that, but it seems somehow that it's even more secret now. Is that possible?"

"Well it said that there's been a change in plans initiated by a change in the mission's overall objective. Don, this is the Army after all. You know what they say; 'Ours is not to reason why; ours is but to do and die'. Things change all the time. There's a briefing in the morning. We'll surely be told more details then."

"Whatever it is, it must be important. That part about us pulling up stakes upon reading these orders and reporting without delay to the base is a bit menacing don't you think?" Don asked.

"These orders were sealed and marked top secret. They clearly instructed us to say nothing, just follow orders. That's what we're going to do. Now let's go upstairs, gather our stuff and get over to the base before they send out the MPs to drag us in." JD ordered.

It took them less than ten minutes to clear out the room and be back in the Jeep heading over to the base. On the way nothing was said between JD and Don. They both had many questions but realized neither of them had the answers so they just drove silently staring out the windshield watching the deserted streets pass by.

That evening upon arriving at Willow Run they were assigned to separate rooms on different floors. In the morning JD arrived at the prescribed meeting room at the designated time for the promised briefing. He waited alone for several minutes before a Captain came through the door followed by three civilians. JD was concerned that the meeting would get started without Don. It was unlike Don to be late for anything. During their time together he had always been the first one up in the morning. On several occasions it was Don who prevented JD from being late. Today Don was late; there was no getting around it. If this briefing was as important as the sealed orders had hinted then Don was about to find himself in serious trouble. JD's attention shifted from Don, he rose from his chair as the men entered the room.

"At ease Lieutenant, you can relax." The Captain said as the newcomers all gathered around the table.

"Good morning Jones, I'm Captain Wentworth these men are with the FBI, Special agents Hall, Andrews and Cleaves." JD moved around to exchange handshakes and greetings before they all sat down.

Captain Wentworth continued, "We have a situation that may have an influence on Eagle Eye. I want to turn it over to Special agent Hall who will take us through the developing situation that has necessitated this meeting. But before I do so let me tell you why Lieutenant Rogers is not in attendance at this briefing. He and sergeant Waters have been reassigned to the Pacific. In fact they both shipped out last night. They are no longer part of the Eagle Eye mission."

JD took advantage of an ever so slight pause in the Captain's delivery to interject. "Sir, may I ask why?"

"Of course, officially they were told that the mission had been scrubbed. Therefore their services were no longer needed here and they have been released to fight the Japanese. This is partially true. Their services are no longer needed on this mission but the mission is far from being scrubbed. In fact, it has been expanded. What you are about to hear will fill in the gaps and answer most of your questions."

JD was more confused than before but waited to hear what would be presented by the agent from the FBI.

Agent Hall started without referring to his notes; instead he began his part of the briefing from memory. He shared all of the information the FBI had gathered so far regarding the potential attack on the two carriers. Once this was complete he continued by reading a copy of the ten point plan developed the day before by the FBI in Chicago. He finished by updating the group on what had transpired in the past eighteen hours as the initial steps of the FBI's plan were being implemented.

Captain Wentworth took over when Agent Hall came to the end of his report. "It is imperative that the mission proceed as scheduled. The outcome of the war may very well depend on what is learned. Let me be more specific. At this point in the European conflict the outcome is no longer in doubt. We will win in Europe. The only questions remaining are when will it end and what will be the cost in lives?"

"If these tests prove successful the war in Europe could be brought to a conclusion much sooner, saving thousands of lives in the process. I'm talking about American soldiers first and foremost.

It would naturally save countless other Allied combatants as well as immeasurable numbers of civilians. Now let me get to the heart of the matter. We have no intention of using the carriers as bait or to allow them to be sacrificed for the greater good just to keep these tests on schedule. The carriers are the key to maintaining our ability to apply the relentless pressure that is shrinking the Japanese Empire back to its own shores. The tests remain top secret. The FBI has been told that the true purpose for the carrier's voyage north is not to promote Naval recruiting but for conducting secret tests. However, they have not been supplied with any information on the true nature or purpose of these tests. This information will remain a well-guarded secret within the military only. The Coast Guard has been brought up to speed as they have now been called upon to escort the carriers to and from the test area. Due to the nature of the tests, during the actual tests the Coast Guard Cutter will be required to stand off quite a distance to avoid any danger to the ship. Lieutenant Jones, you have now been tasked with a duel assignment. Not only will you support the testing as previously outlined, but you will be called upon to fly air cover for the carriers during the tests. If this fishing boat, the *Mary Jo*, appears you are to make it disappear. For that matter, if any vessel sails into the test area you are to attack; removing any threat to those carriers. Assume that everything is a threat. You are to take immediate and decisive action. We'll sort it out later. Any threat to our carriers is to be dealt with using deadly force with no questions asked."

Captain Wentworth paused looking at JD. "Yes sir, I understand." JD answered the Captain's unasked question but he still didn't understand fully. If he now had more responsibility why take away the crew with which he had trained for the past several weeks. "Sir, can you shed some light on what I am to do for a crew? I mean, with both Don and Gary out of the picture I haven't heard anything yet that addresses this important subject."

"Of course Lieutenant, that is a valid concern and I fully expected that it would be high on your priority list, as it should be. Your plane is at this moment having the cannon installed. This, as you were told before, requires that the co-pilot's position be eliminated. Therefore Don is no longer needed. This decision was reached because the cannon now has become a higher priority than the co-pilot. You may very well need the extra fire power the cannon will supply. As for the engineers spot, the mission is now classified as a combat mission due to the obvious threat. An engineer with combat experience has been reassigned from his instructor duties at bomber training school. We want experienced combat veterans along on this mission. Waters is a capable man but an upgrade was available to us so we are taking full advantage of the situation. The new man is also an officer. Due to the sensitive nature of this mission it is best to confine the need to know to officers only. You will meet him this afternoon. We're having him flown in as we speak." Explained Captain Wentworth

JD followed up with another question. "Have you considered additional air cover? I'm referring to more planes."

"Yes but again, the tests must remain top secret. The fewer people that know the better for all involved. Besides, with the firepower placed at your disposal we are confident you'll be able to handle the *Mary Jo*. Commercial fishing boats like her are designed as trawlers which limits their top speed to around eight knots. The tests will be conducted in daylight. The crews of the two carriers will all be issued binoculars and be posted on deck as lookouts. In addition, the cutter is equipped with radar. If the *Mary Jo* appears we'll see her coming from miles away."

JD thought the Captain was correct, in a perfect world. On the other hand, if something unforeseen were to happen it could create an entirely different dynamic. His mind returned to the Pacific Island and the anchorage off the western shore of the island, where all the boats and ships were waiting to fire up at them after they dropped their bombs. This was unforeseen and changed everything. It nearly cost him his life and the lives of his crew. It did cost the lives of *One For The Money's* crew.

If JD had learned anything during his time in the military it was that you can't tell inexperienced superior officers anything, so he didn't try. He just listened while deciding to take proper precautions and plan for the unexpected. Like the Boy Scouts always say, "Be prepared."

Before the meeting was adjourned another of the FBI agents closed it with an ominous statement of warning. "Gentlemen, the public can never learn of this threat so deep inside the borders of the United States. This is top secret. Everyone here is pledged to take it with them to their graves."

JD understood the effect this kind of information would have on the public if it were to be made known. Throughout the war all the battles had taken place far away from the shores of the United States. Such a revelation would certainly alter the perspective of those on the home front and could have a negative influence on the morale of the general population. Nonetheless he didn't like the sound of it. Everyone else in the room could look at the pledge as something they would be required to keep to themselves for a lifetime. Lying on their beds as old men about to take their last breath the secret would die with them. He, on the other hand, stood alone as the only one in the room whose assignment might not require any time to pass before the secret would die with him.

The meeting came to an end and JD headed directly back to his room. There he retrieved the ten gold coins hidden inside the lining of his garment bag. There was a small bank just down the street from the entrance to the airfield. That was his destination.

Inside the small bank there was a line of three teller windows opposite the door and to the right, a few desks behind a half wall. JD walked over to the first desk where a woman who looked to be around thirty-five years old sat behind the desk. She had looked up over her glasses the minute he came through the door. She couldn't help from staring at the Lieutenant and his perfectly fitting uniform, although she did everything possible to avoid making her interest appear obvious to the young officer who was now walking toward her.

"Good morning ma'am." He made his comment in a halting way that seemed to indicate that he was somehow uncomfortable.

"Good morning officer. Is there something I can do for you?"

"Well, I need a safety deposit box. Might your bank have them?" JD was looking over her shoulder as he spoke.

"Yes of course but they're downstairs."

Her answer seemed to relax the young man. She realized that he hadn't seen the boxes and was probably worried that the bank didn't offer the service.

"We have them downstairs. There's more privacy for our customers, you know."

"Oh that's good, well I need to rent one. How much would it be to rent it for two years?"

"We offer a discounted rate to servicemen. Normally they are ten dollars a year but for you it would be five dollars a year for the standard size, three inches by twelve by eighteen."

"Good, that size will do and the price seems reasonable. I'll take it." JD filled out the paperwork and on the line indicating who could access the box; he wrote his name and that of youngest brother Gillas Denver Jones.

A bank clerk escorted JD down to the basement where he inserted the bank's key and JD's key. The two keyed security system released box number 183 from its numbered slot. With the empty box out on a table in a small private cubical, JD placed the ten gold coins inside the box. Then he proceeded to write two letters to his brother.

> *Dear Gillas,*
> *With Russell off fighting in the Pacific, Bill in the Naval Hospital down in New Orleans and Arnold out of contact, I'm trusting you to take care of Momma if something happens to me. Don't be concerned; this is just in case. I have every intention of living out the war but I have come into some money and it would be a shame to see it come to nothing. Enclosed is a key to a safety deposit box as well as the name and address of the bank where it can be found. Your name is on the paperwork along with mine. I want you to hold the key. When I see you again you can return it. If for any reason I don't have the chance to retrieve the key I want you to go to the bank and take the contents of the box. Use the money to help Momma in the coming years. There is another letter which will explain all about it and tell you where to find more. You will also find a journal that I came across out in the Pacific. Read it and it will answer any questions you may have. As far as the additional money goes, after expenses, split it equally amongst all our brothers and sisters with an equal share to Miss Ann Marie Collins at the address below.*
> *See you soon, and be careful down there at Camp Gordon. Basic training isn't nearly as hard as football practice. You can get through it alright. Hold your temper and don't volunteer for anything.*
> *All my love,*
> *JD*

He placed the journal in the box pushing it all the way toward the end. This left a space in front for the coins and the second letter. He closed the top of the box, picked it up and slid it back in its numbered slot. With this done, he called for the attendant and the bank's key so the box could be relocked in its slot. When this was done and the attendant moved away JD dropped his key in the envelope with the first letter and sealed the flap. Outside, down a half block and across the street from the bank, JD found a post office.   With the letter to his brother posted, he casually walked back to the base.

CHAPTER THIRTY-FOUR
OPERATION EAGLE EYE BEGINS

Kenneth Acton didn't need much training. After completing sixty combat missions over the South Pacific he signed on for another ten just for good measure. At least that's the reason he gave to anyone who asked. The truth was he loved the action and a commission came with the deal. With a promotion to Lieutenant he would earn more money for doing the same thing he had been doing for over a year.

When this assignment came up he didn't have to be asked twice. He jumped at the chance to add just one more purposeful flight to his resume. Besides, an increase in pay for hazardous duty went along with the assignment and he wasn't the type of guy to look a gift horse in the mouth. He asked himself, "Just how hazardous can it be? The mission would just be over Lake Michigan after all. The answer is; not very, so I'll sign on and gladly take Uncle Sam's money."

Kenneth Acton wasn't all about the money; he had plans for after the war and would need money to turn his plans into reality. Kenneth had it all figured out. When the war was over the multitude of returning GIs would need housing, a lot of it and everywhere. He was going to build houses. He planned to start slow building one at a time, turning the profits into more material and more land; and then keep on building until he was rich. His buddies out in the Pacific started calling him Kenny Action because he never missed a mission and volunteered for more. He liked the name although he wouldn't say so. He loved hearing the guys use it when talking about him. Kenny Action was a complicated guy but none was braver, harder working, or more prepared.

JD gave no more than a passing thought to the complex personality of his new flight engineer. Instead, JD zeroed in on his ability to do the job. He concluded that when it came down to brass tacks Kenny Action was all business. He was more than an upgrade for Gary Waters. He was the best JD had ever seen. The two men only managed to work in five hours of practice time together before the carriers left port heading north, but it was enough. They were confident, experienced, prepared and ready. Two all-stars just entering the game, but the rules of the game were yet to be defined.

The *USS Wolverine* and her sister ship the *USS Sable* departed Chicago's Navy Pier before the sun came up. A Coast Guard Cutter lay just off shore awaiting the arrival of the carriers. Moments after the two large ships cleared the harbor's outer break wall the three ships linked up to begin the cruise up the lake. The Cutter was armed with two pedestal guns each accurate out to three miles. One was mounted forward and the other was on the aft deck. Both guns were loaded and manned at all times. Two .50 caliber machine guns had hastily been brought aboard and positioned on either side of the bridge for extra firepower. The crew stood their posts armed with rifles and submachine guns just in case. Lookouts scanned the surface of the lake through binoculars. The ship was ready to make its way north on high alert with a crew that never expected such an assignment when they came aboard for duty on Lake Michigan. The ship was alive with excitement and expectation for the adventure that lay ahead.

After a while, out to the west in the distance, the Milwaukee skyline came into view though barely visible through the morning mist as dawn rose over the lake. The sun showed full in the east although still very low. The sky was blue from horizon to horizon creating unlimited visibility. It looked like the dawn of what would be a beautiful day.

An eight to ten knot headwind generated five foot waves. The Cutter's razor sharp bow sliced through the water sending intermittent plumbs of ice cold spray skyward, washing the deck as far back as the bridge. The forward gun crew was decked out in foul weather gear which offered only minimal protection against the freezing spray. They manned their post at the gun undaunted by the harsh conditions. The bow of the Cutter rose on each wave and dropped before reaching the next. Every sixth or seventh wave seemed to be taller than the others. When the ship encountered one of these it would shutter and moan as if it had been hit by a sledge hammer.

The heavier carriers moved forward without nearly as much commotion. The side-wheel locomotion of the converted passenger ships assisted in keeping their bows low as they plowed the water rather than slicing through as the cutter was doing. Heavy black smoke pumped out of their smoke stacks as the coal fired boilers of the two carriers consumed mountains of fuel. The strong headwinds quickly dissipated the smoke leaving no trace in the sky behind the ships. Progress was steady as the small taskforce moved along at fourteen knots.

On the open bridge of the Cutter the Captain maintained contact with the radar operator below decks. "Clear sir, nothing to report."

"Let me know the minute you spot anything on that screen," ordered the Captain.

"Aye aye sir."

The Captain turned to address his first officer. "Doug, keep checking with the lookouts. I want to know if something's out there before they do."

"Aye aye sir."

The Captain had insisted that all hands have breakfast at their posts. Breakfast had been over for several minutes but he still had a half-full mug of coffee in his hand. He drank slowly from the mug while looking out at the water ahead of his ship. The two carriers were steaming at fourteen knots holding a steady course while his ship was making close to twenty knots. The Cutter was now between the carriers moving on a looping course like a Border Collie circling a herd of sheep. He could see the crew members of both carriers standing watch on their decks. With clear skies and all those eyes keeping a sharp lookout he was as confident as he dare be that nothing would get within miles of the ships he was responsible for protecting.

The Captain looked up when he heard the deep crackling sound of radial engines overhead. "Doug, put a pair of glasses on that plane. Does she have the red markings we were told to look for?"

The first mate lifted his binoculars from his chest where they hung from a leather strap around his neck. He brought the plane into focus. "Yes sir, that's her alright, B-25 with red markings"

"That's good Doug, real good. Have the radio room contact the plane and let's coordinate our activity. Ask them to maintain an altitude of three thousand feet and keep within five miles of our location at all times. Have them let us know what they see beyond the range of our glasses. Also, if our long range radar picks up anything alert the plane and have them do visual reconnaissance and report."

The first mate lifted the handset from its cradle on the bulkhead and called the radio room. After a brief exchange he waited on the line. Then he took the phone away from his ear. "Captain, we have the plane on the radio. They're on the line we can speak to them directly."

"Go ahead Doug, relay the instructions. When you finish let me say a word to the pilot before you sign off."

The first mate passed the captain's instructions on to JD, who acknowledged them. "Yes, message received, instructions are understood. We're starting our climb to three thousand now. We'll be in position in approximately five minutes. Monitor this frequency we'll take a look around and report back shortly..."

JD was interrupted by the first mate before he could finish signing off.

"One moment, the Captain would like to speak to you." JD held the mike open while he waited for the Captain to come on. The first mate held the handset out for the Captain who took it while nodding his thanks to Doug. "This is Captain Mac Donald speaking. Good to have you fellows up there this morning. We need you to keep a sharp look out. We're making about fourteen knots. We plan to maintain that speed throughout the day. That translates to ten hours until we can reach port. How long can you stay on station before fuel becomes a problem?"

"Not that long sir. If we conserve fuel I'd estimate we can stretch it out for seven to eight hours."

"I thought so. How long will you need to refuel and return?"

"The best would be an hour but maybe more."

"If the weather holds the visibility will remain good. I need you overhead for the last three hours. This is the most likely time for an attack. Break off and return for fuel when you think the time is right to insure your return within that time frame. Do you understand?"

"Yes sir, understood. We'll monitor the fuel situation throughout the day and keep you apprised."

"Very good skipper we'll keep this frequency open. Again, it's good to have you along."

The Coast Guard had been sending out warnings via marine radio starting shortly after Agent in Charge Barry Coil notified them of the threat. All marine traffic was being instructed to stay a minimum of twenty-five nautical miles away from the planned route of the taskforce.

JD circled around at three thousand feet above the taskforce. He could see clearly for thirty miles or more in all directions. It appeared to him that everyone had gotten the message. There was no marine traffic remotely near the three ships below his plane.

"Kenny, you see anything?" JD asked.

"No sir, just open water as far as the eye can see. What about you, you spot anything from up there?"

"No; nothing, looks like everyone got the word."

The weather held and visibility remained unlimited throughout the morning and into the early afternoon. The B-25 left the taskforce and returned to Mitchell field for fuel. Kenny Action arranged for a quick refueling effort well ahead of their arrival. The gas truck with its refueling crew at the ready was waiting on the grass infield near the end of the runway. JD's B-25 rolled to a stop and as it did the hoses were passed up to crew members who had scrambled up ladders ready to retrieve hoses and start the fueling process. JD shut down the engines and the fuel began to flow. The entire process was completed in a few minutes.

The wind sock hung limp from the top of the pole down at the opposite end of the runway so JD decided not to taxi to the other end. "Kenny, you ready?" JD called to his engineer.

Kenny answered back, "Ready sir, let's get out of here."

"We'll take off from this end, here we go," JD said.

The ground crew pulled the propeller blades through three full revolutions to get rid of any oil that might have settled in the lower cylinders while the engines were off. After a quick restart of the engines JD pushed softly on the left brake to restrict but not prevent the rotation of the left wheel while raising the power on the right engine. The landing gear on a B-25 was not designed to allow a pivot on one locked wheel; the stress would be too great. The inside wheel had to be allowed to roll in a ten foot radius during a turn. The plane came around nicely until it was pointing straight down the center of the runway. JD pushed both throttles full forward and the wheels began to take the B-25 down the runway. At one hundred and fifteen miles an hour and with fifteen degrees of flap JD eased back on the controls and the plane lifted smoothly off the runway.

It had been like a pit stop at the Indy 500. Total time from touchdown to wheels up was twenty-two minutes.

JD radioed the tower. "This is B-25 chase plane to Mitchell tower."

"This is the tower, go ahead B-25."

"Give those guys a well done. We're on our way. Thanks."

"We read and will pass the message along. See you fellows later."

The taskforce had chosen a course that kept the carriers in the middle of the lake as far from land as possible. By the time JD's plane returned and took up its position over the taskforce the western shore of Michigan was only ten miles away from the ships. The captain had been correct in his assessment of the increased risk during this final leg of the voyage. A fast moving boat could appear from the shoreline and be in range of the carriers much more quickly. It would have the element of surprise and reaction time would be reduced.

"Kenny."

"Yes sir."

"Keep a close watch on the shoreline. The ships are on a course that will continue to close the distance between them and the shore. Until they are safely at anchor in port the most dangerous threat would be from there. I'll keep a visual on everywhere else. If something comes out of one of those inlets down there we will need to attack without delay. If you see anything we go, so keep your eyes peeled."

"The view from back here is limited. The wing blocks my line of sight forward. I can see what's alongside and behind but that's about all," Kenny said.

JD turned the steering control left. The right wing came up.

JD asked, "How's that, any better?"

"Good, keep her right there. I can see everything now."

The radar operator had a clear screen. The lookouts posted on all three ships continued to watch open water. JD and Kenny observed nothing.

By three in the afternoon the *USS Wolverine* was moored at the dock along Main Street and the *USS Sable* was at anchor a hundred yards away in Grand Traverse Bay. Military guards were at their posts along the dock. Automobile traffic had been diverted onto alternate roads and local police boats patrolled the entrance to the bay. Captain Mac Donald's Coast Guard cutter took up a position on the lake just outside the Bay.

JD observed the activity below while flying north at one thousand feet. Over the downtown area with the carriers at rest in the bay, then across the bay and out to the lake. He pushed the throttles down and the engines roared as the RPM's increased. Pulling the controls toward his chest the B-25 began to climb on its way to five thousand feet. He leveled out before pushing the left rudder in and gently turning the controls to the left. A slow turn to the left soon changed the plane's course from north to southwest toward Mitchell field and home. Day one of the final mission came to an uneventful end. The carriers were safe.

The Final Mission Arnold D. Jones

CHAPTER THIRTY-FIVE
CAUGHT

The white was now black. Commercial fishing boats were either painted white like the *Mary Jo* was, or black like so many others. Elsa had her hands covered in black paint but the job was done. The *Mary Jo* was now as black as a raven so that's the name they painted on her transom, *The Raven*.

With the new paint job and the torpedoes mounted on ramps hidden on either side of the cabin the work was almost complete. Rinehart was nearly finished mounting the twin .30 caliber machine guns on the ceiling of the aft cabin. The installation looked solid and menacing but no one would see it because he planned to cover it with a tarp for the voyage across the lake. If the hero in that red plane were to try and stop them he would be in for a surprise.

Elsa had her hands in turpentine and the black paint was nearly all gone. Her last task was to fill the fuel tanks with the gasoline stored in four, fifty-five gallon drums. Using the hand pump would take an hour of hard work to finish the job but after that, she was leaving. The thought of getting out of there had lifted her spirits. She wiped off the last of the turpentine and started to fill the boat's tanks.

Rinehart walked over to the open sideboard which exposed the torpedo on the port side. Max was inside the main cabin completing his work. "You ready?" he asked.

"Almost, you want to see how this works in case you need to launch the torpedoes?" Max asked.

"That's a good idea."

"Come aboard, you can see better from inside," Max said.

Rinehart climbed aboard and made his way through the aft cabin. When he stepped down to the forward cabin he was met by a honeycomb of crisscrossing beams. The wood structure had been constructed by Max to act as support bracing for the two ramps that carried the torpedoes. The cabin was so full of beams that it was nearly impossible for Rinehart to make his way any further inside. He stood at the entrance looking at Max through the maze of wood. Max motioned to Rinehart not to come any further and then began his explanation.

"To start with, when we are underway the sideboards will be down, locked in place by this wooden dowel. It's the same on both sides. The two ramps secure the torpedoes. See that small block of wood under the propeller? When the torpedo starts down the ramp it leaves that block of wood which is there to prevent the motor from starting before the torpedo is set in motion. As soon as she comes off that block the motor will start and the propeller will be spinning at full speed before it reaches the end of the ramp. After you screw the detonator into the threaded hole on the nose of the weapon it's ready to launch. You launch it by simply pulling out the wooden dowel. The pin will release the torpedo and it rolls down the ramp. The dowel also releases the latch to the sideboard. On its way down the ramp the torpedo makes contact with the sideboard and the sideboard simply swings open at the bottom allowing the weapon to roll out straight in the water. This wire is connected to the detonator pin. When the weapon travels outside the cabin the wire is made taunt, thus pulling the detonator pin out and arming the weapon just before entering the water. That's the best I could do with what we had to work with, but it should work just fine."

Rinehart could tell that Max was proud of his work and enjoyed sharing the lesson. Rinehart looked past the pride and ego coming through from Max. The fact was Max had plenty of reason to be proud. The job he had done was impressive.

Within two hours all the work was complete. Rinehart came out of the cabin and motioned for Elsa and Max to join him inside. Upon entering the cabin they immediately noticed that Rinehart had a nice fire burning in the stone fireplace. The heat from the crackling flames had already found every corner of the room making the space seem cozy and inviting. A shortwave radio set sat out on a small table just to the left of the fireplace. The tubes were still glowing, Rinehart had been communicating with someone.

"The boat is ready. We will sleep today and tomorrow our mission begins. Elsa, tomorrow I want you to pack all of our personal belongings in the car and wait until the late afternoon to leave for the Lower Peninsula of Michigan. Take a ferry boat across the straights and go to this location." Rinehart handed her a map.

"Those are the directions to a small inlet on the western coast of Michigan. Memorize the directions and burn the map in this fireplace tonight. When our mission is completed we will come ashore here," he pointed to a location on the western shore of Michigan. "You will be there to pick us up. We will head for Lansing where there are trains and buses. We'll split up and go our separate ways."

"Max, I have new identification papers for you; and you as well, Elsa. You will be traveling as man and wife. Along with the papers there is ten thousand dollars in cash. My advice is to disappear and never go anywhere near where you've been before. With that kind of money starting over should not be difficult."

"As for me, it is best that you not ask. When this is over I will have no idea of your whereabouts or you mine. This is the best way."

Max and Elsa looked at each other knowing the mission was so risky that they may never get the chance to start a new life but it was too late. The future was now out of anyone's control. Things would work out however they would. But hope still remained alive; they could see it in each other's eyes.

The next morning Elsa packed the car with everything belonging to the trio. Throughout the day she checked and rechecked to make sure nothing that could be linked to any of them remained. Using the hand pump she filled the Ford's gas tank from the same fuel drums used to fill the boat. She had enough gas to take her all the way out of the Upper Peninsula. She would be two hundred or more miles away before needing to stop. *The farther the better.*

Elsa pulled out of the driveway in the late afternoon as planned. Max and Rinehart waited for the sun to go down before they started out for the other side of the lake. If they timed it just right *The Raven* would be in range of its prey before the sun came up the following morning. If all went according to plan they would strike just after sun up then continue due east disappearing into the secluded inlet. The plan had a better than even chance of working.

Before departing the two saboteurs used the gasoline remaining in the drums to saturate the cabin and boathouse. "You really think that setting fire to the place is a wise decision? Max asked. "It could start a brush fire that might burn for days. If that were to happen there would be an investigation. I mean, is this necessary?"

Rinehart answered back without hesitation. "How are we to be sure that one day this location won't be connected to the attack? I can't take the chance. Something might be found that would eventually lead back to one of us. After all, we've left fingerprints everywhere. I don't want to worry about this for the rest of my life; so we will destroy everything. If they investigate the fire there will be nothing to find and that's the way it has to be. Even if the fire burns down the whole State it can never be tied to us."

The Raven eased away from shore with its running lights turned off. She was the only boat in the vicinity. The water was dead calm and her slow forward progress created only the slightest ripple on the surface as she motored out to the center of the bay. The sky above was covered by a thick blanket of dark storm clouds making the black boat invisible in the darkness.

Then an explosion behind the boat lit the sky for a half mile in all directions as the cabin ignited in flames. Just as quickly, the explosion contracted leaving the dull roar of the fire that was now busily consuming the cabin and everything around it. Rinehart switched on the running lights and increased the boat's speed. They were on their way.

It took thirty minutes to escape the large bay and find open water. The rain was now steady but not too hard. The wind was out of the west and seemed to be picking up. There was a following sea developing as The Raven gradually changed course from south to east toward the coast of Michigan now less than a hundred miles away. It took over two hours to reach the gap between Rock Island to the south and Saint Martin Island to the north. The wind was gaining strength and the rain continued. Once the little boat left the protection provided by the islands they faced nearly eighty miles of open seas in bad weather.

Max watched the compass. Rinehart was at the helm. Visibility was down to nothing. They continued without speaking.

Trepidation best describes the feeling in Max's stomach. As for Rinehart, Max wasn't sure what he was feeling but he looked sick, really sick.

The following seas soon began to push the stern up while propelling the boat forward. Then the wave would continue along the keel passing all the way under the boat forcing the bow up. Before the bow had a chance to settle down the next wave would come along and crash against the transom sending a wash of cold water over the aft deck. Max could hear the automatic bilge pumps running continuously. After an hour of repeated stern to bow heaving both Max and Rinehart were sea sick. There was no place to turn so they vomited where they stood until there was nothing left to give up. Then the dry heaves started. *When will this end?*

Elsa reached the Straights of Mackinaw just before the last ferry of the day was scheduled to depart for the Lower Peninsula. There were several cars and trucks waiting in line for the ferry to dock and unload the vehicles heading north. She could see the ferry's outline and running lights out on the water as the vessel headed her way. It would soon be tying up just in front of the rows of waiting cars. The return trip would be full. As she watched she tried to count the cars waiting ahead of hers in an attempt to estimate if there would be enough room. After a quick calculation her concerns vanished. There would be room.

A man with a change maker on his belt was working his way between the cars collecting the toll from each driver. Soon he was at her window. Elsa had the thirty-five cents out and in her hand having read the posted toll signs as she had driven in. She rolled down the window and handed him the exact change.

"Thank you miss but you can't board the ferry with that hanging on your front bumper."

"What is it?" Elsa asked.

"You need to get that off there or you can't board, sorry."

He had ignored her question entirely. Elsa thought, *What is wrong with him?* The toll collector by this time had moved to the front of her car and was staring down at the bumper.

"Take a look miss. That thing can't go on the ferry."

Elsa turned off the engine, set the parking brake and got out, leaving the door ajar. The ferry was already beginning to lower the ramp to allow the cars and trucks on board to disembark. Elsa didn't need any problems now. Whatever it was she would rip it off there and get on that ferry. If Max made it to the inlet she was going to be there for him no matter what. She marched herself to the front of the car with a mixture of disgust and determination on her face.

In the next second everything changed. They were on her in an instant. With guns drawn three men materialized from behind nearby cars. The toll collector was standing three feet away with a pistol aimed at her midsection. She was surrounded and trapped.

Loud shouts came from everywhere. "FBI, don't move! Show your hands!"

She had no control. Her eyes rolled to the back of her head; and then they slowly closed and she fell to the ground right there beside her bright blue Ford with a white stripe down the side. Elsa was caught.

Just off the road leading down to the ferry dock stood a large maintenance shed. Inside occupying a corner of the building was the ferry company's small office. Elsa sat on a hard wooden chair behind a rectangular table. A few desks and file cabinets lined the walls. There wasn't much room but five FBI agents and the local sheriff were squeezed in the office with her. Elsa was conscious now having awakened just as two agents placed her in the chair. Not a word had been spoken during the thirty minutes waiting in the office. Elsa had no idea what to expect but she feared the worst. Her legs were trembling and in spite of her mental efforts to stop their movement she couldn't gain control over the constant shaking. She kept her eyes down focusing on the pattern in the grain of the wooden table top.

A single knock announced a tall well-dressed man in a dark blue suit. She looked up for just an instant before once more returning her gaze to the table. The man removed his hat as he entered the room. She understood now why no one had spoken. They had been waiting for this man to arrive.

Like subway riders who must squeeze together to allow more passengers onto a packed train the other occupants of the room moved away from the door allowing him access to the room. The man walked around the table until he was positioned across from Elsa. His movements were deliberate and calculated. He placed his hat on the table off to his right. He lifted his left hand; in it was her black purse. He placed it in the center of the table. Reaching inside his hand came out with a hand gun which he displayed for all to see before handing it to one of the other agents. He placed his hand in once more and slowly retrieved a stack of bills, the ten thousand dollars. He held it out for a long moment before once again handing it to the other agent. Now placing both hands firmly on the table he leaned in, bringing his face close to Elsa's. He was staring right at her. Feeling even more trapped than before she wanted to jump up and run and keep on running but her fate was sealed and she knew it. Elsa just sat there waiting for what would come next.

"Elsa, I'm Special agent Ted Holbrooke with the FBI. You are Elsa Menzel an American citizen and you are being detained as part of an ongoing investigation into subversive activity against the United States of America."

Elsa finally looked up. She started to interrupt, to deny the accusations that were about to be made.

"Elsa, I strongly advise you to remain silent until I finish what I want to say. Do you understand?"

Elsa submissively shook her head in the affirmative and once more looked down at the table. She said nothing.

"Good, we know all about the planned attack on the carriers. We are also aware of your association with Max Slavina and of his role in the plot. From the clothes and other personal belongings we found in your car, clearly there are others involved. At this moment that's all it is, just a plot. Before it matures into full-blown espionage you need to tell us what we want to know. Your immediate cooperation is the only thing that will save your life. Let me remind you that in this country we shoot spies with no questions asked."

Everyone in the room was standing around the table staring down at Elsa. She felt as though she couldn't catch her breath. Her legs had been bouncing up and down at a fever pitch. Suddenly, her whole body was out of control. Fear gripped her but now she felt it turning into absolute panic. *"Why, why have I gotten myself into this? Remorse, regret, all of these things mean absolutely nothing now. It's too late.* Elsa's mouth was so dry that even if she could form a thought that led to words she would be unable to speak. Then the tears began to gush from her eyes. Water flooded like two fountains down her face. Ted was having none of it.

"Bullshit!" He screamed. "If one hair on the head of one American is harmed because of this I will personally volunteer to shoot you right between those pretty blue eyes. Now get hold of yourself and start talking. Do you hear me?"

Elsa held up her hand as if to fend off Ted as she slowly but surely managed to seize a measure of control. In a voice so hoarse and so low that the men in the room knew she needed it, Elsa asked for water. One of the men tuned toward the water cooler and filled a cone shaped paper cup with water and without speaking turned back and handed it to Elsa. After receiving the water she slowly took a drink. Elsa placed the empty paper cone down on the table in front of her. Slowly her head came up and she looked directly at Agent Ted Holbrook for the first time. In a clear voice Elsa spoke.

"Special agent Holbrooke, you can kiss my ass on your way to hell you bast...!"

Before Elsa could complete her response the sheriff landed a straight right hand hay maker to the left side of her face. She flew out of the chair and hit the floor hard. Her body twitched then it went still. Blood was trickling from her nose.

All attention immediately turned to the sheriff who looked around at the men staring at him. "What? She's lucky I didn't shoot her."

Elsa lay on the floor, out cold. Quite a bit of time passed before anyone in the room offered to assist her back in the chair.

They got nothing more from Elsa that night.

****

Upon returning to Mitchell Field JD taxied the B-25 over to the refueling area. Kenny and JD were told Captain Brock was waiting inside to speak to them. They headed that way leaving the refueling crew to their work.

"Gentlemen, good work today but I want you to take a look at this." The three men leaned over a map spread out on the counter.

Brock continued, "See that? We have a slow moving storm front working its way across the upper part of the lake. It's a big one but moving very slowly. By morning this side of the lake will be socked in pretty good. I don't think you'll be able to fly out tomorrow so after you're fueled up we need to take the plane over to the other side tonight. The control plane and the test planes are already here." Brock pointed out an airfield on the map just east of Traverse City, Michigan.

"This is a small military base not far from the test area. It's under tight security to protect the secret equipment. I want you to fly over there and bunk with the other members of the team. The test schedule has been pushed up so we can complete the first portion before the storm reaches the test area. The carriers will depart before dawn and the targets will be towed out by tug boat at the same time. You'll take off early and get yourselves in position. I want you overhead before the carriers leave the bay. We have pilots from the company that built them ready to fly the test planes out to the carriers shortly afterward. Final preparations for the radio controlled tests will take place aboard ship. When complete the control plane will take off from the base and take up its position over the test area. If everything comes off as planned we'll have the carriers back at the dock by noon. The storm is expected to reach Grand Traverse Bay at one in the afternoon. That gives us more than seven hours to complete the mission. That's time enough. You men have any questions?"

"Can we grab something to eat before we take off?" Kenny asked.

"Can do, we've arranged for the kitchen to remain open until after you guys take off. They're waiting for you." Brock answered.

On the way over to the dining room Kenny shared his observation with JD. "That Brock is a nice guy, he thinks of everything."

JD thought back to his first meeting with Brock back on the beach south of Mitchell Field. "I guess you could say that."

JD and Kenny had dinner before taking off and heading back to the other side of the lake. After a full day of flying they arrived in the dark at the isolated Northern Michigan military base. They were escorted to their quarters by an Army private who was standing by to greet their plane. They lay down on two small bunks after tossing their clothes over a chair. Sleep came quickly to the two flyers, sleep that would be needed ahead of what would surely be a busy day to come.

CHAPTER THIRTY-SIX
VARIABLES

Wooden hulled ships were perfect for mine sweeping duty as underwater mines are triggered by contact with metal. The United States Navy had requisitioned numerous privately owned wooden vessels for this purpose during the war. Included among these was the recently requisitioned yacht, *Miss Delight*.

Early in the morning, the one hundred and seventeen foot vessel crossed through the Straights of Mackinaw leaving Lake Huron and entering Lake Michigan at its northern most point. Her destination was a ship builder on the Wisconsin side of the lake. There, she would be converted into a mine sweeper in preparation for the upcoming planned invasion of Japan. If she survived the war the government would pay to have her returned to her owners in her original condition.

Due to fuel rationing the *Miss Delight* hadn't left the dock in years. Her owners, Fredrick and Albert Lewinski, a pair of brothers from Saginaw, Michigan decided to make the voyage themselves along with several female companions. After all, the government was supplying the fuel and chances were that they might never see the *Miss Delight* again. With a crew of five, the two brothers and six young ladies, the yacht had a total of thirteen souls on board. A very unlucky number if you believe in such things.

The Coast Guard warnings of the past few days had not gone out as far as the Saginaw Bay which is located all the way across the state of Michigan and on an entirely different lake. For this reason the captain of the *Miss Delight* had no idea he was sailing his ship into harm's way. He did however; see the storm gathering on the western horizon. As a precaution he altered course hugging the Michigan shoreline on a southerly course. The captain was heading at full speed straight toward the protection offered by Grand Traverse Bay.

Preparations aboard the carrier were completed as scheduled and as JD and Kenny watched from two thousand feet above, the first of two test planes to be used this day lifted off the deck of the *USS Sable*. Far to the south and well out of danger from an out of control test plane the Coast Guard Cutter slowly steamed in wide circles. When the tests were completed for the day she would rejoin the carriers and escort them back to safe harbor, hopefully before the storm moved overhead. The B17 control plane was three thousand feet above JD's B-25. The test plane gradually gained altitude. When the test plane reached two thousand feet JD climbed to three thousand feet. If he had to intervene he preferred to do so from above, where he could dive down on his target.

It didn't take long for the first sign of trouble to show itself. Within ten minutes the radio controlled pilotless test plane began to act erratically. JD watched as the nose of the all wooden, twin engine TDR-1 drone pitched up. Then, with what looked to be overcompensation by the remote control pilot who was at the television monitor inside the control plane, the nose was then forced down; putting the plane into a sharp dive. This was corrected but again, over compensation put her into a steep climb. JD feared the plane would go into a stall from which there would be no way to recover. Up and down she went time after time but after a series of heart stopping maneuvers she was flying straight and level.

"B-25 to control one, this is a radio check."

"This is control one, go ahead B-25."

"How we doing fellows, everything under control? Looks a little wild from here?" JD asked.

"Just working out the kinks, this is new to all of us. I think I've got it now."

"Okay, standing by."

JD trailed a half mile behind the test plane as the control plane continued to take it through a series of maneuvers. He was watching intently, ready to intercede if necessary.

"Kenny, are you able to see what's going on?" JD asked.

Kenny answered, "No, I can't see a thing from back here. Why, what's happening?"

"Poke your head up over my shoulder. Looks like they're getting the hang of it, she's flying pretty steady now." JD observed.

Kenny put a foot on the ladder that lead up to the cockpit and took a firm hold on the back of JD's seat while lifting his head high enough to see out the windscreen. They both watched for a long while, everything seemed to be under control. The test plane made several practice dives over the wooden targets which were floating on the surface of the lake. After each dive it regained altitude before executing a smooth banked turn. To Kenny and JD everything looked as it should.

The storm was slowly creeping closer as it moved from west to east over the surface of the lake. Leading the way were stacks of cumulus clouds reaching twenty-five thousand feet into the sky. Flashes of lightening could be seen all the way across the approaching storm front but the weather over the test area remained calm and sunny.

"Control one to B-25."

"I read you control one, go ahead."

We're about to start the final dive on the target. We're taking the test plane up to five thousand feet when she reaches that altitude we'll level off. At five thousand feet she'll maintain level flight for five minutes. I will give you the word just before she starts her dive. There are three targets down there; we'll aim for the one in the center. Please confirm."

"Understood control one, where do you want us?"

"Follow up to five thousand, once I have her in level flight you move on up to six thousand. I'll keep her on a steady course to the north. Once you reach six thousand take up your position about a half mile to the rear. That storm is closing in and it doesn't look so good. We've decided to scrub the second test for today. So after this one's in the books let's head back to the barn."

"We read you loud and clear. It looks like a bad one, see you back at the field." Kenny answered.

JD added, "Okay, we'll follow you, proceed when ready."

On the Coast Guard Cutter the radar operator had his eyes glued to the screen when a blip appeared indicating a lone target hugging the coast north of Grand Traverse Bay. He flipped the cover open and put his mouth up close to the brass tube that lead to the bridge. "Radar room!" he hollered into the tube. The first mate heard the call and responded. "This is the bridge, go ahead."

"I'm getting a target twenty-five miles north of Grand Traverse Bay. Fast moving, on a southerly heading, estimated speed sixteen to eighteen knots, target size one hundred to one hundred and fifty feet in length. She's coming hard and fast, sir."

The first officer relayed the information to the Captain who was standing on the bridge with him. "Doug can we intercept her from here before she reaches the carriers?"

"It's too far to reach her before she gets to the mouth of the bay. But if she alters course toward the carriers we have a good chance if we break off and proceed without delay."

The Captain thought for a moment then made his decision known. "We're not doing any good here. Set a course to intercept the target."

"Aye, aye sir."

The captain contacted the engine room. "Engine room, this is the Captain."

"Engine room reporting, go ahead."

"All ahead full, give me maximum RPMs and keep those boilers stoked. It's going to be a long run."

"Aye, aye sir, we've got good pressure now. We'll keep it up there. Moving to full ahead now sir"

"Doug, contact the carriers. Have them move south. Let's gain some separation between them and the target. We may need it." The carriers changed course as instructed slowly making their way to the southern end of the test area.

Kenny was monitoring the radio and heard the orders being given by the Coast Guard Cutter's Captain. "Skipper, something's going on. The Cutter is heading north at full speed to intercept a fast moving target that they picked up on radar. Should we do a fly over and report what we see?"

JD knew they must stay and guard against the test plane going out of control. "No Kenny, if they need us they'll let us know but check in anyway."

He did as ordered and soon reported back to JD. "Skipper, they told us to stay with the test plane and to watch the Carriers."

"That's going to be a trick. We're heading north and the carriers have turned south." JD had an idea.

"Kenny, can you crawl through the tube over the bomb bay and get yourself in position to observe the carriers from the back of the plane?" JD asked.

"Will do, Skipper. When I get back there I'll plug in my headset to the interphone connection in back. Can you monitor the radio until I'm set?"

"Okay, I'm on it now. Go ahead get back there."

Kenny made his way to the rear area of the plane in good time. "Skipper, I can see the carriers but they're quite a distance back. I might lose sight of them soon if we continue north for much longer."

"Alright stay with them as long as you can then come on back up."

The Coast Guard Cutter was making nineteen knots, closing with the blimp on the radar screen faster than originally predicted. The Captain turned to his first officer who was monitoring the radio room's attempts to make contact with the radar target. "Doug, any luck yet."

"Negative sir, the storm is creating quite a bit of static. We can't raise anyone for very long. It keeps cutting in and out. We're still trying."

The Captain didn't like how events were unfolding. He envisioned trouble if they lost communications all together. Looking out to the west he could see the gathering storm steadily making its way over the lake. "Doug, stay on it. We need to find out why that ship's in the restricted zone before we have to blow it out of the water. I don't want to kill innocent civilians if it can be prevented."

Like all responsible ship captains the Captain of the *Miss Delight* was monitoring his radio but all he heard was intermittent static separated by garbled words. The *Miss Delight* kept coming.

With everyone in position, the test plane was now flying straight and level on a northerly course. Through the static Kenny heard the control plane announce that in one minute he would start the test plane on a gentle one hundred and eighty degree turn out to the west. Just before she came all the way around to a southerly heading he would put her into a steep dive down to the target. If the test plane could be launched from a carrier and then guided in for a direct hit on a target the viability of aircraft carrier launched, television guidance of radio controlled flight would be confirmed. The moment that the scientists and engineers had worked so hard to achieve was about to become a reality. Although JD and Kenny's involvement came near the end of years of effort by many others they were feeling the excitement of the moment.

JD and Kenny had no way of knowing that design work on the TDN-1 drone had actually started clandestinely on November 15, 1937 long before the United States entered the war. Its original purpose was as a pilotless drone intended to be a target for gunnery practice. However, when it was discovered that the craft could be successfully guided to a target, the mission was expanded to include the dropping of bombs or attacking enemy ships with torpedoes. A lighter version the TDR-1 was already secretly in use as a ground-based weapon in the Pacific. Only recently had the mission been expanded to an aircraft carrier based guided missile. With a top speed of one hundred seventy-three miles per hour and a load carrying capacity of two thousand pounds, the war planners hoped that this wooden, twin engine plane would be their answer.

Kenny counted down the last few seconds in his head. Just as he reached zero the test plane began to bank left. Her left wing dipped, the right wing came up as the nose of the plane turned toward the west. As the final test of the day was underway JD saw small droplets of rain hit the windscreen.

CHAPTER THIRY-SEVEN
THE DIVINE WIND

Just behind the leading edge of the storm and hidden beneath the towering, black, billowing, storm clouds *The Raven* fought her way through high seas. Far ahead, out in the sunlight which would soon be obscured by the ensuing storm, Max got his first look at the two carriers. "I see them. They're maybe ten miles to the southeast." Max yelled.

Rinehart reached for the binoculars.

"Take the helm, here let me have a look."

Max changed places with Rinehart holding on to anything he could grab to brace his body against the relentlessly violent pitching they had been enduring for hours. Rinehart did likewise. Max clung to the wheel keeping *The Raven* on an easterly heading. Rinehart tried to steady himself against the bulkhead as he brought the glasses up to his eyes and peered out looking for the carriers.

"Yes," he exclaimed. "There they are, we've made it. I can't believe it."

Max was at the wheel working as hard as he could to stay on course while desperately attempting to prevent *The Raven's* bow from nosing down too deep which could allow the next trailing wave to drive the little boat straight to the bottom.

Max hollered over the sound of waves, wind and rain. "What do we do now?"

"Switch places again." Rinehart answered. After some effort the two men were back as before, Rinehart at the helm and Max at the lookout. Rinehart took a moment before deciding on the best course of action.

"Alright, we'll head for the carriers. Look up there; do you see how the leading edge of the storm front fades back further south of here. Heading in the direction of the carriers will take the boat out from under the protection the storm provides. The boat will be exposed for forty minutes before we'll be within range. We've come this far and I don't want to waste everything by firing prematurely. There will never be another opportunity to do this so we must make today count."

"When we clear the storm I want you to watch for that red plane. He's my biggest concern. After the course is set and the wheel is tied off I'll be free to go up top and uncover the machine guns. If the red plane appears overhead I can fend him off. You can then go below decks to arm and fire the torpedoes."

Max thought Rinehart's plan made perfect sense, he was ready to fight what he hoped would be the decisive sea battle of World War II. The storm that provided cover for *The Raven* was just like the divine wind that came to save Japan during two separate but equally decisive sea battles against the Mongol fleets, first in 1274 and again in 1281. The Mongol forces under Kublai Khan were destroyed with the assistance of the God Wind or Divine Wind which the Japanese call Kamikaze. The Kamikaze had saved Japan before in two epic sea battles which turned those wars in her favor. Max now knew in his heart that he had been born for this moment. With the Kamikaze once again on Japan's side he would do his part.

The Divine Wind had taken them ninety miles across the lake, now he would see that they would safely cover the last ten.

"I'm ready," Max said.

Rinehart pulled the wheel to the right and the bow responded. The waves were soon off the starboard side of *The Raven*. The constant bow to stern rocking was now replaced by pounding waves crashing against the side of the boat. With every wave she rolled forty-five degrees to port but kept coming back. *The Raven* was heading into battle at full speed ahead.

JD watched as the test plane still in clear weather turned west but that's as far as she went. The turn didn't continue through the full one hundred and eighty degrees; instead after only ninety degrees the turn abruptly stopped. The test plane was on a heading of due west and right into the teeth of the storm. "Kenny, something's wrong; she stopped in mid-turn, now she's heading west. Call control one, find out what's happening."

Before Kenny could begin his intended transmission the crackling voice of control one was on the air calling him. The static was heavy making it difficult to understand verbal communications. Kenny had his hands pressed against both ear pieces squeezing them tightly against his ears and his eyes were closed. As he concentrated, he soon grasped that the control plane was repeating the same message over and over. Within a few tense moments he had the complete message. He acknowledged receiving the transmission several times and soon received enough to know that the control plane was confirming that it had received his message.

JD was trailing the test plane anxiously awaiting orders when Kenny's voice came over the interphone. "Skipper, they've lost radio control, the storm has everything screwed up. We have orders to shoot down the test plane."

JD pushed both throttles to full power and the engine noise increased as did the B-25's speed. They were a half mile behind and a thousand feet above their prey. JD pushed the control forward and the plane responded now diving directly toward the target. JD had the twin engine drone lined up perfectly in his sights when he let loose with the eight nose guns. The test plane pulled up and the rounds of .50 caliber ammunition passed behind and below the target. Then the little plane veered to the left, then to the right. She was completely out of control. All the while she was moving ever closer to the storm.

JD spoke in the interphone. "Kenny this is not good. Our target is all over the sky. Try to raise control one. If they are still attempting to send input to the test plane tell them to stop."

After some delay Kenny was back. "Skipper, you were right that's exactly what was happening. They've stopped now."

As the two planes neared the leading edge of the storm front visibility was reduced. Rain was now pounding JD's windscreen but the target was closer. JD let loose with all twelve machine guns. Tracers streamed out in front the B-25 as every tenth round glowed white. The test plane began to take hits to the tail. JD watched as the rudder flew off and the left elevator began violently flapping up and down. The plane started to climb and the remaining rounds from the latest burst again fell short. JD raised the nose of his plane lining up the test plane as she slowly climbed higher in the darkening sky above Lake Michigan. It was in the perfect kill position. The entire upper side of the plane was exposed and the climb caused a reduction in forward speed. JD needed to get this over with before the storm enveloped them. He let loose with all ten rockets. The rockets left the wings in pairs. The first ones off were the two furthest outboard. JD held the trigger button down. The next two left the wings within a split second of the first set. With trigger engaged, all five pairs were on their way within seconds. He couldn't believe how fast the rockets closed on the target. The first two missed long, the next two again missed long but not as long. The third set hit directly on the wings each striking on either side of the cockpit. The test plane shattered into fragments accompanied by a bright orange fire ball. The fourth and fifth pairs went through the debris field and disappeared into the dark storm clouds.

"What happened Skipper did you get it?" Kenny asked.

"Kenny, affirmative we got it. Try to raise control one and report. Hold on to something I'm going to turn into the leading edge of the storm in order to get out of here. Report that we'll proceed back to the carriers just as soon as we can clear this storm front."

The radar operator aboard the Cutter which was still closing on the first target couldn't believe his eyes. Another target appeared to the southwest coming directly from the storm front. "Radar room to the bridge, radar room to the bridge!" he was literally screaming into the mouth piece.

Doug put his mouth to the tube. "This is the bridge, go ahead."

"Bridge I have another target out of the west and to the south of us. Heading southeast on a course to intercept the carriers. Size fifty to seventy feet in length, speed eight knots and closing fast. Range to carriers eight miles."

"How far are we from the target?" Doug asked.

"Sir, the target is thirty-five miles away."

The Captain was standing next to his first officer. He had picked up from the one-sided conversation that something was wrong. "What you got Doug?"

"A second target thirty-five miles south and west of our present location. It's on a course to intercept the carriers. Eight miles and closing at eight knots."

The Captain did the math. "We'll never make it Doug. Notify the carriers of the threat. Tell them to take evasive action, also tell them to split up. Contact the pilot of the B-25 he's the only weapon we have that can get to the target in time. Tell him to break off and proceed directly to eliminate the threat."

The storm was still having a negative effect on radio communication. After more than five minutes of broadcasting the carriers picked up the message from the Coast Guard Cutter.

On the bridge of the *USS Wolverine* the Captain understood the threat. Over the loudspeaker he addressed the crew. "Now hear this, now hear this. This is your Captain speaking. We are under attack. All lookouts focus on the starboard side. We need to locate the threat coming from the northwest, as soon as it is sighted report on the double."

The Captain turned to his first officer. "Give me full speed ahead. That son of a bitch isn't catching us. If we can't attack then we'll out run the bastard. Let's get going. I'll be dammed if I'm going to lose this ship."

"Captain!" hollered a seaman who was on the bridge behind the Captain and first mate.

The Captain spun around in the direction of the shout. "What is it?"

"Lookouts report and confirm the target is off the starboard bow and closing fast."

"Give me a hard turn to port, maintain full speed. That son of a b..."

The Captain was in complete command. He had come out of retirement to take this duty freeing younger captains to command ships engaged in actual combat. Now he found himself in a situation he had never expected. As a veteran of World War One this was not new to him. Experience was on his side and his mind was working through his options just like in the last war. He had the *Wolverine* executing maneuvers that would have been difficult for a speed boat to duplicate.

Rinehart watched in disbelief as the *Wolverine* bobbed and weaved like a welterweight prize fighter in the first round. He decided to head for the remaining carrier which was executing a traditional zigzag pattern. This maneuver would not be enough to prevent a good shot from being attempted by Max. He would go after the *Wolverine* after disposing of the *Sable*. Just like in nature the weakest would be taken first.

Rinehart steered the little boat in the direction of the *Sable* then looped the ropes around two of the pegs on the steering wheel, one on either side. The wheel was now locked in place. "Max, keep a lookout for that red plane. I'm going up top."

Rinehart quickly headed for the stern where he stepped through the rear opening that led to the transom. On the left side of the opening there was a ladder attached to the outside of the aft cabin's rear wall. He took the rungs two at a time. On the roof he untied the line securing the tarp covering the twin .30 caliber machine guns, when it was free he tossed it overboard. Below Max heard the slides click as Rinehart cocked both guns.

JD banked the B-25 into a tight right turn. He couldn't see through the torrent of driving rain pounding the windscreen and the plane. Lighting flashed and thunder roared. The electrical activity within the storm was all around them buffeting the plane like a steel ball inside a pinball machine. JD watched his artificial horizon as he continued the tight turn. He glanced away just long enough to check both the altimeter and the air speed indicator.

The plane was holding at twenty-two hundred feet which was good. Lacking any visual references from outside the plane might easily lose altitude without him being aware. Airspeed was a little too fast for the turn so he eased back on the throttles. The G forces he was experiencing were immediately reduced. The plane roared through the turn, JD held it tight. Then, just that quickly, they were out in front of the storm once again. Visibility returned as the wind quickly cleared the windscreen and the buffeting diminished. JD checked his compass as the sun shone brightly through the windscreen.

They were headed east. Kenny's voice came over the interphone. "Skipper, I'm picking up some radio traffic, it's breaking up but I think… wait a moment."

Kenny was listening intently to the message being broadcast by the Coast Guard Cutter. "Skipper, head for the carriers at all possible speed. They have visual contact with a threat closing from the northwest. It will be on them soon."

"Got it Kenny; radio the Cutter and the carriers that we're on our way. Ask for the position of the threat, we'll head straight for it." Kenny confirmed to JD then began his broadcast as instructed.

"Captain, the B-25 has reported message received, heading for threat at all possible speed."

"Well done Doug, now contact the carriers and pass along the news."

At three hundred miles an hour it took only minutes before JD got his first look at *The Raven* now less than six miles from the *Sable* and still closing.

****

Max yelled up to Rinehart. "I see it, out to the north." Rinehart wheeled the twin machine gun turret around until he had a bead on the fast approaching plane.

JD spotted the machine guns pointing in his direction. The B-25 was still out of range but just to let them know his intentions JD let loose with a short blast from his twelve .50 caliber guns. *The Raven* didn't flinch. Undaunted it maintained the same course and speed.

Now JD was within range. This time he didn't waist ammunition with a shot over the bow. The little boat had its chance; it was too late for chivalry now. He cut loose with a long blast which first peppered the water fifty feet off the port side of his target. The bullets made their way to the boat crossing diagonally through the forward cabin before continuing back to the water off the starboard side. Wood splintered as the forward cabin's ceiling opened up like the top of a can but the boat kept coming. JD's plane roared over the boat at one thousand feet. Rinehart had a clear shot at close range and he was good. Numerous rounds from Rinehart's guns hit with authority against the under belly of the B-25. The cockpit began to fill with smoke, the right engine started to falter.

"Kenny, are you alright?" There was no answer from Kenny as JD banked into a climbing turn out to the east. "Kenny!" JD yelled into the interphone.

"Sorry skipper I was kind of busy back here. Took one in the thigh had to use my belt as a tourniquet."

"How bad is it?"

"I got the blood flow slowed down a little, but it hurts. I don't think I'll be much good.'

Kenny's voice sounded weak, and JD feared for his life. "Kenny, listen to me. Can you get to the life raft? We've got to get out. I have a fire up here."

"Yes sir, I think I can make it."

"Go out the bomb bay when I sound the horn. We're at eighteen hundred feet, plenty of room. Get ready."

"Yes sir."

JD opened the bomb bay and got on the radio. "Mayday, mayday, B-25 bailing out, do you see us, over."

Thank God the radio crackled back immediately. "This is the Captain of the *USS Wolverine*. We see you and are launching a boat now. Check for flares off our deck. Do you see them?"

It took only a short time before the glow from several flares could be seen above one of the carriers.

"Yes I see the flares, will bail out as near as possible. One injured heavy bleeding, gunshot to the leg."

"We'll get you out of the water, don't worry."

JD heard the wind racing through the back of the plane, confirming that the bomb bay door had opened.

"Kenny, are you still with me?"

"Yes I'm ready."

"Okay Kenny, we go when I sound the horn. They have a launch ready to pick us up. As soon as we're over it, we go. Get out as soon as I sound the horn."

The smoke inside the cockpit was now so dense that it was difficult for JD to breath. He pulled the side window open all the way. The noise from the left engine and the wind rushing by were deafening but the smoke instantly began to clear.

JD could see the sailors lowering the launch but they had a ways to go so he flew so near the carrier that he could see the faces of the sailors looking up at him. JD pressed the alarm button then looked over his shoulder to see Kenny disappear out the bottom of the plane. JD closed the bomb bay doors and turned toward the target.

The Final Mission

CHAPTER THIRTY-EIGHT
THE FORTY-FIFTH AND
FINAL MISSION

From his perch atop *The Raven's* battered aft cabin, Rinehart yelled orders down to Max. "It's time, go below, arm the first torpedo. We're well within range, fire when ready. Then get back up to the helm I want that second carrier."

Max did as he was ordered. The forward cabin was unrecognizable. The support beams were splintered and in several cases cut clean in two. Wood fragments, some as large as loaves of bread, lay everywhere. Water covered the floor up to Max's ankles. The bullets from the red plane had cut straight through to the hull which displayed several bullet holes. The pumps were working and the two torpedoes looked none the worse for wear so Max made his way through the debris and started his work.

Rinehart searched the skies for any sign of the red B-25 but it was nowhere to be found. He knew he had hit it and hit it good but there had been only one parachute; and if the plane had crashed he hadn't seen it do so. The sky was clear all the way to their targets.

From the east, directly out of the sun came the B-25, diving down from two thousand feet toward *The Raven* just three miles away. *The Raven* was bow on as JD felt for the button with his left thumb. He found it and mashed down. The cannon fired. The recoil from the blast momentarily reduced the plane's forward momentum by fifty miles an hour. The abrupt deceleration was so unexpected that JD's head was flung forward with such force that it nearly struck the instrument panel over the steering control. He was saved from serious injury when his seatbelt and shoulder harness stopped his forward momentum.

The plane quickly recovered as JD settled back against his seat. The projectile from the cannon was on its way. It reached the water within seconds exploding some thirty yards off *The Raven's* port bow. *Worthless. I have no training with the cannon and I feel like a blind man throwing darts at a moving target. Forget that. Without Kenny there's no one to reload the canon so it doesn't matter anyway.*

The hedgehogs were of little use because they were designed to detonate only upon contact with metal. *The Raven* was made of wood. It was down to the machine guns which should do the job if they didn't run short of ammunition. But, if he could bring the B-25 close enough he intended to release the hedgehogs anyway. It would be a lucky shot but one could hit the machine guns mounted on the top of the cabin. They were made of steel; and if struck the contact just might trip the detonator on at least one and one was all it would take to send the little wooden devil to the bottom.

The explosion and plume of water over to Rinehart's left was all he needed to line up the dark spot coming out of the sun. He squeezed both triggers at once and .30 caliber rounds poured out of both barrels heading up toward the sun. On the plane, JD mashed the buttons with both thumbs and twelve machine guns responded sending a blanket of lead down to the deck of *The Raven*.

Bullets came through the windscreen filling the cockpit of the diving B-25. JD felt his left shoulder being violently thrust backward. His left arm went numb, no feeling, no control. He kept one button pressed down with his good thumb until the eight nose guns stopped. They were dry. Moving his right hand to the left side of the control he pressed the other button and the four blister guns opened up once again. JD fought to maintain consciousness as he strained to look out and see if he was hitting anything. Below, *The Raven* was taking round after round.

JD wasn't thinking, just doing, squeezing the button and flying the plane, attacking the target as he had been trained. He briefly released the controls to open the bomb bay doors. Then he was hit again by incoming rounds from Rinehart's machine guns. His headset and hat were ripped from his head by a bullet which tore through the right ear piece. JD's ear was ringing and the pain from that side of his head was excruciating. His eyes began to tear up making it difficult to see. He gripped the control even tighter not daring to let it go to wipe away his tears.

The Raven's forward cabin received a blast from the eight forward firing machine guns. Max never knew what hit him. The grouping of rounds converged as they entered what remained of the ceiling. It was something like being hit by an eighteen-wheel semi-truck at eighty miles an hour. Max was obliterated.

Rinehart kept firing his twin .30 caliber machine guns desperately hoping that the red plane would disintegrate before his eyes. Closer and closer it came, smoke streaming from the cabin and both engines but it kept coming. Rinehart began to realize the futility of his efforts. He decided to get off *The Raven* and take his chances, but it was too late. There had been a short reprieve from the onslaught but the bullets started pouring down all around him once again. Then they found their mark. Several rounds cut into Rinehart's chest. He stopped firing, dropped to one knee, and fell over the side into the cold water of Lake Michigan.

JD had no idea that the battle was won. All he knew was it was time to pull up and go around one more time. He raised his knees to steady the steering control while he reached down and toggled the bomb release. The hedgehogs slid off their racks and out the open bomb bay door. JD returned his good hand to the controls and tried to pull the wheel toward his chest but he had so little strength that his efforts had little, if any effect. The surface of the water was coming up fast. Annie's lovely face appeared in his mind as clearly as if she were standing before him. The vision brought him back. He wanted to live, to see her again and to hold her as before. In that moment of clarity he dropped the landing gear and lowered the flaps. The drag caused by his actions slowed the plane's forward momentum. Now, with all the strength he could muster, JD yanked the wheel hard. The controls responded as the crippled plane struggled to pull out of the dive.

The crews of the *USS Wolverine* and the *USS Sable* cheered wildly at the sight they were witnessing. Right there on Lake Michigan with lightning flashing and the thunder exploding in the background a battle to the death was unfolding. When the hedgehogs exploded *The Raven* broke apart in flames accompanied shortly thereafter by a cloud of black smoke rising skyward above the burning fishing boat. The sailors threw their caps in the air; and to a man, were elated by the victory that had just played out on a small stage before their very eyes.

The cheers ceased as suddenly as they had begun when the B-25 with glistening aluminum skin and bold red strips crashed into the water, wheels down, just a few yards beyond the smoke that was now slowly drifting to the east above *The Raven* that was never more. The captain and his first mate aboard the *Wolverine* at first, stared in disbelief; finally they both just turned away, unable to speak. Then there was silence disturbed only by the crackling sound of the fire which was consuming the wreckage of the wooden fishing boat.

The smoke pouring from the Cutter's stack announced her arrival on the scene some thirty minutes later. The search was conducted as the storm raged overhead. Two large sections of *The Raven's* hull were recovered but nothing more. These were brought aboard the Coast Guard Cutter. The only real benefit of the search turned out to be little more than to eliminate hazards to navigation from the surface of the water, thus preventing some unsuspecting vessel from striking the wreckage.

The bodies of Max and Rinehart were never recovered. Try as they might, nothing else was found. JD had successfully completed his final mission. That came to forty-five in the bag plus fifteen taken off the board for a total of sixty and a ticket home. JD had indeed gone home.

****

A few days later Agent Ted Holbrook was back at his Chicago office. He took off his hat and coat hanging them on the coat rack next to the door. Carrying his first cup of coffee of the morning he made his way to his desk for the first time in several days. Waiting for him near the phone was a note from Bob. After reading it he placed a long distance call to Mrs. Hammond.

"Mrs. Hammond, this is Special agent Holbrook with the FBI. How are you today?" They exchanged greetings and he continued. "I received information regarding Jane's husband. He's alright, just out of contact for a while. She should receive a letter from him very soon. Could you relay the information to Jane with my regards?"

"I would be happy to; and thank you so very much. She will be so relieved, thank you again Agent Holbrook."

They said their goodbyes and Ted hung up. On his desk was an update on Elsa, she had already been transferred to Washington DC where she was turned over to the Secret Service. A stack of new case files a foot high covered the corner of his desk. Ted reached up taking a folder from the top of the pile. He placed it on his well-worn desk pad and opened the cover to reveal his next case.

Life goes on; but not for all of us. He shook his head, focused, and started to read.

EPILOGUE

I looked over to my dad sitting in the seat next to me. Tears were streaming down his cheeks as he stared straight ahead. We drove on. He remained silent for a long time. Just south of Lexington he was able to regain his composure enough to continue.

"You know son, JD was the best of us. I don't just say that to be saying something nice. He truly was a special human being. I miss him and so does your Uncle Bill. We're the only ones left who really knew him. Your Aunt Fern was too young. JD was out of the house before she was old enough to remember much about him.

"Many times throughout the years I have found myself thinking of JD and wondering what he could have become. Our dad died while JD was missing in action. I have often thought that he died more from worry and stress than anything else. In a way, the war claimed him just as surely as it did the ones who died in action.

"That's war son. Not much good comes out of it but we have yet to find a better way to settle our differences. In war many good and decent people lose everything. Then somehow we get it together and find a way to get along. It seems so strange when you think about it. You would think that civilized nations would see the unacceptable consequences of going to war. Sure, nations win wars but people on both sides lose. So in reality there are no winners. War's end when the people say enough is enough."

I asked my dad why he hadn't told JD's the story until now.

"The FBI was very concerned that the battle on Lake Michigan should never be made public. You need to remember; at the time that this all happened the outcome of the war was still very much in doubt. The invasion of Europe had just happened. It would be nearly a year before the Germans surrendered. The invasion of Japan was planned for after the war in Europe was over. More years and countless lives would be lost to reach the final victory.

"The atomic bomb was still just a science project and a secret one to boot. The bomb shortened the war and saved hundreds of thousands of Americans from certain death. At this time no one knew about the bomb or that it would play a part in the war.

"We were all asked to never speak about JD's final mission. To talk about it would only cause problems. Back then when a man gave his word it meant something. The FBI came to all of us who knew JD had returned to the States and asked for a pledge to take whatever we knew about the mission to our graves. For the good of our country, we all agreed. No one wanted to be a part of aiding and comforting the enemy. If the general population learned that the war was being fought off the shores of Michigan this could have caused a panic or at the very least, second guessing and a loss of confidence. The entire population of this country was involved in one way or another in the war effort. Everything and anything that would keep the American people focused on the goal to obtain the unconditional surrender of our enemies had to be done. Pledging to keep the secret was the patriotic thing to do and without a doubt, it was also the right thing to do. So we did it without a second thought. I would do it again."

After a long pause I eventually asked. "What ever happened to Annie?"

"As for that beautiful young girl Annie, she was devastated by the tragic news. She really loved my brother. She also took the pledge as did her mother and father. I kept in contact with her off and on for years. She got married several years after the war to a guy with two little girls. She raised the girls as her own but never had a child herself. She seemed happy enough. I stopped contacting her after a while because I think hearing from me brought back the past and she had a hard time with it. As far as I know she took the secret to her grave just like everyone else. She might have paid the highest price of us all just for falling in love with a great guy."

"What about JD's war record?" I asked.

"If you look up Joseph Dutton Jones Jr. in the military archives he is listed as killed in action with no body found. His records say he was killed on that forty-forth mission. That's all you'll find. They didn't enter his final mission in the public records. To this day it remains a secret.

"Son, I want you to tell the story. JD deserves the truth to be told. I feel that people should know the story of a fine young man who just happened to be my brother and your uncle. It won't hurt anyone now. The war was a long time ago. It might even help in some way to relive the sacrifices made by so many who fought for our country's freedom.

"This is really about that feeling you get when the national anthem is played with the flag waving in the breeze overhead. Suddenly and quite involuntarily the hair on the back of your neck might stand up as a chill runs up your spine. This country, its flag and its very existence have deep meaning and purpose. The blessing to live in freedom has been paid for by every generation of Americans. That chill is a reminder of those who freely gave their lives that we might enjoy freedom. In some small way this story might help people understand the cost of freedom and increase its value in their hearts and minds. This all might sound a little old fashioned but remember son, we should try to learn from history; if not we will be destined to repeat it."

We traveled on in silence for some time before I asked one more question. "Dad, what happened to the gold?"

Dad managed a little smile. After a moment he added. "Son, now that's an entirely different story. If you can remember to ask me I'll tell you about it on the way home."

The exit at Corbin, Kentucky was coming up. We left the expressway and headed east toward Barboursville, Dad's hometown and the funeral of his dear friend.

Within a year I returned to Barboursville to lay my dad to rest not far from his old friend. I had indeed remembered to ask him about the gold. When he was still young enough to dream of one day finding the gold he didn't have the financial wherewithal or for that matter the opportunity to travel to the island and conduct a search. Being raised during the depression supplied the real reason he never went for the gold. Dad had learned to take a conservative approach; he was not a risk-taker, it just wasn't in him. In later years, when he and my mother were financially secure, the dream faded and his interest dissipated. He never shared the secret with anyone but instead, kept it to himself throughout his life.

Just before his final trip to the hospital we sat side-by-side on his bed. There, in his bedroom, Dad gave me instructions on what to do with his estate. When he was sure that I understood his instructions he brought up the subject of the gold for the last time.

"Son over there in my desk, in the bottom right hand drawer you will find a large steel box. Bring it over here I need to show you something."

I did as instructed and retrieved the box handing it to him as he sorted through his key ring. He found what he was looking for and inserted the small key into the lock on the side of the box. Inside was the journal I had heard so much about and a stack of JD's long unread letters tied with a string. He turned slowly on the bed and asked me to sit down beside him once more.

"Read everything when I'm gone. You can decide what to do after you have the whole story. It's yours now son. Be wise and be careful. I know you and I know your heart. If you decide to act on what you now have, count the cost first. Be sure it's worth it. I have no idea what it might be but there is always a price to pay when you seek a long lost treasure. If you do it, do it for the adventure alone. After all, the gold could be long gone. You never know son, you just never know."

At that moment I didn't know how nor did I have any idea when, but I did know without a doubt that at the very least, I would one day make the effort to find that gold.

Arnold D. Jones was born in Kentucky and moved with his family to Michigan before Kindergarten. He is an entrepreneur in the machine tool industry; spending the past twenty years building several companies, and leaving each as a formidable legacy to his sons. An extensive traveler, Arnold enjoys visiting Mexico, Canada, Puerto Rico, South America, Europe, Asia, several Slavic Nations, and the Far East for both business and leisure. As a teenager, he worked at an airport and opted for flying lessons as his compensation. As a result, he has flown several single engine aircraft of various types.

Arnold is invigorated by a "seven generation view" approach to life and is drawn to storytelling as a way to entertain as well as teach the lessons he has learned gently; with an accessible humanity. Arnold is active in his church's men's ministries and teaches Sunday School to adults. He is married to his best friend; his children are now grown, and he makes his home in Sterling Heights, Michigan.

The Final Mission Arnold D. Jones

Made in the USA
Middletown, DE
21 May 2015